I0740404

Martha E. Berry

Bella, or, The Cradle of Liberty

A story of insane asylums

Martha E. Berry

Bella, or, The Cradle of Liberty
A story of insane asylums

ISBN/EAN: 9783744747745

Printed in Europe, USA, Canada, Australia, Japan

Cover: Foto ©Andreas Hilbeck / pixelio.de

More available books at **www.hansebooks.com**

OR,

THE CRADLE OF LIBERTY.

A STORY OF INSANE ASYLUMS.

BY

MRS. EUGENIA ST. JOHN.

THIRD EDITION.

BOSTON:
PUBLISHED BY N. D. BERRY.
1874.

Entered according to Act of Congress, in the year 1873,

BY N. D. BERRY,

In the Office of the Librarian of Congress, at Washington.

Boston: Printed by Alfred Mudge & Son.

TO

THE PEOPLE OF THE UNITED STATES

This Book is Dedicated.

IT IS A BOOK OF TRUTH; AND AS SUCH
WE GIVE IT TO THE COUNTRY, ASKING THAT GOD'S BLESSING
MAY GO WITH IT.

THE AUTHOR.

2062097

PREFACE.

WE have not collected statistics to show the numbers
of our people who are shut into the large and elegant locked buildings erected and sustained all over
the intelligent portions of our country ; but observing
the daily committals to one, and casting a cursory
glance abroad at the others, we can form an estimate that
will show us that there is a fearful mistake in the nation,
a wrong that the intelligence of the people should investigate, a wrong that is every day deepening into the people's
lives.

A poet gives us an ideal picture of the passage to Inferno,
in which the people are walking with their faces backward.
The ideal finds its graphic reality in prisons and asylums,
where people do walk with their faces introverted upon the
past of their lives ; and, excluded from present happiness,
the past becomes a depth from which Memory draws to
quench the agonies of the terrible present.

An imprisoned American is like a Fourth of July shut up
without a fire-cracker. It wants to explode, but cannot.
It gets angry, and snaps, or, yielding to its fate, sinks,
faints, expires.

One might laugh at the present irrational mode of treating irrational minds, as we laugh at a well-acted farce, were
it not for the tragedies at the end. But farce ceases to pro-

voke merriment when it has lines eternal and immortal in
its acts.

That we may convey to the outside world some idea of
the inner workings of our asylums, and give people some
deductions derived from observation of them, this tale is
written. We can say literally that the facts are truth, but
they are not the whole truth; for, of the sufferings in con-
nection with these legal houses for imprisoning the insane,
the half can never be told. The institutions may bear the
name of asylums, or hospitals, but they are prisons; and
persons who have lived in them as patients know well how
to judge of the effects of imprisonment, both in its moral
and physical bearings.

Mrs. E. St. J.

BELLA.

BELLA;

OR,

THE CRADLE OF LIBERTY.

CHAPTER I.

" My country ! 'tis of thee, —
Sweet land of liberty ! —
Of thee I sing :
Land where my fathers died ;
Land of the pilgrim's pride :
From every mountain-side
Let freedom ring.

CLEAR and loud rang out these words from the stentorian lungs of young Mortimer Beale. They pealed forth into the evening air like a tocsin of alarm. The mists of twilight caught them as they rolled ; and back they went upon the dampened atmosphere, reverberating upon the ears of the singer in full tones of his own creation. Mortimer admired his own voice : its deep bass, its mellow, higher tones, its full development from his strong lungs and broad chest, made his own singing an object of his own admiration.

But not for that was he singing now. A more unselfish
motive prompted his outpourings ,as he went homeward
through the evening of the exciting day, — the day of days
to him, because he had put his name down with the list of
volunteers who were to rush southward for freedom and for
freedom's government.

" My country ! 'tis of thee," —

He had begun, for the third time, that wonderful refrain
that is the very Marsellaise of American hearts, when
he caught a glimpse of the suggestive talisman, — the monument, that, though not living, yet has a voice that speak-
eth. Plain and simple is the shaft; yet it tells to us a tale
of which we never weary, a story that is to us sacred in its
divinity. It tells of the battle of Lexington, that little
skirmish when the untrained yeomen dared the regular foe,
and Liberty spoke through her new and broad highways.

Nearly a century had passed since that battle; and Mortimer had read the tablet till every letter of it was engraved
on his youthful soul, and the history of it was a part of his
childhood's lesson. In spirit he had fought that battle a
hundred times. He had rushed out from behind trees, and
popped at red-coats; he had slung his powder-horn on his
back, and gone bravely forth with his life in his hand.

Mortimer had grown up Freedom's own child. His
mother had nurtured him as such, and his father taught
him its inner essence. Some predicted that he would come
to ruin unless he was curbed; but his father had no fear.
He trusted the innate strength that lay within his only
boy, and felt that he would go through life guided by the
inner light that was his by birth and maternal training.
And Mortimer knew that they trusted him. He knew that
they threw him upon his own strength, asking only that he
should account to them and to his God for truth and
honor.

Of whippings he had none. Not once in his life could he remember that a heavy hand had been laid on him, or a rod, or any coercive punishment. Few were the commands he had ever received, fewer still the cross words; but of instruction in every intelligence known to common life, and of beautiful parental example, he had much. His religious teaching was not precisely of the old Puritanic stamp; but it had in it the eternal creeds of justice, truth, and right.

This night the boy's soul was full. His name stood in fair characters on the enlistment roll. He was his own no longer. He belonged to his Country now: he was one of her champions, ready to do her bidding, and to go whithersoever he was sent. As he passed the monument, it had a new charm for him; for was not he to be like those old heroes? Was not he to fight in a cause as worthy as theirs? And did not his soul burn with a hero's fire? Did not he feel it glow?

> " My native country! thee,
> Land of the noble free," —

pealed the boy.

He had now passed the monument and several houses. He was coming near to a roomy old mansion, — a place that had been aristocratic in its day, and still maintained something of its pretentious character. The style of the house was old; but it was suggestive of comfort and plenty within and without. The apple and cherry trees, the barns and sheds, the spacious kitchen-garden, and the flower-beds well kept, spoke of well-timed industry, thrift, and energy. Mortimer's cottage was beyond this house; but his feet turned toward it as familiarly as toward his own little home, and almost as gladly; for scarce a day passed but he was in and out and all over those premises with perfect familiarity.

It was twilight now; and Mortimer swung himself off

from the highway, and turned toward this house, with the
song still ringing from his mouth, —

> " Protect us by thy might,
>   Great God, our King. "

" Halloo ! " called a voice through the evening air.

" Halloo ! " he replied, the song echoing away, and the
cheerful greeting filling its place.   " Halloo, Bella ! Where
are you ?   I've done it. "

A young head lifted itself above the garden-gate, and a
young face looked sober.

" O-o-oh, Mortimer ! "

" I have !   I've signed, and I am going ! "

" You'll be killed, Mortie."

" How do you know I shall be killed ? "

" Everybody that goes to war gets killed."

" Ho !   No, they don't !   Some only get wounded ; and
some come out unhurt, and some get to be colonels and all
that sort of thing.   How would you like that for me ? "

" Dear me !   I am more afraid you will be killed."

Mortimer straightened up with the look of a brave.
" Well, if I am killed, I shall lie down in the grave of my
glory : and 'nor in sheet nor in shroud' will they bind
me ; but I shall lie in my martial cloak, and they will lay
me slowly and solemnly down " —

" Don't, Mortie ! "

" Why ?   Wouldn't you like to have me enshrouded in
glory ? "

" I would rather have you at home, and the other men
too.   What do they want to go off and fight for ? "

" What for ?   Why, Bella Forresst !   I thought you
knew all about it.   Fort Sumter has been struck, the Union
flag insulted ; and Lincoln calls upon the country to defend
itself.   Isn't that enough ? "

" I don't know.   You'll all get killed by those ugly men."

"Pshaw! Perhaps we shall be more ugly than they. I mean to do my part; and Ed is of the same opinion."

"Ed!" exclaimed the girl.   "Is Edward going?"

"He signed with me."

Bella burst into tears.   The sweetness of her young life seemed suddenly dropped out.   Edward was her youngest brother; and they two, the youngest of ten, were always as comforts to each other in trouble, and joys in happiness. They were the pets of their parents, and were always tenderly cherished by their older brothers and sisters.   Their lives had been as blossoms in the midst of a garden, shielded from rude winds, and sheltered from scorching suns.   But now the thunder of war had rolled over the country; and the two pets were the first to feel the jar.

Mortimer looked at Bella's tears in astonishment.

"I didn't think you was a baby," he said in a surprised tone.   "I thought you had pluck."

"So I have pluck."

She wiped her eyes with a small hem-stitched handkerchief.   "I have pluck."

"The pluck of a girl!"   He laughed as he said it. . "Come, now, be brave! We are only going down to hit those fellows a few shots, just to teach them that they can't insult our flag."

"But you and Edward both! What *shall* I do?"

"Why, you must stay at home, and help keep things going. You must be a heroine, just as the women were in the days of the Revolution, when they fought right here on this ground. You will be a soldier's sweetheart, you know; and I shall be your knight."

"I didn't know I was your sweetheart," she answered, looking up, with a laugh. "I'm only Bella, and you are Mortie."

"I know — But you are my sweetheart, and I shall

2

never have any other; and, when I come back a hero, you will be a hero's bride."

"I would rather you would not go," she responded in a childlike way.

"But you will be my bride when I come back?"

"Do you really mean so?"

"Certainly I do; only you must not tell, because you are only fifteen, and I am only eighteen. Folks would laugh at us."

"Oh, no! I won't tell. But it seems so funny! You and I, Mortie?"

"Yes, you and I,—just you and I,—Bella. That is enough. Don't you like me better than any one?"

"I don't like any one else, only Edward; and, of course, I couldn't marry him."

"Of course not: so now we are engaged. And you mustn't cry any more. And you won't desert me, will you, ever?"

"Oh, no, Mortie! Why, no! I will never desert you, never in my life!"

"Then give me a lock of this." And, as he spoke, he lifted a long, shining black curl with one hand, and, putting his other hand in his pocket, he drew thence a knife, opened it with his teeth, and severed the jetty tress at a swoop. Then he held it up in the twilight, and its coils waved in the breeze.

"There," said he, "that's my token! And now I'll be off. I shall see you again before I go, — a half a dozen times, perhaps. But don't tell. Adieu!"

Then he turned away; and the young girl watched his shadow disappear in the deepening gloom. There was no song on his lips; but there was one in his heart, as she knew. And, as she put up her hand to close the space whence the curl was taken, she felt a sweet young song rising up in her own. The song is really old as the world, old as love; but to every heart there is a time when its strains are new.

"What a funny fellow he is," she thought, "to ask me right here to marry him! But I will. I would rather be his wife than anybody's; and I am *so* glad he asked me!"

Then she turned; and, wending her way through the garden-path, she entered the back-door of the house, — not as she had left it half an hour before, but with a secret, a life-secret, to keep and cherish unknown. She forgot it, however, as soon as she entered the door, in the unwonted scene that presented itself.

There was a family conclave, — the father and mother, all the older members of the family who were at home, and Edward in the midst. As Bella entered, she heard her sister Nellie say, "The idea! That child! Surely, father, you will forbid it."

Before the father could reply, Bella rushed forward, and threw her arms about her young brother's neck. "O Eddie, I know all about it! You are going to the war!"

"I am in a war now," he answered, looking about the room.

Bella, too, glanced around; then released her brother's neck, and rushed to her father.

"O papa! you will let him go?"

"Why, puss! *you* asking for him to go!"

"Yes, papa; because — because — he wants to go."

She was about to say, "Because Mortie wants him," but checked herself.

"But you don't know the danger," said the old father, stroking the long, glossy curls of the child. "War is not all glory."

"O papa! it is not for glory that Edward goes: it is for the flag, you know, — the star-spangled banner."

"What an *old* child!" said Miss Nellie, in mockery. "How devoted to her country! Quite a heroine!"

But the father paid no attention to the speaker. He only looked at Edward, and drew his arm around Bella for a moment. Then he said, "Yes, I ought to be willing; I ought to be willing. Go, my son, but don't talk about it to-night. Let me think, and settle my mind, before we talk."

Bella put one little kiss upon her father's cheek; and the old man, rising, laid a hand for a moment on Edward's head, and then passed out of the room. Not a word was spoken; but Edward felt that a blessing had fallen on him, in which there was richness as of dew from heaven.

The older children knew the uselessness of speaking after their father had decided; and therefore the conclave broke up. There were no more outward murmurings, but plenty of secret dissatisfaction. "Those children" were only fit to stay at home. "The idea" of their feeling themselves so old!

A proud family this was. There was high blood on the mother's side in the ancient times of English history; and the blood still lingered on this shore amongst the descendants.

"Mrs. Forresst was a Montague,—one of the old Montagues; and that's what makes the children so proud."

This was the testimony of Mrs. Forresst's neighbors; and for once "the neighbors" were right.

CHAPTER II.

WHO heard the pæans of Pilgrim praise two and a half centuries ago? Who heard the wooded arches ring as the lofty hymns ascended from the lungs of those brave men? Who listened while they gave free hosannas to the free God of heaven? Did the birds hear? Ah, the birds were flown; for gray-bearded winter was blowing his fierce blasts throughout the woods "primeval," and the rude shore, covered with ice and snow, gave cheerless welcome to the singers of free psalms.

Who heard them, then? Not England. She had other occupation than listening to the songs of a few runaways, who had obstinately chosen a wilderness in preference to her own home-nests.

Who, then, could hear them? Not the Indians; for Providence had cleared a coast where no savages remained.

Who, then, did listen? Ay, who but He who rules the skies, and governs all the earth by his almighty power? He, the impregnating Spirit of all things, heard, and filled those souls with high and holy thoughts. The eagle spread above them on aerial flight; and, as the seasons came and went, they grew in numbers, grace, and earth's prosperity. Freedom dropped her branches, banyan-like; and, in the shadows of her interlacing bowers, chapels of praise arose; and, intelligence keeping onward pace, little squares were rudely hedged in, rough benches improvised, and little boys and girls sat there, and primly conned their spelling-books.

2*

By earthly and by heavenly teachings the Pilgrims hoped to keep their people from grovelling in the dust.

But how difficult it is to cleanse humanity from stain! Even to these men, forms of evil still clung, and elements of perversity still mingled in their natures. The Saviour they sought as guide, and would have patterned him, if their natures had been pure by birth as his.

But that which they did gain from him has given to freedom an impetus that bids fair to reach around the globe, although there have been many standpoints, many rebuffs, and many struggles in the way.

One of these dark points was now at hand; and brother was divided against brother in sanguine fight. There was war.

"Blood!" exclaimed a young Southerner, then standing on the threshold of a Northern college. "I will go back to my home in South Carolina, and dip my arms in blood, in defence of my father's home."

"Blood!" said Mortimer Beale, as he and Edward were on their way to camp. "I dread the thought of shedding blood; but liberty must be maintained, and our country's integrity preserved."

Mortimer's enthusiasm was now unbounded; and as he and Edward, embryo soldiers, were sitting together in the cars, they had a long and earnest talk upon the rights and wrongs of the cause they had just espoused. There is no need to recall their conversation, nor any of those stirring events. They are not forgotten by the world.

The two boys talked a while, and then grew thoughtful. They were going from home; going into they knew not what, nor whether death or life would claim them. They were but boys; and boys' visions came into their minds. Gradually their conversation took a serious form, and home-scenes mingled in their thoughts. Mortimer was an only child. Edward had left behind him a house full of family kin.

Mortimer turned away abstractedly, gazed from the car-window a moment, then put his hand within his coat, and drew thence a thick tin case. From this he took a picture of his father and his mother, and passed them to Edward. Then, holding the case still lower, he drew from it a long and shining curl. This, also, he passed to Edward. The latter started, flushed, and, darting a look at his comrade, murmured, "I didn't know — She gave it to you?"

"No: I took it. You won't betray me?"

"Betray you? I see nothing to betray. I would rather she should give it to you than to any other person."

"Your family will not feel as you do. They will reject me."

Edward thought a moment; then he responded, "I don't think my father would reject you. But I did not know — that is — that you thought of such things yet. We are too young."

"But we are growing older," said Mortimer; "and whatever is to be the end, I do not know. The beginning is made. Bella has promised to wait for me, and I shall do my best for her."

"I give you my hand," said Edward, — "the hand of a brother."

Then they rode on in silent grasp, feeling a new tie between them, and that they were now more to each other than neighbors and schoolmates. The new tie was a comfort to them both; and they thought in silence, as the cars went on, on, bearing them, and a regiment of others, toward the Southern fields. The train was full of brave men, that had bidden good-by to loving eyes, and were going where death might meet them; and all through the cars were hearts of whom we might speak or write. And each heart felt itself alone, as, indeed, we are alone. We enter the world alone; we leave it alone; and, in one sense, we live alone.

As nearly as two hearts can be one, Mortimer's and Edward's were joined; and their spirits mingled now in a new and mutual bond. And then the cars stopped, and the bustle began,— not the bustle of camp, towards which they were looking, but the bustle of the station at Boston, where they were to make a few hours' pause. Here there was a lunch, a march through the streets, a few parting by-words with friends; and then, before they knew it, the hours were gone, as all hours go, into the irreclaimable past. And then they started again; and the whispering wind spoke of sadness, yet a sadness that had in its essence the beauty of hope and the strength of faith.

They were going now to the shelter of tents, to the fields of strife, the days of endurance, and the nights of vigil.

"Not so did our forefathers march," said Mortimer — "not by steam, with armaments all prepared, but by toil of weary feet, and with homespun garments on. Those were brave old times, when

> ' The mother who dwelt in the sea
> Had a daughter, a fair countree;
> And her name was Amerikee.   ˙
> And the Johnny Bulls came to see this young dame,
> And to ask her to buy some tea;
> But, when they got here,
> They were struck with fear;
> For she'd boiled it in the sea.'

"Ha! Jolly old America, wasn't she? I wish I had been there; I'd have put in my help, and roared out a tune " —

"Hush," nudged Edward, " not quite so loud. They'll think you are drunk."

"'Twould be an unlucky thought," the boy replied, " and one that I hope will never be thought of me with truth."

The cars were bowling at headlong speed; and the boys, hushed into quiet, were riding on, as thousands of others rode, towards the broad fields of glory or of death.

Northern people watched, but watched not long; for up over the news-wires came tidings that set all hearts tremulously beating, and made the faces of even grave men lengthen. The news flashed; and everywhere men knew that there had been a battle and a defeat. The name Bull Run is yet remembered. The tidings came to Bella in a letter; and the letter had on the envelope no name but her own, every letter of which was written in a bold, schoolboy's hand. She knew the writing as she knew her own; but yet her young nerves fluttered a little at sight of the letter, remembering, as she did, what Mortimer said at the garden gate.

" I wonder if he will mention it here," was the thought of the child as she looked at the precious missive; and that thought withheld her from opening it while the eyes of her sisters were watching.

" Read it, and tell us what is in it," said Nellie in her authoritative way.

Bella hesitated, took it up, and then dropped it again, while a flush overspread her face.

" You act silly enough," interposed Adelaide. " It is only from Mortimer Beale. Why don't you read it ? "

Still the child hesitated. True it was from Mortimer Beale; but he was more than " only " to her; and an undefined dread came over her, a consciousness, that, if her older brothers and sisters should know what had passed between her and " Chauncey Beale's boy," she would become a mark for their sarcastic shots, — nay, perhaps more: they might forbid her speaking to Mortimer, except as a neighbor and friend.

"Don't act like a baby," said Miss Nellie. "Open the letter, or I will ; " and at the moment she reached out her jewelled fingers to seize the little document. But Bella was too quick for her, and thrust it in her pocket. There might have been a sisterly collision, but for the father, who opportunely interfered, and gave Nellie his particular instructions to let Bella alone, and let her enjoy her letter in her own way.

It was well for the peace of Bella that the father had spoken. Afterward, when she had slyly shut herself into her mother's room, and opened her letter all by herself, she blushed all over rosy red at the very first line, —

"My dear little wife that is to be."

"Dear me!" she murmured. "What a funny fellow Mortie is!" Then she read again, and began it again; · for she liked that funny first line.

"MY DEAR LITTLE WIFE THAT IS TO BE, — This is the first opportunity I have found in which I could write to you. Edward is writing to your father. I have written to my father, and now I must tell you the news. We have had a battle. Of course, you will hear about it in the papers; but I must tell you myself that a battle is a very different thing from what I had supposed; and I think it should be only the direst necessity that should drive men into such positions. I know such a necessity exists now, else. I would not stay to shoot and be shot at. It seems a necessary but a senseless way of deciding a moral question of right and wrong; and it is a very queer thing for intelligent Christian men to stand up in rows, and coolly kill each other; but, after all, there is glory in it when it is for a glorious cause.

"I have my tress; and I think of you often in the midst of the hurly-burly around me, but most often at night, when the stars are glimmering above me, and the night winds stir the memories of my soul. We have grown up together, Bella; and by and by we will grow old together. Won't that be nice? We'll be a good long while growing old; for we sha'n't want to hurry about it."

Bella smiled a little at the thought of her and Mortimer growing old; why, they had only begun to be young. "But then Mortie wasn't like other boys: he always had older thoughts."

At that moment, Adelaide looked in at the door. She had finished sweeping the kitchen, and her busy curiosity was itching about Bella. She wanted to know the contents of that letter; and, all the time that she was tidying the kitchen, she was longing for a peep into her mother's room. But, as she looked in, the letter disappeared in Bella's pocket.

"Do just let me read it," said Adelaide, stealing softly across the floor.

"No, Adelaide, I can't."

Then Adelaide's mood changed.

"O-o-oh! What a wonderful girl you are! You haven't got out of your baby-tucker, and are setting up to receive private letters! From Mort Beale too! What can he say so cunning? Or does he propose marriage? Ha, ha, ha! When shall we have a wedding?"

Adelaide said this by way of torture. She had no idea that he or Bella had thought of an event so preposterous; but Bella was touched. Without speaking, she arose, and went into the dining-room.

CHAPTER III.

LOVE! what is thy name, and what thy mission on earth? Whether thou comest to youth in its dew, or to the strength of manhood and womanhood, thou bearest in thy cup a blessing of blessedness, which thou givest to all such as receive thee in purity, unsullied by passions foul, or selfishness impure. There is nought so weak and yielding as love; there is nought so immovable and strong. The old are made young by its divine essence; the young are matured to age.

Thus it was that Bella was a child no longer. Petted she had always been, but yet not disobedient. Her parents were to her as guardian angels. Her older brothers and sisters had thus far been objects of her childish affection, and by them she had been treated with tenderness. But now a new fealty had sprung up between her and all that she had formerly loved. A new monarch swayed his sceptre over her soul, and his rule was as honey to her taste. She wrote her answer in secret, scarce daring to ask herself what she was doing, or to commune with herself at all. She only realized that it was sweet to love Mortimer, and that, if she told her secret, she would be a target for ridicule, and perhaps forbidden to hold a correspondence with him.

The keeping of " Mortie's secret," as she called it, from her brothers and sisters, did not, in the least, disturb her mind; but to hide it from her dear kind father and mother was indeed a sore trial. Therefore Mortie, in his Virginia camp, received a letter in which was a request for permission to tell their little secret to the dear parents, " because they are so good, you know ; " and, as the young soldier read that sentence, he smiled. " Yes, good: that's so. But what will they say to me ? That's the question. However, I'm in for it ; and so here goes."

He took a pen then, and dashed off a few lines, not very grammatically or elegantly ; but Bella understood by them that she might do as she pleased about telling, only that she must not venture to endanger their happiness. " You see," he said in his frank, open way, " I am but a boy now. I shall be a man by and by ; and then I shall seem a great deal smarter. I mean to be something some time ; but perhaps your father and mother will not believe it."

Bella watched her opportunity, and gave this letter to her father when none were by. A blush overspread her face ; and, shaking back her curls, she stood with a wistful look while he read it. His countenance changed from its gravity to a smile, and from that to a look of incredulity. When he had finished, he chucked her chin ; and, turning her face up to his, he said, " This isn't serious. You do not mean it ? "

" Yes, father."

" Why, you are only two little chickens. What do you know about life ? "

" Mortie says we'll be older by and by."

The old man looked thoughtful. " True, true. You will be older, and I shall be passing away. Well, yes. Tell Mortie, that if he lives, and is a virtuous, honorable man, I shall have no objection."

Thus the girl felt that she had gained a point ; but she knew that plenty of points lay behind. She had not lived all these years without hearing it often said that " Chauncey Beale was a nice sort of a man, but terribly shiftless about getting a living ;" and she knew, that as soon as it should be known that she was "engaged," as Mortimer said, that all her big and "big-feeling" brothers and sisters would rise up, and the poverty of the father would be charged at once to the son. Therefore her wise little heart said, "Keep still ;" and she put her two plump little arms around her father's neck and said, "You won't tell, will you ? "

He smiled as he answered, "No, chicken. You may depend upon that."

Then time passed along. Weeks became months : autumn took the place of the summer, and, in its turn, gave way to winter, furious and cold. Bella received her loving epistles, feeling that she had a right, now that the father had given his sanction. Sometimes she showed him the loving words ; and he patted her head with a meaning smile, remembering, as old men will, his own early days of love.

Notwithstanding that Mortimer was away, and in a dangerous place, Bella was very happy. She felt herself rather romantic as a " soldier's sweetheart," and clandestinely engaged ; and she found great delight in running into Mr. Beale's cottage, and making herself useful there as a daughter, yet knowing, or fancying she knew, that they knew nothing about it, and had no idea that she was really their daughter. All this she communicated to Mortimer, together with the news of the town, and her little love-messages.

It was thus when the winter came, and the snow beat down, covering the roads, the roofs, and the bushes with its fantastic drapery and fleeced blankets. Winter never caught the Forressts unprepared. Come when he would, after November set in, around their house, and all over their premises, he found himself expected ; and he laid his fleeces on, and blew his winds, without harming them. Nor was the elder Mr. Forresst often seen out on stormy days. He let his business wait for the storm-king to pass by, paying obeisance to him as to a power from the unseen.

It was not for himself that he went out this day, when the winds were sifting the snows, and sending them about like Arab sands, filling and flying and cutting and beating into the faces of those who ventured into the drifts. He went out on an errand of mercy. His hands were well incased in double-woolled mittens that his " auld wife " knitted in the days gone by. His overcoat hung to his boots, and its double capes kept his shoulders safe from the cold; while his warm woollen muffler protected close his neck and ears. Altogether he was a very nice-looking old gentleman, and a man whom every one liked, modest and unassuming.

" The pride of the family comes through the wife," people said. " The old English Montagues were a proud set."

When Mr. Forresst left his house that morning, he went in his usual precise manner. Harry harnessed his horse, and brought it to the door. Mrs. Forresst tied his cravat, and placed properly the high, starched linen collar about his neck; Miss Nellie helped draw on his overcoat; and Bella stood waiting with his mittens. There was a little extra tucking of the fur robes at the sleigh, because of the storm; a good many charges to be careful about letting the wind in around him, to keep the muffler close over his mouth, and to be sure to call somewhere and get warm if he felt chilled. And then the old gentleman drove away.

Nobody thought to tell him to be careful in driving. Nobody thought of his needing such a direction; for " father was the most careful driver in the world:" so Mrs. Forresst always said; and it was true. But this day the snow-sifts were hard and ugly, the storm-winds pertinaciously furious; and, in spite of all his exertions for warmth, his old fingers grew clumsy and stiff. The old horse, too, found the elements too hard for him; and in the early twilight, that seemed to hasten on in the middle of the afternoon, when sleet and hail began to add their difficulties, the old horse and his old driver plodded slowly.

There was no one by when it happened; and the driver could not tell his own tale for hours, — not till he had been picked up by a passing neighbor, who found him lying at length upon a drift of snow, incrusted over with sleet, his sleigh overturned, and the horse standing in the crust, with cuts on his legs where he had stamped about in efforts to get away.

Mr. Forresst was carried home; but it was many hours ere he spoke. Then it was as one passing away; and the household sorrowed with deep grief. Proud and stern as some of those sons and daughters were, they bowed before this stroke of God.

But the wife felt it most of all. She had lived by his side through many long years; and they had prospered together. Now, when he talked of going, and held her by the hand, she said, " Don't, father, don't. I can't bear it."

"But we must bear that which the Lord puts upon us," he said reverently. " You and I have had many years together. We did not expect our earthly union to be eternal. The eternity is to come; and you must gird yourself now to hear my few last words. It is of Bella I wish to speak. Our older children are doing well : their characters are formed, their prospects are good. But Bella is young, and has a little secret."

Then he went on and explained this secret, adding, finally, "And now I want you to be to her what I have been. Let her come to you with all her wishes and troubles. Be her shelter and strength."

" And are you quite satisfied with such a match for her ? "

" Quite, quite. I know Mortimer's father never had a tact at getting money; but he is a good man. His boy has been well brought up, and Bella loves him. I intrust them to you; and it is my wish, if Mortimer comes out of this war free from vice, that they marry. Sarah Jane is about to marry. The day is fixed, as you know : do not let it be delayed. Mourning should not be a mere form; and you will mourn for me none the less because there is a wedding in the house " —

"Father, don't!"

The old lady's head dropped to the sick man's breast; she stretched her arms across his shoulders; her face drew near his till her pale, tear-stained cheeks touched his white beard. And, when the children came in, they found her there.

CHAPTER IV.

ORTIMER! O Mortimer!"

There was a wail in the sound of the words; and the young volunteer turned his head toward the speaker. They were reading letters from the camp-mail, which had just arrived; and Edward's face was full of an inexpressible anguish.

"What is it, Edward?" asked the one addressed.

"My father — oh, my father!"

Then he threw the letter into Mortimer's lap, and laid his head down on a stool beside him.

"Read it aloud, Mortie."

Then Mortimer, in his full bass voice, read aloud of the misfortune in the snow, the events that followed, the death and burial of the good old man.

"I shall never, never see him more," moaned the bereaved son. "He feared that I would die; but he has gone first."

The bronzed soldiers gathered around. Many of them knew Mr. Forresst, and all sympathized with the bereaved boy. There is nothing better than sympathy in the hour of sorrow; but even that is impotent when first grief falls in all its fierce attacks. And so Edward moaned and sighed, like a stricken boy as he was.

"Write to mother," said the letter at the close. "This stroke falls heaviest on her."

Then the boy sat up, and the spirit of the man came into him.

"Yes, I will write. Father is gone. We must be mother's right hands now."

"That's right, my brother," was the response of Mortimer. "I would I could lend my aid."

Little time had Edward for manifestations of sorrow; but he wrote a letter to his mother, in which he poured out the fulness of his heart. And the letter carried to the mother just the balm she needed.

"Dear Edward," she said, "he tells me I must remember that I have many loving hearts who will stretch out tender hands of sympathy; and it is true: my children are now my staff."

There was a great change in the Forresst mansion. It seemed that the light of it had gone out. They had been so accustomed to go to father for advice; and he had been always so wise, yet modest, that they all leaned upon him as a rock. Now, however, they must take up the mantle he had dropped, and strive to be worthy a seat in his ascending chariot.

The strong love of the elders was not more grateful to the mother than the weakness of the youngest. Bella sank into her mother's arms like a shocked child. And she *was* shocked. That her father should pass away out of her sight was an event that had never entered her young thoughts; and it seemed that God, whose ways she always heard were right, had done a very strange thing, for which she could not account; and, in her tearful bewilderment, she leaned her head upon her mother's breast, and coiled up into her lap, as though that was the only solace now on earth.

Mrs. Forresst was deeply moved by this clinging helplessness. She took the child into her own room and her own bed. Bella felt that this was now her home; and she brought her clothes thither, piece by piece, till she had made a complete removal. And when the mother told her privately of the father's dying charge, and how she should keep it to the letter, a new life opened before the girl ; and she felt sure that now she was safe from trouble or opposition on Mortimer's account.

"They will none of them dare to speak if mother takes my side."

And now came other changes. Sarah Jane had a wedding in the house. She was married to a man from Salem, —a "heavy man," her brother Frederic said he was. But Bella could not think so. He was a "little, dried-up old fellow," according to her thoughts; and it was a mystery that Sarah Jane could love him.

"I would rather have my Mortimer; wouldn't you, mother?" she asked ingenuously, as they sat together in the mother's room.

The mother smiled. "No doubt you would, my child; but how would you like it if Sarah Jane wanted your Mortimer too?"

"O mother!"

"You see, my darling, it is all right that tastes should differ in love as well as in other matters. Sarah Jane has made a good choice: so every one says."

"Because he is rich, mother. My Mortie isn't rich; but he is *so* nice all the way through."

Mrs. Forresst smiled, and then they went on with the sewing about which they were busy; and afterward Sarah Jane went to her Salem home,— to a house filled with plenty, as none but "heavy" men can fill them.

The oldest daughter, Eunice, had been married some years before, and was already a mother in a sumptuous house in Boston. There remained at home now Miss Nellie, Adelaide, and Bella, with Harry as main man of the

house. The other brothers were established in business;
and no one of them was sufficiently patriotic to leave the
. work of fortune-making for service in the field. It was
better. to scoop in the bills by trading *for* the army than
to risk life and fortune *in* it. This spirit was characteristic
of the family; but yet characteristics do have exceptions.

The home-life glided on again; and time rolled on, bringing no new jars to the bereaved family, till a blow fell upon
Bella, like a second stroke. Adelaide, sly, inquisitive Adelaide, went to the post-office, and found there a letter for
Bella. So strict were the parental commands in reference
to Mortimer's letters, that as yet not one of them had been
opened. But this was from Edward. Adelaide knew the
handwriting; and, walking home at the afternoon's wane
with the letter in her hand, she felt a curiosity to read it.

"I've a right," she said to herself. "It is from Edward;
and, of course, it is meant for us all."

Then with a Maltese purr, and soft silky hands, she tore
off the end of the envelope, and found — ah, what did
she find? Two separate letters. One was for family use,
and the other was for Bella's private reading. To this the
soft sister paid special attention; and the reading solved the
whole question that had often come to her as a possibility.
She carried the letters home in her secret pocket, and
hastened with them to Nellie's chamber. There was a
development then; and the two sisters were fully agreed
in one expression, —

"This must be stopped."

They differed only as to means, each following her own
natural suggestions, by which Adelaide advised a secret
course; but Nellie put her foot down haughtily. The
dainty slipper made quite a noise on the floor; and her clear,
commanding voice uttered imperiously, "No! we cannot
wait for secret measures. The whole thing must be stopped

at once. What can Edward be thinking of! Foolish boy !"

Upon that Miss Nellie arose, and, letter in hand, sought her mother.

But when she found that her mother was already cognizant, nay, more, that she sanctioned it, her astonishment was without bounds.

"Father must have been bereft of his senses."

"I think not," the mother replied solemnly, and with a reverential voice. "He knew it weeks before he left us; and I shall certainly maintain and cherish the trust he left with me."

"Bella has been always hanging about you, and she made babies of you both," said Nellie.

In her excitement she forgot that one of the accused was where he could not reply. But Mrs. Forresst did not forget; and tears came in her eyes as Nellie turned away. The latter, stepping lightly, almost on her toes, as she went, muttered to herself, "This must be attended to at once. The idea !"

In less than an hour the tell-tale letter was enclosed in another envelope, an explanatory note was with it ; and Adelaide was again on her way to the post-office. The letter was sent to Mr. Frederic Forresst of Boston. "He is the best one to manage the business," Miss Nellie remarked as she handed the letter to Adelaide. "He is clear-headed, and will know just what to do."

And Bella sat in blissful ignorance that a letter had come at all. She was in her cosey seat in her mother's room. The mother came in presently, and stroked her hand over the soft, glossy curls, but forebore to speak. Why should she trouble the child, or disturb her dreams of bliss ? She would be her secret friend, and, however they might attempt to annoy her, they should not succeed ; for was not she the dying charge of one whose word should be forever esteemed?

Nellie and Adelaide slept that night in peace. They were confident that Mr. Frederic would immediately attend to the case. He would never permit the son of Chauncey Beale to enter their family; for, though Mr. Beale was a worthy man, he never had the "least bit of a knack at money." It was sure to slip out of his hands if it slipped in; and most likely Mortimer would be just like him.

"I cannot keep it out of my mind," said Miss Nellie. "I would tell Harry; only he's just what he is, and, very likely, will go right against us. But Frederic we can trust."

As it regarded Frederic, the oldest brother, Miss Nellie was correct. In three days he presented his distinguished-looking person in the house of his mother. His plan was formed within an hour from his reception of the letter; and he had come laden with dress-patterns, and every toilet-preparation for the outfit of a young girl.

To Nellie and Adelaide he said, "Silence is the best strategy in such cases. You were wise in sending to me. I planned it at once."

To his mother he said, "Dear madam, I have been thinking of Bella. Now that father is gone, I trust that you will allow me to become her second father; and I propose that we take her out of this common arena, and fit her for a higher sphere. She is growing to be very beautiful; and you, I am sure, would like to see her with a finished education. I propose sending her to a convent for a time."

A perceptible shudder passed through Mrs. Forresst's frame; and she replied quickly, —

"Surely you will not take from me my most precious comfort."

"It is for her good, mother; and surely *you* are not so selfish as to keep her in your presence to her injury. I shall return her to you beautified."

In the "surely" of Mr. Frederic, Mrs. Forresst recognized the voice of her own blood in masculine strength and manhood's prime. She yielded before it; and, wiping the drops from her eyelids, she said, "I am become but a dry and useless branch. Do with me as you will."

"Thanks, madam! I knew you would exercise your usual good sense; and therefore, without consulting you, I have written to 'The Holy Virgin,' a most excellent convent in Canada; and I have brought materials for her outfit. Nellie and Adelaide will lend their assistance, I presume."

The mother's heart was full of misgivings; but, as she had said, she was an old woman now, and her children were her rulers.

"I do not want to go," said the child. "I want to stay with you, mother."

"But I shall not forget you, my daughter. You will not be out of my mind for a moment; and I am persuaded that you will not cease to think of me. We will live together in spirit, if we can in no other way."

"So we will, darling mother; and every night I will put a kiss on my pillow, and think it is you."

Then Mrs. Forresst put an arm around the fair young neck, and said, "Every night I will send up a prayer to my God, and tell him it is for you."

Bella looked up with a hopeful smile. "God will hear your prayers, mother."

And thus, in the midst of the hurrying preparations, they found time to comfort each other; and for one other duty, also, Bella found time. She wrote to Mortimer, and in her simple way told him what had happened, and gave him her coming address.

"You must write often, oh, *so* often!" she said in closing, "or I shall be very, very homesick, and cry to think I am away so far."

CHAPTER V.

A ! That is a new move in our family !"

The voice was Edward Forresst's. Again he was reading a letter; but this time it was not his own. It was the few lines that Bella had sent to Mortimer.

" A convent ! As though there were not plenty of Protestant schools in our country ! And in Canada too ! Cannot patronize our own country in any thing ! Mr. Fred is outgrowing himself."

"He is putting Bella beyond my reach, that is all," responded Mortimer, a troubled flash lighting his eyes, at which Edward caught with a quick reply, —

"Don't worry about that. Going to a convent won't change her; and you have got me and mother on your side. And father *was* there."

"But he is gone; and what can you or your mother do against Mr. Frederic, and Miss Nellie, and all the rest ? "

"I think I am a Montague also," Edward replied; "and they will find me a hard customer when this war is over. Till then, we are soldiers, you know."

Boys are not apt to look on the dark side very long; and these two were but boys. They soon turned their tune of sadness, and planned the glories of a besieging-campaign, — how they would go up to "The Holy Virgin," and waylay their trophy by some heroic means, and make themselves famous as stormers of castles. They were almost glad she was there; for otherwise they might never have had a chance to display their prowess.

Meantime Bella bade the old homestead farewell, and went her lonely journey, encouraged, before she started, by the very mother who would most keenly feel her absence. She was expected at "The Holy Virgin." The great doors opened for her admission, and closed their portals when she had passed through.

"It is not so bad as I expected," Bella thought as soon as she had time to look around, and had been before the lady superior, and seen the sisters. She had forebodings of grimness and austerity and penances and bead-counting; but, if these things were there, she did not see them. It was quite natural that she should not. The reality and depth of things are not apparent till time and stress reveal them.

She saw pleasant ladies with courteous manners and pure grace. They spoke to her with tenderness, and showed her to her room, which was a curtained recess with a little bed behind it, and a long open space, where five or six girls stood grouped, looking with curiosity at the new scholar. Every thing was refined, delicate, and pure; and there was a sweet grace in the manners of the convent ladies. When Bella became more accustomed to it, she thought it a charming life for a little time; but for a lifetime — "Oh!" she shuddered.

There was a charm in hearing the sisters talk of holy joys, the communion of saints, the immaculate purity of the Blessed Mother, and the sweetness of being consecrated to the holy church, whose portals opened to the portals above.

What Bella missed in this community was nature. That which God has implanted in humanity, and which is, therefore, divine was here left out. The natural loves of con-

sanguinity, the ties of kindred blood, and the ties by which
kindred are created, were crushed in this ascetic life; and
to Bella it seemed cruel to shut out nature. God made
nature; and they who restrict its loves restrict and shut
out God. For Bella's warm soul such a life would be
misery; and she wondered whether those sweet sisters
would not be more happy if they had natural homes and
the loves that God himself has implanted on the earth.

In her schoolmates she found natural feelings like her
own, with their different characteristics, like all school-
girls; and like all young, warm-hearted girls, she made
the best of what had come to her. When she had a letter
from Mortimer, it would be "all right," she thought, and
waited patiently for the letter to come.

The days passed away, and she became used to the routine of daily duties; knew which of the pupils she liked
best, and which of the teachers; and began to feel herself
a part of the establishment. She was introduced into the
orchestra, among the chanting-girls, whose dresses of pure
white seemed symbolic of the higher land whose glories
they sang; and the day of her introduction was celebrated
by a little feast of cake and other good things. A new
enchantment was about her, a new aurora encompassed
her. But for Mortimer, she might almost have been lured
to say she would remain forever in this seraphic life. But
she would not have remained happy in it forever. Her
nature was too warm and impulsive, and too full of human
love, to continue happy in a state of this spiritual looking-
forward. In her young soul there were fountains of the
domestic loves; and she waited only for the right master
to kindle them into living flames.

But into this convent-life there came to her no letter
from Mortimer, nor yet from Edward. This worried her;
and she could scarce keep it from her mind. In the pleas-

ant embroidery-room she sat one afternoon, while around were several girls, all busy with their needles, under the care of Sister Nativitie. Flosses and worsteds, silks and linen threads, were lying around; and the girls, sitting among them, looked like fairies in a bower, with a Madonna fairy at their head.

Serene in brow, waxen as a white lily in face, Nativitie seemed as one too frail and delicate for power; yet her power of will was stronger than death itself; for she would have met that monster with fearless eyes.

What an anomaly is human nature! This holy woman would have walked over a field of corpses at dead of night to carry to Mortimer a cup of water for his thirst; but at this moment she knew where lay a letter from him for her young pupil, and she would not even give it to her.

It had been stipulated by Frederic Forresst, that letters from the South should be withheld from his young sister, inasmuch as ·a pertinacious young man was troubling her with an undesirable correspondence; and he trusted to the holy sisters to preserve her from harm. He could not have found a more conscientious trustee than Nativitie.

Bella dropped a tear in that embroidery-room. The tear fell upon the floss of a leaf she had just laid. She looked up hastily to see whether Nativitie was observing, and was relieved at seeing that sister busily engaged on a tangled skein of silk. She had not seen the tear; but somebody else had. A pair of soft blue eyes were looking directly at Bella's face; and a chair was hitched softly toward her by little Lola Street, a Baltimorean, and also a pupil. Lola was a delicate creature, of golden auburn hair; and her work was a gossamer collar of lace, into whose meshes she was deftly interlacing the most fairy work. She moved toward Bella, and stooped, apparently to compare work; but, as she stooped, she murmured, "That

4*

pearly drop — it cannot be a penitent tear. *Me parlez; à l'ami.*"

"It is nothing," was the murmured response.

"*Quoi!*" responded Lola. "I see a pearly drop so fine, so pure. Grief brings it out. Sympathy would be its cure. *Parlez-vous?*"

"No, no, I cannot!"

"*Ma chere amie!* One little word!"

"I dare not."

The cooing voices roused Nativitie. She turned her eyes from the silk, and looked inquisitively at the murmuring girls. How harmless they looked! And how demurely they were comparing flosses, while their innocent eyes glanced furtively, as if modesty itself were sitting there! She turned back to her tangled skein. "It is all right," she thought. The doves cooed on. Lola softly urged, —

"*Ma belle Bella. Je n'ai qu'un ami.*"

"*Je parle l'Anglais,*" answered the more practical Bella.

"*L'Anglais,* then," said Lola, smiling. "I know all about you."

"You know nothing at all."

"I know all. Your heart is aching *for him.* You are desolate here. It is *un sujet de tristesse.*"

"O Lola! how did you know?"

"By love's own light. Have I no heart? Ah, me, *j'aime!*"

"You!" exclaimed Bella. "Do you love?"

"Hush!" responded Lola, and glanced toward Nativitie. "How lovely is this floss! See my vine! So true!"

She held her work before Bella. Nativitie looked up again, and smiled as she saw them engrossed with their labor.

"How happy they are!" she said to herself. "Holy Mother, keep them ever from the wicked one." Then she returned to her silk. Lola touched Bella's arm, and again murmured, —

"Heart reads heart. In the garden, after lunch. Will you walk?"

"Yes."

"*Oui*, then," murmured Lola. "It is enough."

When next Nativitie looked, they were busily at work, and so continued till the hour for lunch. Nativitie praised them for their industry; and they went out together, eager for their *tête-à-tête*. In the passage they met Sister Matildie.

They liked Matildie. She was less austere, and seemed to have an idea that young girls must have natural feelings. They stopped her in the passage: both their faces came close to hers, and they said pleadingly, "It is lovely in the garden. Will you go with us?"

"Now?" queried the sister.

"*Oui.*"

Matildie looked caressingly upon the two young creatures, who stood before her in all the smiles of youth; and a sense of their loneliness stole into her consciousness. She had never been able to "*marbleize*" herself, as Nativitie had. Around Matildie's soul there always hovered the breathings of humanity. She was the music-teacher; and the girls never wearied of listening to her ravishing strains. Pure they were, foretasting the heavenly beatitudes to which she was pledged; but yet they were full of a luscious richness, as though she did not disdain the earth from which she was created, nor wholly discard its God-given, natural loves.

The garden was quiet and beautiful, like a holy retreat. The high wall of its border made it like an island of seclusion ; and the paths winding among the verdure were like paths among the paradisaical spots of earth.

"If we could only open the gates when we choose," Bella thought, "it would seem perfectly beautiful. But those locks!" She sighed as she took Lola's arm within hers, yet not long. She was too young and too healthy to feel for long the shady side of life. Her nature rebounded into gladness; and the hope of something beautiful was always before her.

Matildie walked quietly forward, her fine instincts telling her that the doves wanted to coo alone; and she did not fear to let them coo. Nativitie was in her chamber at that moment, at prayer for the souls of her pupils; and Matildie walked beneath the budding trees, giving to her young charge such happiness as she could.

Before the two girls returned to the house, they knew each other's histories. Lola told Bella of Baltimore, the city of her birth, — of the grand old home where she was born, and how her father and mother died, and she was put under a guardian, who took her to Washington one winter; and there she saw a pair of glorious eyes that flamed out upon her, and seemed to swallow her in their depths, and she was so happy! But her guardian was not pleased with it, and said the young man meant to swallow her fortune as well as herself. "How could he think such baseness of my noble Wilhelm Franz?" asked Lola as she closed her tale.

"That is not an English name?" said Bella.

"No, my Wilhelm is a Swede. My guardian said he was an adventurer; but it is not so. He came to this country to study; and he loves to study; and he has such eyes! You ought to see them, *ma belle Bella*. The first time we met we loved; the second, we were engaged."

"So soon!" said Bella. "Before you knew any thing about him?"

"Didn't I know? Why, I tell you I read his eyes the first time we met."

"Do you expect to see him again?"

"*Oui, ma belle Bella :* so surely as he lives, he will find me in this place."

And she was not wrong in her prediction. If we should go back a little, and take a peep into a large back-parlor of Washington, we shonld see a young man with large, lustrous eyes, busily engaged in packing, not furniture, but specimens of the earth's treasures that he had collected. There were corals from Florida, fish from the Mississippi, rocks, sea-weeds, butterflies, beetles, skulls of defunct animals, shells, skeletons, mosses, and a multitude of other natural curiosities, that all spoke to him a language of life. He was packing them now for storage while he took another excursion.

This time it was Canada he was to explore. He knew of an oriole that had flown thither; and why couldn't he go there also? He went; and, if we had been loitering about "The Holy Virgin" a few days after that, we should have seen another loiterer there also; and we should have seen how a pair of eyes were spying, and yet did not seem to spy, and a pair of ears were listening, yet did not seem to hear; for the owner of the eyes and ears seemed to be busy gathering mosses, rocks, grasses, and any thing that he could find of nature. If we could have read his thoughts, we should have seen a little sentence written there: "I shall get a glimpse of her in some way."

In fact, that which Mortimer and Edward planned in the heroic future, Wilhelm Franz was putting into present execution.

For a day or two past he had been engaged in the boyish employment of flying a kite, but thus far unsuccessfully. This afternoon, however, as the girls were walking and talking in mutual confidence, somebody outside the wall said, "Ha!" Whether the sound of their voices had gone over the wall, or through it, mattered not. Somebody had heard; and in the next moment a kite went flying up in the air. It soared over the garden, and caught the attention of the two girls. Matildie also saw it; and the three stood in silent admiration of its fluttering ascent, when, lo! it fell like a bird with cut wing. Down, down, it came, lower and yet lower, beating about like a defeated eagle; and the three stood watching till it fluttered to their feet, and lay there helpless.

"What a beautiful kite!" said Matildie.

The girls stooped to examine it; and there they read a name stretched across the middle in large characters, "Wilhelm Franz." At the same instant a voice sounded behind. "Pardon, ladies, I was most culpably careless." Turning, they saw a head above the wall; and a pair of luminous eyes were looking directly into the sacred enclosure.

"Pardon, ladies!" and a low bow greeted their upturned eyes. "How shall I get my truant, unless you will be so kind as to bear it up here to the wall?"

Matildie blushed like a girl, and was on the point of rebuking the young intruder; but her natural politeness prevailed, and she said, "True, the gentleman is guilty of an indiscretion; but we will assist him in his trouble, and may the Virgin forgive us! Bear you the kite, and I will follow to see that no harm comes to you."

They did not need a second direction; but, seizing it between them, they bore it across the intervening space, and held it aloft to the extended arms of the young man, who stood there with the coolness of a daring gymnastic performer.

Wilhelm Franz had played his part well. He knew

Lola's voice the instant he heard it. She spoke with softness always; but her tones were clear and musical as the chiming of vesper-bells. Wilhelm had caught their first intonations; and, swiftly rushing to the windward side of the garden, he sent his kite soaring. It went above the enclosed space, as he knew it would; and, when it had reached the centre, he severed the string with his pocket-knife. Now as he saw the kite coming toward him, borne on one side by Lola herself, he took out a paper from an inner pocket; and, as the girls raised the kite to his hands, he dropped the paper at Lola's feet. In the next moment the great bell of the convent rang.

The girls started in affright, and Matildie turned waxen pale. "We have been seen," she said. "Holy Mother, forgive us!"

The three ladies went hastily in. They were met at the door by Sister Cecilie. Her face was long and grave, her manner that of a solemn judge.

"The lady superior desires you," said Cecilie, at the same time leading the way.

Bella was in a tremor, which increased as Lola came close to her, and stealthily pressed into her pocket a folded paper. In Lola's face there was a holy joy. She had seen those eyes; her Wilhelm was near: it was enough. She came before the lady superior with a face serene as a cloudless sky, and impervious as soul could make it. She heard the accusation. Cecilie, chancing to look from her window, had witnessed the proceedings, and said she saw a paper fall from the gentleman's hand. The lady superior looked distressed.

But Lola was calm and firm.

"It is true," she said. "An inadvertence, I suppose. I picked up this."

She placed in the lady superior's hand an envelope.

It was utterly blank. Not a mark, nor even a scratch, was
on it. Wilhelm had been wise.

"Did you pick up nothing?" asked the lady superior
of Bella.

"Nothing," said Bella laconically; but at the moment
she tremblingly grasped the folded paper in her pocket, as
though she would keep it there.

Nothing more could be elicited; but upon Matildie
penances were laid, — not severe, however; for Matildie's
lovely rectitude had hitherto caused her to be a favorite.
Walks in the garden were forbidden for a time; and the
pupils settled down into quiet and unnatural studiousness.

Lola read her letter in silence ere she slept, and on the
morrow she made no outward sign. Not even Bella knew
the contents; but in the thoughts and plans of the delicate
girl a change was progressing. The owner of the kite did
not leave the place. He lingered around, still gathering
mosses, and watching every motion that could possibly be
seen from the outside. The house seemed to him like a
place where humanity was striving painfully to divest
itself of its God-given attributes.

His perseverance met its reward. Before the time forbidden to the garden had expired, the lady superior so far
relented of her stringent rule as to permit the pupils a walk
outside, — a favor not uncommon in ordinary times, and
desirable for the pupils' health. Matildie was not allowed
to go; but Nativitie could be trusted. "No harm will come
to my pupils if Nativitie takes charge of the walk," the
superior said.

Bella was delighted with the thought of the walk, and
almost danced with glee. But Lola was quiet, and, going
to her window, slily suspended a thread therefrom; and at
the end of the thread a white paper fluttered. Nothing was
written on the paper; but it told its tale nevertheless, and

the moss-gatherer understood it. The hour for the walk came; and, as Nativitie led her band up a quiet road, a stout Canadian horse rolled up behind the party; a man leaped from the carriage; a pair of strong arms seized upon Lola; a pair of luminous eyes flashed back defiance; a leap was taken to the carriage again, — and Lola was gone from the convent to return no more.

CHAPTER VI.

IME went on, and glorious, leafy summer came. But not to all did she bring plenty and joy and peace. Beneath her skies trouble lurked; and on that summer's night the stars looked down on a piteous spectacle. Friends and foes lay together; and the night-breezes blew over all. The horse and his rider were fallen together; and the same mandate had hushed both in a rest that would never be broken. Night drew her merciful drapery around the scene, and her dews were like a soft mantle over sorrow and woe.

Deep in the centre of that night, and deep in the middle of that field, a soldier raised his head. The midnight damps were on his brow. His hair was tangled with the gore of fallen men. Near him were corpses, men lying in uniform, staring into the heavens above. The ground was furrowed with seams, and trampled with the footprints of deadly fight.

The rising soldier gazed around him with mute sensations. It seemed that he had heard the voice of the Master calling in the cool of the night; and, rising, he said, "Here am I." He passed his hand over his brow. He stretched his aching limbs and his strong frame. He felt a thirst; but there was no water within his reach. His tongue was hot, and his lips dry. He opened them to the night-wind, and it entered with cooling strength. "I shall live," he said. "I will get up and stand among these who are dead."

But, when he attempted to stand, a pain caught him in the side, and he dropped. He felt a gushing: it was his own blood, and he knew it. For a time he lay quite still, and the flowing ceased; but the thirst, the tormenting thirst, continued: it tortured him. Suddenly, however, his full consciousness returned. He thought of his canteen: it was not empty, and he drank. Then he bound his handkerchief over the wound, and lay quite still. Among all those forms around him he alone had life. He thanked his God for himself; but he sorrowed for the less fortunate, for those who had gone before their time, hastened into the eternal Presence by this sanguinary fight. Then he slept.

When he awoke the sun was gilding the open cemetery about him. It was ghastly; and he closed his eyes with a sickening sensation. He lay a little while. The sun came up, and cleared the mists away. The beauty of the opening day fell upon the ghostly carnival. Then came sounds of voices. Living men were walking among the dead. The sound revived the soldier, and once more he raised his head. Instantly half a dozen men sprang towards him.

"Capt. Beale, Capt. Beale! The Lord be praised! We thought you were gone forever."

"I guess not," said Mortimer. "I am a little damaged, though. How went the battle?"

"Hard enough for both sides," was the answer from one of the men. "There may be glory in war; but there's a pesky sight that isn't glory."

They made a litter, and then carried the soldier away. He was counted among the living, and not among the dead.

But he had been reported dead; and his comrades, who had learned to love him, and had witnessed his promotion with pleasure, had mourned for him as for the departed. A message had gone North to the father; and that father had bowed in grief, — he groaned in his cottage. And the mother wept, for the pride of her life was taken away.

"I will arise and go to my son," said the old man. "I will bring his bones to thee, his mother."

By express-trains, with eager haste, he hurried. Sorrow was in his soul; the lines of grief were on his brow. Over the rails the car-wheels whirled; over the ground the train thundered.

Said a Turcoman chief, "My horse can gallop a hundred miles a day for six days together, and still be fresh."

But the Turcoman steed pales utterly beside the iron horse. He never tires. Feed him with caloric and water, and he will run a race that the Turcoman never conceived in his wildest and most Tartaric moods. Thus the iron horse bore Chauncey Beale to his son. His heart was in his mouth. He trembled as he stood before the colonel, and asked for the dead body of his son. But the colonel sprang to his feet, and grasped the old man's hand. "Your son was dead, and is alive again."

"Alive !" repeated Mr. Beale. "Is Mortimer alive ?"

"I am happy, sir, to say that Capt. Beale is alive."

There is no need to speak· of what followed. Not every father who went to the camp in that war was so blessed.

When Mr. Beale returned home, he. had the living form of a living son; and he had another, who was even more deeply wounded than Mortimer, but who, being taken up among the wounded, had not been reported dead. That other was Edward Forresst. Together the boys had gone out; together the men had come back, thankful that they were alive. As children, they had loved each other; as men, their hearts were close-knit. Mrs. Beale received her son in her little parlor; Mrs. Forresst took hers into her spacious house : but the same sweet motherly love gilded both places.

Now it was a question of time and patience, and strength of constitution, and good nursing; and the boy in the cottage gained upon the boy in the mansion. Mortimer was speedily better; but Edward halted. He was feverish and restive; and the days were a burden to him. His mother worked for him; his sisters worked; and Harry was on constant watch.

"Mother," said Edward one day, "I am going away to that better land."

The mother clasped her hands.

"Say not so, my Edward."

"I say as it seems to me, mother. I am going away; and I want Bella."

"You shall have her," said the mother, and went down to find her other children. She told them what Edward said, and added her wish that Bella should be immediately sent for.

What is human nature? Even in that hour Miss Nellie demurred. "Send for Bella; and here is Mortimer Beale close by!"

"Nellie," said the mother sternly, "think of Edward!"

Something in the words and look made Nellie ashamed. She said no more; but, taking her pen, she wrote for Bella to come to her dying brother.

5*

CHAPTER VII.

THEY were sorry at the convent, — sorry for Bella's misfortune, sorry to lose her. She was both sorry and glad. She wept for Edward, but she was heartily glad to go home; for, though her intercourse with the sisters had been pleasant, she longed for her mother's bosom and her familiar home. She bade the sisters farewell with joy and gladness, with smiles and yet with tears.

Once away, and in the cars, and on the road home, she was a new person. The world seemed larger, brighter, more beautiful, than she ever knew it; and, but for Edward, how happy she could be! When she thought of him, her childhood's brother, the tears came in her eyes, and she looked forward with a shudder. Would *he* die there, in her own home, as her father died?

But her thoughts neither hurried nor retarded her course. In due time she reached the roomy house, stood again on the familiar steps, and entered the well-remembered door.

How natural it seemed! The dear mother met her with a passionate embrace; Harry, with his broad, strong face, gave her a brotherly greeting; and even Nellie and Adelaide softened to smiles as she came joyfully to kiss them.

To Edward her coming was a recuperative power. It seemed that he needed her exuberance of health and spirits. She looked at him, put her arms about his neck, and said, "Why, Eddie, you are not going to die! I shall cure you."

She made him have faith in her. She flew up and down the stairs on tireless feet; she carried him bits of every good thing: she watched her mother dress his wound; she breathed over him her own strong spirit.

Nellie and Adelaide were shocked at this overflow of spirits; but to Edward they were as life-giving cordials. Contrary to all expectations, the soldier began to revive; and the older brothers and sisters were compelled to acknowledge that the returned sister had "done him good."

But now came the vexed question of Mortimer. Edward would have him, and the mother seconded her wounded boy. Nellie pursed her mouth indignantly, but all in vain.

"It had come to fine times if Edward and Bella were to have their way in every thing."

But the mother was firm for her sick boy. He should be gratified; and thus, in spite of Miss Nellie, it came about that Capt. Beale and Bella met often in Edward's chamber, and often, by Edward's own contrivance, were *tête-à-tête* in the chamber adjoining.

They were changed from formerly. The captain's education had been finished at the cannon's mouth; hers had the artistic touch of "The Holy Virgins:" but in affection and soul they were still the same. Edward improved slowly, until he was able to go out. He could go among the neighbors; he could visit Mortimer. There was no longer any need that Mortimer should come to see him. But still he came. He was not a boy in diffidence; and yet he dared not speak to others of the love that he and Bella talked each day. He felt ashamed of his cowardice; but a fear of refusal held him back, until at last he said, "Bella, all this is futile, unless your family like me. After all, I fear you never will be mine. Your friends, all but Edward, are against me."

"My mother likes you, Mortie."

"Do you suppose she would give you to me ?"

"Go and ask her," Bella replied.

"Go with me, then," said he. "I dare not go alone."

"Are you a coward ?" asked she, laughing.

"I would rather face a regiment of cavalry than ask her that."

"Why, Mortimer !" she said, surprised.

"I cannot help it. I am afraid of her. Ask her for me."

"Me !" asked Bella. "Why, that is not the way. The gentleman should ask."

"But I am poor," said he. "I cannot show her an elegant house or lands, or money in bank."

"You can show yourself, Mortie. Come !"

Taking him by the hand, she led him to. her mother's room, led him to the old lady's side.

"Mother," she said simply, "Mortimer wants me for his wife."

Mrs. Forresst looked up. She seemed not much surprised, but only asked, —

"Is that so, Mortimer ?"

"That is just so, madam; if you will but think me worthy."

Mrs. Forresst turned toward her child.

"Your father thought kindly of him, Bella. I shall respect your father's wishes."

"Madam," said Mortimer, "I thank you. I should have asked you long ago, but that I feared denial. I am not ready to take her. I cannot do by her as I would wish. Will you keep her for me till I can claim her by showing you a home of comfort for her ?"

"I will keep her."

"And, when I call, you will give her to me?"

"I will give her to you now; and, when you call for her, you will be claiming what is your own. I say this because some of my family may oppose you, and I would have it distinctly understood that she is yours. In giving her to you, I but fulfil my husband's wishes. Though he is gone, his wishes are my law. It was his aim to give unrestricted freedom to each child, unless he saw them doing what is contrary to the law of God; which, I thank Heaven, they have never seemed inclined to do. I repeat it, then, Bella is yours. I will give her to you, and I will keep her safe till you are ready for her. May God bless you both!"

Electrified at this ready consent, they stood in silence a moment; then Mortimer wound his arm about the girl, and, standing erect, took her hand in his, and with clear voice said, "Mine by your mother's gift, and by the pleasure of our God, — mine forever."

"Even so," responded Mrs. Forresst, standing before them. She placed her right hand on the black tresses of the blushing girl, her left hand on his broad shoulder, and enunciated clearly, "By the consent of the father, now silent in the grave, by my own consent, who soon will lie by the departed, and by the grace of God, who ordained that men and women should love each other, I betroth you till such time as you can wed by public law, by a minister of God."

"It is almost like a marriage," said Mortimer. He was deeply impressed. It seemed as though his highest wishes had been sanctified, and that, from an unseen presence, a blessing had fallen upon them.

"Madam," he said with a trembling voice, "I am overwhelmed. Allow me to sit with my bride for a little time."

"Go," said Mrs. Forresst. "Go, Bella. The parlor is vacant."

"Mother, dear mother," said Bella, "we will come back to you by and by."

"Not to-night, my children, not to-night. I am weary now. Kiss me, and go."

They bent their heads and kissed her forehead, and then went out together. The mother heard them open the parlor-door, then she went up stairs.

Nellie was alone in her chamber. She was thinking of the subject that was engrossing her mother, though all unconscious of the drama that was passing below. She was thinking that Mortimer's visits were quite too frequent. She was thinking that he was too often with Bella, that the consequences would be serious; and, though he was "called Capt. Beale, he was really only Mortimer Beale grown up." She thought that she must speak to Frederic, and they must take Bella somewhere. As she was pondering, her mother entered the room.

Mrs. Forresst looked weary. She was slightly overcome, and yet she was not sorry. She felt that she was but carrying out the wishes of her departed husband. She placed her lamp on the table; and, going up to Nellie, she said, "I have given Bella away."

"Mother, what do you mean ?"

"I have given Bella away. She is mine no longer."

"To that Mortimer ?"

"I have given her to Mortimer."

"Mother, how could you? Are they down stairs now ?"

"They are in the parlor."

Miss Nellie arose.

"Where are you going ?" asked the mother.

"To the parlor."

"Nellie, if you go there, you will disturb that which God has sanctioned. In accordance with your father's wishes, I have given her to Mortimer."

For a moment the young lady hesitated. The sacredness of her father's name arrested her, but served only to moderate her wrath. She was about to turn the daring young man from the house; but her father's name had checked that thought. She went quietly, and, entering the parlor, seated herself by the table, took up a book, and proceeded, apparently, to read. What was there for the young lovers but a few commonplace remarks? Indignation filled Mortimer's soul. Had she been a man, he would have spurned her from his presence; but her sex protected her. He choked and bore it; and at last, with a slight commonplace parting, he arose and left the house. Then Miss Nellie complacently returned up stairs. Bella went to her mother with an indignant tale.

CHAPTER VIII.

ISS NELLIE went to her bed, but not to sleep: she lay on her pillow in all her pride, — the pride that would not leave her even in the hush of repose.

"I must do something decisive," she said to herself. "That fellow is so insinuating, he just moulds everybody in his own way. I must write to Frederic: I can depend upon him."

When morning came, Nellie arose and wrote another letter to her brother Frederic. The sly Adelaide carried it to the post-office. Nellie never did her own errands: such offices were quite beneath her; and Adelaide was but a ready messenger. What mattered who carried the message? It was the letter itself that did the harm. It was an effective document, and did its work. Two days thereafter, there appeared in the doorway of Mrs. Forresst a heavy "swell."

To appreciate Mr. Frederic Forresst, one needs to see him. Description of him runs thus: He entered his mother's house with an air that said plainly, "You are very much honored by my presence." He swung back his circular cloak, tossed it gracefully from his shoulders, hung it upon the hooks at the rear of the hall, and hung his glistening beaver beside it. He placed his ivory stick beneath them. He missed the hall-mirror to which his later habits accustomed him; and, arranging his polished locks by the mirror of imagination, he bowed his way into the family-sitting-room.

Exceedingly polite and bland he was, a finished courtier in every respect. He paid his respects to his mother, then to his sisters, and then went into formal rejoicings over Edward's improved condition. The noontide dinner was served ere he broached the object of his visit. He began by remarking, "You have been an excellent nurse, Sister Bella. Edward is quite recuperated. And I see the advantages of your brief scholastic term have not been lost upon you. I propose now to take you with me to Boston. Those ringlets are quite too beautiful to be kept in seclusion."

"Not to-day, Frederic?" asked Bella, looking up with a frightened air.

"And why not to-day?" he returned. "I am here, and cannot come again. Edward will be down there himself very soon. I will find business there for him."

That decided the question. Bella would go if Edward would. And another secret thought came to her,—Edward could find business for Mortimer. Yes, she would go.

Her manners were softened and refined by her pupilage, and it proved as Frederic predicted. She became quite a favorite in the circle to which he introduced her, and that circle was by no means of the lowest. He also fulfilled his promise to Edward, and found him employment. Then came the last act on the programme. Edward found employment for Mortimer, and Mortimer came; and, as a natural consequence, he and Bella met; and Mr. Frederic himself saw them walking together on Washington Street.

Then Mr. Frederic Forresst flushed. All within himself the tempest was; but it was none the less violent by being pent. The ivory-headed cane writhed about like a spiral cord as he twirled it in his gloved fingers; and his mustache,

6

which, in repose, rested square across his cheeks, and terminated in the finest of waxed ends, went at angles now, until it stopped with both points turning heavenward. That indicated that Mr. Frederic Forresst had arrived at a decision in which temper had played an important part. He walked on with the ends upward, until he reached home; then the mustache went down. He had a part to play, and he was a thorough actor. When Bella came in, he was the blandest, most cordial of brothers. She thought he was never so agreeable, and heartily wished he would always wear his agreeableness, " it was so becoming."

The next morning he was even affectionate; invited Bella to an excursion with him, in which, he remarked, he would show her some new features of the world; and was, altogether, the most tender of brothers. He had a " little business out of town," he said, and her company would make the journey " more agreeable."

She knew that he often made business tours, and she accepted this invitation at once.

" How long shall we be gone ? What shall I need to carry for dress ? " she asked.

" It is impossible to tell," he responded. " You had better put up quite an extensive wardrobe."

They started one sunshiny morning; and she was radiant with happiness, like all young people when going out to see the world. She had money, dress, and all that she needed for comfort; and she thought Frederic extremely kind to take her with him.

And he thought — We will not try to tell his thoughts, but judge them by his acts. They went by rail first, then by stage, and finished their journey by stopping among the Shakers.

CHAPTER IX.

IGHT and darkness! From the noon of day to midnight; from the warm sunshine of love to the depths of arctic frigidity.

Thus it seemed to Bella. Her brother was gone. She was left, without money in her pocket, in a strange place. She felt powerless. Mr. Frederic had agreed with the Shaker family for her board, and she had plenty of clothes. "What more does she need?" was his soliloquy. "If she has money, she will use it to come back; and I cannot trust her here while Beale is here."

In her chamber Bella wept continually. She tried to erase the traces of tears when she appeared in the family; but the eldresses could see that she was in distress. They coaxed her, they flattered, they brought her dainties to eat; but still, when she was alone, she wept, and the eldresses knew it. They were sorry for her. They said, "The cruel world has touched her hard. There is no safety in it. It is a blessing that she has come among us. We will help her forget her troubles."

Then these quiet, industrious women tried, in their way, to make her happy: they let her go about, and took her into their clean, airy kitchen, and among their various industries. She flitted out and in, and wandered about the grounds; she saw the buildings, and the men quietly at work, and they saw her. The staid old men shut their holy eyes, and the women pitied her.

Unconscious of the sensations she produced, she continued to wander, as if in that alone lay her relief. In a few days she knew every nook on the premises.

Not far away, among the buildings of the Shaker villa, was a carpenter's shop; and within it was the sound of a plane. It seemed to be moving briskly, and gave the still air cheerful vibrations. She looked toward the shop. "Who is in there?" her curiosity asked; and she went on till she reached the door. Then, looking in, she saw a bench with a board on it, and a young man was pushing a plane lengthwise on the board. He was unlike the other men she had seen. His brow was open and high: the thick hair, clustering upward, and thrown backward, covered his head in raven masses. He was trim and straight in form; and, as he looked up at her entrance, she saw his eyes of intense blackness.

"How do you do?" he asked by way of greeting.

Feeling embarrassed, she scarce knew how to reply; and, ignoring the question, she said simply, "May I come in?"

"If you would like to," he answered.

"What are you doing?" she asked.

"Can't you see?" he replied, shoving his plane.

"Do you belong here?" was her next question.

"I don't belong anywhere else."

The answer pleased her. It seemed like the world from which she had come. Before she could speak, she found herself the questioned.

"What is your name?"

"Bella Forresst."

"Where did you come from?"

"Boston, last."

"What are you here for?"

"To keep me on my good behavior, I believe."

"I thought as much."

This dry answer was accompanied by an uplifting of the eyebrows and a sparkle of the eyes that showed a keen sense of the situation ; and Bella recognized a spirit kindred to her own.　She seemed to have known this stranger all her life; and she addressed him as he had her.

"What is *your* name ? "

"Elijah Cressy."

The name came through his teeth as if forced; and he added, "It is not so fine a name as yours; but no matter: pretty is that pretty does."

Bella laughed a rippling laugh that restored the young man's feelings; and he asked, "Are you going to join the community ? "

"Would you advise me to ? "

"No."

"What do you stay here for?"

"Well, Miss Forresst, you see" — At that moment, bounding heels over head, an object came in at the door. Bella started ; but Elijah appeared unconcerned.　The object proved to be a boy ; and, as he stood upright, he seemed the most startled of the three.

"Jack," said the carpenter, "this is Miss Forresst, a friend of mine from Boston : I wish you would stand at the door."

As he spoke, he gave Jack a wink ; and the boy went into position at once.　Straight in the doorway he stood ; and, while he did not forget to look within, he rolled his eyes outward in keen glances.　No elder could come unseen.

Then Elijah and Bella talked a little, as congenial spirits on the enemy's ground, and both disposed to fight their own way.

"I want to see you longer than I can here," said Elijah. "Eldress Nancy will do almost any thing to please you. Every night, at half-past nine, somebody locks the great outer doors of both sides of the house ; and the whole house

6*

is stilled. You can ask Eldress Nancy to let you lock them on your side, and I will ask leave on mine. When we get to the middle door, we will slip out and take a walk together. It is the only way we can talk alone."

She looked in his eyes as if searching for truth, and then said, "I will."

That night, as the stars were shining, the two moved stealthily from the great doors, and wandered away beneath the spangled heavens. When they were away, they began to talk. Elijah told her his history, — how from childhood he had been an orphan, and had no other home but this; how he had often marvelled about the world, and whether he could live there as other people lived, earning his own way; and why he could not have somebody all his own to love; and how he had sometimes thought he would run away, but then he knew no place, nor had any friends.

Then Bella told him her story ; and he asked many questions about Mortimer, — his principles, and how he looked, adding at last, "You needn't be troubled about him, Miss Bella: you have only to write to him, and he'll make it straight for you, — at least I would, if I was in his place."

"I have written to-day," was Bella's response ; "and tomorrow I shall send it to the office by Elder Jonathan."

"He won't carry it," Elijah replied.

"Why? Am I in another convent ?"

"No ; but then you know they like to persuade young people to stay here ; and, besides, it is a wicked thing to go back to the world. They would grieve for you."

Bella laughed. The idea seemed to her absurdity. But Elijah did not laugh. He had been under those doctrines too long to laugh at them. He only felt their weight; and he responded seriously, —

"I will mail your letter for you. Elder Jonathan, though an old man, may like you too well. Do not trust him."

"And how do I know I can trust you? You may like me too well. You may want to keep me."

He jerked away his arm, and her hand fell. He stood straight before her : his eyes gleamed, and his hair shook as in anger.

"Miss Bella, do you take me for an idiot? Don't I know that you are a refined young lady, and I an ignorant young man? Why should I seek to keep you or betray your trust?"

Bella laid her hand on his arm. "Pardon me, Elijah! I have seen so much trouble, I hardly know whom to trust. I will give you the letter to-morrow, and thank you ten times over if you will see that it goes."

It was thus that Bella gained a friend; and a correspondence opened that led to wide results. Elijah did not turn himself into a mail-carrier, but he made Jack his messenger; and the boy skipped like a monkey at the joke he felt these letters were perpetrating. Jack was born for fun ; but he found little of it in this staid life, and to carry sly letters for a handsome young lady like Miss Bella was to him a continual feast.

Time passed on, and an event of interest to them was to occur in the Shaker family. A gentle girl had been persuaded to adopt the costume of the sect, and become one of the sanctified. The elders and eldresses rejoiced in her conversion, and bent their energies towards bringing Bella to the same ideas. Eldress Nancy and all the others tried their persuasive methods of arguing, but with no effect. She listened respectfully ; but her nature had no affinity with their doctrines. She grew weary of their teasing, and wrote notes to Elijah, instead of accepting their invitations. In his replies he confessed that he felt like "less than a man" to allow the tender Emily thus to sacrifice her natural hopes and loves, and take upon herself these unnatural vows. To these expressions Bella replied boldly, " Why do you not take her out to the world, and be married like other people ? "

" Where can I carry her, and what shall I do with her ? " he asked. " I should be lost in the world myself. How, then, can I enter it with a tender woman under my care ? "

Meantime the eldresses continued their importunities. They made an entire conventual suit for Emily, every seam and fold of which was in the most approved manner of their sect. Bella looked at it and then at the women whose garments were the same ; and she thought, " Never, never, will I wear such a dress."

Seeing their own failure in persuasion, the eldresses sent for Elder Jonathan. He was an oracle in their eyes ; and they thought he surely could influence her. He came and stood before her. He described the glories of the sanctified, and depicted the horrors of the world. He told her of their safe home, and of the dangers of a tempting world ; and, as he delivered his discourse, she restrained herself by the rules of politeness, but within she was full of merriment. His tall, thin form, his grave, elongated visage, and his conventual garments hanging closely on him, made him ludicrous in her eyes ; but when he came day after day preaching the same words, she grew weary of hearing it, and began to fancy that he came to please only himself, and a great aversion to him seized her mind. This, also, she communicated to Elijah, who sent her a note in reply, and accompanying the note was a letter from Edward and Mortimer. This letter created new hope in her. They wrote of their plans, — how they were going West where lands were cheap, were going to start homes for themselves, and how Edward had found Kate, — Miss Kate Ward, — and when their homes were ready, they were coming back for their brides. " Do not fear," said Mortimer : " we shall come out right yet."   And Edward added, "You will like Kate for a sister, I am sure."

She told this to Elijah, and he was moody.   He said, "In the world, young men have loves and do as they please.   Is there nothing for me?"

Bella answered, "Leave this place, Elijah!   Take Emily and go.   I will help you."

Elijah could not see how she could help him; but the courageous cheerfulness of her manner inspired him.   He said, "Maybe there is some good in store for me."   Then he returned to his shop, and she went to her room.   Eldress Nancy and Elder Jonathan renewed their arguments and persuasions; but she was firm.   Still they did not cease entreating; and on the morning of the consecrated sabbath, when Eldress Nancy carried a new suit to Emily, she also left one in Bella's room.   Bella looked at its plain, sober fashion.   "Wear it!" she said in her heart: "never!   Mortimer is coming to-day: I will wear a dress befitting him."

She closed the door of her room, and opened her trunk.   A delicate perfume arose as she took out such articles as pleased her.   She spread them out, and proceeded to dress, while Emily, in her room, was arrayed by Eldress Nancy.   The time came for service.   The family met in the consecrated room.   Emily sat in her place, attired for her novitiate, her mild young face reflecting its own light.   All the family sat in silence.   All were there but Bella.

Presently along the passage soft steps were heard, and there was a rustle of floating drapery, — not such drapery as the eldresses wear, but rustling drapery, such as the world has.   The sound was strange in that place.   Every eye turned towards the passage; and there, upon the threshold, appeared a vision of wondrous beauty.   Amazement transfixed every face.   The eldresses seemed stricken with horror.   The elders were like dazzled men.   Elijah was petrified.   Jack longed to jump, and cry "Hurrah!"

Bella walked slowly in. Adown from her head flowed her dark ringlets, a dress of pure white muslin floated back in airy fulness, frills of deep lace hung over her bare arms, a fan was in her hand, and her eyes sparkled with brilliant light. Before the scandalized family could regain their usual serenity, steps were heard outside, — heavy steps they were, full of manliness and vigor; and when they entered the room, there came from out that gossamer a little cry, "O Mortimer and Edward!"

To explain what followed would be of itself a little history. Afterward they were alone together. They told her more fully of their plans; and she told them of Elijah's kindness, of Emily, and Jack.

"We ought to reward Elijah," they remarked.

Then she told them the best reward would be to take him and Emily away, and let them be like other people; and, when they had considered her proposal, they agreed to it, except in one particular. She wanted to stay to help Elijah and Emily secretly. Edward said, "No, Bella. Do not stay in this place. Go back with us to mother." She replied, "No. Let me stay, to encourage and assist Emily: she will think she is breaking vows. Let me stay, and show her why she has a right to break them. Leave money with me, and I can get home by myself."

Three weeks after this, when the young men entered the Western-bound train in Boston, Mr. and Mrs. Elijah Cressy were with them. Jack was there also. With a boy's alertness he had discovered the secret, and with a boy's urgency had pressed his claims. He followed the party into the car, pushed into a seat close by, and, looking about him, exclaimed, "Oh, my! ain't Miss Bella a sharp one, to do all this for us, and they not find out? Ain't it fun?"

But the family of sober people were sadly aggrieved.

They wrote to Mr. Frederic Forresst, and bitterly complained of Bella.

"Upon my honor," said he, "if she is fond of playing tricks and of associating with carpenters and boys, I can put her where she will have plenty of such company."

Ere she had time to execute her plan for leaving her post, like a captain who had stood by the ship till all were saved, Mr. Frederic Forresst was on the scene; and suddenly she was transported. She scarce realized his orders, or knew what he meant, but obeyed, as by compulsion; and he took her as by right far away to a new scene. He felt she must be punished. He went to a well-looking house in the secluded village of Sheardown. By his side was the young sister whom he was determined to subdue to his wishes, or chastise according to his own ideas. He drew the bell-knob; and it was opened by a plainly-dressed, but good-looking woman, who responded to Mr. Forresst's inquiry by saying, "*I* am Mrs. Babbette."

Mrs. Babbette was the teacher of a school in her own house; and Mr. Forresst had opened a correspondence with her. She immediately invited him into her parlor, glancing at Bella as she followed her brother. When the three were seated, Mrs. Babbette again cast searching glances at Bella, causing the girl to feel queerly under this unnatural scrutiny. At length Mrs. Babbette asked, "Is this young lady the pupil you mentioned in your letter?"

"The same, madam."

Mrs. Babbette gave the girl another searching glance, and said, "Are you aware, sir, of the nature of my school? Do you know that it is for idiots and deformed children, such as would not be suitable for the larger, more progressive schools?"

"I am quite aware, madam. Do you recollect what I wrote you?"

Mrs. Babbette did recollect; but she only bowed assent. She recollected that Mr. Forresst had written that his sister had a perversity of character; and she wondered at the time how great or of what nature that perversity might be. And now, as she looked at this beautiful maiden, she marvelled still more, and was certain there must be some mistake. But it was too late now to rectify it; for with a sweep and a bow that were gracefully and magnificently appalling, Mr. Frederic Forresst arose, bowed himself out: and the last impression that rested on Mrs. Babbette's mind was that of two pointed mustache ends resting squarely across her doorway in an obstinate, haughty manner, that said, "I am here. I am going; for you two obedience is the only requisite. *I* am ruler."

He disappeared. Mrs. Babbette turned to her pupil. Bella still sat with her hat resting lightly above her dark, flowing curls. Her lips were full and ripe, her form developed as only health can develop a frame, and her chest was heaving as only strong emotion checked by a stronger will can cause the breast to heave. Mrs. Babbette was touched. Her kindly nature felt, and her sagacity told her, that something was wrong; and, going to Bella, she laid her hand on the dark curls. "My dear, there is some strange mistake. Do not feel bad, but trust in me, and I will know how to help you. I shall not take you into my school as a pupil; for I am sure you could better teach me than I you. Come with me now, and see my school as a visitor."

Before morning Mrs. Babbette had drawn from Bella the story of her life; and the next day, taking counsel from her own heart, she wrote two letters. One, directed to Mr. Frederic Forresst, contained her reasons for the course she was taking, and was very explicit. The other was sent to Bella's mother; and Bella was the bearer. On her own responsibility Mrs. Babbette sent her where she felt it was her proper place to be, — to the mother who loved her as no other could love.

When Mr. Frederic read his letter, his upper lip twitched; and the mustache described forty-five degrees of a circle. But he was powerless: the strength of a conscientious woman had been his conqueror. Before he could answer that letter, Bella was in her mother's arms, telling the tale of her sorrows and of Mrs. Babbette's kind act.

7

CHAPTER X.

A CLEAR–MINDED woman had given Mr. Frederic Forresst a strong pill of truth ; and he swallowed it as a sick child gulps down a dose from the hands of a straightforward nurse. He considered now that Edward and Mortimer, the refractory boys, being gone, there was no present danger, and permitted Bella to remain at home. Adelaide was about to marry to the taste of the family, and in accordance with its pride ; and Bella's deft needle was both necessary and useful.

Then came other changes, as they often come to our American families when the children marry one by one, and the old homestead grows deserted. It was Nellie who planned and pressed forward the final change. Nellie, the last of the elder girls, had resolved to make for herself a splendid match ; 'and, as preliminary, she must go where superb men were to be found. According to her ideas, a superb man lived in an elegant house, kept a carriage, wore kid-gloves, and dined in fashionable style. In seeking an elegant alliance, Miss Nellie found Mr. Frederic a ready helper. They carried their point, persuaded the mother, who felt that she was now but a withered branch, and sold the old house with all its associations. Then they took a house in Boston, — a high, narrow house, on a street near Mrs. Boynton, the oldest daughter of the Forresst family, now the wife of a wealthy banker.

Bella did not feel at home in this new house, and would

have cried a little for the old homestead but for the thoughts of the Western home whither her young hopes trended. Mrs. Forresst did weep. The ancestral spirit flamed up brightly in this old woman. She was proud of her home in which her married life had been spent, and loved it as it was. Her heart seemed tearing as she pulled herself away from the long-trodden floors to try her feet in new places. But Frederic said, "Upon my honor, mother, the house is but an old, cracked shell, and wouldn't pay for keeping it in repair."

Only one member of the family deserted home on account of this arrangement, and that was Harry. He could not be hedged by the conventional rules of a city, nor bring his life and habits to the precincts of narrow streets. Therefore he went away to the Aroostook country, where the woodmen felled the heavy timber.

Only Bella, the mother, and Miss Nellie began housekeeping in the new style; and, but for the latter, Bridget would have had an easy time. But Nellie had an object in view; and she gained it. She won Dr. Bergmann, a German physician from Brooklyn, who had come to Boston for scientific purposes, and found himself caught in the meshes of a softer science.

Dr. Bergmann was fifty years old, and had been married. But what of that? He had the nice establishment, money, and extensive practice, that constituted him a "superb man." He was a learned man, and moved in profound circles; but he did not consider it necessary that his wife should be learned. He wanted her to be graceful in figure and elegant in manners, — an ornament to his house, at which he could look when he rested from deep thoughts.

Miss Nellie was very beautiful on her bridal day; and, as she walked through the church-aisles with her orange blossoms and bridal veil, the eyes of her friends followed

her admiringly.　There Miss Nellie Forresst ended.　There
was no more of her in Boston.　Afterward there was a Mrs.
Nellie Bergmann in Brooklyn, elegantly riding in her elegant carriage.　People said Dr. Bergmann had found a very
stylish wife.

Bella and her mother were left alone in their hired house
in the city.　They were lonely, and. could not feel contented.　Bella thought of her Western home, where her
heart had already gone; and Mrs. Forresst felt like a
stranger in her stylish house.　She could not like the city:
it cramped her, and jostled her old-fashioned independence.

Then these two women formed a plan of their own, —
how they would move out to the home of which Edward
had written, and help him and Mortimer, instead of waiting
till the young men had struggled up alone.　The old lady
thought she should like the bracing breezes.　And Bella
said, "Why cannot I be married there as well as here ?"
She wrote to Edward then, and told him they would freight
out their furniture, — told him all their plans; and her
hopes were buoyant with these designs.

We may be sure there was delight in that newly-fledged
home.　Jack crowed like a true chanticleer; Emily smiled
in her quiet way; Elijah's dark eyes beamed with pleasure;
Mortimer felt that heaven was coming down; and Edward
wrote to tell the welcome.

It was then that Bella's trouble began.　When Edward's
letter arrived, Bella and her mother immediately began
their preparations.　They gave up the lease of their house,
wrote to Harry, and began preparing their goods for the
transit.

"Upon my honor !" said Mr. Frederic to himself.　His
anger was roused.　He was not a man easily foiled by any
obstacle; and was a young girl to carry her will over his ?
His handsome face was set in lines of stern defiance: his

mustache worked, and his thoughts worked also. "Is not my judgment superior to hers? How does she know what is best? Long ago I swore that not a cent of my father's property should ever bless Chauncey Beale or his progeny; and my oath is like a Mede and Persian law. Why didn't Chauncey Beale have property to give his son? I have no patience with these thriftless men."

The mustache went up, and the mustache went down, one end at a time, two ends, cornerwise, horizontally, and at angles. Then like a flash it went square across, and rested there. He had thought out his course. His mind was at rest.

That evening, when the rumbling of teams was ceasing in the streets, and the lights were aflame as guides, Mr. Frederic Forresst might have been seen turning a corner, with his gloved hand twirling his dapper cane. He walked gracefully on a few blocks, then paused before a sign, — "Dr. Carnes." Mr. Forresst rang the bell. He was presently ushered into a room, where sat the venerable physician, — a man said to be profoundly versed in mental as well as physical diseases. He arose with a bow, as his visitor entered. Mr. Frederic Forresst was a man often mentioned in the higher business circles. Dr. Carnes knew him, and felt honored by this call. He gave his visitor a suave bow. Mr. Forresst received it as his right.

The next half-hour in that room would have been a study for a philosopher in mind. The way the gentleman and the doctor discussed the science of metaphysics in general, and as applicable to Miss Bella in particular, should be put down in medical journals as showing what can be said on such subjects in these modern times. Surely temper had a fearful hold upon Mr. Forresst, or he could not have spoken of his sister as he did that evening; and, with all due respect to Dr. Carnes, we must say that neither his venerable age nor great learning saved him from a mistake on that occasion. It was strange, that without seeing the young lady, and merely by the representation of a brother whose motives he did not know, this respectable physician should pronounce the word "insane."

Dr. Carnes advised Mr. Forresst to take his sister to an asylum for a time. The doctor remarked that at asylums they have facilities for restoring aberrations of mind; that he was in the practice of sending persons to these retreats, and could recommend them as efficacious. Mr. Forresst was delighted with this assurance. It accorded with his wishes; and he should, he said, "immediately profit by the doctor's advice."

"But," continued the physician, "the law requires that two medical men shall visit the person, and pronounce judgment."

"And to whom should you refer me ? " asked the gentleman.

"I know no better man than Dr. Furbelough."

Mr. Forresst bowed, and was about to proceed to Dr. Furbelough, when a sudden thought occurred to him. "Would Dr. Carnes be so kind as to accompany him ? Dr. Carnes's advice might be invaluable."

For a gentleman of Mr. Forresst's type, people will wonderfully incommode themselves. Almost without being aware that he was condescending from his usual habit, Dr. Carnes arose and prepared for his walk.

They found Dr. Furbelough, a young man of pleasing exterior and rising fame. He received them with a showy dash of courtesy, a profusion of bows and smiles. He listened while Dr. Carnes opened the case. He sighed sympathetically, and turned to Mr. Forresst. "Very sad, sir. Very trying for you. What are the particular manifestations, — violence, or stupidity ? "

Dr. Carnes interposed. "I am sorry to say, sir, it appears to be perverse obstinacy."

"Ah, indeed!" was the medical response. "Very difficult to cure. It would be best to try an asylum at once. Delay might increase the disease. My sympathies are with you, Mr. Forresst. Miss Bella was a very fine girl."

Mr. Forresst acknowledged this sympathy by a bow.

"When shall we visit the patient?"

The busy mind of Mr. Forresst had been preparing for this question. He was not taken unawares. "I am so very busy, gentlemen — Suppose you make out your certificates here, without personal examination."

They glanced at each other, and then replied, "The law requires an examination."

"That is a very necessary law," Mr. Forresst observed; "but it is a law that cannot adapt itself to all cases. Seeing her could not affect your decision. You would find her even more perverse than I have stated: indeed, I doubt whether she would receive you, or answer your questions with any spirit but rudeness."

"Ah! Is she so bad as that?" and again they looked at each other. They seemed to understand each other's glances; and certain mesmeric responses passed between them in silent interchange. "It is contrary to law," said the eyes of one.

"Yes," returned the other; "but who will know it?"

"And it is Mr. Forresst," observed the first.

"Yes, it is Mr. Forresst," echoed the second; and then they both glanced at the gentleman.

"Very rich," said one.

"And popular," added the other.

"What's the use?" asked both. "If we should examine her, we should doubtless find her as he states. Any way, we shouldn't like to differ from him; and — well — what

do you say ?   He is in haste, and we shall get — our pay.
Who'll know ? "

They wrote the certificate then, — the document that was
to confine an innocent, rational girl in an insane asylum.
They did it heartlessly, and then pocketed the fees that Mr.
Forresst drew liberally from a well-filled pocket-book.   They
had earned their money with little trouble ; and, if they
had any regrets, they were that such cases did not oftener
.occur.

Mr. Forresst went home with the certificate in his
pocket; and he laughed softly between his set teeth.
" Cleverly done !   I fancy they would have met a rebuff if
they had paid her a medical visit.   Ha, ha, ha ! "

The next legal step was to procure the signature of the
judge.   This was easily accomplished.   The certificate of
these physicians was sufficient testimony in the mind of
the judicial man.   He might have inquired into the circumstances, might have summoned a jury, and investigated
whether the certificate was a fraud, and whether the person was really a proper subject for the trying ordeal of confined existence ; but he took these things for granted, and
signed a legal commitment in which Bella Forresst was set
forth as an insane person, and a fit subject for an insane
asylum.   Thus her fetters were riveted by a judge who had
never even seen her.   Accused criminals have a public trial,
with a chance for self-defence, ere they are sent to prison.
Persons accused of insanity have no such opportunity, but
are forced into asylums without power to prevent the incarceration.   The statute laws give them ways for proving their
sanity, and for escape if sane; but the arts of physicians
and friends contrive to elude these laws, or destroy their
effects; and statutes, framed to prevent unjust imprisonments, are twisted and executed according to the caprices of
those who imprison, till they become practically statutes
for life-imprisonment.

There is, in papers of commitment, one clause that has a chance for the victim to escape; but practically it is useless. This clause was inserted in this warrant, and stated that the paper of committal should be read to Bella twelve hours previous to her removal to the asylum. Mr. Forresst made this clause void by a short method. He did not read it to her.

"Upon my honor," he mused, "what would be the effect of giving her twelve hours' notice? She would use the time in disappearing, unless I place a guard over her, which is too much trouble. And who will know whether I follow the law? In these cases we must be a law unto ourselves."

Then he went to his sister, Mrs. Boynton, and informed her of these arrangements.

"Surely," she said, "you do not mean to send Bella to an insane asylum? What a disgrace!"

"Upon my honor, Eunice! which is the greater disgrace, that, or a squatter's cabin? And to drag our mother out there too!"

"Mother seems willing to go."

"Yes, she is old, and easily persuaded."

"Does Bella know it? Have you told her?"

"Know it! Told her! Do you think I would cut the strings to my own net, and set my bird a-flying?"

Mrs. Boynton's proud face contracted in meditation. She spoke again slowly. "It is a hard blow to give a young girl, especially one of Bella's temperament."

"It is harder for you and I to see our father's property go to Mortimer Beale," Mr. Forresst replied; "and I desire your assistance without more words." He spoke with unflinching hauteur. "To-morrow morning send your carriage for mother. Tell her that you think it too hard for her to be there in the midst of all Bella's packing. Bring her to your house."

Mrs. Boynton, in her luxurious home, lay awake that night, thinking. But Mr. Forresst did not lie awake. "Thanks to the good laws of Massachusetts, I have found an effectual way," he said to himself. "She will not get out of that berth till she promises better fashions." And then the brother fell asleep.

The next morning, when Mrs. Boynton went for her mother, the old lady said, "What! Go away and leave Bella with all this work on her hands?"

"Never mind the work, mother. We will hire a woman to help Bella."

And Bella said, "Yes, mother. Go with Eunice. Let me have a strong work-woman. I shall do nicely."

Mrs. Forresst yielded; and at half-past nine she went away in Mrs. Boynton's carriage. At eleven another carriage came to the house. Two men leaped from it, and went up to the door. They jerked the bell like men in a hurry, and like men unaccustomed to ceremony. Bella was in a chamber. A morning robe of print, and a large apron tied around, was her apparel. The room was in the disorder incident to packing; and in the centre stood an open, partially-filled trunk. She heard the door open, and heard the men inquire for Bella Forresst. She rushed to the stair-railing, and looked down into the hall. She saw the brass buttons and burly forms of two policemen. She stepped back, lest they should see her; and surprise kept her silent. Bridget came up the stairs.

"An' sure, Miss Bella, an' what can they want o' ye?"

"I do not know. I cannot go down. Go back and ask them what they want."

Bridget went back; but their reply was, "If she cannot come down, we will go up."

"What can it mean?" thought Bella; and she drew back into the chamber with the natural retirement of a women *en déshabille*. She had scarcely thrown the apron from her when the men were in the room.

"This is Miss Forresst, I suppose," said he in front.

"Yes, sir." She looked up at him with a frightened expression; and a strange trembling seized her.

"And this is your trunk, I suppose," he continued, looking at the open trunk with its draperies lying within.

Again she murmured, "Yes." She was afraid of the man with his bold, forward ways. "If I was guilty of any wrong, I should think he was after me," was her flashing thought. In a moment more she understood the scene. The man said, "I suppose our errand is not very pleasing to you, Miss Forresst. We have come to take you to the asylum."

"The what?"

"The insane asylum, Miss Forresst. I·suppose you have heard your committal read."

"Committal? I have heard nothing. What do you mean?"

"Your brother should have read it to you twelve hours ago; but, if he has failed in his duty, we must not fail in ours. If you wish to lay any more articles into that trunk, we will wait a minute. If not, we may as well lock it now."

Bella was stupefied with astonishment and horror. These men were directing her, and assuming full power over her movements. She soon found that the officers of law dispose of their subjects in a very cool manner. Seeing that she did not move, the forward man locked the trunk, and put the key in his pocket. Then he turned to Bridget, who was watching, terrified, at the door.

"Get Miss Forresst a bonnet."

"An' what may ye be goin' to do with Miss Bella?"

"Oh! we are not going to harm her. But make haste: the train will soon be leaving."

Bridget feared the men even more than her mistress. She hastened for a hat, and took out also a sack and a pair of gloves. These she brought to her young mistress, saying, "Whativer it be, Miss·Bella, niver ye fear. The Holy Virgin will protict ye; au' I'll say me prayers for ye day and night."

But to Bella every thing was dark. She stood attired, a victim of — law, we were about to say. But it was not so. She was a victim of law dishonored, and of statutes made null by fraud. One of the men took her trunk; the other took her arm. They passed down the stairs, and out at the door. They put her into the carriage, and drove away. Bridget was left alone. They drove to the railway-station. Bella sat like one stupefied. The two men lifted her out by the two arms. She stood between them on the platform, one on either side. People stared at her. Women drew their garments one side. Men looked her over, and formed their own conclusions. She felt, rather than saw, these stares; and every eye around her seemed as a dagger piercing her soul. She would never forget these looks. She could never forget them, nor forget the cold chills that ran through her system while she stood between those men. Henceforward she would know how it seemed to be in the grasp of law officers. She entered the cars under.a battery of eyes: she rode under the consciousness of people watching her; and when she reached her destination, and stepped out on the platform, she still felt people looking strangely at her.

The two escorts led her to a carriage that was waiting. They put her in : one entered with her; the other mounted the box. It was the asylum-carriage, highly polished, and drawn by a span of sleek horses, expensively harnessed. In this carriage Bella was carried away to the big building. She was transferred from the carriage to the care of the institution, where she was taken out, and placed within the great asylum doors. Then the policemen went away, and she was left " within the bars." She felt as if a blow had been struck in her face, and her life was destroyed. Strangers were about her; and they, too, stared. These were not the rude stares of curiosity, but the professional stares of the asylum. She was not looked *at* now, but was looked *through* and *through*, till she longed to escape into some corner where she could lie down and weep unseen : it seemed that the cords of her heart were snapping.

This professional scrutiny of the " new patient " went against her. She was pronounced " very insane." With her hat, sack, and gloves, no fault could be found; but " what young lady in her senses would ride in the cars in a calico wrapper ? " The long ringlets were declared tô be " frowzled ; " and they said there was a " wild look in her eyes." These were asylum verdicts. No one asked how she was taken from home, — whether she had time to change her dress or smooth her hair. No one thought that her present situation was enough to make her look wild, nor how she must suffer, — a prisoner in the grip of inexorable men. It was " taken for granted " that she was crazy ; and for every action insanity was supposed the cause. She was under the brand.

They led her up a flight of winding, uncarpeted stairs, unlocked a door, led her through, and locked the door again. She heard the key turn behind her; she knew that she was a prisoner. Faintness struck her, and the air grew dark; but she rallied, and looked about her. She saw herself in a long, uncarpeted hall, up and down which women were walking. They paused, and looked at her: but these were not stares of rudeness; deep pity was in their eyes. They glanced at each other, and then at her; and she heard one

8

of them say, "Another.   O Lord God ! how many, — how
many are doomed to this place ? "

Bella felt that these ladies were prisoners. She had come
to be one of their number.   It seemed that the finest fibres
of her heart were snapping.   Darker and darker grew the
air.   Light disappeared.   She groped to a chair, and sat
down. Now she was struggling under the prison-darkness, —
the strange, unearthly sensation that rushes over all human
beings when first they feel the air of a prison, and locks have
closed upon them.   Guilty or innocent, rational or irrational, or whatever be the person's condition, nothing can
save them from that half-terror and half-abjectness that is
the peculiar feature of prison-life.   It fell upon Bella with
wild anguish.   She turned to the woman who locked her
in, and implored for pity ; but never a word did the woman
reply.   With her it was legal, official business ; to Bella it
was as the knell of a life-doom. The woman regarded Bella
as an insane girl, sent hither by her friends, because they
could do nothing with her at home.   She paid no attention
to the girl's pleadings, but went out, and locked the door
behind her.

Nothing could save Bella now.   No human help could
she seek.   Wishing was useless.   Tears would produce no
effect.   Smiles were powerless.   She was a prisoner under
law, held in a stronghold, shut up under absolute power, —
a chattel from which the institution could draw funds. Absolute submission was now her only alternative.   She had
become the property of the institution.   The officials could
hold her, rule her, and subject her to their wills or caprices,
just as men hold animals ; and there was no way for her
to escape.

She sat a while in her chair, palsied and terrified.   Then
she arose and walked through the hall.   Iron-sashed windows were on every side, and heavy doors with locks.   Sad

women sat around, and their eyes turned to hers with pity. In one small room there sat a young lady trimming a hat. She looked bright and joyous,—a contrast to her surroundings. Bella went to her, saying, "Cannot I go out of here? Is that door always locked?" The girl looked up coolly, as attendants learn to look. "No, you cannot go. The door is always locked. Where did you come from?"

"From Boston," said Bella, and turned away, with sickness at her heart. She went to a corner, and dropped into a chair. An old lady came to her softly, and said, "Don't feel so bad, my dear. It is no worse for you than the rest of us. I, too, am a prisoner."

Bella looked in the old face, and recoiled. It was a face on which suffering had written deep lines, — not of active misery, but of rust and solitude, stamping it with an indefinable disagreeableness from which the fresh young girl shrank.

"There, there," said the old lady, "I won't trouble you. I'll go away. You don't know what to make of such a poor old thing. God grant they may not keep you here till you, too, are such as I am!"

Bella shuddered, but did not speak. She saw other ladies looking at her, fresh, bright-looking ladies; and she asked herself, "Are they really insane persons? They would grace a drawing-room."

Presently the girl who had been hat-trimming came and motioned to her. She arose and followed. The stranger girl led her diagonally across the hall, and into a small side-room. She told her that this was to be her room; that she might lay off her things here, and that she "must make herself at home."

"Home!—home!" It was the first time the word ever grated on Bella's ears. "Home, in this place? The very name is desecrated by such a use. ' 'Tis home where'er the heart is;' and my heart" —

She could not finish the sentence, but sat down, speechless, in the only chair the room afforded, and rested her head on the sill of the window. And what a window! The sash was painted; but there was the cold, hard look of the iron of which it was made. She put her hand on it: it felt cold. The attending girl went out and left her. At the tea-hour they brought her a cup of tea and one small biscuit. She ate it, and then leaned back and pressed her fingers over her eyes. Tears trickled through between them; and she wiped them away with a handkerchief that she drew from her wrapper-pocket. A man passed her door. He paused and looked in, but did not speak. She felt annoyed, and arose to shut the door: it would not stay closed. It was a coarse, heavy door; and she examined the fastening. There was neither knob nor latch. There was a lock, with a place for a key, on the outside; but inside there was no way to fasten the door together. She could neither shut it against intruders, nor have any other control over it. She sat down again, distressed. The day was waning. Shadows were gathering. New voices were heard in the hall. The assistant physician was taking an official tour. He paused before Bella, and looked her over. She was his "new patient." He must make a medical examination.

"My dear," he said, "had you no better dress in which to ride here? This is not a suitable travelling-costume."

Bella's cheeks crimsoned, and her eyes flashed. Indignation superseded her distress. She felt that this man must know, or ought to inquire into, the circumstances in which she had been taken from home, and her situation otherwise. She thought of the rough treatment through which she had passed, and answered this smooth-tongued stranger scornfully, "Is it any of your business what I ride in?"

The physician smiled with a peculiar meaning. "Never mind, dear. We hope to see you in a better frame of mind, by and by." He whispered to the attendant, "Very bad!" He passed along; and she was alone again. Evening was fairly set in. There was a light in the hall; but in her room there was no light, save what gleamed through her half-open door. Was she to sit there in darkness? Nay, more. Was she to stay there all night? Was she to sleep on that narrow bunk, and within that cell-like room? She gave her room a careful scrutiny. It was about twelve feet long, and ten in width. In it there was a narrow iron bedstead, dressed with a mattress, and with one pillow in the middle at the head. The walls of the room were covered with coarse paper; and it had that dingy, unwholesome look that comes from closeness long continued, like dust stifled.

There was a bureau, or something they called a bureau, opposite the bed; and over this bureau hung a seven-by-nine pane of glass, called by courtesy a mirror. There was also a washstand in one corner, very much dilapidated, and looking as if generations had used it. Besides these, there was the old chair in which she was sitting, and a cotton curtain at the window. The floor was of a dark, ancient yellow, carpetless, save a strip before the bed.

"And here I am to stay to-night," said the girl to herself. "How much longer? Who knows?"

Suddenly a woman, bearing a tray of glasses, appeared in the doorway. In each glass there was a decoction of some sort. The woman placed the tray on the small bureau; and, taking up a glass, handed it to Bella.

"What is that for?" asked Bella in amazement.

"It is medicine for you to drink."

"Medicine! Why should I take medicine? I am not ill."

"You are to take this, however. The doctor prepared it for you."

"Doctor! No doctor has examined me. I should advise him to see whether I am ill before he prescribes."

"Come," said the woman peremptorily, "I can't stop to parley. Take it!"

But the idea of taking strange medicine without proper medical prescription was horrible to Bella's mind. She had been taught that great care was necessary in administering medicines; and she answered decidedly, "I will not take it. No doctor has spoken to me, except one who asked me about my dress; and that was all he said to me. I will not take medicine without proper prescriptions."

The woman stepped forward, holding the glass firmly in one hand. With the other she seized Bella by the head; and, giving her a twist that made her defenceless, she held the glass to her lips.

"Drink it!"

And Bella swallowed it, she scarce knew how. Then the woman turned, took up her tray, went out, and said to the attending girl, nodding her head toward Bella's room, "You have a hard subject in there. Keep firm."

And still Bella sat there. The potion was doing its work. Stupid sleepiness came over her. She felt it through her frame; and, rousing herself, said, "I may as well go to bed. What is there to sit up for?"

Then she thought of her trunk. Where was it? She remembered that in the bottom of it she had laid some fine underclothing. She must have a nightdress. She called the attending girl, and said, "Where is my trunk?"

"Down in the marking-room, I suppose."

"I should like it. Will you ask some one to bring it up?"

"You can't have it to-night. Your things have not been examined."

"Examined! What do you mean?"

"Why, your clothes must be looked over, and marked."

"Will they take out my clothes, and handle them over?"

"They are obliged to. That is the rule."

Bella sighed with a strange helplessness. She was completely in the power of these strangers.

"What shall I do for a nightdress?" she asked.

"I don't know." The attendant said this curtly, and left the room. Bella retired that night literally without one accustomed comfort. She disrobed in darkness, put a skirt over her shoulders, and lay down on the hard, narrow bed. She heard the sounds of voices and steps, — the women going to their solitary rooms, and the attendant scolding, driving, or coaxing, as the case might be. Then came another sound, — a clicking, harsh sound; and she listened wonderingly. It was the click of the locks, as, one after another, the attendant put her key in them, and fastened the women's doors. So intense was Bella's interest, that the effect of her potion was in a measure counteracted by her quickening sensations. She raised her head, and was trying to look into the hall, when her doorway was darkened by a shadow; and a girl with a key looked in. Bella dropped back into the bed; and the girl stepped into the room. "It is time you were asleep," she said. "Let there be no noise in your room to-night." Then the girl turned, put the key in the lock, and drew the door together. It snapped; and Bella was a prisoner in her cell. She sat up in her bed, and thought, "Wherein am I different from a prisoner in a state prison? Here I am, double-locked from all the world, lying in a room that is close as a felon's cell. God have mercy on me, and forgive those who have done this thing!"

She slept a while, but awoke in the night in the middle

of the darkness, and thought of her situation, her mother, Mortimer, and this sad trouble that had met her in her life-path. She heard the night winds moan around the angles of the large building; and they seemed to her like sighings of the departed. There were other sounds, — cryings and groanings, as of people in distress. She heard them in different directions; and the sounds added to the desolation that oppressed her. Then — but — hark! There was a cry near her, a sobbing as of deep distress. It was in the cell adjoining hers. Some woman's heart was breaking there all alone. There were words mingled with the sobs, — words that seemed to be of prayer; for the tones were those of supplication. How Bella longed to get to the sufferer, that she might console her!

Soon footsteps were heard coming through the hall. A light shone through the aperture over Bella's door; and she thought some one was going to the relief of the sufferer. But, no: the footsteps kept on, died away, and were heard no more. They were the steps of the night-watch, going the rounds with a lantern. The night-watch heard these sobs; but what of that? It was "only a patient" weeping. In that expression, "only a patient," there lies a deep meaning. When persons are committed to these institutions, they become "patients." They lose their human privileges, and are treated as if void of natural affections. They are supposed to have no loves, nor hopes, nor desires; yet, when their friends come to visit them, they are required to show every symptom of natural joy, with not one particle of indignation at their unnatural treatment. They are told to consider their situation as one of God's providences, and that against his will it is a sin to murmur.

Bella had not yet learned the train of asylum argument. To her these cries of her neighbor were the cries of pain and anguish going up there to God alone; and they seemed to her to need human sympathy. The next morning she ventured into the hall, and looked wistfully among the ladies, hoping to find the night weeper: but all were strangers; and it was not till many days after, that she learned which of these prisoners this was. There are no introductions in asylum halls. Ladies, accustomed to civilized proprieties and the forms of etiquette, are taken from their homes and from society without time to say farewell: they are carried and landed within asylums without ceremony; and with broken hearts, without announcement or introduction, they make acquaintance as they can. Bella was not exempt from the general rule. She felt unutterably sad, but spoke to no one. For a time none of the ladies spoke to her. They looked at her, and deep in their souls they pitied her; for well they knew the anguish through which she was passing. They, who had themselves passed through this sorrow knew how to feel for her; and they whispered of her among themselves, —

"So young! So beautiful! What a shame to shut her in here! What do our people mean by banishing so many good and beautiful to these prison-houses?"

Bella did not hear these remarks; but she was conscious of sympathetic glances, and felt that among these ladies there was kindly love waiting for her. She saw that the ladies were well-dressed and refined; and it seemed to her like sin to keep them in this confinement. With a few exceptions, she saw no indications of aberration of mind; but she saw ladies of education and refinement living there in a prison existence of loneliness and heart desolation.

One morning, as she sat in her *only* chair, after breakfast, two of the ladies walked slowly to her door and looked in. One of them had a proudly set head, beautiful blue eyes,

and an oval forehead, above which lay braided bands of
glossy auburn hair. She wore a dress of green and white
silk, flowing in a train behind; and buckled slippers were
peeping out from beneath the ruffled skirt.

Leaning upon the arm of this woman was another. She
had large lustrous eyes, looking out from beneath eye-brows
of jet.   She was tall; and her form was enveloped in a
cashmere robe, over which floated a soft, fleecy scarf of
white. The two ladies introduced each other. The blue-
eyed lady was Mrs. Long; the luminous, black-eyed woman
was the wife of a wealthy gentleman in the suburbs of ——.
The husband of Mrs. Long was a lawyer of rising fame,
"very smart," she said, smiling curiously as she spoke, —
"smart enough to get me in here."

"Excuse me," said the luminous-eyed lady; "but it does
not require much smartness to do that in these days, when
nearly every doctor is a backer to these institutions."

As she said this, lines of fine thought passed over her
face; and Bella was reminded of heroines of whom she had
read in history; and it seemed to her that some imprisoned
princess stood before her.   They opened their hearts there
together.   They revealed to each other the under-currents
of their lives, and felt a chord of electric sympathy in
trouble, — a chord that is ever vibrating through asylum-
halls, and which is the chief, and almost only solace of the
inmates in their troubles.

Between the officers or *employés* of these establishments
and their patients there is very little sympathy. Coercion
and force on one side, and absolute submission on the other,
are like oil and water: they may be shaken together, but
have no affinity. The officers and *employés* of asylums
hold reins of sovereign power over their imprisoned people;
and the people under them live in a state of absolute subjection. There are men and women, by the scores and hun-

dreds, nay, by the thousands, now in these locked buildings, who have lived under these hard rules till the lines of sorrow and discipline on their faces are as graven lines that can never be erased. They have lived as close prisoners, subject to the tempers of different rulers, seeing others 'go in and out till their lives seem as a miserable stupefaction,— a torpor of anguish, out of which they can never come; and the years of their misery may be counted by the furrows of anguish on their countenances. It made Bella's heart ache to see these prisoners of years, they looked so sad and weary. There was one in this hall,—a silver-haired woman, who wore a soft lace cap, trimmed with lavender, on whose face patience had stamped the indelible marks of these long, solitary years. When Bella was told that this old lady had been a patient twenty-seven years, she was shocked, and could scarcely credit her own ears. She went to the woman.

"Is it true, Mrs. Spears, that you have been twenty-seven years an inmate of an insane asylum ?"

"It is quite true, my dear."

"I cannot realize it," Bella answered thoughtfully. " Before I was born, when I was born, and all the time since, you have been a prisoner! I am sure I did not know that here, in our free country, people could be held in prison, unless they had committed crimes !"

"You know little of the world as yet, my dear young lady."

"But it seems, Mrs. Spears, that such a life would be hardly worth the having."

"I have often thought that," the old lady responded, looking tearfully at Bella. "But, life being once given us, we must bear it, with whatever comes in its train. It has been the will of my heavenly Father that I should live this solitary life of hopelessness; and who am I that I should gainsay his will?"

"Is it the will of God, or the will of man?" asked Bella.

The old lady recoiled. "Oh! my dear young lady, do not speak blasphemously. All things are of God's will."

"Then, why do we try to get rid of the wrongs, and uproot evil?" asked Bella. "If wrong is from God's will, let it stand; but if it is from man, who sets up to know more than God, let us tear it down, and put right in its place."

"Well," said the old lady meekly, "you, who are young, may see to these deep matters. I am verging to eternity. I have suffered; and my days are almost numbered. I pray for a spirit to forgive those who have kept these bonds over me; but it pains me more than tongue can tell when I see young girls, like you, brought into these halls."

"Christian prisoner," was Bella's thought. "Could I ever so submit and forgive?"

"Go to your room, Mrs. Spears!" commanded a pert young girl, drawing near. And the old lady went, meekly walking across the hall that might almost be channelled by her feet that had trodden it so long as a patient. She went to her room, and sat down to her Bible, the only solace she possessed; and Bella, too, went to her room. The tones of that pert command were still ringing in her ears; and she longed to reprove that young attendant for such rough speech.

Sabbath came, in its own due time, and the patients were notified to prepare for chapel. The attendants went around, ordering some to go, and commanding others not to go, as their piques and fancies dictated. Bella was told to "Go!" Her trunk, after three days' waiting, and after all the articles had been handled under pretext for marking, had at last come to her; and, with a soul full of pain, she selected from it a dress. When the chapel-bell rang, she was ready. Bands of women began to come out from the different halls and centre towards the chapel. Sad, dejected faces passed by Bella as she stood waiting her turn. The patients from each hall were under the escort of separate attendants, and walked in files, as ordered. Some were well-dressed, and some were clad in a cheapness inexpressible. Some were intelligent in countenance, and some were quite the reverse. Some were fresh in skin and complexion, and evidently were fresh from the world. Others wore the unmistakable marks of long duress, and sufferings borne in solitude.

The women from Bella's hall fell into the ranks, and, walking in a line, descended the stairs when they were bidden. In the central hall the women were gathered, waiting the passage of men, who were coming in file from their apartments. A shadow fell over Bella's soul as she saw these men. They followed each other in regular tramp, each division under its keeper. Some of the faces were demented, but many of them were bright and intelligent; and some equalled, in every respect, the superintendent, who stood in the centre of the aisle, watching the defile as it passed along. To Bella the scene seemed like the passing of mortals to eternity. She was very sad; and as she entered the chapel, guarded as she was, and realized how these were all imprisoned, like herself, she could scarce restrain her tears. Trouble seemed all about her, — trouble, trouble, everywhere. She could not enjoy the service. It was but mockery to her. She could not worship a free God while she was thus bound. Her soul cried, "Let me go. Let me go, my Father; that I may worship thee in peace." But for her there was no release. She must be remanded back to her cell, back to her prison and solitude. And all these who had come out to worship must go back, back to their solitude, heartsickness, and despair.

Bella wept that sabbath night : she could not help it. She wept for herself in bondage, and she wept for others whom she saw suffering about her.   Alas ! she was not the only one who wept in that building.   Hers was not the only anguished heart that was crushing beneath the strictures of those laws.   There were tears in every corridor, there was mourning in every hall.

The next morning Bella met the matron as she was crossing the hall.   The matron said, " Good-morning, Miss Forresst.   How do you do this morning ? "

" Do ? " said Bella meditatively : " how can any one do here ?   Mrs. Matron, this is a house of tears."

" Oh, well, never mind !   *You* do not shed tears."

" I shall, or go mad, if I stay here," was Bella's response, as she turned quickly from the woman who spoke with so little feeling.   " She ought to weep herself," was the thought of the girl : " she ought to weep for the suffering she sees about her."

But the matron was a strong woman : she saw no cause for tears.   Day by day she walked among these anguished women, and never felt one throb of pity.

CHAPTER XI.

BELLA took her first lessons in asylum letter-writing in this wise: the matron was passing through the hall, when a young girl went to her with a letter in her hand.

"Will you please read my letter, and see if it will do to send?" the girl asked in a soft, winning voice.

The matron paused, and took the letter: she opened it, and glanced it through; then she returned it to the writer. "No, I cannot send this letter: it is very improperly written; it has the word 'prison' three times, and you say you want to go home."

"Why is it improper to say prison? I am in prison Why is it wrong to say I want to go home? It would be wrong if I did not want to go home."

"Oh! you do not understand, my child. This is not a prison: this is a place where you come to get well."

"But it is a prison," the girl replied, with tears starting into her eyes. "I am all shut up: locks, keys, bars, and watchful eyes are all about me. I cannot go out unless a guard goes with me. What is it but a prison?"

"You are excited," said the matron: "you had better go to your room."

"Why shouldn't I be excited? I have been here three years. I am worn out with this life."

"Oh, well! You shall go away just as soon as the doctor considers you well enough."

"When will he call me well? I think three years is long enough to be under one doctor or one system of medical treatment."

"But you mustn't tell what *you* think: the doctors know better than you."

"I know enough to know that three years is a very long time to endure this life," the girl replied. "If I write another letter, and leave out the word prison, will you send it?"

"I will read it, and see. Go to your room now, and don't make us any more trouble. Can't you see that it is very unpleasant for us to be teased all the time?"

"I should like to know who we *can* ask, if not you," said the girl. "We are locked in here with no earthly privilege, and no one whom we can ask for the least favor except you, who are hired to take care of us; and if you will not"—

"Hush!" commanded the matron. "Go to your room, and let there be no more complaining."

The helpless girl went back to her room. "I shall never go home," she said to herself. "I shall never go out of here. They mean to keep me: they know I have no father and mother; and they can make my uncle believe whatever they tell him. But I will write again. My uncle told me to write, and to tell him all my feelings. I will try once more."

Bella watched this scene with absorbing interest. It threw a new light upon her own situation. She said to herself, "What! cannot these patients write without being watched? Cannot I write and say what I please? How then shall I get out of here? I want to tell Edward and Mortimer. I want to write. I must write."

She watched eagerly for the *denouement :* it came the next day. Again the matron was passing through the hall.

Again the girl went to her, and laid an open letter in her hand. Neither prison, nor synonym for prison, was in this letter. The matron glanced it through; and the girl watched her countenance. The woman's face was not the index of the most favorable feelings. Looking at the girl, she said, "But you still say you want to go home."

"Because I do want to go," the girl said. And indeed she did want to go. A letter without the expression of that sentiment would not have seemed half a letter to her; and she would have been no happier for sending it. "Well," said the matron, "I will take it," and left the hall with the letter in her hand.

Long the patient waited for an answer to that letter. Her heart sank with hope deferred, and vain conjectures as to why her uncle did not write. Could she have seen the reason, could she have known why he failed to reply, her heart would have gone yet lower; for she would have seen that her letter went — the way of the waste-basket. Her uncle never received it. Instead of it, he received an official asylum-letter, in which was an account of his niece, such as it pleased the officers to write. And the old man said, "I am sorry for my niece. I did hope she would get well; but, if she cannot, why, I suppose that is the best place for her." Then he remitted the sum demanded for her board; and she — is there now.

Absolute power produces different effects upon different individuals. It changes some persons into tyrants; and, as the rule of prison officers over their subjects is absolute, it follows that prison keepers are affected by having this absolute sway. Some rule with moderation; some are calm, some passionate; some are cold, hard, fiendish. Whatever emotions affect the prison-keepers are vented on the prisoners. Are the keepers weary, disappointed, or unhappy? Down upon their hapless victims fall the wreakings of their souls; and there is no way for the victims to escape. Locks, keys, and grates are all about them. A lamb may be locked up under a lion; and in all this broad land not one person can look within to see or pity. Alas! God save prisoners! There are more crimes committed against them than ever they committed.

We speak of asylums as prisons when they have prison-locks and prison-rules, in distinction from open hospitals and houses.

When the nights came on in this place, when Evening drew her sacred mantle down, and Nature called for rest, Bella went into her cell, — for the patient's rooms in asylums can be called by no other name than cells; and there she sought the rest that would not come, for sadness and tears crowded it away. She lay awake, and watched the night-sky through her bars. She thought of the possibility of escape. Could she crowd through her iron-barred windows, tie her sheets together, let herself down by them, and so escape? She thought of heroes and heroines, and of the devices by which they had disappeared from dungeons and towers. She thought of their daring feats and bold escapades. She recalled the tales of queens which she had read, and wondrous sufferers like Marie Antoinette and Baron Trenck. Then she thought of the long list of persons imprisoned and persecuted for right-cousness' sake; and she sighed, "Oh, man's inhumanity to man! Through countless ages, how cruel it has been! Yet God ever shineth the same, even as the sun shines. He sees all this wickedness. He sees it in our fair America, where I myself am suffering, and where thousands of my countrymen and women are sharing in like bondage."

Sometimes she wrenched at the sash of her window, as though she would force it to give way. She might as well have moved an iron mount. Then she tried to sleep; but, if she could compose her own soul, the moans, the sobs, the tears, the wails, the groans, and shrieks about the building broke the stillness of the night air, and kept her awake by sympathy.

Sympathy! Are insane patients capable of sympathy? Ah! What would they do without it? Bella found it her chief outward support. Sympathy for each other is not denied to patients, except when they are overheard to criticise the management of the place. The moment that attendants suspect their patients are speaking of the asylum or hall discipline in terms of censure, the cry rings out, "To your rooms, to your rooms! Every one of you to your rooms!"

Then every patient becomes a solitary prisoner. Silence, utter, drear, and crushing, is their portion. Whatever their needs, they dare not speak. Free speech is a forbidden liberty within these sovereign kingdoms.

Bella often asked herself, "If I were already crazed, would not this life make me worse?"

She saw and heard acts of harshness even in this the best hall; and she was conscious of greater cruelties in the halls adjoining. She saw people brought every day and left, sometimes under circumstances even more distressing than her own; and many of these people had not her health and strength to endure it.

"I thought," she said to one of the ladies, "that this was a land of liberty, of happiness, and of equality. I am sure none of these qualities are in this asylum system. By these asylum practices, people are snatched from their homes as ruthlessly as though barbarians ruled us; and we are held in bondage as abject as tyranny can invent. And how people suffer by such treatment!"

An old lady, who had been a patient many years, interposed, "My dear miss, you must be careful. Such license of speech is not permitted here."

"How ? Will they prevent my talking? They may try, but can they succeed ? "

" They will, indeed, if you talk against the institution."

" I think I have a right to express my thoughts, wherever I am ; and I cannot help speaking, when I see such a scene as that which just passed before us."

What was this scene ? It was the arrival of Mrs. Merrill.

Mrs. James Merrill was a small, pale, delicate young woman. She came to visit the asylum with her husband, as she supposed. She had not one idea that her physician had directed and advised her husband to take this course. She had three darling little children, from whom she had never been separated scarcely for a day. When her husband told her that the doctor thought a ride would be beneficial to her, her first impulse was to provide for the comfort of these little ones during her brief absence. She set apart tid-bit dainties for them, made sure that every thing was comfortable about them, and gave the nurse repeated charges concerning them. Then she kissed them, and went. The day was fine; and she enjoyed the trip in the cars. Her husband proposed that they should stop at ——, and dine. She was happy to do so, and thought she never enjoyed a dinner so much. The freshness of the food, and the change from her home diet, seemed to give her recuperative powers; and, when her husband proposed that they walk about and see the place, she gladly accepted the offer, and went with her arm in his. They walked a while, he purposely going towards the asylum; and, when they came within view of it, she said, " What a large building! What is it ? " — "It is an insane asylum," he answered. " Let us go in and visit it." — "Can we ? " she asked innocently. " Yes. We can be admitted at any time."

All unconscious of what was in store for her, she walked in. They were received politely : no word nor hint was given that could undeceive the doomed woman. They walked through the halls till they reached the one designed to be hers. She stood looking in pity upon the inmates, and thinking that she should go crazy if she had to live there. Seeing that she was absorbed, the official motioned to the husband; and the two slipped out together. She stood alone : presently she looked around. "Where is my husband?" she asked in surprise. "He is gone." — "Gone! I didn't see him go." Supposing he had gone only for a moment, she turned her attention again to the scenes about her. Time passed, and still she was alone. She grew anxious, looked often in the direction of the door, and finally went to it : it was locked. Turning to the attendant, she said, "Will you please open this door for me?" — "I cannot." — "Cannot? why?" — "I am not allowed to." — "Not allowed to! What do you mean?" — "Why, I am not allowed to let patients go out!" — "But I am not a patient." — "Yes, you are to stay a while." — "No, I only came in as a visitor." — "But your husband has gone, and left you?" — "Gone, and left me? It is impossible." — "No, it is not impossible ; it is quite true." — "I do not believe it," the little woman said earnestly. "My husband would not do such a thing by me." — "But he has." — "I do not believe it : he is somewhere down stairs. Please let me go and find him." — "No, I cannot." The voice of the attendant was decided. She turned from the woman, and walked away. Mrs. Merrill was to go through what others had passed, — the struggle of resignation, the strife of passing from life to the grave of imprisonment. The attendant left her to meet this struggle alone ; and it seemed to Mrs. Merrill that she *was* alone. It seemed that her very senses would leave her. One wild despair surged up within her.

She trembled as an aspen leaf. The walls seemed like blocks of adamant around a tomb of darkness, in which she was left. "I will not stay here," she said : "you have no right to keep me." Then she stationed herself by the door; and, whenever a key was inserted, she sprang forward to pass through, but was pushed back, and held back till the door was locked again. An hour or two passed away ; then the attendant said, "I cannot bear this ; send the supervisor to me." The supervisor came, and then the little woman found how truly she was in their power. They took off her bonnet, gloves, and shawl. Seeing, then, that she had a gold watch and chain, they took those also. Then they disengaged her brooch, and drew from her finger a ring set with diamonds. She had no power to resist these acts. Three strong girls were holding her. "Are you robbers ?" she asked. "What kind of people are you ? What do you mean ?" No one answered these questions. The servants went away and left her; the patients, though feeling their hearts leap to their mouths in anguish, dared not utter a word. Mrs. Merrill, thus disrobed, went about to the windows, and felt of their iron bars. "I will break the glass," she said. "I will get out of here. I will go home. I will go to my children." Then the attendant sent out again. This time a man came in.

Then it was that they took the sweet little lady, and put upon her one of their strong canvas jackets, and bound her down like a vile felon ; and there they held her till she shook like a reed : and still they held her, "to take the craziness out of her," they said. "I am sure it will put craziness into her," thought Bella : "it almost puts insanity into me to see her. Is this the way they hold people here? Do our laws permit such things? Oh, I wish that people could see it ! Surely they would not permit it."

And Mrs. Long said, "Another ! How many, oh, how

many are to be immolated here?" Mrs. Josleyn added, "Put thy faith in Christ, O suffering sister!"

Mrs. Spears, who had seen these deeds for twenty-seven years, arose, and walked the hall. "Am I to see these jackets till death puts me where I can see no more of earth? O Father! strengthen me to bear!" Then Marion, the attendant, raised her voice: "Silence! silence, every one! I am going to my room: let me not hear another word."

Then all sounds hushed; and every woman held her bated breath. The attendant went to her room. She had a dress there in process of making: her asylum wages had bought it; it was a silk, with trimmings deep and rare. She folded it about her, admired its lustrous waves, and cared nothing for her patients. And they sat in their solitary rooms, afraid to speak one little word. Say, medical men, wherein does this course benefit injured minds? And why do you allow laws by which virtuous, innocent ladies can be held beneath such rules?

When a few days had passed, and Mrs. Merrill, weary with her first struggling, had broken down into quiet, the superintendent came into the hall and sat down. He looked around, talked a while, and then, turning to the lady, he said, "Mrs. Merrill, what is the matter with you?"

The abruptness of the question startled her. It startled the other ladies also: they were not used to hear the superintendent speak in this manner. Evidently he had forgotten his environments, and for once was speaking his natural mind. Mrs. Merrill answered by asking another question.

"In what respect do you mean, doctor?"

"I mean before you came here. What did you do? I have watched you narrowly, and I see no appearance of insanity. I believe your husband lied about you; didn't he?"

"I do not know, sir; because I do not know what he told you."

" True, true : you do not know."

Here the face of the man clouded into thought. He seemed to be recalling what this lady's husband had told him, and to consider. Then he repeated one of his questions.

" What did you do ? "

" I know of nothing in particular, sir. But," she blushed as she added, " I suppose I was cross sometimes. I had my little children, and my family cares; and I was often very tired, and cross perhaps."

The superintendent's face expressed a sense of incredulity as he responded, " Well, if people are to be shut into asylums for crossness, large numbers would soon find themselves inside. I am not sure but I should get shut in myself sometimes."

He went out then, like a man who has said more than he meant to; and the ladies looked at each other with meaning smiles. Then Mrs. Merrill said, " I am sure I thought the doctor called me insane, because of what I said, and the way I was treated, the day I came in here."

Bella said, " I thought so too. Why did he have you jacketed, if you are not insane ? "

" I said I would break the glass, to go out, and go home to my children, you know."

Afterwards Bella overheard the superintendent say to the assistant physician, " Any true, warm-hearted mother might have said the same under similar circumstances. I do not approve of these deceptions in bringing people here. I do not like to have people brought to my asylum in such harsh ways. It is enough of itself to make them crazy. I do not think Mrs. Merrill is insane."

Bella thought, " Why, then, does he ·not publish his views ? Why does he let the outside world remain in ignorance of these inside scenes ? Why does he not tell people that they must not deceive these sufferers ? "

This question may well be repeated and echoed around. Why do they not publish the reports of the sufferings caused by this system of insane treatment, as well as its benefits ? Why do superintendents report the cures, — of which they freely boast, — and leave unreported the hundreds who are brought into their halls to undergo the horrors of the prison-feeling, and whose broken minds sink into greater derangement under coercive discipline ? Let the public require that lunatic asylums report the sufferings in their corridors, as well as the fair outside shows, that families who have loved members in these institutions may have some chance to know the *real* and *true* conditions of their locked-up friends.

The refrains of "home," running through the halls, are endless and various as the people who utter them. They are borne through the corridors in basso and soprano, in chorus, and in monotones of deepest woe. To Bella, as to others, the place became as a bed of thorns, from which there was no escape. "If Mortimer only could know, if Edward could know, if my mother knew how I suffer here, I am sure they would help me out. I will write, and tell them where Frederic has put me. I *cannot* stay here ; I *will not* stay here."

. She thought she would not write as the other patients did, giving their letters to the matron, or to a supervisor ; but she would ask the doctor himself to mail her letter. She watched her opportunity ; and, when the superintendent entered her hall, she went to him. "Doctor, if I write a letter, and *seal* it, will you send it ? "

He paused before her. "Yes, Miss Forresst, I will send it for you. I have no wish to read your letters. This rule is only for those who are not competent to write."

" Thanks, doctor," said the girl, as smiles deepened on her cheeks. She went to her room. Happiness stole into her heart. "I am *so* glad I asked him," she thought. "How much better it is to go to him direct!"

She wrote then to Edward, and with her own hands put the letter into the superintendent's hand. He smiled upon her with gracious kindness; and she saw in his smiles an augury of freedom. She counted the days she would most likely have to wait for return letters, and nerved herself to bear them. That night her sleep was sweet; and the next morning the hospital hash slipped down almost without a thought of its coarse qualities.

She had not a nature that could become absorbed in her own sorrows, unmindful of others; and she became deeply interested in the women who were her fellow-prisoners. She watched the coming and going of their friends, searched into the causes of these unnatural incarcerations, and inquired, "*Why* are such things tolerated?" She found the causes as various as the people. Some were imprisoned because they were invalids, and their friends didn't feel like being troubled with them; some because they were wealthy, and their guardians and relatives could thus keep their fortunes for themselves, while the rightful owners lived hidden; some were there from poverty, their friends calling them insane, and throwing them on to the State: but by far the larger part were people whose friends were true and sincere, and brought their dear ones here by advice of physicians. Families work and plan to save money to pay for their invalid friends in these halls; and the sick people stay in them under privations that might make them ill, even if carried into them in perfect health. Outside doctors, too ignorant to cure their patients, banish them to these popular houses, and thus relieve themselves, and hide their own stupidity; inside doctors pocket the money and the honors.

The lives of asylum patients are full of aggravations and disagreeable scenes. Bella, like others, found them hard to bear. One of these trials was in the passing and re-passing of visitors. People go through asylums as through a solemn show, — walking with heads straight forward, but casting their eyes to the right and left mysteriously, as though there was some unearthly mystery in the place and people there.

"I suppose visitors think we are wild animals," said a lady to Bella.

"I turn away from them," Bella answered. "I cannot bear that they should see my face."

"Just so do I," responded a third. And this is what thousands do, and what thousands will continue to do, if the system continues to exist. Patients cannot bear to be living as in the cages of a menagerie, the objects of public curiosity. Mrs. Whitney says, "A man might be a little crazy even, and get over it, if he never had it to think that other people knew or mistrusted."

This is true of immense numbers of our modern insane people. Their insanity is often a mere nervous derangement, or a temporary illness, resting on a cause which admits of cure, like other diseases. Home-kindness, supported and guided by the discretion of *good* home physicians, would be far more sensible and successful than crowding people into halls under strictures that drive thousands into chronic misery, and hold them then as public shows. People never recover fully from the shocks their sensibilities receive in the transportations to asylums, and the treatment they see and receive while there. They feel that an ignominy is attached to them. It ought not so to be. There is no disgrace in insanity. It is a disease more likely to fall upon high-toned minds than upon those of rude construction. Therefore in cultivated communities, where mind is brought out in all possible tension, people are more likely to become insane, and are only saved from this and other diseases by

care that their physical developments and health shall keep
pace with the mental. For this reason we have more insane
persons in the more intelligent portions of our country.
Where the climate is a test to strength, and the cultivation
of bodily health receives less attention than education of
the mind, we must expect diseases of all kinds. The most
delicate, refined, and sensitive people fall first. Are we to
go on building asylums, or endowing the present ones, and
continue to confine our people as outcast lepers, shut apart?
Common sense, humanity, and God forbid!

Life in cells is a midnight life. It is the opponent of
light, and the opposite of nature. It feeds souls on darkness. There is neither life nor strength to be gained in its
existence.

But asylum advocates will ask, How, then, do people get
well in asylums?

The answer may be given in the words of an asylum
physician, who, by virtue of his office, should be good
authority. A lady, who had been a week or two under
this treatment, was looking about to discover what was to
cure her. She said to the physician, "Doctor, do you cure
people here?"

"They get well here," was the reply.

"What cures them?"

"Oh! time and nature."

This answer was the text for many after-thoughts.
When the lady had been there longer, she saw, herself, that
those who were cured were indeed restored by these two
agents: those whom these agents alone could not cure
went down, and became patients for life. The lady said,
"If time and nature, working against all these antago-
nisms, can effect cures, what could they not accomplish outside, if judicious help were given them; for time is as

long outside as in, and nature is scarce found within these walls ? "

"To know what patients suffer, we must live as patients live."

This was what Jessonica said to Bella, as they sat side by side in a chapel sociable. They were strangers, from different States. They were patients in different halls, and had not met until now, as they chanced to be seated together, and felt touched by a mutual sympathy.

Bella replied, " I have passed through vicissitudes; but the convent and the Shakers were paradise compared to this place; and the teacher of the idiot's school was a queen, for she had a heart. I wish I could find a heart among the overseers of this place."

"They think they have hearts," Jessonica replied. "They talk about Christian kindness and benevolence, and doing good."

" I know," said Bella, " that it is wrong and hard to judge; but, to me, their hearts seem like those of fat oxen, who, feeding and dwelling in rich pastures themselves, have no thought for the sufferings of others."

Jessonica lifted her dove-like eyes to Bella's flashing face, and softly said, " You are right, Miss Forresst."

And, though such judgment may seem bitter, we, too, are compelled to say, Miss Forresst is right. Observation and experience of life in these halls compel us to believe that the nature of the system tends to take humanity out of the hearts of those who rule within.

Often the nurses, keepers, servants, attendants, and physicians even, are totally incapable of measuring or comprehending the mental requirements of their patients; yet they rule them with absolute power; and there is no possible way for the patients to escape.

10*

The question is not, and must not be, Are these peoplo insane? Are they crazy? but, Is this the way to cure them? Will this "treatment" restore them to mental health, or will it take away what mind they have left, and tend to make them more insane?

CHAPTER XII.

THERE is a general impression in society that asylum doctors possess some peculiar power over minds diseased, and that the patients are under the doctors. The truth is, that asylum doctors are like other physicians: they use the same medical works, have passed through the same course of study, and practise on the same theories. The only difference is, that they work within the circumference of locks and keys, claiming legal statutes as supports. Some of them may be more intelligent and humane than others; and therefore some asylums may be better governed than others: but the underlying-principles of all locked asylums are the same.

The physicians of asylums can be but very little with their patients. Among five or six hundred persons, the doctors can take but cursory glances at each one. The common, daily life of the patients falls under the attendants of the halls. And who are the attendants? They are persons who come for hire, — to earn money. They are hired nurses, or hired servants, as you please to call them. They come from everywhere, — from rural districts where money is scarce, and from service where wages were too low for them. They are mostly young, have a common-school education, and no more. They have no accurate knowledge of the human system, — its wants or requirements, or of insanity, scientifically considered. They have a general idea that crazy people are to be kept shut up, and managed somehow, it matters little how. Keys are put into their hands : they are told to keep the doors locked ; and they do it. Power over the patients is given them ; and they use it according to their natures and temperaments. They earn their money, and spend it for dress, or go home and get married with it ; while a fresh set come, to rule the patients, and go through the same routine as their predecessors. Under these ignorant comers and goers the patients live.

Men, under great mental sufferings, have been known to grow gray in a single night. When prisoners they grow gray by continual disciplinary anguish. The constant going out of hopes, the dying of ambitions, the sundering of all former ties, the gradual extinction of all outward wishes, and the constant submission to the personal power of the keepers, give to prisoners a peculiar misery, found under no other circumstances. All these prison miseries are found in asylums. The lives of patients are lives of absolute bondage, in which bondage they see no avenue of hope nor path to liberty, — not even by serving a term of years as criminals in durance. With this life-imprisonment staring them in the face, is it strange that they grow haggard, wild, or imbecile ?

Patients are commonly told that they shall stay a few weeks, and then are held for years, till life becomes one prolonged suspense and agony, in which they are fitted for neither earth nor heaven. Is it supposed that they are not sensible of their situations ? We answer, they are most acutely sensible of their sufferings, and, being ill in mind, are less able to rise above these depressing asylum influences than if in health.

And this system is assigned by our physicians as a cure for broken nerves and demented wits. Shade of Esculapius, save us !

Living every day amid these scenes, seeing suffering constantly around her, Bella grew dispirited, and looked more and more earnestly for replies to her letters. Encouraged by the superintendent's gracious smiles, and trusting his apparent candor, she had written several letters; and the superintendent took them himself. But time passed, and no replies came. She grew disheartened. "What does it mean? Have Edward and Mortimer forgotten me? Or do they think I am crazy, and so will not write?"

This last was a horrible idea, and it wore upon her. She grew listless and pale. The ladies said, "You are not well, Miss Forresst."

"If I could only have some letters, — even one," she replied. "But my friends seem to have deserted me : they have ceased to care for me."

Confidentially, stealthily, some of the ladies said, "Probably your letters do not go."

"Not go?" she exclaimed. "Why, the doctor himself took them, and told me he would send them unread !"

"And you believed him?"

"Why shouldn't I?"

"My dear young lady," said one of the women, "when you have been here longer, and have become versed in the strategies of the place, you will learn that one of the commandments has a qualification. It is written, 'Thou shalt not lie, except to insane patients.' You see, therefore, that the doctor did not sin. Falsehoods to us are justifiable."

"It is a terrible place," Bella said solemnly. "A system that depends on falsehood, and sanctions it, must be shaky somewhere, and should be destroyed."

"I would to God it might shake to the ground," remarked a woman near.

"Amen !" said another.

"Go to your rooms!" shouted Marion. She had been attracted by the voices, and had come near enough to hear.

They separated, and went to their solitary cells; but, though free speech was denied, thoughts were irrepressible.

"I am on my own native soil, surrounded by the air of my own Massachusetts," mused Bella as she paced back and forth in her solitude; "yet I am a prisoner, held by bonds, and forbidden either to write or speak of my situation! By what right does any one thus hold me? By what right do our States permit laws that can be used for such base purposes?"

She looked through her iron-barred window, and it seemed that the air was not that of America. "My country's air has no smouldering taint of prison belonging to it," she said.

Now the time became more tedious. She had lost faith in the superintendent. He passed her often, and bowed with smiles; but she saw hollowness in the smiles, and they seemed as veneering, put on for show. She began to look for some other way to send a letter. Her soul was sick with her situation. It seemed to her that there must be some way by which to transmit truthful intelligence of herself. Then she ceased hiding her face from visitors, and began searching their countenances, to find one whom she dared ask to take one little missive from her hand. But they all looked solemn, and were closely under the escort of the officials; and she had no courage to ask them. Indeed, her courage and faith began to fail. She went privately to Mrs. Long.

"Do tell me, Mrs. Long," she said, "is there no way to get a truthful letter out of this institution?"

The lady patient looked up quickly. Her blue eyes dilated, and her oval forehead seemed to rise in thought. "Miss Forresst," she said, "I should as soon think of running a gauntlet of trained watchmen as to send a letter from here unless every word pleased the officials."

"But what shall I do?" asked Bella in tones of distress. "How can I stay here in this dead way, with no communication with the outer world, or knowledge of my friends? It will make me crazy."

Mrs. Long thought a moment. Then she said, "My husband is coming to see me in a few days. If you will write, and have your letter ready, I will ask him to take it."

"Thanks, Mrs. Long, thanks. I cannot express my gratitude. You have raised me from despair."

Then once more she wrote; and, because she felt that the other letters had not gone, she recapitulated what she had written before, and explained her circumstances in full. She put the letter in an envelope, addressed it, and waited. Mrs. Long was not certain what day her husband would come.

Well, people get used to waiting, if they are patients in asylums. They are always waiting for this, or for that, or some other thing. Everybody and every thing must be attended to before "patients." If other people are to wait for any thing, they find it easier to know it; but patients are seldom told. They are moved from room to room, taken out and put in, and otherwise managed, without one note of warning.

And these two imprisoned women waited, the one for her husband, the other for the man who would help her seek relief from those who loved her in the outer world.

At last Mr. Long came. A fine-looking man he was, with black hair clustering over his head, and black eyes glancing sharply at whatever he met. Very fond of his blue-eyed wife he appeared to be; but he was a man of legal statutes. He believed in law as laid down by government. Break a statute law? No. The laws of mercy he might break, but not statutes of men. Before he left, his wife asked him to take out Miss Forresst's letter.

"What!" he exclaimed, "shall I come in here and violate the rules of the institution? Shall I bring you here to be cured, and then break the rules of the place?"

"They are very unjust rules," the lady pleaded. "You do not realize how hard it is, nor how much we have to bear, shut in here without privileges of any kind."

"But there is a medical necessity, my dear."

"There is a medical absurdity, you mean," she replied. "If you should stay here as a patient, as I do, you would see this system in a very different light. You would see that it is worse than absurdity: it is wickedness, especially when people are sane, like Miss Forresst."

"Who is this Miss Forresst?"

"She is the girl whose letter I want you to take out."

"Yes; but who is she? Where does she belong?"

"She is sister to Mrs. Boynton, and to Mr. Frederic Forresst."

"Frederic Forresst! Why, he is one of our finest men! If he has put his sister in here, he had good cause. No, pet: we will keep clear of other people's business. It is enough for us to take care of ourselves."

Earnestly the lady pleaded, but without avail. The lawyer was decided. He had chosen his side, and it was the side of power. She gave up pleading at last, and asked when she was to go home, adding, "I cannot see the least good they do me here."

The lawyer put on a look of ponderous gravity, and softly stroked the hair of his fair wife, saying, "Perhaps you are not the best judge, my dear. The doctor tells me you are doing very well."

"Doing very well, am I? That is an old stereotyped phrase that the doctor keeps on hand to use on the friends of the patients when he sees fit. You stopped in the office, and he spread it on to you."

"But are you not doing well my dear?"

"I am trying to keep patient, and endure this life till you take me out. Do let it be soon, please. I shall get better in time, whether I am here or away. You must let me recover slowly. You did not bring me here to remain a prisoner forever, did you?"

"Certainly not. How can you think so? I shall take you away as soon as you are better."

"O my husband! don't wait till these doctors say I am better. I see a great deal of deception here; and it is for their interest to keep me. You pay them as much as twenty dollars a week, I suppose."

"Oh, tut, pet! The money is of no account, if they can cure you.

She talked longer, — pleaded and argued; but Mr. Long had, as she thought, been in the office before he came up to his wife. He was there fortified against all she could say. He was a good customer, paying his twenty dollars a week, that his wife might have extras; while she was taking such as she could get. Such a customer was worth keeping; and they had, as Mrs. Long said, "spread their story well" for him in the office. He went away in the full confidence that they were right, and she was wrong. She kept by his side till he reached the main hall door. Marion followed with the keys. The door was unlocked: he put his foot on the threshold. She clung to him, wept, begged, pleaded. ,, "Do let me go! O my husband! do let me go with you! I cannot stay here without you. This life will wear me out!" Then she kissed him, and hung upon his shoulder. He was touched, for he loved his wife; and the arguments of the asylum office were fading from his mind, when there appeared a supervisor. Supervisors are a middle class of officials, between the physicians and attendants, and are most efficient helpers to the asylum. They are generally ready for any thing, and can strap the patients, starve them, or lock them up, with equal ease. This supervisor, a tall, strong woman, saw the situation at a glance. She stepped into the doorway, and put her hand upon Mrs. Long's hand, saying, "Come, you are behaving very queerly. If you do so, your husband will never think you fit to go. You should use reason, and show him that you are better, instead of worse."

Mrs. Long raised her face, and said, "Do you know what it is to part from the love of your life? Did you ever love?"

The question was unfortunate, since the supervisor was a maiden of uncertain age. She took the patient by the arm; and, though the action was not apparent, she gave it a grip that sent the blood curdling through Mrs. Long's veins, and pushed her back into Marion's hands. Then, with a dexterous movement, she drew Mr. Long through the doorway, and turned the key. There was one loud cry within; then all was still. Mr. Long paused to listen; but the supervisor hurried him along, and keys held the imprisoned woman.

"She will be right again in a moment," the supervisor said, with oily tongue. "It is not uncommon for patients to make trouble when their friends go away; but they soon get over it. I am sorry you should be incommoded, sir."

She took Mr. Long down stairs; and he went into the office again. There he was again assured that she would soon be "all right;" that such manifestations were not uncommon in patients, and that it might be as well for him not to come again very soon. "Give her time to recuperate," said the bland superintendent. "Seeing you and her friends excites her, and puts her back. These cases are very hard, sir: life is full of troubles."

Mr. Long is a good lawyer; but he was "taken in" that time by a doctor. He went home. She went into her cell, the walls of which seemed like fortress-walls, hiding her from hope forever. She fell on her knees, and cried, "If an enemy had done this, I could bear it; but to think that the doctors turn my own husband against me is too much, too much!" She had a fit that night. The asylum gave her fit a medical name; but those who had themselves borne the tension of just such shocks knew that she had an "asylum fit" or "prison fit," whichever we call it. The terms are identical.

Only the rational, strong-nerved, and healthy can bear such fearful isolation. The weak-nerved, the delicate, the broken-minded, the insane, should never be required to pass through such trials.

Bella did not speak of her letter that night. She could not mention her own troubles, she was so affected by seeing the condition of the woman she had learned to love. They took Mrs. Long back to her room; and Marion scolded her for causing so much trouble. For a long time Mrs. Long sat and wept. Her arm ached, and her heart ached. She felt that she had been unkindly treated, that her husband believed the asylum representations, and that there was little chance for her to get release. After a time she drew up her sleeve, and looked at her arm : it was blue-black and swollen. She felt indignant and insulted. She went out into the hall, and walked rapidly up and down. It seemed that she must do something to allay the agitation of her mind. Bella came into the hall, and joined her. They walked arm in arm, talking of their troubles. Just then the supervisor came in again; and her instincts told her that they were talking of her. She approached Mrs. Long, and began, "Ain't you ashamed, making such a piece of work when your husband went away? I shouldn't think he'd ever want you, — such an acting person as you are."

"Hush!" said Mrs. Long resolutely. "I want you to see what you did to my arm;" and she began pulling up her sleeve. The arm was swollen, and the sleeve of a delicate fabric. It tore a little. "That will do," said the supervisor. "You needn't go to tearing your clothes in your craziness. Marion, lock this woman into her room. I will help you."

They took hold of her, and led her away into her room: they locked her door, and left her there. "If she causes you any trouble, Marion, let me know; and I will bring a jacket." These were the last words of the supervisor as she locked the door and went out.

Nothing more was heard from Mrs. Long that night: no sound came from her room. The next morning, when the attendant unlocked the door, Mrs. Long was lying on the floor, stiff and cold. It required all the arts of the physicians to restore her. They said she had a paralytic shock. We, who have escaped asylum fits only by the strength of our natures, know that she had a prison or asylum fit.

When Bella learned that her letter had not gone, she was grieved. "Everybody favors the institution, and presses us," she thought. "Is there no way out of this place?"

She was in the bath-room; and Sarah Tollman, a patient of several years, was there with her. Sarah said, "I will mail your letter, Miss Forresst."

"You! How can you?"

"I will drop it in the street-box the next time we walk out. Such things have been done here; and I can do it."

"But Miss Smiley has Argus eyes. She puts us all in front of her, and watches every motion."

"I know it; but I have been here a great many years. I have learned all their ways. I am very submissive; and I can take privileges. If you will engross her in conversation, and take her attention, I will fall behind, and get the letter into a box."

Hope came again to Bella; and she readily agreed to this plan.

The next morning the walking attendant came in, and made the announcement, "This hall goes to walk." Then Marion went around, and selected such as might go; and Bella and Miss Tollman were of the number. They well remembered their agreement, and went out with little nods to each other. The procession was arranged, and moved on. Bella stationed herself beside Miss Smiley, and began talking as joyously as though a world of happiness was all her own. No one noticed Miss Tollman's tardy movements, nor how she fell back; nor was she noticed when she finally fell behind Miss Smiley herself. Bella did not look around; but she felt that the plan would be a success. They neared a corner, and Bella's heart beat; but she only talked the faster, and kept Miss Smiley interested. They turned the corner; and Miss Tollman glided softly towards the box. Was it her shadow, or what was it that drew the attention of a woman in front? Why must there be a traitor in every company? One would have supposed that Julia Warren had suffered enough in that institution to lead her to help one of her fellow-prisoners; but she it was who turned her head, and raised the warning scream.

Miss Smiley sprang, and pounced upon Miss Tollman. "What are you doing? Give me that letter!" and she grasped the small hand of Miss Tollman.

But the patient was firm, and held the letter in a tight grip. The attendant succeeded only in getting a glimpse of the address, — "Forresst," she said. "Ah, yes! I understand why Miss Forresst was so fond of my company. You have a conspiracy. We will go back to the asylum."

She turned the company then, and headed them towards the asylum. She hurried them back, and let them into the hall. Then she went to make her report.

11*

There had been several recent attempts to smuggle out letters.   Two or three of these had succeeded ; and a patient had just been taken away by her friends, in consequence. The authorities felt tender; and this new attempt increased their irritation.   There must be a stop to these secret mailings.   The face of the assistant physician clouded.

Then these words went ringing through the halls, " Whoever is caught mailing a letter contrary to our rules shall be jacketed and strapped ! "

Who, in free life, can understand the quiet terror that followed this announcement ?   No person who has always been free can judge of a patient's feelings, nor realize how the mandates of such a place fall crushingly upon the helpless people within.   The world knows nothing of the unutterable and inexpressible throes of those who are held beneath these bonds.   It is no wonder that they wail, and that their hearts cry out in anguish.   It is no wonder that they call for friends and freedom and home.   " Home ! " " Home ! "   How often is the name heard in those galleries and halls !   " Shall I never go home ? "   " Shall I never, never again be free ? "   " Must I always stay in these halls ? "   " Am I never again to live with those I love ? " " Have I no friend to take me from this place ? "   " Doctor, when shall I go home ? "   " Doctor, I am homesick. I am tired of this life."   " Doctor, I want to see my husband."   " Doctor, write for me.   I want to see my children."   " Do let me go out of here.   Oh, do let me go out ! "   " What right has any one to keep me here ?   God never gave any one a right to keep me here in prison. Neither father nor mother, wife nor child, has any right to imprison me thus."   " These asylums are blots on civilization, — dark spots in the midst of light."   " I shall go out of here ; God will take me out ; but I do not know what chastisements will first come upon our country."   Then chiming in are foreign accents. "Och! Let me go home to me childers. Home, home!" says the Irish woman.

Such are the cries constantly running through asylum halls, — at least in the women's departments. How is it with the men?

There are other wails, — deeper, darker expressions. The pen refuses to trace them. The public would refuse to read them. Yet that same public puts its most delicate people into the midst of these discordant sounds, where they must listen day and night to fearful words. Mistaken public! Who shall enlighten thy great mind?

CHAPTER XIII.

ORNING dawned.   It was morning in the asylum. But what is morning there?

Click, click, click.

Did you ever hear it, reader?   It is the sound of the key, as it goes from door to door.

Click, click, click, click, click!

Every morning, when the East is flooded with her beautiful light, the patients hear that sound.   Every night, ere slumber comes to lave their brows, the pent-up people hear that sound.   From door to door the attendants go. When they turn, the ladies and gentlemen may leave their cells; and, when they turn, the ladies and gentlemen may go in again.   This system is for the cure of broken minds!

"To live in this way is enough to make one crazy," says a patient.

"Hush!" cry the medical faculty.   "This is the way we have appointed for your cure."

O wise medical faculty!   The remedy is worse than the disease.

But the keys had turned.   The morning had opened. The asylum bell, hung up a-top in the belfry, had struck its early ding-dong.   "Up, up, O sleepers! or else we'll make you get up!"   That is what the bell says, and that is what the keys say.

Some are already up, and are pacing their cells when the

keys turn. They are glad of the dawn, and start from their narrow beds at its earliest peep; and yet they gain nothing by rising but change of posture. The same blank, dreary walls greet them; the same barred windows shut out the light; the same groans and sighs are their morning music. Early risers in asylums do not get up because the morning is a pleasure, but because the bed is a place of agony.

As we said, the morning had dawned. Its hours rolled heavily away. The asylum breakfast had received asylum attention. Bella had folded the spread around the foot of her iron bedstead, and had pinned it in the most approved hospital style. Learning to fold the bedspread in hospital style is among the first lessons for recuperating minds. Bella had thoroughly learned the art; and her spread was pinned square to the inch this morning. She stood beside her barred window, and her attitude was that of dejection. She was looking out upon the free air, and was considering the possibility of getting a letter mailed to Edward. She was sure that Edward had not heard where she was. "He would take me out, if he knew my situation. Yes, I know he would." Then that other thought surged through her, "No. Perhaps he would not take me out. Perhaps he thinks I am crazy. Perhaps they have written him so. And Mortimer, if he thinks I am insane, would not want me. O my Father in heaven! this will drive me to madness! Dost not thou see it?"

Standing there thus dejected, she heard the hall-door click. Then there was a man's step. She did not look up. She neither knew nor cared who passed through that door with keys. They were but prison-guards. The steps of the man came on. They paused at her door. Then she looked up.

"Good-morning!" said the man in a cool, business way.

"Good-morning!" Bella replied indifferently. She had seen this man before, walking through the halls. She knew that he held some position on the staff of asylum keepers; and that was all she knew of him, or cared. She wished no acquaintance with the asylum officials. She had no sympathies with them. If she formed acquaintances there, it would be with those, who, like herself, were sufferers,

But this man did not heed her coolness. He held in his hand a folded paper. He began to unfold it, and drew near to her as he did so. His manner was imperturbably calm, and of a pure business demeanor. He addressed her as though the business was desirable, and to her pure advantage.

"Miss Forresst, how would you like a guardian ? "

" A guardian!" she repeated in a tone of surprised inquiry.

"Yes, a guardian over yourself and property. Your brother has sent us a paper, in which he himself is appointed in that capacity."

He laid the open document in her hand. She glanced at it, but scarcely comprehended its dread import.

" A guardian!" she repeated, and tried to read the paper. There were printed words and written words, technical and half-intelligible: she read enough to bring a giddy feeling over her; and, with the words staring before her, she put her hands to her eyes. A mist had gathered on them, and a weak tremor seized her whole frame. To what end was she coming? What power was this that was forging and binding these fetters? Without her knowledge, physicians had put their names to papers that deprived her of every right; and, on the strength of this, a judge had exiled her from home and freedom, and consigned her to ignominy and misery. Now, when she was

•

powerless, unable to get out, or appeal to any person for help, another legal weight was laid upon her.

With a thrill of new anguish, she looked from the paper up to the face of the man before her. She was about to ask him to intercede for her; but his countenance was hard and cold. He seemed to enjoy the scene, and remarked, "You are fortunate to have a brother for a guardian."

"I do not think so," she responded curtly.

"Oh, yes, you are! Many of our people are under the guardianship of strangers; and it is not so pleasant for them. Strangers have less feeling."

"I do not see that anybody has feeling," she replied, tossing the paper upon the narrow bed.

"No, you do not see, because the state of your mind is not right just now. We hope to see you better by and by."

He turned then, and went out, leaving the patient alone with her guardianship paper. She might destroy it, or keep it, it mattered not which: it was but a copy. The original was safe.

Bella knew very little of the forms of law, or its technical terms; but she understood that the paper lying there was as a rivet, fastening her fetters tighter. There was no one to whom she could apply for redress or protection against this usurpation of power over her. She could not get outside, to present her case to any person: she could not send out a letter with the truth in it; and inside she could get no help nor pity save from those who were equally powerless with herself.

Overcome by the helplessness of her position, she resolved to lay her whole case before the assistant physician. Was not she his patient? Was it not his place to attend to her wants and needs? If she ought to be released, was it not his place to know it, and to help her? Was it right for him to permit people to stay in that bondage, when he knew that every day was an injury?

"It is his place to ask me, or to find out in some way whether I am unjustly kept here, and whether it injures me; and he ought to be honest enough to tell me, and to help me. But then, if he should do that by his patients, he would soon have a thin house; and it is not for the interest of the institution to have a small number of patients. However, I will try."

She did try. She told the assistant physician that she wished to see him alone.

"I can give you a few moments," he replied, taking out his watch; and she was thankful for even that. He went into her little room, and, closing the door, leaned against it in default of a latch. Briefly, then, but truly and earnestly, she related her history, and described her situation. He listened; and, when she had finished, he said, "It is a sad story, and your situation is very trying; but what can I do for you? I am not your brother, nor relative of any kind. I have no power in the case."

"You can set me free."

"I have no power for that. Your friends keep you here."

"But you are my doctor : you have power to say whether I am insane, and whether I ought to stay here."

"And suppose I say that you are not insane. What then? Where would you go? What would you do? You and your property are under a guardian. You can have no money without your guardian's consent. If you go back to your friends, they will return you here again, or you will be a homeless wanderer. Depend upon it, you are better off here than anywhere else."

"I have friends who would not turn me off."

"Why do they not come to you, then? They must know where you are."

"No, they do not know where I am. There is some deception practised over them. If they could know where I am, they would come and take me away."

" Why not write to them ? "

"I *have* written. I have given the letters into the superintendent's own hands."

" And do you get no replies ? "

"Not a word. He does not send my letters. They do not go into the mail."

" Does not send them ? Then they were unsuitable."

"They were not unsuitable. They were plain, simple letters, with just the statement of my situation. But how should he know what was in them ? He promised me he would not open them. He said he considered me competent to write. You do; don't you, doctor?"

He might have said, " Yes, *too* competent for our interests: you would write too much truth." But he did not. He said, " Certainly; and, if the superintendent told you he would send your letters unread, he did send them. You may depend upon that."

And the man, standing there and telling her that, did not blush at the lie he was speaking. Why ? Because she was an insane patient. He looked at his watch again.

"I must go, Miss Forresst. I hope I shall find you in a happier frame of mind when I come again. Contentment is one of the greatest blessings of our lot. Try and learn it. Learn wherever you are, and whatsoever you have, therewith to be content. The Lord will be your comforter."

He went out then ; and Bella said, " Heartless man ! yes, the Lord is my comforter; and I thank him. But he is outside of here. I do not need to stay here to find him. Contentment! yes, it is a very good quality; but if we should all sit down supinely, and say, ' Wheresoever we are, and whatsoever we have, therewith let us be content,' what

12

would become of the world of people? No, I will not be content in such circumstances as these. I will run away."

The thought had been in her mind before, but never so definite as now. It took root, and grew into shape in her mind.

It was a resolve more easily formed than executed, and she knew it; but her determination was strong, and she set about watching for an opening. She made herself agreeable to the servants, and tried to get into their favor. She begged walks, offered to work, and tried various devices to get near the outer doors. There came a chance at last. She had begged her way to the laundry under the escort of a servant; and, while the servant was busy, she slipped through an open door. But they were after her in a moment, and brought her back in triumph. "Ho, ho!" said one, "you didn't do it, did you?"

"You needn't try to come that dodge," said another: "we shall be too much for you."

"Tried to run away! Ha, ha! ha, ha!" said a third. "'Tain't so easy done, my lady."

Bella did not care for their sneers; but for the fact that she could not get away she did care, and resolved not to give up her efforts for freedom.

"I will do it," she affirmed in the silence of the night; and the walls of her room heard her. Those walls had heard and received the wails of deeper agony than hers; but she did not see their record. Only God and the angels had the key to these hidden tablets, and only they recorded what was written there.

"I will leave this place." Bella said it over to herself, and found comfort in the words.

She began now to plan in earnest. Every sense was on the alert; every chance was canvassed; every avenue for escape was studied. And, sooner than she anticipated, the chance came. Miss Smiley had gathered her walking company at the outer door, when a disturbance occurred among them, and Miss Smiley stepped back to quell it. Only for an instant was she out of sight; but that instant was enough for Bella's quickened purpose. Without one moment's consideration, with not one studied plan, she glided from the steps and down the path. Like a bird whose feet were wings she went, swift, yet quiet, flying, yet not seeming to fly. One woman saw her go; but she was no traitor. She saw the girl disappear around the building's corner, and deep thankfulness went through her heart. "God speed thee!" was her unspoken thought.

When Miss Smiley returned, she looked around, and counted her number. "There is one gone," she said; and again she counted. "Yes, there is one gone. Who is it, — who? Miss Forresst? Yes, it is Miss Forresst. Who saw her go? Did anybody see her go?"

No answer; but all looked one upon another. One woman's heart still said, "God speed thee, my sister! God speed thy flying feet!"

Back to their cells the women were remanded: there would be no walking now. And they went back, secretly wondering where and how Miss Forresst managed to slip away; and also secretly hoping that she would have the good fortune to keep away. In less than a moment, as it seemed, the officials were on the alert. One might have thought a fire-alarm had sounded, so suddenly those men started. And not as men who knew not what to do did they start, but in trained organization. Thoroughly bred to the business were the hunting-bands of this asylum. The leader, the man who had given Bella her paper of guardianship, was keen on the scent of runaway patients. Small chance had they of escaping him. In the words of his townsmen, he was "a smart man." He had represented

them in the State legislature, and looked quite dignified as
he held his head erect among the lawmakers.   But now he
reminded one of a class of animals that scent their victims'
tracks by instinct.   The comparison is rude and barbarous,
perhaps ; but those who suffered by him felt that it was
true, and that he did indeed lower his humanity.   However just or necessary it may be for patients to leave an
asylum, they are pursued as relentlessly, and brought back
as heartlessly, as fugitives from penal imprisonment.   By
our asylum practices, good, honorable, virtuous people hold
the same rank as criminals in state prisons.   This man was
securing his property when he took escaped patients.   He
had legal power over Bella, and could send police or other
persons after her, and bring her back, and then subject her
to whatever his caprice might dictate.   He knew this, and
began his pursuit methodically, saying, " Which way did
she most likely turn ? "   He answered the question himself.
" She must have turned the corner, and crossed the yard.
To the yard, men ! and branch from there every way.   I
will take the hill."

He had selected the most difficult ground for himself,
feeling himself most competent.   They started in swift and
earnest pursuit.   They thought they should find her in the
yard ; for how could she get beyond the high picket-fence
in the broad daylight?   They expected to carry her in
amid triumphant laughter; and they rushed among the
bushes with mouths all ready to give the shout of discovery.
But they hunted in vain.   All in vain they peered into
nooks, searched corners, and ran around the buildings.   She
was not there.· " To the street, to the street ! " was now
the cry ; and away they went.   Women were in the streets,
but no Miss Forresst.   Nowhere was she to be seen.   The
leader took the hill-track.   It was difficult searching there.
The ground was broken and broad, the houses sparse ; and

in the fields around she might be hidden anywhere. His practised eyes left no crevice unsearched, no hillock un-scanned, no yard unexamined.

Other men were trying other grounds. They visited the railroad stations; they went up and down the streets where shops were; they traversed lanes and byways. Then the· leader called his forces in. A new method was adopted. The telegraph-wires were struck. Despatches were sent to Frederic, and to every other place where it was likely she would go; and men were stationed at the dépôts to watch. The police were informed; and the leader went out again, giving information, and notifying people that a pa-tient was gone, that, wherever she appeared, people might be ready to secure her. But the hours wore into the night, the night became morning, and the patient was not found. The face of the assistant physician wore a solemn look. "Poor Miss Forresst, how unwise she was! Where can she be ? What will she have to pass through ? If she goes home, her friends will surely bring her back. How much better for her to stay here !" And the one woman who had seen her start, silently thought, "God still speed thy flying feet, my sister, and put thee far from here ! I wish I was with thee."

And the first day passed, and the second, and the third dawned. No tidings came of the lost one. The patients whispered to each other in joy. Mrs. Long spoke to Mrs. Joselyn, Miss Tollman skipped blithely, and old Mrs. Spears said, " Thank God ! she comes not back."

And where, all this time, was Bella ? For hours after she fled, she hardly knew where she was. She never could realize how she sped across the asylum yard, nor how she went over the picket-fence. If she had been told she could do it, she would not have believed it; but it was done : she was outside the prison bars, and outside the

12*

yard. Fleetness must do the work now. She paused not
to see whether she went towards the hill-region, or to the
busy streets. "On, on !" was her thought; "on ! somewhere, away from there. On, on, anywhere, anywhere;
but forward, on !"

Like a flying chamois she went, and yet she did not run.
She dared not run, lest she should attract attention, and
some one should arrest her. She felt like a fugitive, and
feared every moment that some one would suspect her.
Her heart beat, but she dared not stop : she dared not even
look behind. The trot of a horse frightened her; the sound
of men's voices gave her quivers of alarm. The day was
pleasant, and she did not pause. When her heart throbbed,
she pressed her hand on it; when her breath came hard,
she drew a longer inspiration. And still she went on.
Men saw something pass them, — what, they never knew :
they had no time to think. And so night came, and darkness settled over the place where she was. Where was it ?
She did not know. How far had she come ? She could not
tell. She only knew that she began to breathe more freely.
She began to feel that she was away; that the wide world
was before her, that she was free. Something seemed to
rise up in her mouth : it felt like joy. She thought it must
be joy ; but it was long since she had known the sensation,
and she was not sure. Perhaps this feeling was sudden
freedom. There was a strange lightness all over her : it
seemed as though a pressure had been suddenly taken from
her, and she was rising into light. "Oh! had I the wings
of a dove, I would fly," she murmured, as she saw the
broad-spread sunset sky; and then she dropped. She fell
wearily upon a bed of grass, and its soft tufts were as fragrant down to her tired senses. "My mother Earth, I
welcome thee !" was her ejaculation ; and, for the first time,
she realized that it was night. Yes, it was night. The
hours of darkness were coming ; where should she stay ?

"I am a homeless wanderer," she said, half aloud; "but oh, how happy I am!"

There were some houses in the distance. She knew not what kind of people were in them, but they would give her shelter. She arose, and went towards them. Now she found that she was tired: her feet ached, her limbs trembled, she walked wearily. Then she began to think what she should say if she called at a house. "They will ask me all kinds of questions, I know. Mother always used to ask people all about themselves, when they came along begging food or lodging. Of course she didn't know whether they told her the truth, but they had to tell her something; and I shall have to answer questions, for I am a beggar now."

Pausing, then, new thoughts came. To the left were the houses; to the right stretched dark, concealing woods. They seemed to invite her to their privacy: they said, "Come to us, for beneath our shadows there is rest;" and the tired girl turned that way. She crossed the intervening field, felt the night-dews about her feet, saw the shadows deepening, and entered the wood. At first the trees were sparse. No shrubbery was among them, and she walked from trunk to trunk without finding an inviting place to rest. Then low bushes appeared, and quiet nooks were frequent. Then she came to a stone wall, and to a place where two walls met. In the angle there was brushwood, and huge piles of leaves were drifted in and dried.

"Here I will rest," she said. "I will slumber here; and the free winds shall sing my nightly song, and the leaves overhead shall be my canopy."

She took off her hat then, and hung it on a broken limb. She spread her shawl around her shoulders, and her long tresses fell about her neck in clusters. Then she smoothed a bed of leaves; and, lying down, she drew the piles of dry leaves about her, and snuggled back beneath a low-spreading branch. "My God, I thank thee!" was her thought. The stars were coming out in the azure above, the tremulous leaves whispered peace, and night was now upon her. In the distance a dog barked; and this was all she feared. She reasoned thus: "In our woods, there are no large animals; only squirrels and birds are here. I am not afraid of them. Dogs might come; but here in this out-of-the-way corner, what is there to attract them? No, I will not fear. I will sleep here in this cradle of my God."

Then she folded her hands, and the soft-winged spirit touched her eyelids with soothing rest.

It was deep night when she awoke, startled by some sound. She was conscious of a crackling, snapping sound, and something seemed to fall. There was a twittering overhead, and she strained her eyes as she listened; but no more noise was heard, though she held her breath that she might hear. A star glimmered through the foliage above, and afar the trees seemed to tower like giants in their strength ; but all around her there was peace, and the leaves about her person were warm and soft, soothing her to rest. Then she said, "It was only a dry branch that snapped and fell in the night air. I will sleep again."

When next she awoke, the dawn had overspread the earth, and light was gladdening the sweet, dim woods. Fresh aromas were in the air; health and strength were in their odors ; the old earth was awake again.

Bella had some troubles that day ; but yet they scarcely seemed like troubles, so confident was she that she should worry through, and come out right. It was ten o'clock before she broke her fast ; for she did not feel like calling at a door for bread till hunger drove her. She evaded the peoples' questions, and still went on, pausing now and then to rest when some by-place allured her. In one of these pauses she began to plan. "I will not go to Boston. I will not go home. I should be sent back to the asylum if I should. That is the way patients are always served. If I only had the letter I wrote to Edward, I could mail it somewhere. If I had only had it with me when I came away ; or, if I had paper, I could write."

This last idea impressed her. She must write to Edward ; yes, she must write ; but how could she get paper ? Beg it ? Yes : anybody would give her a sheet of paper, and lend her a pencil. She walked briskly then ; and when she came to a small white house, whose neat yard bespoke tender women, she called. She trembled a little as a stranger woman opened the door, but ventured to ask for a sheet of paper and a pencil. The woman stared. It was such an odd request for a beggar. She was about to refuse ; but a man appeared. He looked at the girl, and said, "Give it to her, mother: a sheet of paper isn't much."

"And would you give me an envelope too ? "

Again the woman stared ; but the man said, "Give her an envelope too ; what harm is there ? " Then he spoke to Bella. "Keep the pencil ; keep the whole. You are welcome to them."

"I am all right now," she thought, as she turned from the door. It seemed that real strength was given her now ; and she walked briskly away. She would write, then beg a stamp, then mail her letter ; and — no thanks to the hospital ! "If I have nothing else, I have my freedom," she said ; "and with that I can do all things." Then she turned into a field, sat down on a mossy stone, and wrote. Smiles dimpled on her cheeks ; Hope guided her pen. She wrote a page, a second page ; and then she paused. A troubled look was on her face : she held the pencil suspended. The troubled look deepened. She arose finally, and put the pencil in her pocket. She walked and mused. She wrote no more that night; nor until late the next forenoon did she write again. No, nor even then. But she had come to her decision; and she announced it to herself in this wise. "It is just here: I cannot tell Edward where to direct a letter, or where to come, even if he would come on. I must have a place where I can stay till I hear from him. I know what I will do: I will find a place to work somewhere. That will give me a home and wages. When I have engaged my place, I will finish my letter. It is a splendid plan: I am glad I thought of it; for then I can tell Edward where to write."

Every thing was fair now. She brushed down her dress, put back her hair, smoothed her hat, and saw her way clear. And she began to call at houses; but the more she called, the less seemed her chance. Some looked at her with incredulity; some said outright that they never hired strangers; some asked her where she came from; and some inquired what she could do. But nobody wanted her. She came to a village, and tried at the large houses; but no one wanted a stranger. At last she grew discouraged, and said, "What shall I do? I must have a place. I cannot keep tramping. Where should I come out? I cannot send Edward word where to write, unless I have a home."

In this mood she entered a large village. A signboard swung in the middle; and it gave her a thonght. "Here is a tavern. Maybe they would hire me."

With eager steps she hastened to the door, and made known her errand. The landlord himself came to her, and asked her in. She saw a roomy hall; doors were opening on either side; and the place had a half-stylish air. But style was nothing to her. A home and a refuge was what she wanted.

"What can you do?" asked the landlord.

"Any thing, any thing that you want me to."

"What have you been doing?"

"This was close; but she was used now to questions. She made a random answer: "General housework."

"Where did you come from?"

"Boston."

"Ah! You have come a long way. Couldn't you get work nearer?"

"I didn't try."

"Ah! How is that? Been cutting up, and want to get out of the way?"

She longed to turn on her heel, and flee: color came and went in her face; but she stood firm; and the man went on with his questions, puzzling her as a cross-questioning lawyer. There seemed to be listeners in an adjoining room, and occasionally a face peeped out. At last a man motioned to the landlord, and he stepped in there. A sigh of relief gushed from Bella's lips. The man in the next room spoke low. "Landlord," said he, "that 'ere's the gal what Billings was tellin' on. I know her by her curls."

"You don't say so!" said the landlord; "yet it is! I know it too! The description answers exactly. She is the lunatic just escaped. Yes, yes! What shall we do?"

"Hush! She'll hear you! I tell you, landlord: you let me have a team, and I'll take her back again. They'll pay me handsome."

"But my team," said the landlord: "they ought to pay something handsome for the use of that.".

"Oh, they will, they will! That 'ere feller that goes round huntin' arter runaways, always pays. That's the way he gits everybody to help him. I tell you what, landlord, I'll pay you for the team, and go snucks besides.

That feller'll give me a good V or X, I'll warrant. He'd give a good deal to git that gal back. Jist you let me manage."

Then the man went out to the hall: "I say, gal, the landlord here don't want no more help; but I know a man what does want jist sech a gal as you are, and he'll take you, I'll be bound."

"Where is he?" asked Bella, trembling with disgust at the man's rude manner.

"Oh! he's down here a few miles. You'd have to ride; but I can take you right down, ef you will ride with me."

"I want work so much that I will go anywhere," Bella answered, while cold shivers ran over her at the thought of riding with that man!

"Well, he'll give you work, I'll be bound."

It was with some misgivings that Bella entered the wagon with this "creature," as he seemed to her. She ventured but one question.

"What kind of a man is he?"

"Oh, he's a gentleman! Don't think he's like me, 'cause he ain't. He wants jest sech a gal as you. I heerd him say so. You see, you're right smart. You show it in your looks. Why, I shouldn't wonder ef he would pay me for bringing you to him."

They rode on silently then; and miles passed behind them, till at length something in the landscape became familiar. She was sure she had seen it before. She looked earnestly. Yes, it grew more natural. Yes, she knew the place. She turned, and clutched the man's arm. "You are taking me back to the asylum. I know this place."

"Asylum! What do you know about the asylum?" he asked coolly.

Sure enough; what did she? She was betraying her-self. She fell back heavily, and was still; but her heart beat with wild leaps, for every moment the scenery grew more familiar. At length the tops of the long asylum building came in view. She gave a spring. "You are taking me back. I will not go! I will not go!"

But, as she sprang, a powerful arm was thrown about her. "No, no, my hearty, you don't get away from me. Yes, they want you down here. I heerd 'em tell about them 'ere curls o' yourn." And thus they drove in at the great asylum gate. His coarse arm was about her, her heart was throbbing with lightning velocity, her eyes burned in her head. Now she was a bound prisoner. That night she slept in the blinded room. The stern supervisor came, and they bound her down with leather straps.

"You won't walk out any more," said the attendant. "You have fixed yourself this time. You'll get no more privileges, I'll warrant you!"

In whispers the patients spoke to each other. "It is dreadful, isn't it? There is little use in trying to escape these miseries. If we get away, there is always somebody willing to bring us back. Patients have no real friends."

Darker than ever were the days to Bella now. She was not allowed to walk, nor even to leave the hall. The strictest rules were enforced upon her. But these severities brought no submission into a soul like hers. Every independent fibre of her being roused into action. Loving, warm-hearted, sensitive to true emotions as was her nature, there yet was within her a deep, ingrained sense of freedom, an independence inherited, and trained by education among free people. To true and genuine love she was submissive as a child; but, against this continued repulsive bondage, her young soul incessantly rebelled. She would not be silent. She thought, she watched, she observed, criticised, and talked. Her sister patients were alarmed.

They tried to hush her, to persuade her through fear; but she would not heed them.

"You will bring more trouble upon yourself," they said.

"Trouble!" she repeated proudly. "I expect trouble. We all are surrounded by trouble in here. What I say is true. If my garment did not fit, they would not, could not, put it on."

"We know it is all true," the ladies returned; "but we fear for the consequences to you when you say these things."

"Fear," she replied. "I am past fear."

"What shall I do with her?" asked the attendant of the assistant physician.

"Put her at work," he replied. "A great healthy girl like her should be at work."

Marion attempted this, but was met by a flat refusal. "No, I will not work for this institution. I will not lift my hands for the prison that holds me in this bondage."

"But you should not be angry with *us*. It is your *friends* who keep you here."

"Friends!" echoed the patient. "What are they? People who pet us while we are in prosperity, and desert us in the hour of our trouble? Do you call them friends? And as to you, if you choose to let yourself for pay in this building, you may do your work. I am not a hired servant in this place."

Marion told the assistant physician that Miss Forresst flatly refused to work. "There ought to be a law for enforcing labor in asylums," he replied. "These healthy people ought to work."

"I'll be a law for you," the supervisor remarked. "Leave Miss Forresst to me. I can fix her."

What selling South *was* to a Virginia slave, removal to a lower ward *is* to asylum patients. They chill with sadness when one of their number is removed to a lower hall. Their hearts go out in sympathy for that person; and pity followed Bella now, for this removal had come to her.

The supervisor entered the hall, and walked straight to Bella's door.

"Miss Forresst, I wish you to change halls. You will please go with me."

There was peremptoriness in her tone. Bella looked up.

"Now?"

"Yes, now."

Bella glanced around. She had a few articles lying about, and she began to gather them up.

"Don't stop for your things," said the supervisor in a tone of command: "come!"

Bella knew it was useless to resist, useless to remonstrate, or even to speak. She looked around, gave one wave of her hand to Mrs. Long, and went out through the rear door of the hall, and into the open portico; and the place that had known Bella knew her no more. She had entered that hall without introduction; she left it without ceremony. She was now in a passage with only her stern conductress. She was to enter another hall, a new arena, where the faces were all strange to her, and the "treatment," she had reason to suppose, was much harsh'er than where she had been. As she followed her guide through the corridors, and inhaled the mouldy, musty air, she asked herself, "Am I really on American soil, or am I in some country where tyranny rules? Is this the land to which those grand old men came, that they might sing the psalms of the free?

"Then the wild woods rang
With the songs of the free,
And the glorious tones
Of liberty;

> And the joyful sound
> Rolling far around,
> Echoing back on the sea,
> Pealed liberty."

" And I," mused the girl, "a lineal descendant of those heroic spirits, am an innocent prisoner on their soil ! "

It was a mighty struggle through which the free young soul of Bella passed that day. She had cause to thank her God who created her with health and strength to endure.

As she passed from corridor to corridor, weird, wan faces looked out at her. She shuddered for them ; and her quick thoughts whispered beneath her breath, " Poor, dear, suffer-ing women ! Shall I ever be like you? God knows ! Perhaps so, if I am held here years, as you are ; for this is a wearing existence, — a death in life, a slow wasting into despair."

And back in the hall she had left, women went to their cells and wept. "Dear, bright, and beautiful Miss Bella ! What lies before her? For her sympathy with us she was removed. Because she could not sit still, and see justice outraged, she is punished."

CHAPTER XIV.

DO the spirits on that other shore quiver at each new advent? Why should they? It is but another who has passed, by Nature's appointed way, to another clime of God's creating. Do we tremble at a new advent into our life? Nay. We rather ring bells of acclamation, crying, "Another child is born : a new being is added to our earth." But the birth into this life is of Nature's appointing. Therefore we *should* rejoice; for that which is created by the unseen natural forces is the result of laws of grandeur and magnificence, mysteriously working above and around us. At these results we should be glad.

Therefore, at every advent into this life, we should be glad; and, at every advent into the next life, we could be glad if the laws of God in Nature were kept. For, if the laws of Nature were fully kept by men, all persons would live in health and beauty, and would enter that eternal passage as ripened shocks of corn, gliding, from the close of long years, into spheres of beauty and eternal joy.

But advents into asylum halls are not of God. They are men's contrivings, and they show their origin. With all the art and reason that men possess, they are imperfect workmen beside the great artistic Intellect. No painter has ever yet equalled one flower; no sculptor has ever put life into a bust; no scientific man has yet perfected his science. Man, compared with any other earthly creation, has wonderful powers; yet, at his best estate, he is but an imitator of his Creator, and men should feel honored when they succeed as his imitators.

But, when men attempt to do that which God has not done, their deficiencies are made more apparent; for their plans are out of tune, friction and pain ensue, and harmony is lost in discord.

Such are men's efforts in constructing and governing prisons. God has given the human race but one environment; and that is the pure, big atmosphere in which we live and breathe. Never has he given to man a model for prisons, nor for causing other pain. The sweet, fresh atmosphere, when it enters and emerges from the healthy lungs, causes them no agony; and as we move in this atmosphere, and observe the beautiful creations that flourish in it, it does not seem like a prison, but like a wonderful palace that our Father has given us for an inheritance.

But men and women sadly mar this beautiful floating palace on which they are created. They mar it by many mistakes and violations of infinite, eternal, natural laws; and they mar it by their unwise methods of punishing those who have violated these laws.

Human nature is wise and glorious when it walks in the path the Creator has appointed; but when it stretches up its hands, and says, "We can make laws, O God! for we are wiser than thou," it creates Babel instead of the order the Lord intended. More than one Babel on this globe has towered up as an insult to Heaven; more than one still towers. The futility of such works is always apparent on near inspection. Let us draw near, and see this invention into which Miss Forresst was now entering, — this patent for the cure of minds.

She followed the supervisor into the hall. It was longer than the one she had left; but its sides were lined with the

same kind of coarse doors, and its aspect was all prison.
The floor was unpainted, and coarser than that of the hall
she had left. Along the sides were ranged a few stiff settees or lounges, put there apparently to use, but not much
permitted to the weary women, from fear of the injury the
settees might sustain. The building and furniture of asylums must be preserved intact for the inspection of trustees.

Bella looked up and down this hall; and a glance told
her that it was full of a deeper misery than any she had
seen. The women seemed lifeless and dejected. Their faces
were dulled, and an asylum apathy was settled on them.
They looked at each other as Sorrow looks in the eyes of
Sorrow, and as Despair watches Despair, saying in heart-
language, "How long, O Lord! how long?" As Bella entered, they turned their eyes upon her; and their *eyes* spoke
as *lips* oft spoke in "the best hall." "Another, another.
How many are doomed?"

Bella felt a deeper chill. Her bosom heaved, and her
long black ringlets quivered as from deep emotion. As she
followed her conductress, they paused at the door of a dor-
mitory. Six cot-beds stood side by side. Every night six
women were locked in there, strangers to each other, from
different ranks in society, but called insane. How insane
were they, if six could be trusted together in one small
room, locked in by themselves, without power to get out?

But Bella did not think of this. She only thought that
she was to be one of the six; and involuntarily she shrank
back. "Not there; oh, do not put me there!"

"I do not intend to," the official replied. "I intend you
shall have a room alone; and I wish you to stay in it. I
wish you to form no acquaintances in this hall, but to remain in your room entirely alone. This is your room."

She paused at an open door; and Bella glanced within.
An unpainted, coarse board floor; an iron bedstead at the

right hand; a small chest-of-drawers at the foot of the bed;
and on the opposite side of the cell another bed, — a sort of
wooden frame a foot and a half wide. This was taken out
into the hall at night for some poor mortal to lay her tired
body on, while she sought the rest, that, being sought, often
could not be found. Between these two beds there was
barely room to walk; between the foot of the iron bedstead
and the drawers there was just room for a small chair. For.
a moment the young lady stood at the door, and asked herself whether it was possible for any thing to be more cheerless. But she did not speak; for speaking would bring on
an altercation, and an altercation would only result in
heavier trouble for herself. Therefore she silently walked
into the disagreeable place; and the supervisor turned away.
She went to the attendant, Annie, and said, "I have brought
down Miss Forresst to your hall. I wish her to have her
room entirely to herself. I wish her to have no conversation or communication with any of the patients. You will
please not allow her to go into any of their rooms, nor allow
any one of them to enter hers."

Annie received this order without comment, simply bowing her assent. Annie had but recently come to the asylum.
She was a lady in heart, thought, and feeling. She had
come, not with the idea that these were crazy people whom
she might " thrash " about, and take pay for it; but she had
come with the feeling that they were unfortunate people,
for whom she was to do all the kind acts that were in her
power. The ladies under her appreciated her tenderness
toward them. She kissed a poor haggard woman one day,
and the woman was overwhelmed with a grateful delight
that she could not forget. Often the women said to her,
" If we could always have attendants like you, Annie, we
should not be so wretched."

But Annie's kindness was frequently counteracted by the

supervisor, who, calling Annie "too soft-hearted," took upon herself the government of the hall. She went about now among the patients, and gave them all particular instructions to keep out of Miss Forresst's room, and not even to speak to her when they met her in the hall, as she was "a very troublesome patient; and the less they had to do with her, the better it would be for them."

The consequence was, that, whenever Bella stepped into the hall, she was the immediate object of scrutiny, although, as the women looked at her, they kept at a respectful distance, much as they would from a lioness that had suddenly been thrown among them. They expected some violent outbreak or fearful manifestation; but hours rolled into days, and still the patient was quiet. She went to and from the table, and, when necessary, crossed and re-crossed the hall. No one spoke to her; and, knowing herself to be under a ban, she spoke to no one. But for her speaking eyes she was not responsible. Nature had given her eyes that *would* speak; and, though she suppressed her lips when she met these women, the blue-black Montague *would* flash out. And as the language of the eyes is not easily mistaken, it came about, ere many days, that the women all felt acquainted with Miss Forresst. They began to suspect a hoax, and to see that Miss Forresst's "troublesome" qualities were not from insanity, but from her quick perception, which made her "troublesome" where there was so much wrong to discern. Annie formed the same opinion; but she made no remark. Presently the women began to question her.

"Annie, do you see any thing dangerous about Miss Forresst?"

"I see nothing," was Annie's mild reply.

"We all thought she was violent, from the orders given about her; but she does not show any thing of it, and we have changed our opinion."

"You have a right to your opinions," said Annie, smiling.

"Yes: we can think them, but not express them. We dare speak to you, because you are so kind."

"I speak myself sometimes," was Annie's response.

There was in this gallery a small, frail woman, who was one of the objects of the supervisor's especial attention. It seemed that she could not be satisfied unless this woman was under discipline. Mrs. Jones was the sufferer's name. She was the wife of a respectable young farmer; and she was also young, though she had been the mother of five children. She wandered up and down this hall, heart-broken and forlorn. Somehow she had incurred official displeasure; and, as a consequence, she bore the whole force of discipline. She had walked in jackets day after day, till jackets seemed her normal condition. And it is not a light thing to wear a jacket made of strong canvas, with heavy sleeves coming down over the fingers, and sewed tightly at the ends, to which are attached straps that bind the hands tight to the body. When these straps are tied, the hands cannot be raised from the body, nor has the person the least chance to use them. Mrs. Jones had worn jackets till it seemed that she must be worn out herself; and she was. She grew pale and thin, and her eyes looked staring and wild. "She's a terribly crazy woman," the assistant physician said; and therefore he justified the acts of the supervisor. Mrs. Jones had been dragged on the floor, by her two arms, the length of the gallery. She had been pulled across the hall by the ears; she had been jerked by the hair of the head; she had been struck by the keys, and carried on her forehead the scars of the gashes they had made! She was among those who had been silently watching Bella, and had read the young girl's speaking eyes. Softly, one morning, she came to Bella's door, and cautiously looked in. Bella saw her wild eyes, and thin, wan face, and was startled. Mrs. Jones said, "May I come in?"

Bella hesitated. Then she said, "You know I am not allowed company."

"Yes, I know," said Mrs. Jones. "Is it because you do not want them, or because the people over us do not want you to have them?"

"Oh, it is the people over us! I should not shut myself up of my own will."

"Then I am coming," said the woman; and, gliding in, she partially closed the door as a screen behind her.

"But the supervisor"—Bella suggested.

"She has just been through the hall," Mrs. Jones replied. "She won't come again quite yet."

"And Annie"—

"*She* won't tell. She is always good. She has been here only a short time; and, if we could have such attendants as she is, it wouldn't seem so terrible here. But there! after all, it can't be good here. The best of attendants could not make things right. There are the supervisors, and the matron, and the doctors, all coming in and giving orders, and spoiling all comfort. Annie says, if we could be let alone, and do a little as we please, she thinks we might have a little happiness, if we *are* prisoners. And then there are such rules! Did you ever read the printed rules hung up in this hall, Miss Forresst?"

"I looked them over."

"Did you notice that every rule has a *not* or *never* in it?"

"I did not observe that. I only thought they were very close, hard rules."

"Well, you read them again. There are ten of them, and every one reads, 'The patients shall not,' or 'the patients shall never;' till one wonders what we *may* do here. Don't you think it is wicked to keep people shut up so, and deprive them of every privilege of natural life?"

"My opinions are well known here," Bella replied.   "It may not be best for me to repeat them."

"And that is why they order us not to speak to you," said Mrs. Jones, her face lighting up with intelligence. "I understand them. You know too much for them. You see through things, and there is so much here that won't bear being seen through. They tried to make us think you a wild maniac ; but I am sure I don't see but you are as rational as they are. *Are* you insane ? "

"I never knew that I was ; but I don't know how soon I shall be, if I stay here."

"That's it ! " said the woman with a sudden thrill. "They make people crazy here. I know all about it. I have borne their discipline ! "   Here her eyes dilated. "Yes, I have borne their 'treatment.' I have been harnessed to an iron bed in the blinded room, and staid there, bound, all night, — alone, except my God. I was sane when I came here. I was sick, but sane. I am not sane now: I am insane, insane ! I felt myself grow insane. They drove me into it. And, oh, it was such pain, such terrible pain ! I shrieked in my agony ; and then they sheeted me. Do you know what that is, Miss Forresst ? "

"No.   What is it ? "

"I will tell you.   They take a poor woman, like as they took me, and they take her into one of these little cells. Our supervisor is very fond of that kind of discipline. When she sheeted me, she took me into that little room opposite this. She had two attendants with her, great strong girls ; and she is a strong woman, you know ; and they laid me down flat on the bed, and held me there. And while the two girls held my arms and feet, she took the sheet, and wound it around and around my head, closing my mouth and nose from the air. I could not breathe. A feeling came over me as of death, and a gurgling noise

was in my throat. I thought I was going to my God;
that I could never breathe again. Then they unwound the
sheet. I suppose they did not want me to die outright.
Oh, when I was sick, and needed comfort, this was what I
had! And my little children at home — when I think of
them! But oh, I must not think! And we are so hungry
here: we have so little to eat. Don't you get hungry, Miss
Forresst?"

"I do, in this hall. In the other hall there is enough
such as it is; but here there is not enough of any thing.
I think the ladies must all be hungry."

"They are, they are. Sometimes we divide out the bread,
so as to be sure that each has her portion. At other times,
some of us feel so hungry that we hurry to the table like
greedy pigs; and then the last ones go without; for we
can't all have enough, you know, and hunger makes people
selfish. Don't you think so, Miss Forresst?"

"I have heard of its making people wild and insane,"
said Bella. "But here they use it to cure insanity; and,
as this is a scientific and approved institution for the cure
of diseased minds, I think people are mistaken in eating
enough out in the world. They ought to know that plenty
of good food is injurious to mental health. And when they
provide dinners and entertainments for celebrities, they
should have a few baked beans, or a little corned beef and
cabbage, or a plate of bone-soup, or a bit of salt fish, followed by a dessert of half-made hasty-pudding. My father
used to make better puddings for his horse. It is a pity
the world should be ignorant of the scientific methods for
mental cure that are used in these large establishments.
Somebody ought to make this system public."

"If you ain't splendid!" said Mrs. Jones. "I do not
wonder they keep you alone. Why, you could stir up the
patients till there would be a rebellion right here in this hall."

14

"Which I should be sorry to do: for they can neither get out, nor help themselves, in; and I should only cause them more trouble. No: it is not in here that these matters should be discussed. It is out in the world, the open, free world, everywhere, in every house and family. For are not homes broken, and family ties sundered, to feed these institutions? People outside of here should know just what goes on inside, —just what we know, — we who suffer."

Click.

"Hush!" murmured Mrs. Jones. "Somebody is coming." And, with terror in her face, she darted behind the door, forcing her way in at the foot of the narrow bed.

The click was that of the supervisor. She passed through the hall, looking keenly each way at the weary, dispirited women. She saw Bella sitting in her one chair, and said to herself, "It takes *me* to manage patients."

She did not see Mrs. Jones behind the door. But Bella saw. She saw how Mrs. Jones's eyes dilated, how she grew wild at the sound of those stern, hated steps; and Bella did not wonder. She reflected on the "treatment" this supervisor had given this pale woman, whose insanity was caused by a physical disability that should have received the tenderest care; and her reflections opened to her mind new and broad views of this appalling disease. She marvelled that the doctors looked on complacently, and winked at the cruelties the attendants committed; and she marvelled also that the physicians looked only superficially at their patients, holding them in bondage while their disease worked deeper and deeper.

Mrs. Jones's visit emboldened the other women to try sly visits; and, within a week, nearly every woman in the hall had been in Bella's room. Sometimes Annie would look in and say, "Be careful, or you will be caught."

"Oh! you keep watch, Annie, and let us know if you see her coming."

The kind Annie did watch, both for their sakes and her own; for she knew that if she was discovered as a partisan with what would be called insubordination, she would receive reprimands, perhaps dismissal, though as to the latter, she expressed herself as considering it would be no disgrace if she was dismissed for being too humane. "I should be proud to have that said of me," she remarked.

As connecting links between the halls, there are porticos with large windows, where the patients can walk, and fancy themselves out of doors. But the windows are iron-sashed, and the doors locked. Bella sometimes walked in these porticos, for exercise and variety to her life. Many and sad were the sights she saw here, many and sad the lessons she learned. She saw women thrust out there at the caprices of their attendants. When it was rainy, and when it was cold, early and late, and at any other times, they were rudely pushed out and locked out at the commands of their attendants. There was one poor, thin, hollow-cheeked woman, who had been for more than a score of years in that house, who was regularly, every morning, thrust out there to pace, or crouch down, regardless of the weather. In the depths of winter, when the ice crackled around the building, and the hoar-frost covered the windows, at five o'clock in the morning, when the great bell rang, this woman's attendant went into her room, pulled her out of bed, threw a calico gown and a thin shawl over her shoulders, and thrust her out to walk in that cold, cheerless space. The poor creature shivered and chattered there for an hour. Then she was taken in; and the rest of the day she was locked into her desolate cell, sitting all day alone, without fire, occupation, or comfort. She had brothers and sisters out in the world, in luxurious homes, with plenty around them.   They were healthy, robust people.   She, the invalid, fared no better than a vile felon on a dungeon-floor.

Many faces did Bella see as she walked these porticos. They came to the windows of their halls, and looked out into this dreary space.   There were young faces, delicate, refined and beautiful, looking out in wistful agony.   There were old faces, from whom the hope and joy of life had flown.   There were women in middle life, cut suddenly from all they loved; and hopeless prison stagnation rested on them all. There was one woman, sent out there every day in the pitiless cold to eat.   With her plate of meagre food in her hand, she was turned out and locked out.   There was neither chair nor table.   The floor was of bare boards : she put her plate on it in one corner, and, crouching, ate her daily food there.   Bella shuddered at the sight.   It seemed like a dog crouching to his food; and, when a human being falls to this state, it is pitiful indeed.

CHAPTER XV.

ONNECTED with our asylums are chapels, where God can be worshipped by patients in bondage. The chapels are airy, prettily-finished rooms, and are used for all public meetings of the asylum inmates, such as sociables, lectures, prayers, and any amusements that the superintendent sees fit to provide. But all these arrangements are subject to stringent rules, and do not at all partake of the nature of free meetings in the open world. First, the majority of those present in these asylum assemblies are driven together by the orders of their attendants; for comparatively few are so trained that they walk submissively in the circumscribed, plodded paths that the managers mark out.

Second, the manner of going from the halls to the chapel gives patients strange sensations of bonds and prison horror. The patients are filed from the halls under guard; and, to reflecting minds, this filing is a sad sight. It seems like mortals filing through passages to eternity, without freedom, joy, or hope.

Some very good lectures are given in these chapels. If delivered outside, they would be both pleasant and instructive. But here the listeners feel their chains, and are too burdened and unhappy to find real enjoyment in any thing. During long days they have been sitting within sounds of woe, — have been in misery themselves, and know that they are to go from the chapel back to those same locked

14*

halls. They think also of the numbers left there, too miserable to come out, even for an hour; and that over them are left guards, whose business it is to keep them there.

Realization of these circumstances prevents the patients from finding real pleasure in any thing within these walls. Their nerves are tremulous with fear; their hearts ache with suffering. From beginning to end, the "treatment" of insane patients is made up of shocks to their already weakened nerves; falsehoods that are uttered to them as freely as though God had not forbidden falsehood and deceit; and violent acts committed *upon* them, such as, if committed *by* them, would consign them forever to cells.

The false ideas of the cure of insanity, which have given birth to the corroding system now eating the hearts of our people, are sanctioned by laws, that, though framed for the protection of persons accused of insanity, can be easily evaded by unscrupulous men; and rational people can be, and are, as cruelly confined as the truly insane. Not only are rational women there, but men also, on whose brows are the stamp of intelligence and the seal of truth. Bella met one of these gentlemen, one evening, at a chapel sociable. Surprise almost compelled unbelief in her own eyesight when she saw Mr. David Wright sitting among the patients in the chapel. She had met him often in Boston, and thought him one of the finest men of her acquaintance. He, too, was equally surprised at meeting her. He spoke with her.

"Is it possible?" he said. "Do I really see Miss Bella Forresst in this unfortunate place?"

"It is quite true," she answered; "but you are not more surprised than I am to see Mr. David Wright here."

Then followed the usual questions; of which one was, "Do you think you are benefited by being here?"

"I think," was Mr. Wright's reply, "that I am in a constant anxiety about my family; that my wife is struggling with her four boys to manage, and no husband to help her; and that she is paying six dollars a week for me here, for board that is of the meanest quality; and I see no benefit to myself. But I am in. When I shall get out, time will show. The institution claims law, and has the credence of the people outside, which gives it power. I have my simple protest; and the protest of a patient is — that!"

He snapped his thumb and finger together, with a schoolboy's twirl; for his soul was irritated with his situation, out of which there was no egress.

Bella learned now something of her neighbors, the men who were imprisoned in their own departments. She had seen them in the chapel, and had sometimes had glimpses of them through the windows when she was outside; but now, for the first time, she learned of their inner life, as Mr. Wright, talking low, ventured to communicate.

" How do the men employ themselves ? " Bella asked.

He glanced carefully around, lest some attendant might be listening; then he said, "By way of amusement, the most popular employment is playing cards. Rather doubtful as a mental improver outside of here, Miss Forresst, but considered very efficacious within. When the physician sees a company engaged in it, he says, 'Ah, glad to see that! The more of it the better.' By way of labor, the occupations are various. Washing dishes is extensively used as a mental renovator. If wives only knew how beneficial this employment is to the mind, they could set their husbands at it at home, and thus save the expense of sending them to asylums. Then we have washing windows, cleaning paint, knives, floors, brasses, and so on. Some are detailed to the laundry, some to the cook-room; and some are permitted to go outside and work on the farm, provided they submit themselves to their overseers, do not try to run away, and work faithfully hoeing and digging in the hot sun, while their attendants loll and lounge on the ground, earning their money by watching their slaves. This is said to be an excellent thing for the patients; and land is purchased by the institution purposely for this labor. If its excellence consists in toiling in the hot sun, why may we not work in free life, and work as we please, where the wages would be our own? If its excellence consists in working under overseers as slaves, I must say I beg to be excused from receiving its benefits. It would not agree with my constitution to cultivate land with an overseeing taskmaster at my side. I should bolt; and then I should be marched back to my cell.

"There is another method of improving the minds of men here. We are allowed to walk out. I tried it once in the yard. We were told that we might walk up and down the terraces, provided we kept on the front of the house, and within view of our walking attendant. Well, I began the solemn tread; but scarce had gone half one length before the attendant came down upon me with arms uplifted, a heavy cane flourishing in his right hand, and vociferating boisterously, 'Back, there, back!' He shouted as he came near me. 'Back to the next terrace! This is too near the street!' I quietly stepped back, and he marched on to the front terrace himself, brandishing his cane; and there he walked back and forth with pompous steps, while we cowered humbly, and listlessly paced beneath his eyes. I tell you, I never saw so abject a spectacle; and I could scarcely believe myself in my own country. I do not know by what rule of mental philosophy physicians prove such methods beneficial to their patients, in this enlightened, independent country; and I"—

"Ah, Mr. Wright! you seem to be having quite a chat with Miss Forresst," said a man's voice near.

Mr. Wright looked up. The supervisor stood there. At the same instant some one touched Bella's arm. It was the matron. "Miss Forresst, there is a lady out here wishes to be introduced to you."

Bella followed the woman outside the chapel, and here the matron paused. "Miss Forresst, I am shocked at you talking so long with that man. I cannot permit such an impropriety. This young lady will take you back to your hall."

A tall, stout girl here stepped forward, and, twirling her keys, deigned to speak. "This way, Miss Forresst." This was said in a tone of insolent command. Bella followed, quietly and speechlessly; but two red spots burned in her cheeks.

The supervisor disposed of Mr. Wright more summarily, by hissing into his ear, " Dry up your slang, now, or *you'll* not get out of your hall again ! "

Thus the mutinous conversation was suppressed, and the asylum had its way. Mr. Wright might sit his lifetime in his cell, thinking of his struggling wife and children at home. His feelings were of no account. He was a chattel of the institution, and chattels are valuable only for the gain of their possessors.

We may as well add here that Mr. Wright did continue to sit there. Week after week, and month after month, he waited patiently for the word of release. He was an honorable, law-abiding man, and wanted to leave the place " honorably," as the asylum keepers call it. Mrs. Wright went often to see her husband. She sent him to this institution by the advice of her doctor, who told her a few weeks' stay would be sufficient. It *was* sufficient, but not to cure. It sufficed to reduce him, to take hope and health from him. Months passed; and the superintendent repeated to her the backneyed phrase, "He is doing very well.

A little longer stay will be sufficient." She told this to her husband, and he resigned himself. He waited. The hot weather came, and the superintendent told him he might go as soon as it was cool. He waited all the fall for the word of manumition, but no such word was spoken. Then winter drew on; and, when Mrs. Wright came again to see her husband, she was told that he would be better to stay through the winter, until warm weather came. He staid on, dragging out a miserable existence, which he endured with what fortitude he could summon. His wife paid his board as long as her means lasted; but the failure of money gives no release to lunatic prisoners, whatever their condition. The law magnanimously provides for those who have no other means of payment, and it seems like kindness; but when, practically, this charity is used for the purposes of gain to the institutions, it becomes a cruel bondage to thousands whose board-money thus goes to swell the asylum coffers. State patients are small in cost within asylums. They are crowded into spaces scarce larger than their bodies; they are hustled together in rows; the corridors become miasmatic with their exhalations; and all this is for the cure of their minds! Such situations would demoralize the finest minds! How, then, do physicians thus expect to elevate their lunatic patients?

Without a word to himself, Mr. David Wright's name was, by the asylum managers, transferred to the list of poor patients. He suspected it. He knew his wife's resources, and knew that it was impossible for her to continue to pay the stipulated sums; and, though no one told him, he felt that he was made a pauper as well as a prisoner. The thought was like a vulture gnawing at his vitals. How could he escape? His fetters were as iron, and his mind might well go lunatic under his trials. But what cared the asylum? He counted *one;* and *each* of these *ones* was just so much gain to the institution. Mr. Wright grew haggard, and his clothes became shabby. He felt that he *could not* and *would not* stay. He *would* have freedom! His poor wife had become disheartened. The brightness of her eyes was dimmed. The prolonged imprisonment of her husband led her to fear that he would never be well. She wept when she saw how thin and haggard he was growing. It did not occur to her that scanty and improper food, constant incarceration, homesickness and heart-sickness, were the powerful stimulants that were wearing her husband away; but he knew it, and it wore upon him. By stealthy contrivings he managed to get at some points of law. He found that by application to the judge of the Supreme Judicial Court, he would be entitled to a hearing or trial, as to his sanity, or fitness for release.

But who would make application for him? Should he himself send out a letter? Who would take it out? Not the superintendent, nor any of the asylum officials. When he asked them to help him, they said, " Oh, don't hurry! Your wife will take you out some time." But his wife was disheartened. She had been so often told, " He had better not go just yet," that she fully believed the "just yet" would never come. She was timid, and afraid to appeal to so dignified a personage as the judge of the Supreme Court. This law thus became a "dead letter" to Mr. Wright. He turned then to lower powers, but to powers that were absolute over him. He appealed to the trustees. He wrote a letter in which he stated his case clearly, and appealed to them to give him a hearing, and, if it should be proved that he was not insane, to release him from his confinement. By law the trustees had this power; but in practice their power was of no avail, for they immediately referred the matter to the superintendent, and he assumed his blandest smile, assuring the trustees that Mr. Wright was "a very nice· man, but," here he lowered his voice significantly, "better off where he is. He is not quite right, gentlemen," he continued in the same tone, "not quite right."

Thus the case ended, though Mr. Wright tried again and again to interest the trustees. As they passed through the hall, he arose and spoke to them; and he prepared other letters which he put into their hands, but they never gave any attention to his pleas. The opinion of the superintendent governed them. They never asked what motives ruled the superintendent. They never thought he could have a selfish motive. Time went by. Lines of disciplinary sorrow gathered on Mr. Wright's brow, and deep anguish furrowed his cheeks. He walked like a man under fear, and his whole manner was subdued and hopeless; but still he did not quite give up. His integrity and purity served him as props, and bore him up. He still hoped for justice. At last another opportunity offered, and his heart leaped for it. He heard there was a law, that, upon complaint of any person confined in a lunatic asylum, or other place, or of any other person in his behalf, to the general agent of the Board of State Charity, that such person ought no longer to be confined, the agent should have power to investigate the case, make report to the board, and, if they so direct, should make application to the justice of the Supreme Judicial Court for the discharge of such person. Mr. Wright learned of this law, and again he wrote. He prepared a true and touching letter, and sent it out to mail by a brother patient who had the privilege of going about town. He was more successful than Bella, when she sent her letter by a patient; and his letter went. It was received by the person to whom it was sent, and was made the subject of action. A hearing was ordered; and Mr. Wright, pale and weary with his long duress, felt happiness once more surging into his soul. Freedom seemed before him. Once more he was to walk without a guard watching every movement, to sit at a table where wholesome varieties of food would invite him, and to feel that he was a man among men. He talked of his coming liberty, thought of it by day, and dreamed of it by night. He felt a halo about him; and, in its glow, he expanded till his face seemed renewed and glorified. But alas for his hopes! One by one they perished; one by one they withered away. Just as the superintendent influenced the trustees in Mr. Wright's previous efforts, he now influenced the Board of Charity. How could they gainsay his smooth words? How could they deny his assertion that Mr. Wright was unsuitable to go? One word from the superintendent outweighed all other testimony in the opinions of the gentlemen of the board. They said to each other, "Surely the doctor knows better than we."

Thus again the well-meaning law was prostituted, and became as blank paper to this long-suffering patient. He could not get out by it. The asylum had more power over him than the law; and asylums will have more power than law as long as the words of the officers are taken for absolute truth.

Mr. Wright did not get his freedom. He still sits in his cell, a tall, gaunt man, in seedy, rusty garments, with silver streaks threading his hair. His wife has no husband, his children are fatherless. The superintendent says, "He is not suitable to go."

When will he be suitable? When will his mind be uplifted from its pressure, and gladness once more step in? Not while he dwells within these walls, a prey to sadness, lonely, desolate, and wretched, among men as desolate as he.

15

Of what use to him are the laws, save to keep him forever in prison ?   To be effective, laws must have executors. How can patients, shut up from every avenue of outer communication, procure executors ?   The persons who are keepers over them can utterly prevent their making known their situations ; watching them with a closeness that precludes letters, or any message, from going out.   There might as well be no laws for the release of such persons ; such laws are valueless, except to show the fine powers of the law-makers.   Practically they are of no avail to persons held in locked asylums.   Boards of charity, judicial wisdom, and legal acumen, can all be thrust aside, and rendered useless by ingenious devices, and shrewd management ; and people at large know nothing of the many evasions. Laws and patients all glide by together, while the printed reports, and suave smiles of the superintendents, are eagerly accepted ; and the patients suffer on, each in his or her own pinched compartment.   " It would be better to abolish the laws for shutting in, than, being shut in unjustly, to find no way out."   So said Mr. Wright, and so thought Bella as she still continued looking through the grates.

CHAPTER XVI.

OUT in the broad lands where west winds blow, and civilization's axe cleaves bold strokes, there had stood the rude cabin of a settler. Its owner was a native of Norway, who had come from Europe with a band of his countrymen. He settled with them at first; but, straying one day in a hunt by himself, he chanced upon a lovely, isolated spot, one of Nature's oases. It flashed in sheen, and it sang the hymns of the ages; for a stream of clear water purled glitteringly through the verdure, and the adjacent "timber-land" echoed the wind-chorals of the "forest primeval."

The attractions of the place caught the eye of the Norwegian. The trees would give wood for his fires; the stream would furnish fish for food; while the fertile banks invited the hoe and the plough. It might be cold in winter; but what was cold or snow to him? Cold was his native element; and frost and ice were pastime playthings. He brought his wife and little ones to this place; he upturned the soil by his own strength; his cabin was filled with plenty; and peace sat at his fireside. But there is one law of Nature to which all must bow. It passed its hand over him. His wife became a widow, his children were fatherless. The "neighbors" talked about it. They were miles away; but still they were neighbors, and knew the widow wanted to sell her improvements, and go to a settlement of her countrymen.

This was a subject of conversation among the scat ered families, as Capt. Beale and his little company were searching and inquiring for a location suited to their wants.

"Stranger," said a rough-bearded, roughly-dressed man, with a shock of grizzly hair covering his head, and a flapping specimen of a hat surmounting that, "I reckon I know the place that'll suit ye. It's a moity fine sitooation: a leetle out o' the way, perhaps, jest now, but la! Ye can't git fur out o' the way in this yer country. Ef ye try to be by yerself, the fust ye know, there's a city behind ye. This is a big country, stranger. We don't have no hills a cuttin' off the 'rizon as they say they do in that ar New England, whar I reckon you hail from. Why, I've heern tell that them ar hills are so high, that a man can't see but seventeen acres of sky ter one time!"

The speaker cocked his old felt hat, and cast up his eye at the same time, to see what effect his remarks had produced. The captain replied pleasantly, "I don't much like your hit at New England, my friend. I have grown up there; and I like the hills, the sky, and the people. But every man has a right to praise his own country, and I am sure I have no wish to speak disparagingly of yours. I have come here to find a home; and, if you will pilot me and my friends to this place you have mentioned, I will see you well paid."

Under the guidance of this man, the party reached the little spot; and, as it had charmed the Norwegian, it now charmed the New Englanders. Its beauties were not of the prairie type, but of that undulating character that never wearies by monotony.

Trading, in this case, was not a haggling, but a matter of pleasant intercourse. The widow was ready to sell at any price; the young men, full of chivalrous honor, were ready to empty their purses for one upon whose sorrows they looked with sympathetic pity.   Between the two over-generous parties, the Westerner came with his knowledge of valuation ; and, by his aid, the transfer was successfully completed.   The Norwegian cabin on the isle of beauty became the property of Capt. Beale and Edward Forresst. The widow went to her people, and the New-England family settled in her place.   Emily became housekeeper; and Elijah, the carpenter, worked on the buildings with a carpenter's eye and hand.

Jack was in ecstasies.   The place to him had all the charms of fairy romance.   He peeped around into the corners and crevices, within and without.   He was up and down the banks of the stream, and plunged into the glens of the wood.

"It's cute," he said with a grin ; "and, when you get *her* here, cap'n, we'll sing, 'Oh, be joyful!' all the time."

Bella was Jack's ideal of womanhood.   From the first, in the Shaker family, he had invested her with the most wondrous halos; and the glory still lingered about her. He admired the captain chiefly because he was Bella's chosen.   Jack thought he must be different from other men, or *she* would never have liked him; and all Jack's plans looked prospectively to the time when *she* should come to their home.   It was, indeed, the era for which they all planned.   In reconstructing the house, Elijah was ever thinking, "How would Miss Bella like it?   Would she have it this way, or would she have it that?" while Mortimer and Edward were asking each other, "How soon shall we have the means to take our brides?"

Into this home, with pleasant surprise, came Bella's letters, announcing that she and her mother were coming, furniture and all.   The Western cabin was full of happiness then.   The very rafters vibrated with the echoes of joy.

15*

Jack crowed like a Yankee cock-a-doodle, and Emily's face lighted up with delight.

"This is scarcely a fit place for mother's furniture," said Edward thoughtfully.

"We will make it better sooner than you expect," Elijah replied, his eyes kindling with energy.

The captain was silent; but his thoughts were busy. "At last, at last, I am to be happy."

He felt that his day-star had arisen, and in his soul a new morn was appearing. "At last," he repeated, "I am to begin life. What has been my life hitherto ? A speck, a moiety. What shall be my life henceforth ? One eternal rhapsody. Thank God! I will write to her, and bid her welcome."

.   .   .   .

"Ah ! upon my honor."

Mr. Frederic Forresst held an open letter. His upper lip was taking its peculiar curve, and the mustache was at angles. The letter bore a Western post-mark. He read on, and then commented. "This is the cream of love's eloquence. Capt. Mortimer pours out sentiment like a romancer. He will have time to cool before it is answered. My foolish little sister must have a different letter." Then he tossed this into his drawer, and sent her the paper of guardianship. Her Western letters she had no more chance of receiving than if she had been in a monarchical stronghold. Frederic met every emergency with perfect skill, aided by these institutions, and in secret muttered his old oath, "Never, never, shall Chauncey Beale or his progeny inherit one penny of my father's property."

Then he gave his shoulders a shrug, and his mustache another twitch. "Grand institutions these are ! Once in them, and you are snug as a bug in a rug. How would people manage their crazy friends without them ? "

Mr. Forresst went home after this peroration, and the tip of his cane tapped cheerily at every impediment in his path. He entered his elegant house in- a particularly amiable mood, and rested his invincible person on a velvet lounge, where he meditated in a self-satisfied frame of mind.

"Upon my honor! Does Chauncey Beale's son expect to get the better of *me?*"

Meantime the home-circle grew anxious. Letters from Bella had ceased. A letter from the old mother, written tremblingly, informed them that Bella was ill, and had gone into the country for her health. Poor old mother! Overcome by the fate that had overtaken Bella, how could she write otherwise than as Frederic dictated?

"Mother," said he, "the girl is insane."

"It will break their hearts out West! It will break *my* heart!" she answered.

"No, mother! You must summon more fortitude. As to Edward, tell him she is ill, and gone into the country for improvement. Upon my honor! She causes us all sufficient trouble."

"Ill — gone into the country for her health — but why does not she write to us?"

That was the light, out West, in which the matter was discussed. And the days passed on, giving them no more news. Summer melted into autumn, autumn faded into the cold that precedes winter. November whistled in premonitions, and still there were no more tidings. Anxiety came in, and settled as a guest in the family. They consulted and surmised.

"She has yielded to Frederic, and given me up," said Mortimer in a discouraged tone.

Edward clinched his fist. "More likely he has got her into some tight place, — the convent or Shakers again."

"And there is no Elijah there to help her," said the carpenter moodily.

"By jingo and all the coons," exclaimed Jack, starting up. "If they *have* got her again! Just give me the rhino, cap'n; and I'll go there, and dig her out, as surely as I live to get there."

Mortimer looked thoughtfully at the boy, and then slowly said, "I have a mind to go myself, Jack."

"No, no," Edward responded quickly. "This is Fred's doings. You are no match for him. It takes a Forresst to manage a Forresst. I will go myself."

"You, Edward! No. It is I who have caused her trouble. It is for her truth to me that she suffers. Let me go and work for her, or suffer with her."

Edward laughed. "Come, this is no time for sentiment. Let the one go who can be most successful. I think I understand my family better than you do. I have the same blood as Fred; and I'll fight him with his own cool weapons."

"And I am poor," said Mortimer moodily.

"Pshaw, now! What matters it who has the money, you or I? You have been as a brother to me since we toddled out of our cradles, and played horse astride our sticks together. Do you think I am going to desert you now? Besides, there is my Kate, you know. I haven't made a spread about her; but, ever since I have had her acquaintance, she has been in my deepest thoughts, and we may as well be married now as ever. So I'll come back with my own bride and yours."

"Jolly!" said Jack. "You are the man for us. You are Bella's own brother."

"That is what I am, Jack. So lend a hand, all of you, and I will be off."

The "leetle out o' the way," of which their guide spoke

when he told them of the Norwegian's home, was just enough to make the mails a rarity not enjoyed every day; but, the day after this conference, Elijah undertook the task of going to the distant post-town for family supplies, and also because there might be letters in waiting. He found the precious missives; and when he had brought them home, and laid them on the plain table, the household gathered as to a feast. Among them was a square envelope of large dimensions, not scrupulously clean, and covered with "pot-hooks and angles."

"That is from Harry," said Edward. "Let's see what the old fellow has to say."

He read it aloud, while the company listened.

"BOSTON, Nov. 16, 18—.

"MY DEAR NED,— As the girls say, I take my pen in hand to inform you, — not in girl's language, however, that there is some confounded villany at work. Bella is in an insane asylum. I " —

"Hold!" groaned Mortimer. "It cannot be! Read it again." And Edward read it again; but it was just the same, and he went on : "I have just come down from the Aroostook, and am not posted in the way the thing was done; but Fred has managed it, and we must manage over him. If she is insane, Fred has made her so. If you or Mortimer want to do any thing about it, let it be quick. You will find me on your side. HARRY."

Edward folded the letter, and said solemnly, "Let me be off."

Two days after, as the November cold blew over the prairies, and the iron horse steamed his way Eastward while the breath of his nostrils curled in the frosty air, the noise of his iron feet echoed in the ears of Edward Forresst. He was on his homeward mission.

Shall we say that Mortimer was weak and deficient in duty toward Bella during all this time ?   We say nothing on that point.   We give the facts, and leave others to censure or vindicate him, as they choose.   Our pen has other duties.

CHAPTER XVII.

THE cold and frost and dreariness of November deepened around the asylum. Within, the pipes were
full of steam, and the furnaces, were kept full of
burning coal. The galleries were comfortably warm;
but the opened cells had only the warmth that came
through the doorways, and the locked cells had no warmth
at all. Those who sat locked into them sat shivering,
with not a soul to whom they could speak, and not a single
diversion to occupy their minds, or turn their attention
from the thoughts of their own distress. Bella looked
through between her iron bars, and saw the trees with their
naked branches, and the brown earth bare and desolate.
No letter had come to her. The letters that had come from
the West had fallen into her guardian's hands, and had
gone into his private drawer. Bella longed for a letter,
for one little word from her friends; and said to the assistant physician, "Doctor, I think of my mother all the time.
She loved me, and she is an old lady. I think her heart
will be so sad for me."

"Why don't you write to her?" asked the physician.

"Of what use is it? I have tried writing letters in this
place."

"Oh, but you were writing very improper letters! You
were writing against us, and contrary to the wishes of your
guardian."

"My brother Frederic has no right to make himself my

guardian. He shut me up here; and now does just as he pleases with all my property, and nobody seems to care."

"Oh, yes, Miss Forresst! We do care. We do not wish to see injustice. Write a good letter to your mother, just such a letter as will make her happy, and we will send it. Don't fill it with complaints, but tell her you are doing nicely, and mean to try to do well, and hope you will be well enough to go back to her by and by, and conform to the wishes of your friends."

"Doctor," said Bella, "it would be a series of false-hoods."

But she considered the matter; and there in her loneliness she concluded to write. "Dear mother will be glad of any thing from my pen," was her thought.

But it was not easy to say just what the doctor advised her: she could not be so false; and she wrote in her own way, telling her mother how much she thought of her, and keeping silent as regarded herself.

"It may not be a lie, but it is all a suppression of truth," she observed, when she handed it to the doctor at his next round. "Read it, please, and tell me whether it will answer."

"It is a very good letter, Miss Forresst. I knew you could write properly if you tried."

"It is just the same as a lie, doctor. There is nothing true in it."

"Oh, pshaw! You are not in your right mind yet. Things look queer to you."

That was the only letter she succeeded in getting out of the building. She could not and would not write soft, smooth letters, such as many patients stooped to write, just for the sake of getting a message to their friends. "It must be truth or nothing," she said, "if I write."

Having all these restrictions about her, being compelled

to stay where, day and night, she continued to see and hear this life, her intelligent young mind roused into renewed activity. She broke the bounds of prescribed silence, and criticised openly. She even defied the supervisor; and one day, when an act of injustice passed before her, she went boldly to the woman, and confronted her face to face. She laid her hands on the two shoulders of the employee; and, looking straight into her eyes, she said, " Do you know what you are about ? Do you realize that these women are locked in here without power to get out, or to escape from your temper or cruelties ? What is it that you mean ? "

For a moment the woman's eyes fell; then she said, " You know nothing about it, Miss Forresst. You do not know how I am tried and aggravated and worried."

" I do know; I see it all; but I also know, that, if you were kinder and less arbitrary, you would have far fewer troubles, for we should all like you better."

There were, in this hall, many "chronic cases," as they are called; and Bella did not wonder they were chronic. Said a workman who was repairing the hall, " I have worked for this institution twelve years; and, during all that time, that woman has sat in that chair." He pointed to a woman near.

Can we imagine it ? For twelve years that woman had sat in that one chair, eating her food from a corner of a table that was guiltless of a cloth, sleeping on one of those narrow cots that are put into the halls at night, and never did she ride or walk. And yet she was not old nor a cripple nor ill, but seemed stricken with mental apathy: was it wonderful that that apathy increased ?

By the workings of the inner machinery, those who most need privileges and attentions get the fewest. There are carriages kept for patients to ride, but only the best dressed and healthy go in them. The same rule prevails with walking, choice of rooms, and amusements. Those who most need these recuperative agents are most deprived. The best-furnished rooms are given to the employees or servants, except in a few cases where the friends of some person pay large prices, and make frequent visits to see that the patient gets what was agreed.

Bella could not see the justice of these things; and, as the system was more fully revealed to her by her prolonged stay, she became bolder in speech. She reasoned with the matron, close-questioned the assistant doctor, and remonstrated with the superintendent. "I wish," he remarked, "that people would not put these intelligent women into my institution. I do not want them."

This remark was overheard, and carried to Bella. "Tell him," she replied, "that these intelligent women do not want to be here."

Persons of sensitive, high-nerved temperaments, confined within restricted spaces, are often subject to peculiar horrors and strange sensations, that induce them to march, or pace back and forth, or go in circuits, swift or slow, according to their natures. It is not alone the insane who do this; but it is an impulse that seizes the rational and healthy when held in small, close spaces. We read of prisoners in despotic countries, who have channelled paths in their stone floors. In asylums, we do not have stone floors; but the patients pace, nevertheless, and often to their own destruction. We may call this the prison-march; or we may call it the death-march, since it leads to death of the soul. Those who follow it long can never be the same afterwards. It becomes an infatuation, an outlet to the repressed emotions. At first it seems like a relief; in the end it becomes paralysis, or wildness, or slow sinking into apathy, or death : its termination depends upon the peculiar natures of the individuals attacked. Patients are often seized with it, and often walk till their nerves are overcome. In this asylum an educated, accomplished lady was seized by these sensations. Her friends had been to visit her one day. "She is doing finely," said the superintendent. "She will go home soon." The friends went home delighted. The word "soon" seemed encouraging; but to the lady it had a different sound. She had known that word prolonged to weeks, from weeks to months, and thence to years, when applied to other patients. When her friends were gone, she asked the superintendent, "Doctor, what do you mean by soon? When shall I go?"

It was evening when she asked this. He replied, "Don't worry! You will go when you are better."

The lady's heart was stirred with deep, repressed emotions. She could not sleep that night. The next day she began to pace from the piano to the wall, and from the wall back to the piano. In a few days she paced up and down the hall, and then in her room. Her senses seemed to benumb, and fail her. The attendants began to make sport of her, then to weary of her; and then they turned her out into a back-yard. The enclosure resembled an old-fashioned impounding yard for unruly cattle. There was a tree in the centre. She walked around and around this tree till her feet channelled a path in the earth. Then she sat down weary and listless. Two sides of the yard were made by the walls of the asylum wings; and crumbs were sometimes thrown down from the windows. Out from beneath the building, rats came. They ran across the woman's feet. She had no energy or power to drive them away: but she envied them their freedom; and, when she saw them run out at apertures beneath the fence, she thought them the happiest of creatures. Faces came to the windows, and looked down at her; and she could hear people say, " Who is that poor crazy thing?" In her heart she answered,

"Who am I ? What does it matter now who I am ? The beauty of my life is flown, — the friends who knew me will know me no more forever!" Now she is a hopeless maniac.

Wearied, worried, and worn, Bella was seized with this infatuation. An old lady flew to her in alarm. "My dear girl, do not walk! I beg you to stop! It will injure you beyond recall!"

"But I cannot keep still."

"You *must* keep still. I have seen a great deal of asylum life; and I never saw one get well after long continuance of this death-march. Do not begin it. Hold yourself quiet by some means. I know these hardships, my dear, by sad experience; but do not try to walk them off. You will walk yourself into irretrievable ruin."

The old lady saved another at the same time. A woman of middle life had sat three years in her cell without yielding to this impulse. Then she arose, and began to walk, to and fro, to and fro, while her countenance assumed a pallor and rigidity as of death. The old lady went to her, and took her hands in hers. "Don't you know, my dear, what you are doing ? Have you been here all this time without seeing the effects of this marching ?"

"I have seen," said the woman. "I know; but I must walk. When I came here they told me I was to stay three months. I have sat still three years. Now let me walk. For what should I live ? To stay here another three years ? I would sooner lie down in my grave, and have it over. I wish they had laid me on a funeral pyre before they brought me here. I would rather be hung from the gallows; for then the struggle would soon end. Give me any thing rather than this long, slow-torturing, prison-life."

"I know," said the old lady, — and an inexpressible pain

passed over her brow, — "I know all the trials of this place.
Yes, yes, I know, —

> ' But still I say to thee,
> Fear not, but trust in Providence,
> Wherever thou may'st be.'

Do not walk the walk of ruin.   Do not lose your God."

"God" — said the woman, and she did pause then.
"He is not within these walls.   He stops outside."

"No!" said the old lady.   "He stops not.   He is
here."

"But his laws are not here.   His truth is not here."

"True," the old lady replied.   "His truth cannot dwell
under such rules as govern this place; but still I find him
here.   Come with me, and I will show him to thee."

Then gently the old lady led her to her own room; and
Bella heard the words of Holy Writ, and the voice of
prayer.   And her heart said, "O.Father! teach me also
to pray, that I may trust in thee, and be quiet under this,
my great calamity."

The officers of asylums never mind this march.   They
see patients pace and pace, and never take any notice of
them, or try to check the fatal proceeding.   It is considered
"a part of their insanity."   And when the suffering victims
are worn haggard or into wildness, they are put down into
lower halls, to be counted among the lost, living in wretchedness, agony, and woe.

The old lady who saved Bella had saved many others
from yielding to this impulse.   She was a kind old woman,
and her sympathies were tender; but she could not always
keep patients bright and happy in such isolation.   Nor
could Bella always endure.   She felt exhausted and faint
with accumulated trials; and, though she had learned the
hollowness of official promises, yet she could do no better,
and once more appealed to the superintendent.

16*

"Doctor, when shall I get out of here?"

He turned toward her, and replied, —

"When you give up your foolish notions."

"What notions?"

"About that man, I suppose."

Her eyes flashed. The Montague blue shone out from the black, and the old English blood quickened in her American soul. She flung back her raven curls with a toss of her head, and the physician was startled as she looked at him with her awakened nature.

"If you mean Mortimer Beale," she said, "and that I am to stay here till I give up my thoughts of him, you will keep me till the end of my life; for neither you nor any other person, neither this nor any other place, will ever drive him from my mind. You cannot *force me.*"

"We do not wish to force you, Miss Forresst. We wish you to use your own good sense; and I have no doubt but you will come out right by and by."

Bella thought long on this conversation. She seemed to have a revelation by it. "So I am to stay here till I give up my 'notions' about Mortimer, and I can never do that. I have known him from childhood. He is part of my life. They may as well ask me to forget my mother, and Edward, and myself, and my God! I wonder what kind of a representation has been made to the doctor."

The days grew short and cold, and the nights were long and tedious. The sounds of lamentation within, the mournful winds without, the narrow room, and her own sad heart, made the nights into periods of dread, when thought piled on thought, and time seemed bitterness, and the " silver clouds" lost their lining, and the "golden bowl" of hope was broken.

CHAPTER XVIII.

THE street was broad and airy, the house modern and elegant; and the sea-breezes, floating inward, brought with them their own savory freshness. Mrs. Nellie Bergmann lived in one of the pleasant parts of Brooklyn, and was herself an ornament to the place. She had her own standard by which she measured society; and Mr. Frederic need have no fear but her standard was high enough to suit his most fastidious taste. She was the personification of grace in manner, as she reclined in her cushioned chair in conversation with the young man by her side. His ruddy cheeks, full chest, and healthy physique bespoke a man of the open air, one who dwelt in it, and inhaled it, till his soul was broad as the world, and his heart open as the day. He had been speaking; and Mrs. Bergmann replied, "Indeed, Edward, you must not tell him."

"But, Nellie, if Bella is insane, your husband is the one to know it. He is a man of judgment, and a skilful physician. Let her case be submitted to him at once."

"But think of the disgrace, Edward."

"What disgrace?"

"Of having my husband know that she is insane."

"I see no disgrace. If she has gone out of her mind, there is a cause for it. Let us search for the cause. If it is physical illness, who can prescribe more learnedly than your husband? If Frederic has driven her to insanity, the disgrace is his. Let us attend to him." Mrs. Nellie adjusted the lace on her wrist, thus displaying a diamond ring, and a marvellously beautiful bracelet. Then she said, "Edward, I do hope you will not mention this to my husband. He heartily despises family disagreements."

"Very well," the young man responded, rising. "I have hastened East purposely to aid my imprisoned sister. If I can be of no service to her here, I will leave my regards for your husband, and go on to try what next I can do."

"But you will stay and dine?"

"No. I think aloud sometimes: I might unfortunately say something that would shock you. I should be thinking of Bella: I might speak my thoughts."

"You think too favorably of her, Edward. She has caused us all great trouble by her obstinacy."

"You mean that you have caused her great trouble by your meddling," returned Edward.

Mrs. Nellie tapped her foot impatiently, precisely as she used to tap it when she was Miss Nellie Forresst, except that now she tapped it beneath a slipper of greater elegance, and on a carpet of more costly material.

"Edward, Bella is insane. Frederic had the names of two physicians who certified to that effect. Is not that sufficient evidence?"

"No: it is not sufficient. Certificates can be bought, or obtained in various ways. I would not trust a physician's certificate unless I knew how it was obtained, and whether he was competent to give it. Nor would I trust Frederic, if he is my brother. We cannot always trust brothers. I shall go to Boston, God willing, and shall investigate the whole case."

With a sturdy farewell, the young man left his sister; and with his heart in his work, and his mind on its execution, he hastened on. The wintry winds and freezing air made no impression on him. His soul was nerved by a higher thought than the elements, or bodily comfort.

But of his movements Bella knew nothing. To her it was as though all the world had forgotten her; as though she had died, and yet lived, lived to know that she was dead. There was no world for her except that little space within that locked and barred enclosure. There were no people, or society, or friends for her, except such as were within that hall. Natural life was losing its meaning. Her heart was quivering and withering; the winter of despair was coming. She was ill one morning. The attendant said Miss Forresst had taken cold; so said the matron; and so said the physician, no wiser than the others. Her brow was hot, her hands and feet were cold. She had pain in her bones, pains all over her, but, most of all, pain in her heart. The asylum physicians and em-, ployees saw her physical condition ; they said she was feverish ; but no one saw or thought of her heart, her affections, or her desires. All the intellectual and soul parts of people are ignored by asylum treatment. The assistant physician walks through each morning, and, parrot-like, repeats certain stereotyped questions ; but they are all questions relative to physical conditions, and of the plainest parts of those. The soul and spiritual natures are utterly passed over; and " treatment " is only given to the most superficial, plainly-apparent, physical disturbances.

Annie saw that Bella was ill; and she did for her just as she would have done for a sister at home, as far as was in her power. But she had few conveniences for taking care of the ill : the hall was barren of comforts for the sick, as of food for the well. Every thing medicinal, even the simplest herbs, were locked in the dispensary ; and there was no way to procure a cup of gruel, or one taste of something nice, or one extra necessity, except to send down through a series of official channels, — a series often worked on a circumlocution plan, — by which what was needed at the moment reached the patient after hours of delay.

Annie had no patience with such ways of caring for sick people. She looked at Bella a moment, and said, "Don't try to get up. You have taken cold, I fear. I do wish I had something to give you, but there is absolutely nothing. The doctor will be through soon, however."

He came. Bella heard him unlock the doors of the solitary, and give them the customary glance. She heard him approach her own door. "Ah!" said he, looking in, "how is this ? "

"Annie thinks I have taken cold," was the reply.

An application was made to the pulse. "Ah! rather quick. Now your tongue. Yes, — I see. Nothing serious, Miss Forresst. When did you take your last bath ? "

Now, Bella had heard questionings and orders and commands about baths till she was disgusted. It seemed that her keepers thought a dip into their baths was a sovereign remedy. They used the bath to cure religious diseases, domestic diseases, love-diseases, and all other soul-troubles. She looked up at the physician quickly. "Doctor, do you think I came here to learn to bathe ? Do not you suppose I knew something of that sanitary and healthful art before I entered your institution ? "

"Yes, yes; but then there is nothing better. I will see that you have a bath immediately."

He went into the hall; and Bella heard him say to Annie, "As soon as possible I wish you to give Miss Forresst a bath. Draw the water as hot as she can bear it. I will send up some salt to put in it."

The physician passed along; and Annie entered Bella's room. Bella looked up at her. "I heard it, Annie. If I *must* go through it, let me go by myself."

"I dare not," said Annie. "I must obey the doctor's orders, however disagreeable."

"But, Annie, do you think you can bathe my heart-sickness and my home-sickness out of me?"

"No, Miss Forresst, I do not. If salt-water would cure trouble, the sea would be full of bathers. I think there is but one remedy for you; and it is not here. All that we do injures you in this place."

Just then a heavy step was heard; and a large, middle-aged woman appeared, bearing a bowl of rock-salt. Her voice was coarse and strong; and she did not repress it as she said, "Dorctor sent this to put in Miss Forresst's bath. Dorctor said as how I'd better stay and rub her, 'cause it ought ter be done moity hard."

Annie cast a glance at Bella, and she glanced back. The two girls then understood each other. "Dorctor" must be obeyed, or "dorctor's" messenger would go back and report.

That was a fearful bath. The salt was duly dissolved in the hot water, and the patient thoroughly immersed. Then the woman began the "moity hard rubbing." With one hand she held Bella down, with the other she scrubbed, till the patient was uncertain whether she had a skin, or whether it was rolled off into the water.

"I should think that was sufficient," Annie said at length. "She can't bear too much."

"Too much! Why, Lor' bless ye! I've been moity easy, 'cause her skin seems so tender and baby-like! You ought ter see me rub some of the patients, when I put in the whole strength of my arms! Why, I could fetch either o' you to blisters! You wouldn't need no mustard draughts. Ha, ha, ha!"

"Oh, don't!" said Bella, shrinking involuntarily.

"No, I don't 'tend to! But I must do my duty; else what sort o' a report could I make to dorctor?"

Bella was silent. She remembered what she heard in the bath-room a few days previous. She knew now whose voice it was that had spoken those words. What she heard was this: "Git in there, I say, moity quick!" There came from the patient a tone of remonstrance. Then the voice said again, "Don't care nothing about yer bolderdash! Git in there! Dorctor says you are to take a bath, and I reckon you will! So git in!"

A gurgling sound and a splash followed. A strong arm had pitched the patient in. Again there was a remonstrance, this time more earnest. The remonstrance was followed by blows. Heavy, thick, and fast the blows fell; but not a groan was uttered. Bella had held her breath during those blows. She marvelled who was in the bath-room, and began to look about the hall to see who was missing. Then she heard the voice say, "Wall, you'll stand more poundin' than anybody I ever see in my life." No one replied to these words; but in a moment more there was more pounding; and Annie, coming to Bella, said in an undertone, "I do believe that nurse will kill Mrs. Brown."

"Mrs. Brown!" exclaimed Bella. "Is it possible that that poor little Mrs. Brown is taking all those blows?"

"Yes," was Annie's response. "That big nurse has got her locked into the bath-room, and she is pounding her all this time."

"Annie, this place is horrible!"

"It is indeed," said Annie. "It is so horrible that I shall leave it. I shall give my notice before many days."

A cloud came over Bella's brow. "There you have the advantage over me, Annie. We live here in friendly intercourse; but you are a free girl. I am bound. When the place becomes unbearable to you, you can leave it. I must stay, and still stay; and who knows whether I shall ever get away?"

Both Bella and Annie thought of this conversation as they were now in the bath-room with this same nurse; and both submitted to her requirements lest there should now be some demonstration of her strength.

"Thar, I'm done!" said the woman at length. "The dorctor he'll be satisfied with my work, I think! I'm a moity smart 'un on these patients, I tell ye! You can go to yer room now. I've got to go to 'nother hall."

Whether the bathing was too much or too little, it proved not a cure. Bella was worse after it; and the fever, instead of being rubbed out, was well rubbed in. Young and healthy as was Bella, with scarcely a day's illness that she could remember, she would not have broken thus beneath a slight cold, if her affections had not been tried beyond her powers of resistance. She had by nature a fervent, warm, outgushing heart, and men were trying to crush out of her that which her God had put within her. By their bolts and bars and legal statutes they were depriving her of her inherent rights to "life, liberty, and the pursuit of happiness." Her eyes became full of delirious anxiety, and her lips parched with her heated breath. She talked of Mortimer, murmured of going, going, and called "Mother," "Mother," "Dear mother!" in her fevered sleep.

Meantime the cold deepened. The ice-king was hastening apace. Boston, full of hope and energy, had fires glowing in its furnaces and grates. Women wore their furs, and men walked in overcoats, stepping briskly in the clear, cold wind. Boston looked solid without, and felt solid within, as it smiled in its carpeted rooms, and read in its newspapers notices of current events. Amusements, concerts, and lecturers were flourishing, and charity was not forgotten.

In a large easy-chair, in a richly-furnished chamber of a luxurious house, with her feet on a hassock, and her head resting quietly back, reclined an old lady. Her hands were folded in her lap, and her silver-streaked hair was smoothly parted over her high, clear forehead. She was a proud-looking woman, and yet her eyes were love-lit, and her face serene. Two cherubs were playing near. One looked up at the old lady, and said, "Hus, teep still! dramma sleep!"

The other looked up, and said, "No: dramma make b'leve sleep. I see dramma peep."

The old lady smiled; and at that moment the door-bell rang.

"Who tome?" exclaimed the cherubs; and away they bounded into the hall. The next moment they were hanging to the balustrade, and looking cautiously down to see who should appear. A servant opened the outer door, and the voice of a man was heard. Then there were steps in at the door; the servant made some slight remark, and the man replied, "Don't trouble yourself. I will leave my coat here, and run right up to her chamber."

At that voice the old lady started, her hands unclasped, her eyes flew open, and she stood upright. She was old no longer. Her eyes grew bright, and her step was elastic as she went lightly through the door. She reached the head of the stairs. A man was bounding up. Two steps at a time he came, his broad shoulders, broad face, and brown whiskers seeming as wings to uplift him. He spread his arms; the old lady fell into them; and while he cried, "My mother!" she cried, "My son! O Edward! my son, my son!"

Then Mrs. Boynton came, and gave her brother a cordial welcome. She was not a heartless woman, except when fashion ruled her with its dogmatical decrees; and fashion did not ostracize a man like Edward Forresst, even though he had made his home in a wilderness. He was a grace to the wilderness. Its freshness gave him health; its rusticity seemed not to touch him. Nothing in his dress or manners offended Mrs. Boynton's cultivated taste, and he was in no way out of keeping now as he passed through her elegant hall to his mother's room. She wished that Harry was like him; but bluff Harry would never conform to conventionalities. He would not live in a city. He loved the open country, the wild, free woods, and life in simplicity as he found it there. Nature had endowed him with every attribute of manliness, and he had not sullied one of Nature's gifts. In integrity and sturdy strength of character, he was "every inch a man," and bowed to no bondage, not even to the forms of society. To Mrs. Boynton he was a constant trouble. His boots were too thick, the cloth he wore was too heavy, and he sat awkwardly in her elegant chairs. Reproofs for his misdemeanors he received with a laugh, but did not reform; and Mrs. Boynton was forced to consider him her incorrigible brother.

In the evening, after Edward's arrival, three brothers sat in Mrs. Boynton's private parlor. One was thoroughly attired, with his waxed mustache pointed artistically; the second was square-shouldered and firm, free in action as the breezes of the woods; the third was graceful, but ruddy-brown with the Western winds. Opposite the three sat Mrs. Forresst and the fashionable Mrs. Boynton.

In his own resonant tones Edward remarked, "I was never so surprised as when I read that letter. You know, Frederic, that Bella is not insane. You have played false."

"I know that she was committing a very insane act. Upon my honor! I thought it best to arrest her before she should throw herself away, and squander our father's patrimony."

"The money that father left her was as much hers as yours that he left you, or mine that he left me!" said Edward.

"Let her keep it, then," Mr. Frederic replied. "It cannot be used to enrich Chauncey Beale's son."

"You prefer that it should enrich an insane hospital."

"Until she is restored to her senses, I do."

Mrs. Forresst sighed as she looked upon her children "Alas!" she said, "that I should live to this day, when one of my children unlawfully holds another in prison!"

"Your pardon, madam," said Mr. Frederic bowing to his mother, "it is not unlawful."

"In the sight of God it is unlawful. Men's laws are frail constructions."

"Again I ask your pardon, madam. We may differ as to our views of God. I feel it my duty to save Bella from throwing herself away."

"Which you are doing by holding her in a confinement that is worse than throwing her away."

A tear glimmered in the eye of old Mrs. Forresst. She did not attempt to wipe it away, and Frederic responded, "I regret, mother, that you should feel this so deeply, since it is a necessity."

"Enough of that," interposed Harry. "Bella is coming out of there! You say you are going to see her to-morrow, Edward?"

"I shall."

"Fetch her out with you; that's all."

"You forget, perhaps, that I am her legal guardian," said Mr. Frederic.

"I do not forget that you have procured for yourself that honor. We will see about the guardianship afterward."

The mustache twitched, and then settled firmly. Frederic replied again, —

"Perhaps you are not aware, that, as she was consigned under the forms of law, she can only be taken away legally. The institution has no right to surrender her to every passing caller."

"I shall take her by the rights of a brother," said Edward in a clear, ringing voice.

Mrs. Boynton arose, and the rustle of her dress seemed as a quieting breeze. "That will do," she said softly. "You are worrying mother too much."

Edward cast a glance at the old lady, and said, "Forgive, me, mother. I will say no more, but I will do my duty."

They talked of other subjects then, but did not forget; and, when they parted before retiring, Harry quietly grasped Edward's hand, "Go ahead, I am with you."

That was all he said, but Edward felt strengthened by the words. Frederic walked home, apparently alone. No one said, "I am with you." And yet Frederic was not alone. He had an ally more powerful than a brother. That ally was the locked institution founded by the laws of his own native State, and claiming these laws as a shield in all its usurpations. On the breast of the old Commonwealth lies the cradle in which our liberties have been rocked. Now that liberty has grown, shall we build prisons in her eyries, and permit brother to hold brother in bondage? Let the States of our Union ask this question, for the Commonwealth is not alone in its mistake.

The following morning, clear and cold, saw Edward Forresst on his way to the asylum where his sister was held. He remembered that sister as she used to be, a frolicsome girl making his youth merry; and his heart warmed with his boyish love as the train hurried him to the town where the asylum was located. He took no carriage when he left the cars; but, with strong steps, he

17*

clanked his boot-heels over the frozen ground. The air was cold, but what of that ? The great building was in view, and Bella was in it. He drew near it, entered its yard, and, hurrying in at the main door, inquired for Miss Bella Forresst.

Asylum officials become very expert in reading the countenances of visitors to patients. They saw at once that Miss Forresst's visitor was a man whom they could not easily delude, and with whom they dared not trifle. There was no use in telling *him* that " it would be better for the patient not to see her friends," nor to tell him any thing but the bare truth. He was honest in his love for his sister, and they saw it. He was too discerning to be duped, and they saw that also. Therefore, not having any subterfuge concocted for the emergency, they told him frankly that Bella was ill, and took him up to see her. He followed an official up the winding stairs, stopped while she unlocked and re-locked the doors, and filled with indignation as he saw the close prison in which his own beloved sister was held. He passed the rows of cells, passed the sad, dispirited women, and his free nature recoiled. The broad, breezy West had scarcely fitted him for this cloister of men's devising. It seemed utterly unnatural, and had a dismal look of darkness in his eyes.

As he passed from corridor to corridor, the eyes of the women followed him. There was a free and easy briskness in his step, a self-possession in his manner, and a genial heartiness on his countenance, that instinct.vely attracted the attention of all. " Who is he ? "— " Who has he come to see ? " These were the questions that passed from lip to lip.

We will not describe the meeting between this brother and sister : why use awkward words to tell that which can be felt, but not described. Nor can we repeat much of their conversation during the interview, nor depict with vivid-ness the sensations of the brother as he sat by her bed, with her soft hand lying in his, and her pale face before him. He was not only pained, but shocked, and roused to stern denunciations.

"Is it possible!" he exclaimed. "I had no idea that we tolerate laws under which such reckless perfidy can find shelter! We have just had a war to liberate our colored bond-people — what shall we do for our white sufferers?" The eyes of the soldier dilated with the intensity of his emotions, and he felt that his country was still not thoroughly free.

"I meant to take you to Boston with me to-day," he remarked at length. "I did not expect to find you ill."

"Only to Boston?" she asked anxiously.

"Only there to-day; but when I go back, I hope *la belle Bella* will go."

"I shall be well in a few days."

"I hope so, Bella; for I cannot go back home without you: I promised Mortimer you should go. You do not know how much he thinks of you."

"I know how much I think of him. Not all the arts of this place can drive him from my mind."

Then Edward described his Western home, and depicted its future. He told her of Elijah and Emily and Jack, and how Mortimer felt meanly at not coming on himself; "but," continued the young man, "I told him it was better that I should come; for I understand Frederic, and I shall not go back without you. Do not fear."

When Edward left, he told the attendant and asylum officers that Bella would leave in a few days, or as soon as she was able, and it was a subject of rejoicing among the patients. Nothing creates such thrills of joy in these halls as to know that one of their number is to be

released.   She who is soon to go is looked upon as sacred.
The halo of freedom seems about her, and an invisible
light irradiates her.   The more the patients love her, the
more do they rejoice in the good fortune that has come to
her.   Though they know they shall never see her again,
yet they are glad she is going; for is it not freedom to
which she is hastening?

A slaveholder, in the presence of Isaac T. Hopper and
another Friend, remarked that his slaves were happy.
" Friend," said the Quaker, " give thee a palace, enclose it
in a ten-acre lot, plant it all round with Lombardy poplars,
and ornament it with beauty, and give thee thy pen and ink,
and thy books that thou lovest so well, and shut thee up
within it, and thou wouldst look over the wall with longing
eyes."

And just such longing as this our physicians prescribe
for restoring injured minds !

CHAPTER XIX.

EDWARD FORRESST returned to Boston with a keen sense of Bella's situation. "It is enough to drive her crazy to stay there," he said to his mother, "and it has made her ill, else I should have brought her back with me to-day."

"I feared it," the mother replied. "I told Frederic, if he was not careful, he would make the child insane."

"I believe she would be after a time," Edward returned; "but she is only feverish now. She brightened wonderfully when I told her I had come for her; that I should take her out in season to prepare herself to be present at my wedding; and that then she should go on with me, and there would be another wedding. When I came away, she seemed like a new person; and we'll have her out of there in a few days."

Edward told Harry his plans; and Harry said, "Go ahead. Get her out, and I am with you."

But Frederic sniffed the air like a wild Arab steed. His curling lip went upward, and his eyes flashed defiance. In business circles he was known as a man of uncompromising energy, invincible will in conquering difficulties, and stern in the hour of danger. He never turned his back to obstacles; and all the qualities that carried him over the waves of business bore him on in this matter now. He went to the house of Mrs. Boynton.

"Eunice," said he, "what is that boy doing? Does he

expect that he is going to take that girl from where I have put her for safe keeping, and carry her to the wilds with him? I am the eldest of my father's family, and who will direct these children if I do not? "

" We can scarcely call Edward and Bella children," Mrs. Boynton replied.

" Upon my honor, Eunice, they act like children, or like simple young people, trying to make romance out of a very practical part of their lives. I want you to use a little common sense, Eunice. I want you to go and ascertain, and bring back word to me, that I may know what Edward did and said there, and whether those people suppose they are to let her go out of there without her guardian's consent. Edward is not her legal guardian : I am."

Even when Eunice and Frederic were children, there were times when she yielded an involuntary submission to his will. Such a time had come to her now, and Frederic knew that he had this power over her. He knew that she would not question this mandate, issued in his most princely way. He went out of the house confident that she would be his faithful agent. ·

In early winter, when late autumn is struggling for a breath more of warmth, there are days that partake of autumn's mellowness blended with winter's elastic clearness. On such days ladies appear out in costumes befitting the weather, and the bright sun welcomes them in brief, coquettish smiles. On such a day a lady ascended the asylum steps. A bonnet of velvet and a feathery spray lay on the top of her stylishly-dressed hair, a double-frilled travelling skirt floated coquettishly above her boots, and from her gloved hand there hung a reticule of costly elegance. The front asylum doors swung wide on their hinges, and the porter bowed blandly as she passed in. The style and richness of her apparel, her innate self-possession, and her quiet assumption of superiority, were sure passports to attention. The lowest of bows, and most flattering words, were showered upon her in the office. With a grace that was all her own, she inquired for her sister, Miss Bella Forresst; and with a grace that was all *their* own, they replied to her inquiries, and conducted her through the halls to Bella's room. She glanced not around as she went, but passed through with that peculiar air that seems not to see what all know must be seen, or it could not be thus avoided. Such cognizance is an indefinable, acquired art.

Bella had been very happy that morning. Since the visit of Edward, she had recuperated wonderfully; for she had been drinking the elixir of hope. Blessed hope! Sweet cordial of the soul, pure nectar of life! Thou art more than medicine, thou art life.

On the strength of hope Bella had arisen, and light was once more coming back to her eyes. "In a few days I shall go home; yes, in a few days I shall go home." These were the talismanic words that were flitting through her mind as a shadow darkened her door, and a voice spoke.

"Miss Forresst — a lady to see you!

Bella looked up. "Eunice — why Eunice — is it indeed you? I am so glad."

The patients who heard it said, "It is Miss Forresst's sister, come to take her away." They had no thought that the beautiful lady was an agent, a spy.

Mrs. Boynton laid her bonnet on the narrow bed, — a bed she would not have given to a servant in her house; and then she sat down on the other bed, — sat down as coolly as if it had been a sofa standing there. No remark, no censure of the place, nor apology for permitting Bella to stay in it, escaped her. She opened her reticule; and, after the fashion of people who visit friends in these places, she took out the bonbons, fruit, and delicacies she had brought, as though people could be kept imprisoned at starvation's point for weeks and months, and then be made happy by a few sweetmeats !

Bella looked on with surprise. " What do I want with those, Eunice? Am not I going home?"

" Not to-day, Bella; not till you are well. I came to see how you are. You are ill, they tell me."

" I am well enough to go home with you, Eunice. This place makes me ill. Let me be out, and I shall be well. I need to go out."

" Then, why not go out here? There are attendants to walk with you I suppose."

Bella looked up earnestly. " Eunice, I do not want to go out here ! I want my freedom ! Why am I held as a prisoner? Why was I taken from home as a felon? By what right does Frederic hold me in this bondage?"

" Don't get excited, Bella. Keep calm."

" Put yourself in my position, and see if you could keep calm," said the prisoner. " Just try it ! That is all I ask."

" I know your position is very trying," Mrs. Boynton replied; " but you brought it upon yourself by your persistency in your absurd course."

" Eunice," said Bella, " when you wanted to marry Mr. Boynton, was it absurd?"

With a stifled scream the lady lifted her two hands. " Don't, Bella! do not compare Mr. Boynton with the man you have chosen ! It is absolutely shocking ! I could *never, never* have descended to such a choice !"

Then it was that Bella stood up straight in her prison cell, in the narrow passage between the two beds. Into her eyes came the fire of determination; into her face shot the proud old spirit of ancestral inheritance; her head placed itself erect on her firm, white neck, and her long ringlets floated back of her round shoulders as she answered, "Eunice, if you have come here to force me or to frighten me till I yield to Frederic, know this: You have come on the most fruitless errand you ever undertook. I have been driven hither and hither; I have been scolded, and commanded, and my youth has been a broken pathway; but my heart is still true as a needle to the pole, and you can never turn it by any such means as you use. You are too late now in trying to change my mind. I have suffered for Mortimer; and, if I cannot marry him on earth, I will wait and marry him — in heaven."

There was a sublimity in every lineament of the patient's face. Her two hands were folded on her breast, her brow was calm, her lips firm, and her pulse beat with full, strong, and clear vibrations.

For several moments Mrs. Boynton did not speak. When she did, it was on some trifling subject of dress. She appeared not to have heard the words of her young sister, or, if she did hear, to regard them as a summer tale, to be forgotten as the changing breeze.

But the banker's wife did not forget. When she was passing out of the asylum, she paused at the office, that official room where the destinies of human beings are decided as coolly as though no soul or immortality was attached to our existence, and men had a right to dispose of each other as their finite fancies and judgments see fit.

Mrs. Boynton here expressed her regrets that her sister was no better, suggested that her correspondence be carefully guarded, as her brother was extremely anxious that she be protected against the influence of certain obnoxious persons, and so on. Mrs. Boynton knew exactly how to express her meaning, without saying too much; and, when she was gone, the asylum officials vied in her praise.

"So elegant in manners," "So exquisite in costume," "So delicate in expression," "So careful not to say that it was a lover from whom they were shielding Miss Bella." Mrs. Boynton might have blushed at her praises had she been a listener; but then, people who listen are seldom the ones who hear good of themselves. It was best that Mrs. Boynton could not listen, even to her own praises.

She went home with her report. "Frederic, you will never overcome her obstinacy. You may as well let her go with Edward."

"Upon my honor, Eunice! You have the weakness of a woman! Let her marry Beale — indeed!"

"I formed my opinion from her own words. She told me directly, that, if she could not marry him on earth, she would marry him in heaven."

"Heaven! ha! Well, we are not there yet. At present we are dealing with earth."

Mr. Frederic bowed himself out from his sister's house, and walked home. The evening lights shed their rays upon him; and he soliloquized. "In heaven! I do not understand those ethereal marriages. Ha, ha! It is quite prophetic love — this of theirs."

In the asylum Bella laid her head on her pillow. The thorn of bitterness had come back to pierce her. The hope that Edward gave, Eunice had taken away. Annie came to her softly, and tried to comfort her; but her sorrow lay too deep for her to soothe.

"Annie," said the supervisor, "put Miss Forresst at work."

"I do not think she is able: I should not like to ask her," was Annie's gentle response.

"La! you need not feel delicate about *her!* Something has got to be done to keep her in order. Her folks don't want her at home, that is plain. Her sister did not say so, but she might as well. We could all see what she meant; and she is a splendid lady! I think it is a shame for Bella to give her so much trouble."

"But what shall I have her do? There are more women in the dining-room than I need now."

"Put her into the hall, or send her into the sewing-room, or let her work for yourself. Any thing to keep her busy."

Annie considered; and recollecting the embroidery she had seen among Bella's clothes, and knowing that patients who could do any fine or fancy work were always taxed by the attendants, she went into Bella's room, in her own soft, loving way, and said, "Miss Forresst, didn't you tell me that your embroidery was your own work?"

"Yes; I always do my own. I learned in the convent."

"Will you do some for me, if I will get the materials? I should like some as a token of remembrance."

Bella hesitated. "I may not have time to do much, Annie; for, notwithstanding my sister, I believe in Edward. I know he will come for me."

"If he comes, you can leave the work, and go; and I will follow you with my love, and keep the stitches you have taken as a token of the happiness I have had with you, for you have been a comfort to me, Miss Forresst. This life is weariness for me, as for you. I cannot shut my sympathies away from my patients, as most attendants do."

And Bella kissed Annie, and said, "I will work for you."

Whoever passed Bella's door, in the days that followed, might have seen her bending over the fine embroidery, her skilled needle going through the cambric in patient stitches. It brought back remembrances of Natinitie, and Matildie, and Lola who fled with him of the glorious eyes. Where was Lola now? And then her thoughts would roam away from that to the home where Elijah and Emily waited, and Mortimer was preparing for her.

One of the women who had seen much experience in these halls watched her opportunity, and stealthily followed Bella into the bath-room. Closing the door by shutting a paper within the marginal space, she said earnestly and emphatically, " Don't you do it! Don't you work for one of them. You may work, and work, and work, till you are tired and sick; and you will get no privileges, nor even thanks in return. These girls are hired here. They are paid by the institution. They stay until they replenish their pockets, get all they can out of the patients, and then go again. They do not care what becomes of us who are left behind; and when the patients become worn out, and can no longer work, then they are crowded back, jostled out of the way, told they are crazy old things, and trampled on as though they had no feelings. I know a woman who has earned more than two thousand dollars for this institution; and, if she was justly compensated, she would receive that amount; and yet she cannot get even one small favor. The other day she asked the supervisor to let her go into the next hall to see a woman there whom she knows; and the supervisor said sharply, ' No! do you think we are going to let patients run around from hall to hall ?'

" ' After all the work I have done,' said the woman humbly, ' surely I ought to have some little privilege.'

" ' After all you have done !' the supervisor returned contemptuously. ' You ought to be thankful that we gave you the honor of doing it.' The supervisor walked grandly off; the poor woman went towards her solitary room. I saw tears in her eyes. Do not work for them, Miss Forresst ? "

" I shall not work long," Bella replied; " but I like Annie, and will do this as a token. I expect my brother every day."

" You may be disappointed in that," the elder woman

responded. "I have known a great many to be told they were going soon; and then they were kept years, till hope died, and death came to close the scene."

"I know it is so," Bella returned; "but I have a brother whom I can trust."

That afternoon Bella sat at her window with the embroidery in her hand. She was watching the declining sun through her bars, and thinking how it was going to see that far-away cabin where she was soon going; and how she should love to watch it there; and the embroidery fell from her fingers. She leaned her head upon her hand, and her elbow on the window-sill. Thought sank into reverie, and reverie was followed by sadness. Click. She heard it. The sound had become monotony and weariness. She knew the hall door opened, but what of that? The servants and officials were always going in and out. She sat unmoved, and steps drew near. The steps of a man they were, heavy and firm. She started then. Perhaps it was Edward. He had just such firm steps. She dropped the embroidery: she stood upright, and counted the footsteps as they drew near. The man did not speak; but the steps were surely Edward's. A tremor thrilled her. Her lips parted in expectancy. A shadow came in at the door, then an employee, and the steps ceased. The employee said, "This is Miss Forresst." Then the employee turned away; and a living form of solid strength stepped into the doorway, and paused. One glance the patient gave, then with a cry she sprang forward, and fell upon the broad chest of — Harry Forresst. He put his strong arms about her, and said in a voice of woman's tenderness, "Bella, — *my little sister Bella*, — is this you?"

"Harry," she answered, "my own old Harry, is this you?"

"It is just nobody else, you may be sure of that," was his reply.

18*

"I thought it was Edward."

"But you are glad to see *me*, I hope?"

"Glad! Why, Harry! I was never so glad of any thing in my life."

She gave him her chair, and he sat down. She also took a seat, but it was in his broad lap; and her hands went twining about his neck, and she kissed his bushy brown beard.

"Why, little one," he said, in his off-hand way, "you are hungry for kisses. Haven't had many lately, eh?".

"I haven't had any thing that I want. You have come after me, I hope."

"Why — not exactly — little one; though, confound it! if I had known," here he glanced around, "that you was in such a cow-pen of a place, I shouldn't have let Fred off quite so easy."

"O Harry! you won't join Fred against me, will you?"

"No, no, Bella, you may be sure of that. Once I might have thought you could do better than to take Mortimer; but the way Fred is treating you is enough to drive you mad, and I have had hard work to restrain my temper with him. He has intrenched himself under the forms of the law; and, in order to oust him, I must examine the statutes. He has legal power on his side, while we have only our sense of right."

"That ought to be more powerful than law," said Bella, "or, at least, that and law ought to agree."

"*Ought* and *are* are two things, little one. The men who make laws study all their lives, and work so hard getting the laws straight, that it puzzles even a lawyer to wade through the crooks of the statutes. Now, I find by investigation, that the laws relative to these asylums, imperfect as they are, are yet more imperfectly executed. In fact, they are evaded, twisted, and made void, by relatives, doctors, and the asylum managers, while the numerous institutions seem like a ring, or brotherhood, in which one member is bound to uphold and support the acts of the others. Why, Bella, here are you, a young, innocent girl, put in here by your brother, who asserts that you are insane, and assumes authority over you! Now, you might stay here till the end of your days, unless we who are your own flesh and blood get you out. Nobody else cares, of course; that is, not particularly; or, if they do care, they have no legal right to get you. I have been looking into it, and have got one of those sharp-eyed lawyers to search it out for me; and if Fred doesn't let go his hold upon you, and let you come out of here fairly and squarely, so that there shall be no hitches or drawbacks to prevent your being free, and the mistress of your own property again, I shall go into law myself, and try what can be done by knocking law against law. I mean the laws of men, Bella. The statutes of God do not conflict in that way; but law processes are expensive. Once in them, a man does not know how deep he may need to dip into his pocket; and, before I enter, I must be sure of my ground. I must know how every thing is, according to the statutes; and I must have money ready to back myself. You see it, don't you? Well, I came down from the Aroostook with a lot of unfinished contracts on hand. It will take me all winter to carry them out. When I got to Boston, I found out about you, and my sense of justice came up. I determined to look into the case, and this is my decision. I must go back to the Aroostook, and stay till spring, till the ice breaks. And then, when the rivers give way, I will come down; and, if Fred does not change, I will spend every cent of my property, or you shall be free. Don't run away again, though I think it is all right to go in that way; because every innocent man and woman has a right to liberty, and there is nothing dishonorable in taking it.   But you see this institution holds you legally ; and, if you go off surreptitiously, the people here have legal power to go after you, and they will do it, and hunt for you as if there was a price on your head. They do not mind whether you ought, or ought not, to be free.   You are their property, and they go for you.   Now, that would be no freedom for you: you would feel like a hunted criminal. You see it, don't you ? "

She had listened attentively to every word; and she answered, " Yes, Harry, I see it.   You want me to stay here till spring, and let Edward go back without me."

" Just so, little one.   Edward cannot stay on here. He cannot afford to ; and, besides, the family of his bride have made preparations for her to go. And he ought to go. And when you go, Bella, I am going. I think I will go out there, and settle with you. I am a rough kind of a man; but you would give me a place at your fireside, wouldn't you ? "

" O Harry, I would be so glad, so happy ! " And she kissed him again.

" Well, then, little one, the matter is settled ; and you and I will sink or swim together, eh ? You can trust me. You do not fear to trust me ? "

" No, Harry, I do not ; but," and she raised her eyes to her surroundings, " I do hate to stay here. It is such a disagreeable place ! "

" I know it. No, I do not suppose I know it ; for we can only know such things by personal trial. But you see how it is : I can do no better for you just now. And you have high blood, Bella ; and you will not disgrace your ancestry by flinching in the hour of trial. Bear bravely; and remember there is a God who is always with us. Keep with him. I am rough, Bella. People might judge that I am not God's ; but he looks at the heart and at the soul, at its integrity and truth. And when I am out in the pine woods, and hear the wind roar among the trees as if the sea had broken bounds, and the waves were dashing on in desolation, and, looking up, I see the little birds sitting fearlessly on the branches, and the squirrels frisking their bushy tails in happy contentment, I say, ' Behold, all things are in the hollow of thy hand, O Lord! and lie there safely; for thou givest them peace and rest. In the hands of that God I leave you, Bella; and, with his permission, when the ice goes roaring down the rivers, I will come; .and it is you and I together, then, my little Bella. Kiss me once more; for I must go, and you must bear.

> ' For men must work, and women must weep,
> And the sea goes on with its moaning.'

There, I am getting poetical. But good-by! Give me a good, hearty shake of the hand.   I like a big grasp."

He turned. then to go out, but turned back again. " I came near forgetting: don't you want some money ?   I imagine Fred doesn't make you much allowance."

" He hasn't given me any."

" I thought likely. Take that. If you can't use it for yourself, and do not need it, you will find somebody that does."

Then he laid a roll in her hand; and, drawing his own rough hand across his eyes as if to brush away a mist, he went out. Bella heard his heavy steps recede, heard the door click, and then she could hear no more. She sat down in her chair again, and rested her elbow on the window-sill, where it was before he came; and there, close by the iron bars, she unrolled and counted her bills.

This visit of ' Harry's was a great comfort. She knew now what she must expect, and the hard features of the situation lay in her mind; but suspense was gone, and Harry had given her strength.

"I shall write to Mortimer," Harry had said. "He knows he can trust *me*." She remembered this when she recalled the conversation; and remembered also the volume of meaning that he put in that one word *me*. It was not arrogance, nor vanity, nor self-conceit, but a simple, honest, outspoken trust in himself; and she understood it.

"Yes," she said, "Mortimer can trust him. Good old Harry never fails."

The patients looked at each other in disappointment when Harry was gone. "Poor Miss Forresst! We did hope she would go!"

But the supervisors and employees said, "La! we knew she wouldn't go! Her folks don't want her! She is love-cracked."

Changes of halls and cells were constantly taking place, the supervisors and physicians never seeming satisfied with the way the patients were; and among those who were brought into Annie's hall, Bella saw Jessonica. Three months before, Jessonica Wade was brought to the asylum by the basest treachery. A doctor had been hired to sign a certificate, and a second doctor signed in compliment to the first; and the judge completed the documents. She was carried to the asylum by two men, and left standing within the doors, a friendless prisoner among strangers. The superintendent pitied her. He drew her hand within his arm, and himself led her up the stairs. As they went, he gently pressed her hand within his own. She glanced up with a timid air, and said, "You need not hold my hand so tightly, doctor: I shall not run away."

He looked down upon her kindly. "I did not think of that, my child; but you are so young, so tender, that I pitied you for what has come upon you; and I pressed your hand to show you that we are not all unkind, and that we surely will be tender of you."

She learned, afterwards, that attendants do not always fulfil the medical assurances. She was very lonely. There was a sociable gotten up in the chapel by the superintendent. Jessonica, fresh from Washington, dressed for this occasion as for a party. With the license of a blonde, she wore a tissue of azure on which were spangles of golden stars. The matron, seeing her beauty, placed in her hand a rose-bud, and threw over her hair a spray of green. Thus attired, she enteréd the asylum chapel, a prisoner among prisoners. She was a gem in an oasis. So thought Mr. Gervase as he saw her enter.

And who is Mr. Gervase? He is a gentleman of fine countenance and noble demeanor, heir to a large estate. His father died while he was yet young. He was consigned to an asylum. To pay his board required but a small sum from his inherited income; and, from that time to this, he has lived within barred walls. A visitor, in passing through, struck with the noble face and demeanor of Mr. Gervase, turned to the attendant, and asked, "What is the matter with that gentleman? What caused his insanity?" — "He is not insane, sir," was the reply. — "How?" queried the gentleman. "Can you keep gentlemen here as patients who are not insane?"

"His friends do it, sir. We are not responsible."

"On what grounds can they do it?"

"Oh, sir, it is easy enough! He was a minor, sworn in here by those who thought his inheritance convenient for them. The reason that put him in keeps him here."

The visitor gave Mr. Gervase a searching look of pity, and passed along. Mr. Gervase still continues to live in asylum halls, an American gentleman who has never known his rights. He was in the chapel when Jessonica entered. Struck by her fairy loveliness, he went to the superintendent, and requested an introduction. The superintendent

complied; and Mr. Gervase, with graceful ease, stood beside
the lily girl. He admired her flower, talked a little, and
pleased her by his courteous ways; but in the midst he
suddenly paused, and, looking admiringly in her face, he
remarked, ",Pardon me, Miss Jessonica, but allow me to
say that you are very beautiful."

He bowed, but Jessonica was offended. Her eyes turned
up in disapproval.

"Pardon me," he said, seeing her disapproval; "but we
gentlemen who reside here see so very little that is beautiful, that, when we do find it, we must of necessity forego
etiquette, and speak our thoughts. But allow me to say,
that, if you stay here six months, I shall not wish to see
you; for you will not be as beautiful then as now."

Jessonica was impressed by this remark, from one who
thoroughly knew the effects of this restricted existence.
Alas ! she lived to know how truly he had judged. Three
months had scarcely passed, and the superintendent, who
had promised her tenderness, had permitted her to be
removed from hall to hall, to be the butt of coarse girls,
and to be placed in juxtaposition with low minds, till her
delicate system was shattered. She no longer wore or cared
for the azure, her beauty was tarnished, she wailed for her
mother, and cried for her lost hopes. In the night-time
Bella could hear her cry; and she said, "I would I could
lay bare these secrets, and open these doors, if but for thy
sake, sweet Jessonica."

There came into this hall, or rather there was put into
this hall, another young girl, a tall, dark-eyed girl, with rosy
cheeks, and pleasant countenance. She was a factory girl,
paying her board from her own hard-earned money, to be
cured ; and she, too, wandered up and down in loneliness.
The three girls formed a band of friendship; and Jessonica,
resting her head on the tall girl's bosom, said, "Dear Benedicta ! what should I do without you ? "

"Why call me Benedicta?" said the tall girl, stroking her fair hair.

"Because you are my blessing, my Benedicta; and, without you, I should faint in this weary place."

When mental science takes a new basis, when society is dispossessed of the idea that insanity is a disease to be treated with isolation and barbarity, then people will look back upon present methods of treating it with as great wonder as we look back upon the past methods of its treatment.

It was not the original design of asylum-founders that the buildings should be used to make people insane. When it was urged as a plea for building them, that there were miserable lunatics confined in attics and almshouses who could be made comfortable in these halls, it was not supposed that they were to be filled by young girls and boys fresh from school, or gentlemen and ladies from comfortable homes, or old people thrown into them by the heartless young; nor were they designed as receptacles for persons whom ignorant physicians sent to them to hide their own stupidity.

A generation back, — and many of that generation are still living, — when doctors had a difficult case, they disposed of it by calomel. It was the sovereign resort, and was administered to people till their swollen tongues and cancerous mouths made them hideous, and their teeth fell out in consequence. Persons who were salivated never again had pure, healthy systems, and doctors knew they could not; yet they persisted in administering this poison till the common sense of the people drove it out of sight. What calomel was then in the medical science of physical treatment, insane asylums now are in mental diseases.

Chains and cages are not used in our asylums; but blinded cells take the place of cages, and for chains we have

coarse jackets, — camisoles they are called, — and strong
leather straps; while the attendants practise, at their own
wills, poundings, kickings, pushings, pullings, jerkings by
the hair, jerkings by the ears, lockings in and lockings out,
and that never-ceasing method of discipline, the free and
varying use of the keys.

Annie practised none of these things; but Bella saw
them, and heard them all about her. She saw gangs made
up for the work-rooms, — the laundry, the kitchen, the sew-
ing-rooms; and she saw how "handy" the keys were for
mallets on the heads and shoulders of the lagging. She
saw these things, and they stirred her soul.

CHAPTER XX.

SITUATED as Annie's hall was, in the centre of the wing-divisions, Bella heard the cries. above, below, and around her. This hall was used as a passage for the working bands. They often paused and waited here, while their leaders chose other workers from this hall; and Bella saw sad, pale, sorrowful women among them; and often they were weeping on their way. Bella saw one thin, sad woman walking in tears, and her sobs became audible in her distress. "Dry up, there!" shouted one of the leaders; and, reaching his hand across another woman, he struck this woman on her head with his keys. The blood came out, and saturated her hair. Bella's heart leaped with horror; but the man said, "That'll teach her to behave herself, and not be whining along." This man came from the laundry.

"Come along," he said to a young Irish girl in Annie's hall, one day. "You are just what we want down in the laundry. You are young and healthy. Come along."

The girl was young and pretty, more intelligent than most of her class; and she had formed a secret attachment for Miss Forresst. The independence of Bella, and her evident sympathy, made her a sort of heroine among the patients; and many who never spoke to her felt a chivalrous trust in her, that, under other circumstances, might have led them to organize, with her as leader. This young girl turned away from the harsh laundry-man, and fled into Bella's room. Bella was sitting in her chair, the girl dropped by her side, and buried her face in her lap. "Save me, Miss Forresst, save me! Don't let him take me!"

"I cannot save you," said Bella. "I have no power. I could not save myself. If I knew how to do that work, they would make me go too."

"Come along here!" ejaculated the man in a loud voice, forcing his way into Bella's room. "You needn't come in here to hide. Come along, I say."

"I can't, I can't!" said the girl. "I have ironed and ironed till I am tired all out, and my wrist aches, and my feet ache with standing, and I am hungry. I ironed all this forenoon; and I have had nothing for dinner, except a few spoonfuls of that sloshy soup, and I can't work, and I won't work. O Miss Forresst, save me!"

Bella looked up into the man's coarse, unfeeling face. "Can she not rest this afternoon?"

"What is it to you?" he said. "If she don't want to work, she must get a reprieve from the doctor. When he tells me not to take her out, I shall leave her in; not till then. Come along, I say."

Bella stooped, kissed the young face, and said, "Go, Margey: it is best. I hope you will not always be here."

The man cast upon them a look of contempt; and, seizing Margey by the shoulder, he jerked her up from the floor, and pushed her out of the room. A crowd of women were gathered there listening. He raised his keys, and swept them in a semi-circle into their faces. "Get out of the way," he said. "Be off with you. Here, where's my lot? File up here I can't waste no more time!"

He pushed Margey into the column, and filed them all off together. That night, when Margey was returning with the file, they met the superintendent. "Doctor," said Margey, looking up pleadingly, "I am tired."

"So am I," he answered coolly; and, turning on his heel, he walked away.

Bella was sitting quietly in her room one sunshiny morning, when the matron paused at her door. A lady was by the matron's side. "Good-morning, Miss Forresst," said the matron. "Allow me to introduce to you Miss Dix."

Bella's eyes opened. "Is it the Miss Dix of whom I have read and heard so much?"

"Yes: it is the same."

"You have come," said Bella, "to visit us prisoners."

"No, not prisoners. You must not consider yourselves prisoners. You are only staying here for your health." And Miss Dix smiled in her endeavor to impress this idea.

"We *are* prisoners," Bella responded, "*close* prisoners; and if you lived as we do, Miss Dix, you would find it out."

The matron touched Miss Dix, and said, "We will pass along." Then the matron said, as they went out of hearing, "It is of no use to talk to her. She is incorrigible."

And Bella said in her heart, "Yes, Miss Dix would find it so. She visits asylums and prisons, but she knows nothing about them, after all. To know these places, we must live in the bondage of them, and endure."

What Bella said of Miss Dix is true of all visitors. Especially is it true of trustees.

These gentlemen, appointed by legal authority, and selected from very respectable classes, are too polite to investigate. They see the surface, under such colorings as are given by official representations; and it is impossible for them to see otherwise. Gentlemen of their breeding and habits would feel that they had broken the laws of courtesy, if they went into such methods of examination as are absolutely necessary for discovering the real condi-

19*

tion of asylum life. The regular trustee-days are days
set apart by themselves. From end to end of the buildings, in every department, everybody is in preparation.
Patients who have scarce seen light since the last trustee-
day are brought out, and dressed, and are perhaps, when
the trustees pass, playing back-gammon, or reading, or
sewing. Music-rooms and reading-rooms are thrown open,
— rooms that are never opened except when visitors are
coming ; and patients are warned not to cry or complain,
— not only warned, but commanded; and not only commanded, but threatened with punishment afterwards if they
dare utter one word of complaint in the presence of the
gentlemen.

Nor do trustees succeed much better if they drop in
unawares. They can get no farther than the office until
they are escorted. The keys that lock the patients in hold
trustees and visitors out; and there are inner telegraph
wires of communication, that is, the means of transmitting
intelligence from hall to hall are so complete, that, almost
with electric quickness, the most distant hall attendants
are apprised when visitors are likely to come. Five minutes
sometimes makes miraculous changes under this complete organization. And then the supervisors always know
in which halls there is trouble ; and, among so many wards,
there are generally some quiet ones. These are selected
for the inspection of visitors.

The great work of preparing for visitors does not con-
sist in tidying the halls, for uncleanliness is not a cardinal
fault in our asylums. The housekeepers are generally
thrifty, cleanly, and thorough in work ; but to suppress
the cryings, hush the moanings, and put the unhappy
people into comfortable positions, is an art. All this also
did Bella see, and she talked about it. She would not
keep still, for her heart was in pain.

Nor would she be silent with reference to the food. "I would like to send some of our dinners to Boston for exhibition," she said. "I think people would be astonished at both quantity and quality. Do you think, Annie, that the food here is fit for human beings?"

"I think," answered Annie, "that it is not fit for dumb animals, much less for us; and I am ashamed to preside at a table of ladies, when I have so little to offer them. I sometimes see them look nauseated at the quality of the inferior messes. Sometimes they leave the table as hungry as they sat down; and sometimes I am hungry myself, because I cannot relish such dishes."

"It's a mystery how the women can live so, year after year," Bella remarked.

"They acclimate, Miss Forresst. They get sick, faint, nauseate, vomit, then rally, until at last they get broken in, and can eat any thing. They have told me about it."

"I don't see why they need starve us," Bella returned. "The institution has pay for every patient. They can afford to hire laborers, to keep carpenters and other workmen; the tables of the superintendent abound in plenty, the trustees and visitors are dined elegantly, the kitchens are full of good food, and the lowest servants luxuriate in nice tea and coffee with cream and white sugar. But we patients, boarders, for whom the place was founded, sit in these cells day after day, famishing. There are. farms connected with the establishment; but the nice products are either sold, or consumed by the employees. Very little good fresh food reaches the inner, desolate halls where the need is greatest. Unlocked, open doors would remedy this kind of abuse."

Now, this talk was treason. If the girls had been overheard, one would have been locked into a cell, the other discharged.

At the next dinner Bella tried to swallow her cold watery potato, but could not. She arose disgusted, and went to her room. There she took the roll Harry left, and counted out what she thought necessary. Then she hied to Annie, and said, "Dear Annie, I am so hungry; and here is money. Do you think you could get leave to go out, and buy me something? Or are you afraid to ask ?"

"I am not afraid to ask, Miss Forresst; and, if I go out, I do not know that what I buy or do is anybody's business. I am not aware that I have sold my liberty."

Bella then gave her the money and the order, saying, "You shall share with me."

"Oh, no !" said Annie, "don't buy for me. There are others here who need food more than I do."

That night there was a general surprise and gratification through the hall. Bella went from room to room, and from woman to woman, with her little gifts. Cheese, pickles, cakes, oranges, and other relishes, such as they never saw in that place, gladdened many sad persons, and thanks went to Miss Forresst from every direction; and she, speaking freely her thoughts, ate her own purchased supper that night.

Such boldness of action and speech did not escape unobserved. The matron came to Bella. "Is it true, Miss Forresst, that you report our patients as being hungry ?"

"It is true that they *are* hungry," Bella replied firmly. "When I was in the other hall, I always saw enough in quantity, but here there is not enough even of this mean quality. There are twenty-three women in our dining-room; and this noon I am sure ten would have eaten every mouthful there was on the tables."

"But you know it is always best to live plain."

"Plain, plain !" said Bella, "what do you call plain ? A

piece of salt fish as large as your finger? You do not live so at your table, Mrs. Matron."

"We have salt fish at our table sometimes."

"But you have other things?"

"Ye-es, of course we do. I am not particularly fond of salt fish myself."

"You are not, are you? I presume not. Nor am I. Nor are these other ladies who are boarding here; but they have to eat it, because they are locked in here where there is nothing better."

"But we cannot afford to board you any better. Our means do not allow it, and patients should not expect it."

"Then give up the institution," Bella responded. "I would not try to have an institution, if it must be so poor as to starve its patients. These women live in constant, systematic, half-starvation, and we all feel like famished wolves. Last evening I asked Annie for one mouthful of something to stop my faintness. All she had was half a cup of black molasses. I ate it, and tried to sleep; but I could not sleep for hunger, and I cried; yes, I wept for myself and for these others shut up here in a land of plenty to half starve. Mrs. Matron, you know these things; and you countenance them: you do it coolly. You officers of these asylums join together in these plans. You correspond," —

"Miss Forresst, hush!" said the matron sternly. "You must not say such things! You will raise rebellion among our patients."

"Let me out, then," answered Bella. "I stay here day and night: I hear the groans, and see the tears. If I must not speak, let me out."

"We cannot let you out. It is your friends who keep you here. But you must be quiet, and cease to criticise our arrangements, or we must put you still lower. There are lower halls than this, you know."

"Put me there, then. I want to go. I wish I could go. I want to see what is done down there. When I hear the terrible noises that come from there, I want to know what makes them, and what is done to those poor haggard creatures. Yes, put me there; and then I shall see for myself what is done."

"Miss Forresst, you are wild! Go to your room, and stay there!"

That night an official order went to the kitchen department. "Send an extra loaf of bread to the hall of the upper wing."

"Hall of the upper wing is always grumbling," came back from the kitchen. "It has more now than any other of the wing halls."

This answer was transmitted to Annie. It was true that she had several times sent to the kitchen for more bread. As this reply was given her, she said, "God save us! If the others have less than we, I do not wonder they are crazy." And this response was also transmitted. It reached official ears. The matron entered the hall again, and met Bella walking. She had not remained in her room as she was bidden.

"Miss Forresst," said the matron, "you are at the foundation of this trouble. For your own credit you should not be talking such things."

"For *your* own credit," responded Bella, "you should have an institution that does not require such things to be said!"

"But, Miss Forrest, this is an old established house, patronized by the best of people. We have, among our patients, gentlemen who write, and support their families by their pens."

"The greater the shame, then," Bella returned. "If gentlemen are capable of supporting their families by their pens, they surely ought to have some different life from this! To shut men of brain and thought into these narrow, barren prisons is an outrage upon nature."

Without another word the matron turned away. Meeting the supervisor, she said, "I do not know what to do with Miss Forresst. I see no way to quell her."

"I do!" was the supervisor's emphatic reply.

CHAPTER XXI.

have brought the patient, Miss Darius," the supervisor remarked.

This was all she said.   She went out; and Bella
was left alone with her new mistress.

The supervisor was right when she said she knew
what to do with Miss Forresst.   She did know.   She knew
how to hush complaints, or, rather, she knew who did know
how.   Not an instant's warning did Bella have, when she
left Annie's hall.   "Come with me," the supervisor said,
and laid her hand heavily on Bella's shoulder.   Bella went.
Out again through musty passages, toward a far-away, low
hall, a hall that in itself was musty as the passages.   It
seemed that the very walls were full of miasma, such miasma as accumulates from the breaths and effluvias of innumerable human beings through a long period of close
confinement.   Persons unaccustomed catch their breath,
and almost reel, when they enter such air.   Insane prisoners
live in it for the benefit of their minds.

Mercy wept when Bella Forresst stood before Miss Darius ; but Bella did not weep — she was past weeping.   She
had entered on the heroic stage.   She felt somewhat as
martyrs may be supposed to feel when first they resolve to
do, and dare, and die.

Miss Darius rolled out her great white eyes, and scanned
every line of her captive's countenance ; but Bella did not
flinch.   She looked up steadily under the ordeal, and then

she smiled. It was not a smile of happiness, but of defiance and disdain. Miss Darius understood it. "I'll fetch *you* down, Miss!" was her inward thought.

Miss Darius understood her profession. There was no insubordination in her department. Ladies or ladies' maids, Yankee, Irish, Swede, or French, young, middle-aged, or old, feeble or healthy, insane or sane, whatever or whoever came under her dominion — "stopped." That was her favorite word.

"I do not need anybody to teach me how to handle patients."

That was her boast.

"I can manage the refractory."

That was another boast.

Bella was not consigned to her as refractory, but as troublesome. Miss Darius understood the difference. She understood that Miss Forresst was discerning, and inclined to look behind the scenes.

"I'll take her high head down," was the continuation of Miss Darius thoughts; but she only said, "This way!"

Bella followed her then, and was ushered into a room, — could it be called a room? — ushered into a cell, — could it be called a cell?" It seemed more like an iron box, with an iron-barred hole in one side. It was the most comfortless place Bella had yet seen. The asylum horses were standing in much nicer rooms.

There was literally nothing in this room but a small hospital bed, and an old chair. There was not a vestige of carpeting on the floor, and the boards had never seen paint. The plastered walls had been whitewashed, and re-whitewashed, till the successive layers were peeling off like the coats of a moulting animal. Without speaking, Bella sat down in the chair.

Miss Darius had one of those natures, that, being placed
20

in charge over people, many of whom were her decided superiors, felt a sort of savage delight in "taking them down." She conceived an instantaneous dislike to Bella. First, she was younger than herself; second, she was handsome. It was hard for Miss Darius to forgive these two faults, even in free life; but when she saw them here, and had power over their possessor, she found an exquisite pleasure in the use of the peculiarities of her vocation.

She left Bella a moment alone, and then returned with the first order.

"Miss Forresst, the last patient who slept here complained of bugs. You had better examine your bed."

Bella cast a glance at the iron bed with its square-cornered foot, but made no reply.

"Miss Forresst, did you hear me ?"

"I heard."

"Well ? "

"Well ," was Bella's response.

"Will you attend to it ? "

"Is it my duty to clean your beds ? Am I hired here for that purpose ? "

Miss Darius's eyes flashed. "None of your sauce to me ! I am hired here to attend to such people as you ; and you will find that I am capable. I am not one of your soft heads ; and, if you want to save yourself trouble, you will take off those bed-clothes, and do your duty."

Bella gazed at her mistress with a feeling of disgust, and hasty words came into her mind ; but she repressed them, for she remembered her position, a prisoner in the power of this woman ; and she well knew the futility of resisting one of these employees. With a feeling as if a dead weight had fallen upon her, she arose to comply with the disagreeable command, while her mistress stood by, watching eagerly to make sure that the work was thoroughly done. Her keys were in her hand.

The women in this hall seemed as people in constant fear. Their countenances wore an habitual expression of what may be called " cowed." They were disciplined until all natural spirit was disciplined out of them. They crouched and shrank away at the approach of Miss Darius.

When Bella came to the table, she saw table discipline in full force. One by one the women came, — not one staid away, not one came cheerfully ; but as if driven by unseen thongs they took their seats at the cheerless table. Miss Darius stood in the centre of the room, turning her eyes to the right and left. Not a woman escaped her scrutiny. She motioned to a chair opposite herself for Bella. The " troublesome " patient must be under the eye of her mistress.

What a meal that was ! What meals they all were at Miss Darius's table ! The food was divided out, and distributed by Miss Darius, before the patients entered the room ; and, as they sat down, they knew what was each one's allowance. If any woman refused to eat what was on her plate, she was reminded of the force-pump ; if 'any asked for more, she was told, " Go to your room ! You have had enough ! "

Miss Darius ran a secret express to the kitchen, and al ways had delicacies hidden away for herself.

The cleaning of the bed was the only work required of Bella on the first day. The remainder of the time was occupied by Miss Darius in watching her new patient ; keeping her eyes fixed on her as though to awe her by power of supremacy. It was very annoying and wearing to the patient ; but then Miss Darius knew how to manage insane patients. The superintendent said she was one of his best attendants.

The next morning Miss Darius's method for Bella became apparent. She was not to be strapped and jacketed, nor dragged and pounded; but her cure was to be in *work*. As soon as breakfast was over, Miss Darius said, "Miss Forresst, you can wash my dishes."

Bella paused a moment, then walked on toward her room. "Miss Forresst, you can wash my dishes!"

This time she spoke with emphasis. Bella turned, "Washing dishes is not my business in this house. You are hired for that purpose."

Miss Darius stepped in front of her. "Miss Forresst, be careful! *My* patients are not allowed such expressions! You — will — wash — my — dishes!"

Bella looked at the two eyes glaring at her; and, for a moment, felt as if she should like to put her two fists into them; but better thoughts prevailed. She scorned to quarrel with the woman. She scorned to even dispute with her. Harry and the Penobscot ice came to her recollection. "'Tis but for a time," she said to herself, and proudly turned to her assigned work.

"It is not because I fear you," she remarked to Miss Darius, "but I should be ashamed to contest with you."

"I did not ask for your motives," was Miss Darius's reply. "It is your work I want."

That was the beginning of days of toil for Bella. To see her work was Miss Darius's especial delight, and her name was continually ringing through the hall. "Bella Forresst, you may scour the brasses! Bella Forresst, scrub the dining-room floor! Bella Forresst, sweep the hall! Bring my water, Bella Forresst."

Thus Bella became one of the asylum slaves. She toiled till her hands were soiled, and her feet tired; while Miss Darius sat with folded arms, and rocked in her chair, her keys lying within reach. She was fond of using those keys; and if a blow from them raised a protuberance, why, what matter? It was only on "a patient."

But Miss Darius was not confined to keys as instruments of discipline. She choked one woman for refusing to wash dishes. The woman could not swallow for a month without pain. She kicked another woman down a flight of stairs. The woman was sitting on the top stair: Miss Darius wanted to pass. "Get up!" she said; but, before the woman could comply, Miss Darius put out her foot, and sent her to the foot of the flight. It did not kill her, but it broke her hip; and now she hobbles on crutches,— a cripple for life.

Miss Darius knocked an old lady to the floor, and broke her shoulder. They picked up the poor old creature, and laid her on her bed. When the physician had set the broken bone, he said, "I hope you will not cherish hard feelings towards Miss Darius."

"No," the old lady replied, flushes of pain passing over her brow. "She was a little more hasty than usual, that is all."

It was true. Much that old lady had suffered from Miss Darius. She had been jammed into chairs, and held there for hours; Miss Darius had seized her by the neck, and ran her the length of the hall, till it seemed that the old lady must fall; and she had been jerked and pulled in every conceivable way.

Miss Darius also was expert at keeping women locked into their cells in constant solitude; but she was not alone in that. Other attendants kept them locked, forever locked, day and night, in darkness, cold, and desolation, in rooms barren of comforts, and only pittances to eat.

When Miss Darius ordered women to their rooms, if they did not step quickly enough to suit her, she had a way of going behind them; and, with her fists doubled, she rat-tat-tatted on their backs with all her force, and thus drove them in. Those who have had the misfortune to receive

20*

blows on the spine know the cruel sufferings these rat-tat-blows produced.

Miss Darius also had a habit of catching women, by hooking her arm about their necks, and, with their bodies dragging behind, she pulled them into a dark closet, and there administered punishment. But she felt that she had reached the acme of hall management, when, after dinner, she marshalled out all her women, and seated them in chairs along each side of the hall. Every chair stood square in its niche, and every woman sat square in her chair. Miss Darius was ready for visitors then ; and when visitors, passing through asylums, see women sitting thus, let them think of Miss Darius.

The asylum officers, passing through the halls, and seeing the patients sitting thus in quiet order, give praise to the attendants. Miss Darius was considered a model attendant. Her women, looking at each other with eyes of silent anguish, moaned softly, "How long, O Lord! how long?" One said, "Why did they not hang me ere they brought me here? Hanging would soon end, but this will never end." Another whispered, and her hollow eyes glared, "Oh! why was I not laid on a funereal pyre, and my body given to the winds? 'Twere better than this." And another said, "Why did they not put me in my coffin alive, for then my sufferings would soon have ended; but this goes on and on, like a great revolving wheel, crushing me at every turn."

It is, indeed, the endlessness of imprisonment that adds the last dread bitterness. Penal prisoners, serving their terms, can count the days, and feel each night that there is one less, and that, if they endure, freedom lies once more before them ; but prisoners in asylums, consigned and held by medical advice, have no such hope. They are life prisoners, and they know it. Deep into their hearts sinks this terrible consciousness; and, "forever, forever," rings from soul to soul like echoes among the lost. Is it wonderful that they shriek, and cry, and tear their hair? Is it strange that they grow haggard, or lifeless, or wild, or sink into imbecility, or despair, losing beauty and life, and becoming unfit for earth or heaven?

Over these wretched people, attendants like Miss Darius tyrannize. Patients have no privileges under such attendants. They cannot even call their clothes their own; but trunks and garments are taken from them at a moment's notice.

Miss Darius supplied herself with delicacies, by eating what was sent to the patients from their homes. Said a gentleman one day, taking Miss Darius one side, "Here are some oranges, figs, and bottles of wine, for my wife. She is a very generous woman; and, if I leave them with her, I fear she will give them away. I want she should eat them herself. Will you take charge of them, and see that she has them, a few at a time?"

Miss Darius simpered, "Ye-e-s." She had a very soft way of speaking to visitors. The gentleman went away thinking how pleasant she was! That night Miss Darius handed an orange to the lady; the next morning she gave her a fig; two days after she gave her a small glass of wine.

"Oh!" said the lady. "How nice it is! Where did you get it?"

"Your husband left it," Miss Darius replied. She felt "gracious" at the moment. Her own mouth was fragrant with the nectar. For three days she continued to supply herself and the patient; then the patient's allowance was withholden.

"I would thank you for another glass of the wine," said the lady a few days after.

"There is no more," said Miss Darius curtly.

"I will take an orange, then."

"They are gone."

"A fig, then."

"I tell you they are gone.   Did you think your things would last forever?"

"I wonder why my husband left so small quantities?" the lady remarked, and then went to her room.

"I wonder where Miss Darius expects her soul will go," whispered a woman near.   "I saw her carry twelve bottles of wine, more than three dozen of oranges, and a drum of figs, to her room."

It was true. The gentleman was no niggard, and had supplied his wife freely with these nourishing articles. Miss Darius sat in her room, and regaled herself for many long days.

Well, — that patient is dead now. We read her death in the papers. "Died in the asylum at ——, &c., &c."

We asked ourselves, "Did she die of slow starvation, prison paralysis, home-sickness, or heart-sickness?   When last we saw her, all these diseases were on her.

"If I only had some apples!" said an old colored woman to a lady visitor. The old woman was for many years a highly-valued servant of this lady, who had now come to visit her in her misfortune.

"You shall have them," said the lady. "I will send you some."

The next day there came to the asylum a basket of beautiful rosy apples, labelled with the name of the old colored women.

"She is in Miss Darius's hall," said the persons in the public room. A passage-sweeper took the basket. A supervisor joined her. They carried the basket to Miss Darius. Half an hour later the old colored woman saw several attendants eating large rosy apples. She was reminded of the promise of her mistress; and venturing to Miss Darius, she asked, humbly, "Have any apples come for me?"

"*You!*" said Miss Darius, staring. "Who would send apples to *you?*"

The poor old eyes drooped, she turned away, and tottered to her chair, and sank into it, murmuring, "I thought she would send me some. She used to be good. But nobody cares for us when we get in here."

Sad, sad, is the fate of asylum patients! Nowhere, save in these corridors, can be found such weird, down-trodden women, or sad and hopeless men, sitting stultified in these living tombs, while outside their walls the free sun is shining, and the birds are carolling their songs, and animals run each in their own natural way.

"I wish I was that rat," said a woman, looking through her grates, "for then I should be free;" and her face lengthened into a soberness that settled into lines, marking her with grim despair.

"But," says an asylum apologist, "all patients do not feel thus. There are those who go and stay awhile, get better, go home and stay a few weeks, and then go back; going back and forth, willingly and pleasantly."

We grant it. There are such women; but the asylum does not cure them. Asylum doctors do not touch the causes of their disease. As a general rule, they do nothing for their patients except to hold them as prisoners. If they give medicines, it is chlora, or some soporific that stupefies, from which patients wake more miserable than before. The real disease is usually untouched.

Women go back and forth uncured. "Willingly," it is said. Perhaps so. But what is the state of persons who go willingly to prison? Ought they to be allowed to remain

in such an apathetic stupidity ? The Lord made the glad
earth for the uplifting of souls, and the broad sunlight for
their healing. He made no prisons for men ; and a soul
that is so broken as to live contentedly in little enclosed
cells is the very soul that should be lifted out, and held beneath the smiles of God. The fresh, glad wilderness, the
sea with its foam and bracing air, the mountains, the valleys, plains, babbling brooks, limpid lakelets, and broad
rivers, — all have health in their scenes, and nature in their
beautiful recesses. Let people seek health by Nature's
rules, and they will find it. Let them have Nature's freedom. Remove artificial rules ; give free rein to Nature in
her purity, not in her perversions. The Creator made
people for freedom, guided only by his pure laws.

What the theories are that fill volumes of works on insanity, we do not know, — we do not want to know ; for
theories that produce such results should be studied only for
the purpose of exposing their fallacies.

Insanity should not be treated in masses. Each individual case requires its own individual treatment. Neither in
locked cottages nor locked halls should insane people be
massed. They require deep scientific treatment, and remedies that reach the cause. They are unhappy together,
some in cells, some pacing the halls, and all feeling that a
ban rests upon them. If people are not insane, they certainly should not be in such prisons ; if they *are* insane,
they need the natural companionship of natural persons to
keep and sustain them till they are restored ; and such
restoration depends on remedies applied to the *cause* of the
insanity, and not to the insanity itself. This is a disease
that touches the souls of men and women. It should not
be the subject of ridicule, cruelty, or contempt ; but should
be skilfully and tenderly removed by removing the cause,
or giving the sufferer strength to bear the cause.

"If it were not for hope, the heart would break." Bella most certainly realized the truth of that adage during that winter under Miss Darius. She counted the months, she counted the weeks, and almost counted the days, before the spring opening; and, as she toiled like a servant for her unthankful mistress, she felt to say, "Every day is one less; and how do these bear who have no brother they expect?" And echo answers, How?

Miss Darius had no faith in the fulfilment of Bella's expectations. "I have heard patients talk before," she said. "They are always expecting to go; but they are pretty apt to stay. What does her brother want of her, a crazy, love-smitten thing? He only talks; but she'll stay, I'll promise you."

And Miss Darius had good grounds for this opinion, if she judged by her experience in the past, and by her observation of large numbers of patients left there by friends to linger. But Harry Forresst was not of that class of friends. His promise was his bond. His soul was truth. All winter he bore in mind that prison and his young sister. Every plan was governed to conform to his pledge; and when the snows softened, and the ice gave way, he was ready to go. He shook the hard hands of the woodsmen, exchanged farewell greetings, and felt that the men were sincere when they said they were sorry they should "see his face no more." He, too, was sorry. He had spent many genial evenings by their wood-fires, smoked with them, read their newspapers, and heard their evening tales. Pleasant memories lingered about them; but now Bella was in his heart, the Western home on his imagination, and the Aroostook would know him no more. He steamed to Boston.

Straightforward in his actions, he went from the boat to Frederic, and plunged into business.

"I say, Fred, I am going West."

"Ah !"

To Mr. Frederic it mattered little whether Harry was West or in the Aroostook. Harry was "a rough member of the Forresst house, who made money fast enough, but whose social ideas were far astray," Mr. Frederic often remarked.

"I am going immediately," Harry continued; "and I must take Bella."

"Ha !"

Mr. Frederic opened his eyes, and his mustache went up-ward. Harry went on, "Yes, I am going to take Bella. The sooner you let her out of that place the better. I want to be off."

Frederic looked Harry in the eyes, and said, "There will be two words to that bargain. I am her guardian by law."

"I know you have procured that situation for yourself; but I intend to give her to another guardian."

"Ha !"

Frederic uttered this ejaculation, and then coolly turned to some figures before him, as if to say, "Why talk any more? I am master of the situation. Go away !"

But Harry was not the man to be turned away from his purpose. He spoke again, and this time peremptorily.

"I say, Fred, I never quarrelled with you yet; but if you don't let Bella out of that place, and give up her prop-erty, *I* will try a game at law. I will ascertain where justice lies."

"Very well," was Frederic's response. "The law has pronounced the girl insane; she is proved so by the certifi-cates of two physicians; and that she is no better is evident from the fact that they have had to put her in lower wards to keep her in subjection."

Harry Forresst squared his shoulders, his head set itself upright on his firm neck, and for a moment astonishment held him silent.   Then, in a low and solemn tone, he asked, —

"Frederic, are you a devil?"

"Upon my honor," said Mr. Frederic, "you can call me by that name if you please! Your own humor seems of that kind to-day."

"It will be of that kind shortly, I fear," was Harry's response.   "I will leave you now.   I shall see you this evening."

Harry turned then, and walked into the street.   He felt that he needed the air.   He would have liked a bath in the pine-woods atmosphere, that he might cool his temper with its sweetness.

Frederic was already cool.   In fact, he never allowed himself to be heated.   He was quite still after Harry went out, and considered.   At first he was buried in reverie; then thoughts flashed over his haughty face, and then they passed away.   In that moment his decision was made, his course decided; and when he went home to his fashionable dinner, and walked up the street, with one glove off, and his small cane carelessly swinging, none could see that the destiny of a human being hung in his thoughts.   Some young ladies, meeting him, remarked after passing, "How superb Mr. Forresst is!   He grows splendid every day."

When Harry kept his appointment that evening, he was utterly taken aback.   Frederic was affable and polite as at a dinner-party.   Before Harry could speak, Frederic said, "I have considered, my brother; and as you are resolved upon entering a law-case unless I yield, why, I yield, for the credit of the family.   I will send Eunice for her to-morrow."

"I will go myself," said Harry.

The next morning saw Harry on the alert.   He break-fasted early, strode to the dépôt, and was off.

What a day that was! Miss Darius's white eyes stared
with astonishment as that big, bluff man came through her
hall. It was spring-time ; and there was extra cleaning.
The beds, the cells, windows, and rough old paint, were
having their spring scrubbing ; and Bella had been assigned
to a heavy portion. With a weary feeling she had dressed
herself in a scouring-suit, and was down on her knees at
the mop-board, in obedience to Miss Darius's command.
It seemed to her that spring had done every duty except to
open the Penobscot ice ; and she wondered whether that
was bound by the satyrs of the ice-king as closely as she
was bound by the satyrs of the prison-king. Suddenly her
mistress appeared before her.

"You may leave this work, and go to your room. You
have company."

"Company ?"

Down went the cloth, scrubbing-brush, and all appurte-
nances. Up came the patient from her knees. Back flew
the curls, and the eyes flashed. She had no time to *think ;*
but she *felt* that it was Harry, and away she flew.

"That's always the way," Miss Darius muttered. "Company are sure to come when we don't want them. He'll
bother round as much as an hour, I'll warrant. I must
get work. Oh, I know! There's Mrs. Murray! I'll make
her work !"

"I am thankful for Miss Forresst," said Mrs. Murray,
when Miss Darius entered her room. "It is the very
brother for whom she has been looking. She will go home
now."

"Pshaw ! no, she won't ; and, if she should, it's none of
your business."

"I have a right to be thankful for her, if I have no other
right," meekly said the woman, as she arose from her chair
to do the prison cleaning.

Bella, meantime, had gone to her room, — no longer a desolate place, for a noble man stood in it. His soul was full of a good purpose: does not that ennoble any man?

She saw him face to face, saw him smile; and, closing her door, she rushed straight into his arms; and, laying her head on his shoulder, she wept. She did not speak, nor kiss him, nor say she was glad; but she sobbed, and her tears wet his bushy brown beard. He lifted up her face, and looked at her anxiously.

"Why, little one, what is the matter? I thought you would be glad?"

"Glad, Harry? Am I not glad?"

"I don't see it. I thought you would jump for joy?"

"I will, when I have cried enough. I must cry first, you know."

As she looked up then, there broke through her tears, deep smiles; and all over her face, bright colors seemed to glow. Harry thought of a rainbow after a shower. She brushed away the misty drops, the smile deepened, her eyes looked up with their old-time hope, and then he felt re-assured. He began to understand her. A bit of a tear came into his own eye; but he brushed it away, saying, "Confound it, Bella, don't make a man weak!"

"But, Harry, I thought I should drop right down with joy."

"Drop! Why, what are you women made of? Come now, stand up like a man. Be yourself. Make ready, and we'll be off. I have bidden farewell to the Aroostook, and am going out to marry you to the captain."

The words were like an electric shock to her. The thought was familiar; but the words, uttered in this open way, produced a re-action. She blushed. Blushing — the most natural effect of such a remark — brought nature to her aid. She looked up in her old quick manner.

"Sit down, old Harry, and I will pack my trunk."

"That's it!" he exclaimed. "Now you are Bella again That's jolly. Go ahead, and I will not speak of the captain again for full five minutes."

She obeyed him with willing hands, working rapidly as in a dream when the mind rushes, it knows not how. She had been expecting this event; yet now that it had come, she could scarce believe its reality. "It was a dream, and yet, not all a dream."

The great event was soon known through the hall. "Miss Forresst is going, — going home." One day of true happiness, and only one, does the asylum patient prisoner know: that is the day of release. The world seems suddenly larger. The air is more wholesome, life puts on new bloom. The women who were to remain gathered in groups as if their whole interest centered in her. "Dear Miss Forresst," said one, "I wish I had a letter ready for you to take out. You could mail it for me."

"Why cannot I write for you after I am away? I shall be my own mistress then, you know. Nobody can control my letters," and Bella smiled triumphantly.

"Oh, do write, do! I shall be so happy! Write to my Aunt Ransom, corner of Pine and Grosvenor Streets, L——, Mass."

"Yes," said Bella, "I will tell her what you suffer. I will tell her how you are situated; but will she believe me? Sometimes it seems impossible to make people believe even that which is before their eyes, with reference to these asylums. They attend only to that which the head ones say."

"I know it, I know it; but there is no hope for me save in somebody's letters; and my aunt used to love me."

"Will you write for me too?" asked another. "Write to my brother at Willimet Centre, Mass. O Miss Forresst, how happy you will be! But you will not forget us who are left behind, will you?"

"Indeed I will not," Bella said earnestly. "I could not forget you if I should try; and I shall not try."

Bella felt her heart come in her mouth, as she looked upon these women, and considered the weary, dreary months that lay behind them, and the weariness that was yet to come.

"What is such a life worth?" she asked herself.

There is a strange contradiction in asylum partings. Patients rejoice most when those go whom they love most. Bella knew that when these women said, "We are so glad you are going," it was because they loved her; and that she herself would have so joyed in their departure that she would have parted with every one, and would have walked those corridors alone, and thanked her God that the others were free.

When she was dressed, and the partings were over, Harry drew her hand within his arm. Then she hesitated a moment. She had not said good-by to Miss Darius. Should she? Could she? "No — yes — I will. Poor Miss Darius! It is not her fault that she is unkind and cruel. The place and the business make her so."

With this charitable conclusion, Bella said "Good-by," then walked through the open door, heard the key turn behind her, felt that for her entrance it would no more unlock, and went down the stairs, thanking her God and her brother, who seemed to her like a rock of salvation, a present help in time of trouble, a saviour whom God had sent. Harry helped her into a carriage, and they rode away. She grasped his hand, and looked out upon the broad landscape. "O Harry! Isn't 'out-of-doors' larger than it used to be? I do not believe I shall know how to behave, I have been shut up so long."

"You will soon find out. You must put up your courage, and make ready to receive Fred. Do not let him

think he has cowed you down. But here is the station."
They were driving to the dépôt.

"Now I feel free!" she said as she sprang from the carriage, and saw the waiting train. "Farewell, prison! Come, old Harry."

He smiled at that appellation. He himself taught it to her ere she could scarce lisp it, or knew its meaning; and he felt young again as she uttered it with her old-time joyousness. He helped her into the car, and took a seat beside her. It would be hard to say which was happier, he in protecting her, or she in being protected. Thus beautifully has the Creator harmonized nature between strength and weakness, that both are happy in their appropriate spheres.

While they were riding, Harry unfolded his plans. "The captain," he said, "wants his father and mother to go on. I have made arrangements for them to go with us. They are two lone old people, with only their one ·boy to love. I suppose you have no objections to their going."

"No, indeed! I shall be so glad. · Dear Mrs. Beale, I always loved her."

Then, as she settled back, an expression of ineffable gladness stole into her face. Harry watched her in silence. Neither spoke; but the bachelor brother mused, "It is strange what this is that comes over women! There is Mortimer Beale full fifteen hundred miles away; yet the thought of him makes her face shine as though angels were blessing it. Heigho! I wonder how a man feels when a woman loves him so! Well, I shall never·know. I never had a knack at women."

She spoke but once again on the road. Then she looked up, and said, "Is it really, truly true that I am going? I hope it isn't a dream, Harry."

"It is a wide-awake dream," he answered.

They steamed on. All around them were other people, each with his or her own emotions, interests, and loves; and yet they two were alone. Around themselves they carried the halo of their own mutual love; and, in the midst of the world of people, they were alone. Alone, yet together, we all are. Souls speak to souls; yet each soul has its own organic laws, its own individuality. Each is alone.

Of all the crowd in the station that day, none was more manfully strong than Harry Forresst, with his sister under his care; and no woman walked more buoyantly than she, with her hand on his solid arm.

CHAPTER XXII.

THERE was no need for Bella to assume, in order to show Frederic that she was not crushed. Thanks to a good constitution, she arose from her sorrows, and life seemed to re-act. She entered her sister's comfortable home under Harry's protection;. and was gathered to her old mother's heart in one long embrace. Harry left her there; and went down to Frederic.

"H'm," said Frederic, "I suppose you have been for her."

"Bella is now with mother," was the response. "She needs new clothes, and a young housekeeper's outfit. I have come to you for a check."

"Upon my honor! How much do you calculate it will take to furnish a squatter's cabin?"

Harry's eyes flashed, even with Frederic's own sheen.

"It will take the whole of her property; and, unless you pass it over immediately, it will take some of your own to pay your lawyer's fees." This was the second time that Harry had threatened him with law. The mustache twitched with an ominous jerk; and he drew forth a check which he filled as Harry dictated, but his hand had a convulsive movement as he wrote. It was not the amount of money that convulsed his fingers, as he signed his name: it was the fact that he was overmastered. When Harry was gone, he stood and mused.

"Upon my honor! They all are lunatics together.

The whole family ought to be in an asylum. Harry threatening me with law! As though I do not know the ground I stand on. The girl is insane. I have proved it; and that she is no better is shown by the fact that twice she went to lower wards. Well, I bide my time."

Then Mr. Frederic settled his face; and over his inward determination his habitual blandness fell as a screen. What he thought could not be deciphered then by what he said and did.

The succeeding days were full of new life to Bella. On Summer Street, on Winter Street, up and down Washington Street, crossing and recrossing she went. The world was beautiful and bright again. She was living in a present of happiness, with a future full of the halo of promise. She thought sometimes of those imprisoned women whom she had left, and who had no brother to take them from their galling bondage; and when she sat at her sister's luxurious table, she thought of them trying to subsist on their pittances; and often she said, "If people only could know these things! Isn't there somebody to tell?"

"It seems wrong for me to go out and be happy, while they are all left miserable," she added; "but what can I do?"

Mrs. Boynton's house became a busy scene. She opened her heart to the occasion; and, in truth, she was not sorry that Frederic had taken this turn. Much as she deprecated Bella's "low marriage," she yet thought it preferable to an asylum. "That seems such a disgrace," was her frequent remark.

The most marked feature in Mrs. Boynton's house at this time was the frequent presence and cordial civilities of Mr. Frederic. His magnificent presence illumined every department. The dressmaking, millinery, and household linen all passed under his observation; and he seemed to have entirely forgotten his animosity.

"It is the part of the conquered to yield gracefully," he remarked to Bella, "and I wish to show you that I can bear defeat. Wouldn't you like to visit Nellie on your way as you go West?"

"How can I? Harry has no time to stop at New York."

"Allow me to be your chevalier to Brooklyn. Two days precedence of Harry will give you time to visit Nellie, and also to look about the Empire City. I shall be most happy to show you about."

Bella looked up at him in astonishment; but his face was as calm as if he had been in his own counting-room, completing a business transaction. He saw her searching glances, and said, "You are surprised at my offer; but you see, when I do give up a point, I do it thoroughly and completely."

It seems impossible that the girl could have believed him sincere in this offer; and, in order to show that she did thoroughly believe him, it would be necessary to delineate the characteristics of Frederic Forresst, and to depict the perfect control that he possessed over his fine features. To this power, much of his business success was due. He could utter absolute falsehoods with a bland and honest expression that deceived even shrewd men, and drew from their purses thousands that went into his own. He thoroughly deceived Bella now. She thought him full of regrets for his past course; and he was, but they were regrets that in the end he had been defeated. It seemed to him that he had become imbecile to allow a girl to "get the better of him," even though half a dozen younger brothers abetted her.

"Am I not the eldest of my father's house?" he asked himself. "If I were in England I should have rights as eldest; but, upon my honor, in America we have no rights."

Mr. Forresst was no republican at heart, though he passed outwardly as such. In fact, no one had ever read him, or knew exactly what he was.

But when Bella mentioned Frederic's proposal to Harry, he started, and said, "The deuce."

"Why, Harry! Oughtn't I to visit Nellie?"

"But there is something wrong about it. How came Fred to offer?"

"He wants to show me courtesy by way of amends."

"H'm. You see, Bella, I have very little confidence in this show of acquiescence he is making; but then I don't care whether he is sincere or not, as long as I can keep him harmless."

"But what harm can he do me now? I am free. You have my money, and you will be only two days behind me. I can meet you at the New-York dépôt; and I do think Frederic is sorry for what he has done, now that he sees it has never changed me; and we must forgive."

"I have no doubt but he is sorry he did not conquer you; and as to forgiving, — well, let him go to God. If he gets forgiveness there, I shall not withhold mine; for which latter Fred cares very little, I fancy;" and honest Harry shrugged his broad shoulders. "But, as I have not the power of God to read his heart, I cannot know whether he is sincere, and I cannot trust him."

Frederic, in his home, thought that Harry would say this; and he came again to his sister's house. With consummate tact he repeated his proposal in the presence of the whole family, and, to prove his sincerity, offered to take his mother along as guard.

"It would do mother good to visit Nellie," he said, "and, upon my honor, Bella ought to go there; and now that I have given in, and am conquered, I want to show how I bear it."

All but Harry acquiesced. He looked at Frederic, and said keenly, "If you play me false in this thing, you shall rue the day."

Frederic smiled, and tapped his boot with his ivory cane. Harry afterwards said to Bella, "I have no faith in him; but, if we can avoid another rupture, we will. Mother will be with you to New York: you will meet me at the station there. Mr. and Mrs. Beale will be with me, and we will be off."

It was on a lovely, balmy day, toward the even-tide, when the broad street seemed quiet as a country road, and the salt-water breezes came over Brooklyn in ocean fragrance, that Bella stood on the steps of an elegant house, bidding her sister her last adieux. Nature was wearing her gorgeous spring robe. The air was full of life and love. The tiniest hum seemed of peace. The grand houses stood around in spring-time freshness and quiet. Far away the ships studded the sea, and the sailors enjoyed the bright, warm day. On land, grand carriages rolled; and the occupants, enrobed in luxury, inhaled the aromatic air without a thought of suffering in such a beautiful world. A policeman, standing near, found·no occupation, and idly gazed at the carriage drawn up before Dr. Bergmann's house. Bella threw her arms about her sister's neck, and gave her a long embrace.

"I have had a charming visit," she said; and smiles rippled over her happy face. She kissed her sister and mother; and then, stooping, she kissed a German-looking child, and tripped lightly down the walk. Frederic stood at the carriage-door. She entered, and waved her last farewell as the carriage rolled away. Frederic sat on the seat opposite her. His face wore its blandest smile; and she thought how handsome he was, and how proud she could be of him as her brother. His hardness towards her was forgotten and forgiven. At that moment every thing was forgiven. She was too happy to cherish resentment. She forgot the unhappy past, and thought only of what was to come. She was now on her way to meet Harry at the cars that were to bear her to her home whither her heart had long since been borne.

Steadily forward they went. The sleek horses obeyed the impulse of the driver, and they soon left the quiet of Brooklyn behind. The scenes changed. They entered the thronging city, went up into the busy thoroughfares where men trade for souls, and women walk in pride, measuring each other by gold. Frederic was silent. Not even the ends of the mustache stirred, and Bella watched the multitudes.

Suddenly the carriage stopped. Another carriage stood waiting. Frederic said, " All right," and the driver leaped to the pavement. Frederic pushed open the carriage-door. The door of the other carriage was already open. Bella looked on with surprise.

" What !" she exclaimed. " Are we to get out here ? "

" I must leave you here," he answered, with unwonted suavity. " I have some business engagements. These gentlemen will see you to the cars. Keep up good heart, whatever comes."

He drew out his watch, glanced at it, and added quickly. " Upon my honor ! I have need to hasten."

A chill went through the soul of the girl as she left her carriage, and entered the other carriage with the two strange men. She looked wistfully at Frederic. He was her brother, and she was going far away. She might not see him again. " Forgive me, Frederic," she said, " I have sometimes thought hard of you."

"Don't speak of it," he responded. "Some time you will be brought to reason, I hope."

Then he turned away. The men had transferred her trunks. One of them sprang into the carriage, the other went up with the driver. The two carriages parted, even as we often part to meet on earth no more. Bella felt a pang, but it was quickly followed by a gush of relief. She thought of Harry, and how he would be relieved at finding Frederic gone. "There will be no danger at the station now," was her silent thought. "Frederic will not be there to see Mr. and Mrs. Beale, and we shall have every thing as Harry has planned. Dear old Harry! He is waiting for me now! A few minutes more, and I shall be with him, on my way to " — happiness, she was about to add; but something in the street attracted her. Looking out from the carriage, she watched the people hurrying to and fro, and her soul filled with a quiet such as a tempest-tossed mariner might feel as the shores of his haven came in view.

And Frederic rode away to his business with a manner composed as of one who had accomplished an important purpose. He had no misgivings; but said in his heart, "Upon my honor, what else can I do? Shall I see her throw herself away? She might have married into the highest family of the land, and she would have adorned the sphere. Can I see her wilfully throw herself away on a Beale? Never; and, if Harry had the sense of his family's dignity, he would not be led around by the folly of a girl. Pity he hadn't married, and had a woman of his own to attend to. Then he wouldn't be so susceptible to whimpering tears. As to Edward — well, the truth is — I mean no aspersion on my parents — but Edward and Bella, the children of old age, were spoiled by petting. Well, I must do what I can with such refractory young people. And now for business. I may as well make the best of my trip, now that I am here. Let me see."

He took from his pocket an ivory memorandum, and glanced at the leaves, then drew the coachman's string. "To No. — Broadway."

Yes, Harry was waiting. He stood on the platform beside the long Western train. Hurry and bustle were all around him; but he was cool and calm. One thumb was in his vest armhole, one foot akimbo, and he seemed as carelessly at ease as a clear conscience and firm health could put a man. The two old people were snugly placed on a seat where no window could betray them, and Harry felt like a sentry whose charge was safe. He watched the carriages drive down, watched each fresh arrival, and grew impatient. He whistled, consulted his watch, placed his other foot akimbo, then stood on both feet square, put up his watch, and drew a long breath. He heard the signals of the approaching start; saw people hurrying in; saw baggage-men hurling the big trunks; heard some speaking in haste; and pulling off his hat, he wiped the perspiration from his brow. But no Bella came.

"The deuce!" he ejaculated, jamming his hat on, and stepping forward to scan the carriages once more.

"Yes; there they come, at last. Thank God! No: it is not they. It is an old man with two young girls. Great heavens! Don't they know the time? Will they miss the train?"

He broke into increased perspiration. The cars were beginning to tremble. The passengers were in. The platform was deserted. Preparations were complete. Steam was ready, but no Bella. "Good God!" he ejaculated. "Where is she? Are they all stark mad?"

The train began to glide. He saw it with one eye cast backward; and those old people were on it. What should he do? What could he do?

"Great heavens!" he muttered breathlessly. "What — shall — I do?"

The train still moved. Car after car glided on. He gave one searching glance through the streets. No carriage coming. Nothing like Bella to be seen. The cars were going. Mr. and Mrs. Beale were in them. He whirled, flew, his coat flew after him, — but he did it. He reached the train, caught the last rail of the last car, and stumbled on to the last step. He was safe, except a bruise on the hand by which he swung. A man helped him up with a reproving caution. "Risky business, that, sir. You should be more careful." Harry made a slight reply, then straightened himself, and pressed through from car to car. He found the old people in a fever of anxiety. They calmed at his approach, but trembled again at his tale.

"We cannot go," said Mrs. Beale decidedly. "We must get out, and wait for another train." She arose as she spoke.

Mr. Beale laid his hand on her arm. "Sit down, mother. We *must* go. Don't make yourself conspicuous. Don't you see the cars are moving?"

"But they haven't gone far."

"What of that? We are in them, and we cannot get out."

"True — true," she murmured, and sat down with a blankness in her face. "What shall we do?"

Harry mused, and then said, "There is only one way. At the first town where there is a hotel, I must leave you while I go back. Of course we cannot go without Bella."

And thus, in the midst of anxiety, they steamed on, with the great train thundering in their ears.

"I won't! I won't! I won't! I will never step my foot in there as long as I live! I never will! Let me alone!

Let me alone! Let me alone, I say!" and, as the speaker ejaculated, she struck her hands out wildly each side of her. The two men who had her stepped back. Another came forward. He was a stranger. His hair was combed lightly up, his forehead was broad and serene, his countenance pleasant and fair, and his manner genial. He was a gentleman, a true-hearted gentleman. It pained him to see a beautiful young lady in such excitement. He extended his hand gently. His smile was winning, his voice pleasant.

"My dear young lady, do not be agitated. We will not hurt you."

She struck his hand, and turned away.

"Take me back!" she said to the two men. "Take me back, or I will walk back."

But at her first step, the pleasant gentleman laid his hand upon her wrist. The grasp was gentle, but firm. It held her like a vice. Then he motioned the two men.

"Bring her trunks right in. We will take care of her. She will be all right soon."

Then he took her hand, and started forward. She jerked away, and turned upon him.

"I will not go in! I say I will not go in! It is an asylum! I know it is! I will never go in!"

"Reckon she has seen such places before," said one of the men who had brought her. "She has been raving ever since we took the cars. She was peaceable enough till then. Then she began to rave that we were wrong, and to talk about her brother whom she was going to meet. But, you see, it was her brother whom we took her from; and "—

"It is another brother," interposed the girl, turning upon her jailers. "Haven't I more than one brother?"

"There, my dear, do not talk," said the pleasant-faced
22*

gentleman. "These men are going away, and then you shall tell us all about it. We would like to know about your brothers."

"My brothers," the girl repeated slowly, and emphatically: "I have one who is killing me."

"No, my dear young lady.. You are mistaken. Nobody wants to harm you."

He bowed a farewell to the two men, and once more attempted to lead her in ; but she jerked from him like a lightning flash, and leaped for the door. Alas! The man was not alone, and there was no escape for her. Another man rushed forward, intercepted her, and held her till his superior reached her again. The superior spoke more sternly now, and his pleasant face darkened with decision. "Miss Forresst, you must submit yourself quietly. Do not compel us to use force."

"I will never go in there, never, never!" she said firmly. "I have been cruelly treated, basely brought here. It is a house of torture. It is a house of death. I will never step a foot within its halls, never, never!"

A third person now appeared. She was a woman of mature age. Well dressed she was, tall, straight, and firm ; and a woman who never failed in an emergency.

"Miss Partridge," said the leading gentleman, "you are just the person I need."

Bella saw her coming, and raised a piercing scream. "I know what you are," she cried. "I see your keys. You are the supervisor of an asylum. Go away from me! Go away from me! O Frederic, Frederic! what have you done to me?"

They carried her to a settee ; they brought in her trunks, and set them down. Then she bounded from her seat, and started forward wildly.

"Where are those men? They must take me back. I

must go to Harry. I must, must go. What will Harry think? What will he do? O Harry, Harry! Frederic will kill me."

"We had better take her up stairs," said the pleasant gentleman. Miss Partridge called him "Dr. Gracio," and assented to his suggestion.

They took hold of Bella's hands gently but firmly. She jerked again, but there was no escape. Then she stood upright, and assumed the dignity of a princess. Her eyes flashed till the very sparks emitted seemed royal fire. It was the latent, ancestral fire of the ancient English Montagues; but these people knew it not. They thought it insanity.

"Doctor," said Miss Partridge, "this business is not proper for you. Send for Moreton."

Then Moreton came, a stout, sandy-whiskered man, the supervisor of the men's department. Tender Dr. Gracio stepped one side. He never liked to see the hard side of his institution. Every thing must be pleasant around him. He retired to his own room, and his emissaries took up the work. They carried her up the winding stairs, they "led her to the den." They laid her on the narrow bed. Then Moreton went out, and Miss Partridge removed the beautiful hat, the gloves, and other outer attire. Bella wept. Great gushing tears poured from her eyes. This was well. Without those tears, she would have been what they pretended she now was. Ah, blessed Nature! Is not she her own best restorative? Weeping saved her from madness; and when her tears had assuaged the heat of her excited system, and she lay calm, Dr. Gracio came up to see her.

"I am very anxious for her," the doctor said to Miss Partridge. "Her brother's letter described her case feelingly. She has an hallucination that she is going to be married, and has even left home prepared for her bridal. Of course her friends are greatly pained."

"She has been in an asylum before, I judge," said Miss Partridge.

"She has just escaped from one. Her hallucination is of long standing. If we could banish it from her mind, and restore her to herself, it would be quite an addition to our fame."

Bella watched them speaking. When they were done, she raised herself and said, "I wish you would let me tell you how it is." Dr. Gracio smiled approvingly ; and, sitting there, she told him her history, briefly but truly, ending with her appointment to meet Harry. "And now," she added beseechingly, "I do wish you would let me go back to New York. What will Harry think?"

"But, my dear, you could not find Harry now. He must be gone ere this."

"No, Harry is not gone. He would not go without me. He is somewhere looking for me. He does not know where to find me."

"Yes, my dear, he knows. Your friends know where you are."

"Harry does not know. It is Harry I want. Do help me find him. Do let me go out of this place. Oh, these cruel, cruel prisons !"

Dr. Gracio stepped gently forward, and laid his fingers on her pulse. The beats were quick and feverish. He turned to Miss Partridge. "Do the best you can. I will send up an opiate."

He went out, and Bella raised her eyes imploringly. "I do not want an opiate. I want to go free. Do tell the doctor to give me my freedom. Nothing else will do me any good."

"By and by we will see about it. Keep calm now, my

dear young lady. Do not distress yourself. We will do
every thing for you that lies in our power."

"I do not want you to do any thing for me. I know
what I want. Nothing that you can do will be of the least
use, as long as you keep me here."

But what did her entreaties avail? Only to be met with
smiles and gentle persuasions, and in the end a quieting
potion. She fell into sleep. The powerful opiate laid her
physical frame in 'slumber, and her soul was obliged to rest;
but when she awoke she was still more distressed, for time
was passing, and every added moment seemed an age
separating her farther and farther from her goal. Three
days passed. Three days of hopeless waiting, walking,
watching, thinking, longing.

She was treated here as a private patient, but she was
none the less a prisoner. Mr. Frederic had forwarded to
Dr. Gracio a check for heavy advance payment, with directions to draw upon him for any amount necessary, and a
request that his sister should receive every available luxury.
Frederic had tried hospital roughness as a cure for her obstinacy; now he would try the opposite course; and
smiling Dr. Gracio complied with his request. He liked
patients backed by men with big purses and generous
minds. A few such inmates were worth halls full of the
other class. He began his work vigorously. He gave
Bella ingress to his own family circle, kept her within his
own well-furnished apartments, took her to ride in his own
private carriage, and his wife even condescended to ride
with them. They rode through the streets of the town,
and skirted its most pleasant borders. They conversed
upon chosen topics, and entertained her with the choicest
bits of their social lives. But what did she care for these?
Even while they were talking, her heart cried in secret
agony, cried for her own, for freedom, and for those she

loved. These strangers were nothing to her. She did wish they would let her alone. She might have lived thus during all her life without seeing unkindness, or hearing any thing that indicated wretchedness in the buildings about her. All disagreeable sights were kept from her; but she felt, notwithstanding, the bands of force, and even in all this kindness she saw the hidden elements of their power.

But Dr. Gracio did not consider himself as using force. He brought in every appliance of kindness. He put his patient into a large, well-furnished chamber, around which there was no appearance of prison or restraint. The windows were natural as all house-windows, even the door was not locked. Seeing this, Bella said to herself, "I will watch my chance. I will get away." But however stealthily she left the room, by day or by night, she could not get beyond the passage; for there sat all the time a guard, a special attendant: and often as Bella entered the passage, the attendant said, "Do you wish any thing, Miss Forresst?" Receiving a negative answer, the girl went on. "Are you going out? I will go with you, and guide you wherever you would like to go."

"Guide me to the station," said Bella.

"Certainly, if Dr. Gracio will give me permission."

The girl spoke in the kindest tones, and made herself into an obsequious servant; yet she was a prison-mistress, and Bella felt it. What cared she to walk with such a guard at her side? What was all this kindness but barbed arrows.

Dr. Gracio set apart servant waiters for his distinguished patient. They carried food to her from his own table. Delicate frostings, rich meats, luscious fruits, and sweet preserves went to her every day; and her body was nourished with the choicest food. It was indeed a blessing;

and she contrasted it with the food in her former asylum, and said to herself, " If we could live by bread alone, then surely we could be contented here: •but we cannot live by bread alone; .there was One who said we could not. We must have words from the mouth of God, and those words are love and truth and peace. I cannot find them here. These people are kind, wonderfully kind; and yet my heart will break, break! Where is Harry? What will he think? Can he ever find me? Who knows where I am except those strange men and Frederic? And Frederic will not tell. The strange men Harry will not see. How will he find me? I will write. No: I cannot write. With all their kindness they would not let me mail a letter. No. Crazy people must not write unless their letters are supervised, *because they worry their friends by writing.* And, under cover of this excuse, all sorts of deceptions are practiced, and cruelties too. I wonder if there are such cruelties here as I used to see. Dr. Gracio is so kind, would he permit such things? And Miss Partridge is an intelligent lady. If I were in the halls, should I see her do as I have seen supervisors do ? "

For an answer to these questions we must not look in the rooms around Bella. We must follow Miss Partridge to the corridors and distant halls, where she is a different person. She is not a woman of hasty temper; but calm, precise, and disciplines for the sole purpose of obedience, with a cool resolution to keep order, and have the patients know their places. Is she a Christian? She thinks she is. Let us see how she cured Lucy Brown of "sauciness."

Lucy was the daughter of poor but virtuous parents. She had been disappointed in love; and being of a delicate, high-toned temperament, she was bewildered after it. Her doctor said she was insane, and prescribed an asylum. Perhaps she was insane. Her great disappointment may have overwhelmed her tender mind, and caused aberration. But, in all his pharmacopœia, had he no restorative but this? To a mind already crushed under its sorrow, why did he add greater sorrow, putting the young girl where there was nothing to make her happy, nothing to take away the poignancy of her grief, and where no new love could come to soften the pain, or alleviate memories?

Lucy's father had no money with which to meet the expenses of the asylum; but the doctor told him that was of no consequence. The State provided for that. Thus Lucy, in reward for her virtue, was made a poor patient. She was carried to the asylum, and added to the long list whose names helped swell the funds. They gave her a cot two feet in width. During the day it was packed away in a cell; at night it was brought out into the hall, and Lucy slept on it. She had no room to herself, nor even a drawer for her clothes. She felt like one in punishment. It seemed to her that she must have done some wrong, and she tried to recall some blot or stain; but her record was clear, her conscience pure. Then she felt that her situation was unjust. Young and high-toned, she could not submit to this life, and to the caprices of the attendants. She could not believe that girls, in no wise her superior, ought to order her from day to day, driving her to work or sit still, as their whims seized them. She determined she would not submit, and answered them back with words as high-spirited as their own. They appealed to Partridge; and she undertook to "break Lucy in." She put her in a chair, and bound her down with a leather strap. Two attendants assisted. Then they procured a bucket of cold water, dipped a sheet in it, and then threw the wet sheet over her head, gathering the folds behind her neck, and tightening it until the points of her features showed through the cloth. Then they seized the wet folds behind, and shook her with force. She shivered; and cold chills ran from her head to her feet.

Then Miss Partridge said, "There! will you stop being saucy now?" Poor Lucy bowed her head. She could not speak; but they understood her assent. She was released, and turned again under the attendants, who tantalized her more than before. She hated them now, and told them so. This time Miss Partridge took her away to a blinded room, strapped her into a chair again, and fastened the chair to the floor. Then, throwing a shawl over her shoulders, she left her there all the day and all the night. Alone, through the dark hours, she sat there. She heard the night-winds moan, heard the nightly, groans, the night-watch tramp; and all those dark hours she sat in her bound chair. It seemed to her that the morning would never dawn; and the striking of the clocks, at one, two, three, four, were so many knells. Alas! they *were* knells. They struck her sensitive system with thrills of unearthly dread. She grew cold; but her hands were tightly bound. The shawl slipped from her shoulders; but she could not draw it up. She could reach neither blanket nor extra garment. While the world around slept, she sat thus in the house where the doctors had put her for cure. What shall we call this remedy? Does science or Christianity afford a name? We call those murderers who kill the body: what shall we call those who shut up minds, and let them slowly die?

To Lucy those night hours in that lone cell were fearful beyond description; and darkness in loneliness had a meaning she had never suspected. Miss Partridge came in the morning; and said solemnly, as if duty laid upon her, "Now do you think you can be obedient to your attendants, and stop your sauciness?"

Lucy answered faintly, " Yes." She was released then;

and Miss Partridge said, " I think she is conquered. I have known women to sit out three such nights before they would yield. Some are subdued at two; and some give up in one."

Miss Partridge was correct. Lucy was conquered. She obeyed the slightest word of the attendants. She obeyed everybody. She never again had a will of her own; never again had a sparkle in her eyes, nor a smile on her checks; never expressed a want; never had natural sense. She was cured of sauciness.

Dr. Gracio, tender-hearted man, never saw the hard acts of his institution. He said to his officers, "Take them away, take them out into the corridors;" and he liked officers who were self-reliant, and could discipline without his aid. For this reason he prized Miss Partridge; and for this reason he also prized Moreton, chief supervisor in the men's department. Moreton was a huge man, with a stolid face, and a chin deep-set and massive jawed. He was perfectly self-reliant, considered himself competent to manage insane people, and boasted of his prowess as Miss Darius did of hers. He was experienced in the business, and liked it.

"Shet up yer head!" said Moreton to a pale, sickly lad who was worrying about home. "Blast yer! I'll put yer carcass where yer can groan to the silent walls!" With that he seized the boy, and dragged him by the heel across the hall, one hundred and eight feet, and then jammed him into a cell. The floor of the hall was full of splinters and rough slivers, that pricked through the boy's clothes, and remained sticking in his shoulders; but what of that? It was but a source of amusement to Moreton, who laughed loudly at the boy's moans.

"Take that, will yer?" said Moreton, thrusting his fist into a man who was attempting to pass him at an open hall door. The man was a new comer, who had not yet learned the strict prison discipline, and seeing the door opened, he started to go out. "And that!" added Moreton, a second time planting his fist in the stomach of the patient. That blow laid the man flat on his back. Then there came an attendant, and helped Moreton. They pitched the poor man into a cell, and there stamped upon and jammed him till life seemed expiring. Then they left him there, and for several weeks he was not seen again.

Dr. Gracio's establishment had a reputation for superior management, and Moreton was an excellent representative of asylum government. Jeremiah Hurd, a man of forty years, had been promised to go home, but, like many others, had to live on promises (there being no fulfilment), and was still held in bonds. He grew discouraged, felt that the promises would never be kept, that he should never go out of his prison, and grew still more discouraged. Then he took the prison-march; and, as he walked back and forth on the rough floor, splinters of the boards peeled up, and, piercing through the soles of his slippers, entered his feet, and remained in the flesh till festering sores were produced. These increased in numbers and size, till they spread and joined together. His feet became like jelly, and began to swell. The inflammation increased, growing higher, till it reached his body. Then his jaws began to set, no food could be got between his teeth, he grew sick, and death drew near, so very near that the attendants even grew alarmed. Still death drew on: nothing now could save the man; and the doctor, seeing the necessity, sent for the wife. She came; but every moment while she sat by her dying husband, Moreton sat there also. He feared the wife might turn back the bed-clothes, and see those feet. That night Mr. Hurd died. He was carried from the asylum in an elegant coffin, provided by his wife. The jellied feet were hidden deep within it. Thus was ended the man who had been repeatedly told that he should soon go home. One patient, bolder than the others, asked Dr. Gracio why he did not let Mr. Hurd go home when he promised him. "Because he was a stubborn man," said the doctor; "and his persistency in his determination to go home was from his insanity."

"It is very curious," the patient responded. "The other day I asked you wherein Chase was insane; and you said because he did not want to go home. You said that rational persons would want to go home."

Dr. Gracio's pleasant face clouded. He turned from this patient. By what right should a patient question him?

Moreton's example, as supervisor, was contagious among the attendants. There was a Mr. Hames suffering from physical disease. He begged for medicine, but did not get it. He grew worse, and begged yet more earnestly. But he was not humble and suave; for he was a man of natural independence, and could not brook the lordly manners of the attendants. He reproved them: they were angry, and would give him neither medicine, nor food such as he could eat. He failed, grew weaker, and sank every day. He begged for something better to eat, or for milk to drink; but nothing was given him. He was a man of property, and offered to pay for what they would bring him; but they would not stir, and he lay there moaning and groaning with pain, and with piteous cries implored them to give him a drink of milk. They called his cries "howling," and let him moan. He became exhausted, suffering thus from day to day. At last the doctors were alarmed, and came to him with offers of help. He said, "Gentlemen, you are too late! I am dying from neglect." At ten o'clock that night, the attendants covered him for the last time. They drew up the bed-clothes, and turned away, saying, "Howl now if you want to!" Then they went out, and locked the door. Mr. Hames was left alone, a prisoner at the mercy of his keepers. Nobody saw him again till morning. No one knew when he passed away; but, when they unlocked his cell door the next morning, he was cold and stiff. He could beg no more for medicine or milk, he could "howl" no more, nor would he any more hear the harsh voices of the attendants.

There was Mr. Sharon, who was the particular object of Moreton's experiments. Mr. Sharon was slightly deranged, and sometimes talked a little flightily. Moreton put him down in a lower wing, where there was no fire, jacketed him, and held him there in the cold days of December, "to take the insanity out of him." He sank beneath such hardships, and ran still lower. His hands were bound tight in the jacket; and he could not move them, even to cover himself when lying in his bed at night. If the bedclothes slipped down, he could not draw them up. The weather was freezing; he had neither light nor fire; and even healthy men could scarce keep warm with the scant hospital coverings. Shivering with cold, Mr. Sharon, still bound in the jacket, weak and trembling, arose and paced the floor. The death angel hovered over him, and was visible on his face. The patients saw it; but what were they? Who heeded their opinions? He still ran down, fainting daily under his strait-jacket, hunger, and the terrible cold. At length death stared out from every lineament. The attendants could no longer hide it. Even Moreton saw it, and Dr. Gracio's oily words could no longer smooth the rough place. Mr. Sharon was then unbound, carried up to a warmer hall, bottles of warm water were put to his feet, and nourishing drinks were brought him; but he had run too low for restoration, his chills were too deep for warmth to remove. They telegraphed to

23

his friends, who came to see him die.   Then they carried him away, and the sad scene was ended.

Charlie Peabody was a young man who had become insane.   Moreton kept him also in that cold wing.   Dr. Gracio and Moreton believed in scientific classifying.   They put the insane sick, or "worst cases" as they called them, down into the lower wards, and had no fire for them there, nor any comforts, holding them there in positions of misery.   Charlie grew weak and feeble and more insane.   He became too weak to walk even to the bathing-tub.   Moreton bade him go.   Charlie said he could not.   Then the attendants took him and dragged him to the bath; and, filling the tub with cold water, they plunged him in.   This was to subdue him.   He chilled, benumbed, grew livid, and could not recover from the shock.   The next day he died.   Thus another victim passed away.   Another coffin came to the great doors of the asylum; and the patients, looking through their grated windows, saw it.   How often are coffins seen at those doors!

But there is a worse affliction than death, and it fell upon John Gould.   Mr. Gould was a man of excellent character and sterling principles.   He was sent to the asylum, as thousands are, by his doctor.   Mrs. Gould had said anxiously, "Is it a good place, doctor?   Will he have kind care?"

"The best possible," was the medical reply.   "Dr. Gracio has not his superior in the country."

Two years had passed, and Mr. Gould still sat beneath this noted physician's care.   It seemed a long time.   His wife and family came to see him occasionally, but were met by the suave words of Dr. Gracio, and went home, leaving the husband and father still there, and leaving, also, liberal sums for his board and care.   Mr. Gould sat still, and felt it all.   He read also the scenes that passed

around him, and roused at last to a belief in his own
rights.

"Doctor," said he, as Dr. Gracio was passing through
the hall, "I have written a letter to my wife, and sealed it.
Will you take it, and mail it?"

"Oh, yes!" smiled the doctor; and, extending his hand,
he took it, and passed along.

Days lengthened into weeks, and no answer came. Mr.
Gould grew anxious. He had his suspicions, and determined to inquire.

"Doctor," said he when next he saw Dr. Gracio, "did
you send my letter?"

"Yes, sir," replied the doctor, hastening on through the
hall.

"Where?" called Mr. Gould.

"Into the fire;" and still he hurried along.

Mr. Gould had not expected this blunt acknowledgment.
He was accustomed to seeing subterfuges and deceptions.
But here was an open, daring acknowledgment of wrong.
Mr. Gould was an upright man, who scorned such usurpations. He sprang after Dr. Gracio, and seized him by the
shoulder. Then he looked him in the face, and said, "Are
you shameless? Dare you say that you have burned the
letter you promised to send to my wife?"

Almost before the words were uttered, two attendants
pounced upon Mr. Gould. They bound him down, they
kicked him, jerked him, and stamped upon him with their
nailed boots. One or two ribs broke; but what of that?
They took him to a cell, laid him on an iron bedstead, and
strapped him down, arms, body, and legs. Shall we say
how long he lay there? The patients could not get into
his room, therefore they could not tell; but several weeks
passed ere he was again seen in the hall; and then what
was he? A wreck of humanity, a shadow of himself

He would no more write letters, he would ask no more for freedom.   His life henceforth would be a living death.

What were the objectionable words that the inquisitive doctor found in that letter?   They were these : "My dear wife, I have always endeavored to live a true and godly life ; I have. helped you rear a family of good children ; I have gathered and saved enough to support me in my old age ; and now to be thrown into prison, to subsist on prison rations, and spend my days in misery, seems hard. I fear you are deceived," and so on.   These truths cost Mr. Gould his reason, which is more than life.

However many grow chronic or die within these walls, no blame is ever attached to the institutions.   The doctors count up the cures, so-called, and publish them exaggerated : the chronic and dying are of small account.   Reformed drunken men* help greatly in increasing the numbers of cures.   Sometimes one man is cured four times in a year. He stays a while, is pronounced cured, goes out, drinks again, is re-committed, and so continues.   Every discharge is recorded as a cure.   Some people are cured, or roused from mental illness, by the antagonistic effects of the surroundings.   The injustices they see and hear rouse them to a defiance that restores them, if they have strength to recuperate : if they have not strength for defiance, they sink to chronic states or die.

Moreton was fond of "breaking in" patients, as hospital managers call it.   He tried to "break in" Mr. Randall, a New-England man of fifty years, — a man whose sons were in Chicago, and other parts of the West, among the enterprising of those places.   Mr. Randall had the misfortune to fall into the hands of the medical faculty, and thence into the asylum.   He was a sturdy, solid man, and could not see the justice of his "treatment."   Moreton and the attendants "put the screws to him."   We beg pardon of the public for using this expression; but, if we describe prison-scenes, we must use prison language. Mr. Randall was kicked and stamped with nailed boot-heels till the marks covered his body. Hope and life paled under such cruel-ties. A patient, looking on, exclaimed, "Good God! We have societies for the prevention of cruelty to animals, where are the societies for the prevention of cruelty to human beings? Shall man, created in God's image, in this day and generation, be thus subjected to man's brutality? Why is it that intelligent men shut up here, and witness-ing such horrors, do not tell of them to the world?"

"Because," said another patient, "when men get out of here, they want to shake off the dust of these remem-brances, and do not care to publish their sorrows to the world from very shame."

Reports of the cell-deaths do not often reach the outer world. The witnesses of these deaths are angels and the unseen God. The records are kept in the archives of the place whither we are all going. We shall meet them there; and then we shall read how the people were lying alone in their little cells; and there was no one by to wipe the death-damps from their brows, or to whisper in tones of soothing love. Then we shall read, also, how the spirits and angels of the great God came and took the sufferers away. Earthly tablets bear no stories of these lone depar-tures; yet such deaths are occurring in every asylum and prison and locked-up house.

In those cells people lie, and die as they live, helpless, hopeless prisoners. The trustees walk through the halls; and many patients look forward to their coming with hope, but their hopes fail when the gentlemen come. The eagle eyes of the overseers and attendants prevent approach to the men, as they walk through with the doctors by their sides. Or, if patients do dare to speak, the ears of the trus-tees seem not to hear.

"Gentlemen," said a patient one day, rising boldly, and meeting them, in Dr. Gracio's establishment, "if you wish to know how things are here, you should stay day and night. You can find out in no other way."

Moreton, following in the rear, ground his teeth, and glared at the patient.

"The Devil take Jones," he muttered. "I should like to lay hands on him; and I *will* by and by. I'll shake daylight out of him, by G—."

Dr. Gracio cut the scene short by hurrying the gentlemen forward; and going out of the hall door, he locked it behind them, saying, "Mr. Jones is a very crazy man. You must excuse his speaking."

Mr. Jones, standing within, helpless, thought, "They may pass us by, nor listen to our complaints; but there is One whom they cannot shut out. His eyes see; his ears hear; and he will rise in judgment to save his suffering ones."

Sometimes, for successive days, and even weeks, Dr. Gracio's sensitiveness would not permit him to go through the halls, except a supervisor walked by his side, to prevent the patients speaking to him. If he walked through alone, the patients, feeling that he had absolute power in the house, went to him with complaints and requests. Miss Partridge told the women that they annoyed the doctor exceedingly by this course; but they only answered, "Who *shall* we go to? If Dr. Gracio cannot listen to the wants of his patients, let him resign, and let the place be filled by some one who *can* listen."

Miss Partridge turned, disgusted, from such unreasonable. remarks. "As though a man like Dr. Gracio was going to wear himself out in listening to such as *you!*" she curtly observed.

Therefore he walked sedately through; and Miss Partridge walked sedately beside him.   Not a woman dared to speak, however pressing her wants.   When he finished his tour in the women's halls, Moreton took him through the men's; and he was safe then.   Misery dared not speak in his presence, nor could anguish utter a word.

Out in the world Miss Partridge would have passed as a very nice woman, a lady of decision, but none the less respected on· that account.   And Moreton was not more brutal in free life than thousands of uneducated men; but this prison-life is a test, a- touchstone, that develops qualities unthought of in open social life.   There are people who will not, and cannot, stay as servants or attendants in these institutions: their sensibilities cannot endure such scenes; and they leave.   There are others who can harden into the life, until nothing is too cruel for them; and these are the people who remain, as a general rule.

Dr. Gracio wrote very excellent reports for printing and public circulation.   His words were as "apples of gold, fitly chosen."   His sentiments, as he expressed them, were Christlike.   He also had a flattering way of speaking, among his patients, of the superior arrangements of his house.   It sounded like boasting; though he intended to inspire them with the idea, that, under his care, they were more comfortable than they would be in more illy-regulated establishments.   The patients to whom he talked were the elegantly-dressed ladies in the "best hall."· To the wretched, in the long, dreary corridors, he never talked. He said to a visiting lady one day, "We have no filthy under-ground cells, where we keep patients; nor rooms four feet square, in which they lie coiled; nor rooms without ventilation."   He often remarked thus to the friends of the patients; and always with a bland, benevolent expression of countenance, that led visitors to think him the most excellent of men, and to publish his praises wherever they went.

A patient, to whom he said the same, replied, " Doctor, if you know of institutions where such cells are used, and that human beings are suffering in them, why don't you make the facts known to the public ? "

He made a slight reply, and turned away. " Patients have such absurd ideas that there is no use in talking with them," he murmured.

Thus asylum officials often say, " Patients have such insane ideas, that no trust can be placed in what they say. There is no use in believing in them."

Thus by the word " insane," the officials disparage the testimony of the persons who suffer under them, while they go on in their unfeeling barbarities.

Asylum cruelties differ in different institutions. If Dr. Gracio had no dungeons and underground rooms in use for patients, he permitted his attendants full sway ; and the very tenderness that he considered a virtue, by keeping him aloof from whatever was disagreeable, left his attendants to their own devices ; and the patients endured the consequences. Hence the sufferings in bath-tubs, when ill-tempered attendants let cold water run over shivering bodies ; and hence, too, the agonies in the blinded rooms, when women, and men too, lay bound all night in leather straps.

Was this fastidious superintendent ignorant of these actions ? He certainly knew that the house was furnished with camisoles, straps, and other instruments of bondage. He knew, also, that attendants were 'constantly changing, bringing in all kinds of tempers to rule his house.

Bella did not see these hard parts of Dr. Gracio's establishment. Her chamber was near his own rooms ; consequently she was free from all unpleasant sounds. She saw only the smiles of Miss Partridge, the pleasant face of Dr. Gracio, and the obsequiousness of the servants. But she felt — her own troubles. Secluded from all that was disagreeable in the house, and supplied with the best they could bestow, she yet could find no happiness. She thought of Harry, and walked her beautiful chamber, considering and pondering. Time was passing. No news of her own came to her. She was a stranger in a strange land, a prisoner without hope. She passed and repassed before her swinging mirror. She clasped her hands, her eyes upturned to heaven, and her raven curls floated back in wild disorder. Her lips moved in agonizing prayer. There were no tears in her eyes; but they burned like coals of fire, and the light in them turned to wild despair. She said in her heart, "No — no. Harry will not come. He will not find me; for though he's a firm, strong man, though he is good and true, Frederic is as firm and strong as he, more polished, more subtle, as wicked as Harry is good, as deceitful as Harry is true. Fred will not tell Harry where I am. No, he will never tell. What *shall* I do? I cannot bear it. I cannot, cannot, cannot bear it. I will not, will not bear it."

The marble-topped table and bureau became as mere dust in her eyes; the carpet was as sand beneath her feet; and even her own flowing curls were matted and unkempt. Her whole life was centred on the one point, freedom against bondage; and her soul was fearfully strained in the contest.

"Calm!" she exclaimed in soliloquy. "They tell me I must be calm! Why, I cannot be calm! I do not want to live! If I cannot have freedom and peace on earth, let me go to heaven. There are no iron bolts and bars in that blest land. Here I can have no peace. Wherever I go, Frederic will pursue me. Oh, what a wicked brother he

24

is! But I could escape his wickedness, I could get away from him, were it not for these prisons! Why does my country build these prisons, with their locks and keys? To shut up the sick and suffering, and cause them to suffer more; to shut up people that they may weep unseen; to give wicked relatives a chance to rule the good; to give blinded relatives a chance to show their want of sight; to give foolish doctors a way to get rid of patients whom they are too ignorant to cure at home; and to give a few officers of the institution a chance to get rich. I know enough about asylums. They are cruel prisons. They feed on the blood of families, and devour their victims. I hate their cruelties, and I hate their kindnesses, so unlike free-life kindness. I want my freedom. I want my mother. I want Harry and Edward and Mortimer. If I can have none of these, I want heaven. O Father above! if there is nothing more for me but these imprisoned days and nights, take me to thyself."

While she was walking thus, a servant looked in; but Bella took no notice. She continued walking and talking, with her hands still clasped, her eyes upturned, and her dishevelled tresses flowing. The servant ran out in affright, flew across the passage, and down the stairs, calling, "Miss . Partridge, Miss Partridge, Miss Forresst is dreadful!"

Then Miss Partridge went up, other women went, and Dr. Gracio followed. They laid Bella on the bed. Fever was in her eyes, fever was on her brain, her head was as fire, her feet as ice, her breath came thick and hot, her speech grew incoherent. She tossed and turned and raved, and uttered half-formed phrases of Mortimer and Harry, of Edward and Emily, and the Norwegian home. Thus she lay, while the fever burned. Her eyes grew hopeless and dim, she took no notice of those around her; the thoughts she had were far away, and she moaned as in great pain. They watched and tended her, staid by her day and night, gave her cooling drinks, and sought by medical arts to assuage her distress. But she heeded not. Her lips were parched, and her hair tangled as she turned in her agony. They tried to comb it, and to keep it smooth, but it would not stay. Miss Partridge said, "We must cut it off;" but Dr. Gracio answered, "It is a pity to cut it. We will try a little longer."

Then they tried, but all in vain. She tossed and raved, the curls matted yet more, and at length they severed them, one by one; and there she lay, with wild, glassy eyes, and shorn locks.

CHAPTER XXIII.

IS there any thing more I can do for you?" asked Harry Forresst, as he stood in the centre of a small hotel parlor beside old Mr. and Mrs. Beale.

"Nothing," they answered in concert. "We shall be every way comfortable. Take good care of yourself, and bring Bella back with you. That is all we ask."

"Never fear for *me*," said Harry, with a full metallic ring in his words. "You can trust *me*."

"Yes, yes, we can. Good-by."

"Good-by," said Harry;" and in the next instant he was outside the hotel, and on his way to the station to take the train for New York.

"The old people will be comfortable," he said to himself, as he hurried on. "A little lonely perhaps, but they won't mind that. It is well I did not tell them all my suspicions. How they would worry!"

Indeed, it was well that he kept his thoughts secret. He only told them, that probably some mistake as to time had delayed Bella. In his heart he thought, "It is Fred, — at least, I fear he has done this" —

What he meant by this, he hardly knew. He was not given to speculative thoughts, and did not attempt to imagine *how* Frederic had prevented Bella's going, but hastened on, resolved to learn *how*, and to find her. He reached New York, and, as soon as possible, appeared in

Brooklyn, at his sister's house. He found company there, guests whom his sister was entertaining; but he heeded them not. With a pre-occupied air he asked to see Mrs. Bergmann in a private room. He was shown into a small room, and Mrs. Bergmann soon entered.

"Why, Harry!" she said, advancing to take his hand. "I am quite surprised."

Harry did not take her hand. He was standing; and he turned towards her, his earnest eyes piercing her with their inquiring expression.

"Nellie, where is Bella?"

For a moment Mrs. Bergmann quailed. Then she said, "I thought Bella was going with you."

Harry's eyes dilated. He looked at her more searchingly.

"Is not Bella here, in this house?"

"No, Harry. I told you I thought she was going with you."

"Is mother here?" he asked.

"No: mother and Frederic have gone back to Boston."

"There I am going too! Good-by."

He was half way out of the room before she comprehended him.

"What do you mean, Harry? Where are you going?" she called after him.

"To Boston," he answered; and, closing the door behind him, he was in the street ere she moved from her position. Then she went to the window, and looked out, to be sure she was not dreaming. She saw him going away with the utmost velocity, never once turning his head to look back. She watched till he disappeared from view; then murmuring, "Strange," she slowly returned to her guests.

Did you ever see a strong man rouse from a lifetime reverie? Did you ever see a firm man when he first be-

came conscious that he had inward powers? Such a man
at such a moment might have been seen by watching
Harry Forresst in that journey between New York and
Boston. Powers that had slumbered in him hitherto awoke
now, and he felt deep emotions such as he had never
dreamed he possessed.

As he stepped from the car in Boston, and moved majes-
tically away from the station, he thought, "Yes, I am a
match for Frederic. I believe I have his strength of will;
but God grant I may use it for a better purpose than
he."

Then his thoughts assumed a prayerful form; and he said,
"Let me do right, O Father, — help me now ! "

He entered his sister's house, and he went straight to her
room.   He stood before her, holding his hat in his left hand,
and said, "Eunice, where is Bella ? "

She was frightened, both at seeing him there, and at his
manner. Rising, she said, "I do not know. I thought
she went with you."

At that moment the mother entered; and Harry turned
to her.   "Mother," said he, and a strange tenderness filled
his voice, "where is Bella ? "

"Harry," replied the old lady, a tremor seizing her,
"isn't she with you ? "

"No, mother. I have not seen her; but somebody knows
where she is, and I shall find out."

He started toward the door; but the mother intercepted
him.

"Harry," she said solemnly, " do not go to Frederic now.
Wait."

" Why should I wait ? "

" My son, I see a strange light in your eyes; and Frederic has a temper. I dare not have you two meet now."

Harry stooped, and put his arm gently about his mother.

Then he said, "I know I am angry, as I never was angry before; but I shall curb my temper, in the strength of the Lord I shall govern it. I shall do Frederic no bodily harm; but I must find Bella. Pray for me, mother, while I am with my brother: I shall need your prayers. Eunice, be tender of her."

Then he gently placed his mother in Eunice's arms, and went out.

Frederic was busy as Harry entered his office. Some gentlemen were with him. He was settling the details of some business with them. A clerk was industriously writing.

Frederic did not see Harry, nor hear him, till he was aroused by a tap on his shoulder. He turned, and met Harry face to face.

"Frederic," said Harry, "where is Bella?"

"Upon my honor," was Frederic's reply, "I thought she had emigrated with you."

Harry looked Frederic steadily in the eyes, and repeated his question.

"Where is Bella?"

Frederic recoiled slightly. For the first time in his life he retreated one slight step. The light of Harry's eyes was too strong for him. He rallied, however, in a moment, and replied haughtily, —

"What should I know of her? You took her under your care. Couldn't you keep her?"

"Frederic!" said Harry, and his voice was hollow with suppressed emotion, "*where is Bella?*"

"Upon my honor!" responded Mr. Frederic. "You seem a little beside yourself, and have chosen a very inopportune time to trouble me with your vagaries. Take a seat, will you, till I have finished with these gentlemen?"

Then, with polished ease, he turned to the gentlemen

who were staring with half-suppressed curiosity, and blandly said, "Pardon this interruption, gentlemen. We will go on."

They went on, and every minutiæ was as carefully attended to as though no interruption had occurred ; and yet Frederic knew that Harry's eyes were every moment fastened on him.

At last the two brothers were alone; and there, in that business office, they stood and looked each other in the face. Harry repeated his question.

"Where is Bella ? "

"You are very presuming," Frederic returned. "What do I know of Bella? You took her yourself, as you well know."

"Frederic," said Harry, "you know she never came to me. Tell me where she is, or I shall never leave your side, nor cease to ask you where she is."

"So, then, we are to have two lunatics in the family ! Upon my honor, you are as crazy as she is ! "

Harry made no reply; but he fastened his eyes upon Frederic's face, and remained quiet. Frederic arranged his papers, wrote a little, but grew uneasy. Those eyes were too powerful for him. He arose, called his clerk, gave him a few directions, then took his cane and gloves, put his hat upon his head, and went out. Harry followed; and, as Frederic came upon the broad sidewalk, Harry was at his side.

"Upon my honor," said Frederic, turning angrily toward him. "This is unbearable. What do you want?"

"Bella."

Frederic swung his cane, the mustache twitched, but he did not speak; and the two walked on. Frederic walked at random, up one street, down another; but Harry was not to be wearied. Sturdily and steadily he marched by his brother's side.

At last Frederic's patience gave way. With an upward fling of the cane, he turned to Harry.

"One would think you had lost your senses! Why do you follow me so?"

"Tell me what you have done with Bella."

"You are making a bold assertion," said Frederic. "I — indeed! — what have I done? You took her yourself."

"Frederic," said Harry, his eyes emitting suppressed wrath, "we will waste no words. I told you you would rue the day you played me false. Tell me now into what asylum or other hole you have put Bella, or "

Frederic interrupted him.

"Upon my honor! If you have an accusation against me, the law is open. You have threatened me with it: now try it. *Prove* that I have put her anywhere."

"It is too late for law," Harry replied. "While I should be getting out writs, and procuring evidence, she would be pining, perishing, or going mad in those mad-houses! Besides, after I had proved every thing against you, she would be still *unfound;* for these institutions are all over the country, and you can move her from place to place, keeping her always out of my reach. No: I shall not try law, except the law of strength and right. Tell me what you have done with her!" and once more Harry's eyes pierced Frederic's soul. It was a contest of strength against strength: the strength of truth and right was pitted against falsehood and wrong. Truth showed her supremacy. Frederic felt that Harry's power over him was mightier than men's laws. He could have equivocated in court, and could have brought witnesses to sustain his position; but this silent witness of eye to eye was more than his nerves could sustain. He turned towards his home, his mustache and his cane twirling as by one spiral impulse. Harry kept steady pace with every step. Frederic ascended the elegant steps of his house.　Harry went up by his side.　Frederic entered the hall and the drawing-room.　Harry silently entered with him.　Frederic turned then, and glared at him.

"How long do you intend to follow me ? "

"What have you done with Bella ? " asked Harry.

Frederic turned, and went swiftly to the library.　Harry followed as quickly.　The servants were attracted, and soon notified Mrs. Forresst that her husband's brother had come home with him, and they were " having a frolic in the library."　She ordered an extra plate laid, and presently they were both summoned to dinner.　They did not go. Mrs. Forresst soon came in : she kindly asked if either was ill.

"No: pre-occupied."　Frederic answered.

She returned to the table, wondering.

An hour passed.　Frederic had neither moved nor spoken. Nor had Harry.　Then Mrs. Forresst came again, and pleaded to know the trouble.　Neither of the men explained it.

Another hour passed.　Frederic opened a book.　He tried to read, and to appear indifferent; but he could not. Those eyes — he never knew Harry had such eyes !　He turned every way to get from their gaze, but he could not. He rushed to the door to escape.　Harry rushed with him. He went silently back.　Harry also returned.　The doom he had given Bella had recoiled upon himself.　He was under guard in his own house.　The servants whispered together.　They began to suspect it was a serious frolic.

It was one o'clock that night when Frederic's wife came in, and, seating herself between the two men, began seriously to inquire the cause of their strange conduct.　Little by little she found it out.　Slowly the truth came to her. Then she turned to Harry.

"But this man whom Bella likes is very unsuitable for her, I am told," she remarked.

"That is not the point," said Harry. "I will enter into no discussion as to that. The question is this. Has Frederic a right to imprison her, and bring upon her a life-blight of misery, because she does not please him in all she does?"

Mrs. Forresst turned to her husband. "Tell us how it is," she said.

It was not simply because she asked, nor because the hour was late, nor because he was weary, that Frederic answered. It was because his falsehood had yielded to the continued pressure of Harry's truth. Harry's clear eyes had conquered. The almost indomitable spirit of Frederic Forresst succumbed and yielded then. He arose, took his wife's hand within his arm, and, turning to Harry, he said, "You will find her at the asylum in ——. I could do no better for her than to put her under the care of Dr. Gracio, the most celebrated mental physician of the country."

He bowed, and turned to go; but Harry waved his hand imperiously, and pointed to the writing materials on the table.

"Give me a permit to take her out," he said. "I will have no obstacles in my way when I get there."

Once more Frederic looked at Harry. It was eye to eye, and face to face, for a moment. Then the battle ended. The victory was won. The clear eyes of Harry looked unflinchingly upon Frederic's face. Frederic's eyes drooped. His mustache relaxed, his hand trembled. He soon steadied himself, and wrote the permit. As he handed it to Harry, he said, "It would be better to put *you* in than to take *her* out."

"If the places are so beneficial, it would be well to go in yourself," was Harry's response.

Thus they parted. Harry went from the house, Frederic to his room. Harry said, "Father above, I thank thee." Frederic said, "Don't ask me any thing about it," and petulantly pushed his wife from him.

Harry thought of his mother, but would not go to her at that late hour. He sought her in the morning, and comforted her by telling her the result, and assuring her that he would find Bella, and then it would all be right. He kissed the old checks, and said, " I shall come back and see you. It may be I shall take you out there yet, when we get settled." Then he went steaming across the country with Frederic's permit in his pocket. He took it out, and examined it as he went.

"Writing those few lines was the hardest thing Fred ever did," he said musingly. "I saw the perspiration on his brow. Well, what will not a man's temper lead him to do ? "

He went on then. The way seemed easy now. " I will get her," he thought; "and Fred will be punished enough by knowing that we have conquered him."

Thus Harry thought, and tranquillized as he drew near Bella. He felt like a man emerging from darkness, and like a conqueror in the cause of right. He looked forward to his greeting with Bella, thought of Mr. and Mrs. Beale in waiting, and also of the coming journey, and of the expectant family to whom he was going.

With all these thoughts in his mind, he came to the establishment of Dr. Gracio. He entered the public office, and inquired for Miss Forresst. They told him she was too ill to be seen. They should not have said it. Harry roused at the words. "Too ill! Let me see her." Dr. Gracio assumed his most professional blandness, and began a description of her situation; but Harry only said, "Let me see her ! " Miss Partridge cast a deprecatory glance, and feared lest the patient could not bear a visit: "It might injure her." Harry said again, "LET ME SEE HER!" His voice had the ring of decision, his manner was impetuous, like the rushing of a fresh mountain torrent. To resist him was like resisting Nature itself, and the law-constituted guardians gave way. They led him up the stairs. He entered her beautiful chamber, and paused beside her bed. He looked in her eyes, and saw them glassy and vacant. He laid his hand on her forehead and spoke to her, but she knew him not.

Then the heart of the man went into agony. He bowed his bearded face to hers, he touched her parched lips, and said in a hollow voice, "Bella, *my belle Bella*, speak to me. Don't you know me? I am Harry, old Harry. Do speak to me one little word!"

But a moan was her only answer; and as she turned her burning head, and he saw her short, shorn hair, his soul went down like lead. One deep groan went through him, such a groan as only a strong man gives. He turned, and waved his hand. "Please go out from me: let every one go out. I want to be alone."

There was a dignity in the tone of his voice, a majesty in the expression of his face; and they who looked upon him were awed. They went out, one by one, silently and softly disappearing: the door was closed; he was alone, with the shorn head and the glassy eyes before him.

Then he clasped his iron arms about her, laid his broad, bronzed face upon her cheek, the dew of his breath fell over her like fragrance, and the warmth of his earnest soul penetrated the closed, burning pores of her system; and, in the depth of his earnestness, he groaned, —

"O my sister! my sorrowful, broken sister! I had none that I loved as I loved thee! And now the curls that our mother gave thee are shorn, thine eyes are glassy

25

and wild, and when I speak thou knowest it not!   Accursed be these asylum walls, and accursed be these
asylum laws; for, without their aid, Frederic, with all his
strong will, could never have brought thee to this!"

As he stooped and enfolded her thus, the magnetic power
of his breath, the old home influence, the old home love,
stole from his honest frame; and his breath went into her
soul, thrilling over her face, and warming it with natural
heat.   It was the breath of her own, for which she had
yearned.   It was the breath of one who drew from the
same mother's life, of one whose father gave to them both
incipient birth; and now as he leaned, pressing his brawny
face to hers, the spirit within him whispered to her soul.
Not a word was spoken, not a sound was audible; yet the
maiden heard, and her spirit revived, for it felt the soul of
its kindred calling.   It was as the voice of God: yea, it
was the voice of God; for God, who created flesh and
blood, created it male and female, to be husband and
wife, from whom should spring brothers and sisters, thus
creating the natural relations of blood, and thus forming
ties that are to be sundered only by him.   Neither
physicians nor prisons nor asylums nor governments
have a right to sunder ties of blood, of which the marital
tie is the fountain.

And there the rough man sat, breathing into the maiden
the breath of life.   Unconsciously he did his work.   Unconsciously to himself, but not to God.   He watched them
both; he heard the still prayer; he saw the work that
it was good; he breathed upon it the "breath of life;"
and Bella became "a living soul."   The Master came
down, and, touching her heart, said, "Maiden, arise!"
The blessed Master! He saw his servant unwittingly
doing God's work.   Yes, Harry was healing spirit by
spirit.   He was not forcing the soul to love that which it

could not love, to be contented within a hedge of prison-
bars, to tread a path of bondage, nor to abandon its sacred
oaths. He was calling kindred spirit back to its own.

"Bella!" said he in tones of earnest depth, "Bella,
speak to me! Oh! my Bella, my sister, speak to me!"

Then she turned slowly her head, looked up in the eyes
that were looking in hers, and her suffering spirit seemed
to recognize its own life-blood. She looked up earnestly in
those kind eyes, and a new light darted into her own. It
was the blue, her native blue, the blue that was latent in
his. He saw it, he knew it: hope came in his heart.

"She is not quite gone," he thought. "Love can call
her back. Kindred love can waken her dying soul. She
wants her own. *La belle Bella* always loved her own."

Then he passed his hand across her brow, touched sadly
her shorn head, and, still breathing his warm breath over
her, groaned, and his spirit yearned in speech. "Bella,
come back to life! Bella, I have found you; and I will
never leave you again! Speak to me! Speak! One
word! Speak!"

Slowly her spirit seemed to come. Slowly through the
burning tendrils of her frame, slowly through the wild
raving of her face and eyes, her own sweet spirit came,
and, forcing itself up through the tortured faculties, found
its way out. Her own true soul gleamed forth, and recognized its kindred. Then her lips moved, her eyes spoke,
her cheeks flushed naturally, she threw her arms about his
neck, and his soul thrilled in deep emotion. He heard the
words, the thrilling words, "Harry! my Harry! my own,
own Harry."

Thus was she rescued from madness and soul death.
Thus God restored her spirit, and gave to his servant
Harry the fruition of his labors.

Harry gave Dr. Gracio no explanation of the family

troubles, but he showed him the paper that Frederic had written and signed; and, when Bella was able to ride, Harry dressed her head with some false hair that he bought, and took her away. He watched her as a mother watches an infant, while they rushed to the broad Western field in an easy car; and his heart swelled with a gratitude he had never known before. He had earned his happiness; and she, leaning on him, said softly, "Harry, my own, own Harry!"

Thus they went, and Mr. and Mrs. Beale sat by in grateful silence.

CHAPTER XXIV.

IN "Old and New," February, 1872, there is an article by Oliver Dewey, from which we quote a few lines. He says, "Infancy comes into the world like a royal heir, and takes possession as if the world were made for itself alone. Itself is all it knows. It will by and by take a wider range. There is a natural process of improvement in the very progress of life. . . . Selfishness, which is the excess of a just self-regard, is the one form of all evil in the world. The world cries out upon it, and heaps upon it every epithet expressive of meanness, baseness, or guilt. And let it bear the branding scorn; but let us not fail to see, though selfishness be the satirist's mark, and the philosopher's reproach, and the theologian's argument, the real nature and value of the principle from which it proceeds. Self-hood, I have preferred to call it; self-love, be it, if you please. . . . This magnificent *I*, — and I emphasize it, because all meanness is thought to be concentrated in that word, — this mysterious and magnificent *I*, this that one means when he says I, we may utter, but can never explain, nor fully express it. . . . 'I think, therefore I am,' said the philosopher; but the bare utterance of the word 'I' yields a vaster inference. No animal ever knows what that word means. It is some time before the little child learns to say 'I.' It says, 'Willy or Ellen wants this or that, will go here or there.'

25*

"What is insanity but the wreck of this personality? The victim loses himself. And the morally insane, the prodigal, when he returns to reason and virtue, returns to himself.

"A man's self," says Thackeray, "must be serious to him, under whatever mask or disguise or uniform he presents it to the public."

These remarks on insanity are true. An insane person has lost himself or herself. The *I*, the tenant and owner of the earthly tabernacle, is gone, or has become an injured tenant; and, in the close interlacing of the human house and its occupant, neither can be injured without hurting the other. The *I* of a man fills every space and particle of him; is in every fibre, atom, construction, and interstice. In his physical frame, his nerves, his delicate fibrous skin, all over him, through him, bounding, rebounding, acting, doing, quickening, and leading hither and thither, *I* is the spirit that animates, and the spirit is the *I*. It wills, and thinks, and moves the organic clay by which it is environed;' and, in its turn, it is moved upon, and acted upon, by the earthly body that it animates. We are children of law, and our organizations are ruled by the same laws that govern Nature in all her departments. Of all constructions on the crust of this globe, the human system is most complex, most artistic, delicate, and wonderful; yet to nothing are we so savage and unthinkingly cruel as to these very organizations. In us dwell thought and reason and immortal loves. We have each a personality, — an individuality that cannot be disturbed without creating pain.

What each individual needs is his or her own individual self in purity and freshness. An Irish woman weeping "behind the bars," expressed herself thus: "I want meself, meself, me own, own self. Why don't they give me **back** me own, own, self, and make me what I used to be?"

Ah, poor woman! How could the hospital give her back her own, own self? Have hospitals a self for each individual applicant? Are they God, that they have the mobile power of furnishing selves to Irish, French, German, Swede, English, American, young, old, learned, unlearned, grave, or gay? Have they all kinds of selves, with their multiplicities of attributes and peculiarities of natures? Is it possible for one set of human-made, stringent rules, to restore to each person his or her God-stamped individualities? Insanity is a disease, but it rests on a cause. Something produces it, and that *something* should be the subject of " treatment." The causes of insanity. are as various as the persons diseased; differing according to age, sex, temperaments, pursuits, and other conditions. No two persons are alike in these respects, and no two should be treated alike for mental diseases.

When insanity is caused by physical disorders, the body should be healed. This can be done outside of asylums more easily than within. When insanity is caused by stricken affections, domestic troubles, or pecuniary difficulties, these soul afflictions should be healed by appliances of their own nature. When insanity is caused by the patient's own sins, reformatory measures are needed, but not the crushing, soul-trying measures of prison-asylums. It is cruel to keep people in locked rooms, suffering from nervous, physical, and soul derangements, while the causes of these derangements are unnoticed, never receiving medical or other attention. Mind, soul, spirit, intellect, — all are under law; and Nature is intimately and powerfully associated with these departments of humanity, and must and will have sway. In asylums Nature is denied.

If a farmer has a field of stunted, badly-growing grain, does he build walls about it, and shut it in from the sun and rain? Or does he let it lie open to the mists, the storms, and clear warm sky, looking anxiously towards these things as helps to bring back the wayward field ? Does he let the earth lie dormant ? or does he stir up the fallow ground, so that the smiles of God may enter in ? That which thou doest for thy stunted field, do also for thy wife or daughter, or poor old father ! Take them out of the asylums and locked-up houses, and give them the free winds and suns and storms of life ! Have patience with them. Shall men have patience with fallow ground, and not with their own flesh and blood ?

The human system is a harp of ten thousand strings, a lyre of exquisite finish, a lute of symphonies. The prick of a pin will cause shivering thrills in a whole body ; a word of unkindness will create unutterable agonies. We are full of delicate nerves ; and a chord touched by accident in one part of a human body will vibrate through the whole system. And yet the possessors of this wonderful mechanism grow up and live in almost total ignorance of themselves constructively. They neither understand their own organisms, nor what they can endure, nor for what they are fitted, nor how to repair themselves if injured.

It is time for the intelligence of mankind to be directed to the study of itself. Shall we have our land covered with asylums, penitentiaries, prisons, and other tortures for erring minds ? Let the intelligence of the country save the country from these evils, by giving the people such instruction as will help save them. Many aberrations are the result of absolute ignorance among the people. Hundreds and thousands are now lying in asylums, ay, and in penal punishment, who fell into those conditions from utter ignorance of themselves.

Our common schools teach grammar, geography, arithmetic, and the arts of reading and spelling. There is another science that should be added immediately, — the

science of *man*, as he is wondrously and beautifully made;
what will injure the human system, and what will preserve
it, should be as universally taught in our public schools as
are reading and writing. Little children would be delighted in the study of themselves. Their own internal constructions are sources of wonder to all young people, and
proper instruction would save thousands in life and happiness. Children value themselves, and prize the life that has
been given them. They would not knowingly injure themselves, and they would not forget true instruction as they
advance to mature life. Text-books on human life should
be elemental'and progressive, just as in grammar and other
sciences.

When we think seriously of the myriads of contingencies
surrounding human lives, the extreme delicacy of the
human system, and the ignorance of themselves in which
people live, it is not a marvel that insanity, crime, or other
diseases, should appear to mar the exquisite workmanship.

We teach children spiritually. We tell them, that if
they sin they will be punished, and will never go to heaven.
But this is not all we should teach them. We should
teach them the penalties of errors and wrong, just as we
would teach them any natural science; thus enlightening
their understandings as well as touching their emotions.
Vague fears, or anticipations of something in the dim
future, have not sufficient power to hold people against the
seductions of passions. Passions clamor for instant gratification, and the victims risk the vague, spiritual future.
Children should learn that crimes, diseases, and insanity
are the natural results of broken natural laws; and we
can never have a healthy vigorous country till people
understand themselves as creations of laws fixed by Nature
with physical penalties for violations.

A recent writer has attempted to prove that insanity is

a crime. If insanity is a crime, then all diseases are
crimes ; for insanity is a disease. It is caused, mayhap,
by people's own mistakes and perversities ; but we may
say the same of all diseases.

Nearly akin to insanity, almost its counterpart, is nervousness ; and innumerable women who have no disease
but nervousness are shut into our asylums by physicians.
In these weak states, they are expected to endure the trials
and aggravations of imprisonment. No one has patience
with nervous people. They bear their sufferings without
sympathy. Yet pain of the nerves is the keenest, the
most distressing, of all pain, except soul pain. Why do
not physicians know, that to treat either soul or nervous
pain with impatience or harshness is to be impatient and
harsh with the very Divinity itself? The soul is God in
man. The nerves are *God's* electric telegraphs. These
rest on the physical organizations for earthly supports.
To touch them is to touch the Great Unseen.

We talk of cohesion, gravitation, heat, motion, electricity, and numberless hidden adjuncts ; but behind all
these there lies a power that defies our capabilities to
understand. This is the power that we call God. The
mighty forces are his nerves. The material part of the great
cosmos is his garment. We, being made in his image,
have a soul which is his essence ; nerves that are to us as
forces ; and the material body, which is our garment.
When we touch the human nerves with pain, we touch
that which touches the soul, which touches God. The
nerves are ethereal, delicate, higher than the body, and
made by God as messengers between the priceless soul and
its garment. When physicians, or others, treat the nerves
lightly, the sin is scarcely less than mistreating the soul.
Nerves are *our* electric soul telegraphs. They are deftly
intertwined within us, responding to every thought, vibrat-

ing to every thrill. If they become diseased, the consequences to our bodies and souls are on the same plan that the consequences would be to creation, if the mighty forces that lie between God and the material universe were destroyed. If these great forces were disturbed, the power of the great eternal Spirit over the material universe would be gone, and destruction of present existences must ensue. So in the human system, the most intense agonies, and certain destruction, follow injured nerves. They are the visible wires on which the powers of thought run, as electricity runs on wires of iron. Break a wire, and electricity no longer uses it. Sunder a nerve, and soul no longer uses it; but the body quivers in pain. With these delicate organisms we live in ignorance.

It may be said that all people cannot become physicians. We do not want they should. We would have fewer doctors, not more. But all people can learn the primary rules of life, its foundations, laws, methods of preserving nature in its purity; how to avoid that which injures, and why it injures; how body and soul are combined; and how to judge of themselves and their families, and thus save themselves from quackery, inebriated doctors, and doctors who can never practise properly, because Nature never gave them suitable judgment.

J. G. Holland says, "My physician shall walk hand in hand with my pastor, in my esteem, confidence, and affection. He shall be welcome to my table, my hearthstone, and my heart; but I utter no more than a self-evident truth, when I say, that, because a man passes an examination before a corps of medical professors, he is not, necessarily, qualified for a physician; and that there are members of the profession who sit in their offices, with their diplomas signed and sealed, ay, and framed and glazed before them, impatiently waiting for patients, who vulgarly look upon their profession as a trade, and in whose care it would not be safe to risk a sick horse worth twenty-five dollars."

This is the testimony of J. G. Holland, given to a public that will readily indorse the sentiment; and yet that public allows these physicians, by law, to sign certificates that banish the finest people to cells of prison-like chill, and to hopeless misery. The great public lays its head on the block before these physicians; and they do with us as they will. Our people, intelligent as they are, are powerless before physicians, because of ignorance. When we are ill, we all lie down together, the old and the young, the learned and the unlearned, — all classes; and doctors gather over us. They write their prescriptions in unknown tongues; and we are satisfied. They talk in big-sounding words; and we are dumb before their faces. They concoct strange compounds; and we swallow them. They send us to prison; and we go. We know nothing of ourselves, and dare not dispute their words.

At present, if young people learn how to take care of themselves, to guard their health, or keep themselves from the encroachments of inward passions, it is by chance. A maxim here, or an ignorant direction there; a chance word from some relative, or a religious precept of eternal judgments, — are all the sources from which the masses of children learn of themselves. Never a lesson on the natural and scientific retributions which the God of nature and revelation has implanted in humanity is taught our children; and yet there is not one violation of natural laws but has its penalty. Crime, in all its forms, has its own penalties affixed in the secret alchemics of creation. These penalties cannot be evaded. Violations of physical laws are followed by physical ills. Violations of moral law have penalties of moral bearing. These penalties are as sure, and may be as absolutely depended upon, as the fact that cold follows the absence of the sun, or heat accompanies its presence. These human laws and penalties should be reduced to science; and, beginning elementarily, should be taught in every school of our intelligent land.

With our church-spires everywhere pointing heavenward, our ministers preaching the words of life, our Bibles lying on home-stands, our public schools where our children seek the streams of knowledge free, our colleges, libraries, printing-presses, and orators, there is no need that we be overrun by asylums, penitentiaries, catastrophes caused by sin, or any ignorance. We have the means to spread among the people such knowledge as will preserve them from evil, re-create them, and bring to the next generations pristine strength and purity.

26

CHAPTER XXV.

"God pity the wretched prisoners, in their lonely cells to-day!
Whate'er the sins that tripped them, God pity them! I say.
Only a strip of sunshine, cleft by rusty bars;
Only a patch of azure, only a cluster of stars;
Only a barren future to starve their hopes upon;
Only the stinging memories of a past that's better gone;
Only scorn from women, only hate from men;
Only remorse to whisper of a life that might have been.
Once they were little children; perhaps their little feet
Were led by a gentle mother toward the golden street.
If, therefore, in life's forest, they since have lost their way,
For the sake of her who loved them, God pity them! I say.

And you who judge so harshly,
    Are you sure the stumbling-stone
That tripped the feet of others
    Might not have tripped your own?
Are you sure the sad-faced angel
    Who writes your errors down
Will give to you more honor
    Than to him on whom you frown?

Or if a steadier purpose unto your life is given, —
A stronger will to conquer, a smoother path to heaven;
If, when temptations meet you, you crush them with a smile;
If you can chain pale passions, and keep your lips from guile, —
Then bless the hand that crowned you, remembering as you go,
'Twas not your own endeavor that shaped your nature so;
And sneer not at the weakness which made a brother fall,
For hands that lift the fallen God loves the best of all.

> Oh ! pray for the wretched prisoners,
>   All over the land to-day,
> That a holy hand in pity
>   May wipe their guilt away."

.   .   .   .

The Rev. E. H. Chapin says, " In nine cases out of ten, crime is no proof of special depravity, apart from general depravity; and that the circumstances have just so much weight as this, that, put you or me in just those same circumstances, in nine cases out of ten we should be criminals too.   In the same circumstances involves a great deal.   It involves an hereditary taint stamped in the very mould of birth; it involves physical misery; it involves the worst kind of social influence; it involves the pressure of all the natural appetites, rioting in the need of the body and this darkness of the soul.   And it implies no suspicion of a man's moral standard, it is no insult to his self-respect, to tell him, that, under similar conditions, it is extremely probable he would have been a criminal too.   Reasoning in an arm-chair is very proper, and often very accurate; but the logic of starvation is too peremptory for syllogisms.   We have grown up in pure light and air, appeased with the comforts, and braced by at least the current morality, of society.   But concerning these degraded ones, what some call ' charity ' is no more than ' justice.'   It is no more than justice to say, — all the conditions being considered, — that, as to the vast majority of them, crime is no proof of special depravity.   It is the genuine humanity that is there, no base metal.   It came from the common mint: somewhere you will find upon it a faint scar of the divine image; but the coin was pitched into this bonfire of appetite and blasphemy, and it has come out a cinder.   God made them complete souls, and stamped his image upon them; but they have fallen into the dark and dreary ways; the fierce flames have hardened them; the foul air has tainted them; and their special depravity, over and above the common depravity, is the infection of circumstances."

Thus says one of our influential clergymen. But what avails it for our learned men to see these truths, if no practical results are to follow? If criminals are still to feel the execrations of mankind binding their fetters of bondage, this insight into the causes of their crimes is useless.

Relevant to this subject, and as though the Lord had sent them for use on these pages, two little books appear at hand. The books were published A.D. 1845. They were written by L. Maria Child, and entitled, "Letters from New York." She says, "I was once visiting a friend in prison for debt; and, through the grated windows, I could see the outside of the criminals' apartments. On the stone ledges beneath their windows alighted three or four doves; and hard hands were thrust out between the iron bars to sprinkle crumbs for them. The sight brought tears to my eyes. Hearts that still loved to feed doves must certainly contain somewhat that might be reached by the voice of kindness. I had not then reasoned on the subject; but I felt, even then, that prisons were not such spiritual hospitals as ought to be provided for erring brothers. . . .

"The wisest political economy lies folded up in the maxims of Christ. . . .

"The cure for all the ills and wrongs, the cares, the sorrows, and the crimes, of humanity, all lie in that one word, LOVE. It is the divine vitality that everywhere produces and restores life. To each and every one of us, it gives the power of working miracles if we will. . . . Even the poor, despised donkey is changed by love's magic influence. When coerced and beaten, he is vicious, obstinate, and stupid. With the peasantry of Spain, he is a petted favorite, almost an inmate of the household. The children bid him welcome home, and the wife feeds him from her hands. He knows them all, and he loves them all; for he feels in his inmost heart that they love him. . . . The best tamer of colts that was ever known in Massachusetts never allowed whip or spur to be used; and the horses he trained never needed the whip. Their spirits were unbroken by severity, and they obeyed the slightest impulse of the voice or rein with the most animated promptitude; but rendered obedient to affection, their vivacity was always restrained with graceful docility. He said it was with horses as with children : if accustomed to beating, they would not obey without it; but if managed with untiring gentleness, united with consistent and very equable firmness, the victory once gained over them was gained forever.

"In the face of all these facts, the world goes on manufacturing whips, spurs, the gallows, and chains; while each one carries within his own soul a divine substitute for these Devil's inventions, with which he might work miracles, inward and outward, if he would. Unto this end let us work, with unfaltering faith. Great is the strength of an individual soul, true to its high trust, — mighty is it, even to the redemption of a world."

Having visited Blackwell's Island, Mrs. Child says, " As I looked up at the massive walls of a prison, it did my heart good to see doves nestling within the shelter of the deep, narrow, grated windows. I thought what blessed little messengers of heaven they would appear to me, if I were in prison; but instantly a shadow passed over the sunshine of my thought. Alas! doves do not speak to *their* souls as they do to *mine ;* for they have lost their love for gentle and childlike things. *How* have they lost it? Society, with its unequal distribution, its perverted education, its manifold injustice, its cold neglect, its biting

26*

mockery, has taken from them the gifts of God.   They are placed here in the midst of green hills, and flowing streams, and cooing doves, after the heart is petrified against the genial influence of such sights and sounds.

"As usual, my organ of justice was roused into great activity by the sight of prisoners. 'Would you have them prey on society?' said one of my companions. I answered, 'I am troubled that society has preyed upon *them*. I will enter no argument about the right of society to punish these sinners; but I say she *made* them sinners. How much I have done towards it, by yielding to popular prejudice, obeying false customs, and suppressing vital truths, I know not; but doubtless I have done, and am doing, my share. God forgive me ! If he dealt with us as we deal with our brother, who could stand before him ? . . .

"'The secrets of prisons, so far as they are revealed, all tend to show that the prevailing feeling of criminals, of all grades, is that they are *wronged*. What we call justice, they regard as an unlucky *chance;* and whosoever looks calmly and wisely into the foundations on which society rolls and tumbles (I cannot say on which it rests, for its foundations heave like the sea) will perceive that they are victims of chance. . . . That criminals so universally feel themselves victims of injustice is one strong proof that it is true; for impressions entirely without foundation are not apt to become universal. If society does make its own criminals, how shall she cease to do it? It can be done only by a change in the structure of society, that will diminish the temptations to vice, and increase the encouragements to virtue. . . . In the mean time, do penitentiaries and prisons increase or diminish the evils they are intended to remedy?

"The superintendent at Blackwell told me, unasked, that ten years' experience had convinced him that the whole system tended to *increase* crime. He said of the lads who came there, a large proportion had been in the house of refuge ; and a large proportion of those who left afterwards went to Sing Sing. ' It is as regular a succession as the classes in a college,' said he ; ' from the house of refuge to the penitentiary, and from the penitentiary to the State prison.' I remarked that coercion tended to rouse all the bad passions in man's nature, and, if long continued, hardened the whole character. ' I know that,' said he, ' from my own experience. All the devil there is in me rises up when a man attempts to compel me. But what can I do ? I am obliged to be very strict. When my feelings tempt me to unusual indulgence, a bad use is almost always made of it. I see that the system fails to produce the effect intended ; but I cannot change the result.'

"I felt that his words were true. He could not change the influence of the system while he discharged the duties of his office ; for the same reason that a man cannot be at once a slavedriver and missionary on a plantation. I allude to the necessities of the office, and do not mean to imply that the character of the individual was severe. . . . The world would be in a happier condition if legislators spent half as much time and labor to *prevent* crime, as they do to punish it. The poor need houses of *encouragement*, and society gives them houses of *correction*. Benevolent institutions and reformatory societies perform but a limited and temporary use. They do not reach the ground-work of evil ; and it is reproduced too rapidly for them to keep even the surface healed. The natural, spontaneous influence of society should be such as to supply men with healthy motives, and give full, free play to the affections and the faculties. . . . I by no means underrate modern improvements in the discipline of prisons, or progressive meliorations in the criminal code: I rejoice in these things as facts, and still more as prophecy.   Strong as my faith is that the time will come when war and prisons will both cease from the face of the earth, I am by no means blind to the great difficulties in the way of those who are honestly striving to make the best of things as they are.   Violations of right, continued generation after generation, and interwoven into the whole structure of action and opinion, will continue troublesome and injurious, even for a long time after they are outwardly removed.   Legislators and philanthropists may well be puzzled to know what to do with those who have become hardened in crime.   Meanwhile, the highest wisdom should busy itself with the more important questions, How did these men become criminals?   Are not social influences largely at fault?   If society is the criminal, were it not well to reform society?

"It is common to treat the inmates of penitentiaries and prisons as if they were altogether unlike ourselves, as if they belong to another race; but this indicates superficial thought and feeling.   The passions which carried those men to prison exist in your own bosom, and have been gratified, only in a less degree; perchance, if you look inward with enlightened self-knowledge, you will perceive that there have been periods in your own life, when a hair's breadth farther in the wrong would have rendered you amenable to human laws; and that you were prevented from moving over that hair's-breadth boundary by outward circumstances, for which you deserve no credit.

. . . "I have not been happy since that visit to Blackwell's Island.· There is something painful, yea, terrific, in feeling myself involved in the great wheel of society,·which goes whirling on, crushing thousands at every turn.   This relation of the individual to the mass is the sternest and most frightful of all the conflicts between necessity and free-will.   Yet here, too, conflict *should* be harmony, and *will* be so.

"Believe me, the great panacea for all the disorders in the universe is love. For thousands of years, the world has gone on perversely, trying to overcome evil with evil, with the worst results, as the condition of things plainly testifies. Nearly two thousand years ago, the prophet of the Highest proclaimed that evil could be overcome only with good. But when the Son of man cometh, shall he find faith on the earth? If we have faith in this holy principle, where shall we find it, on our laws or our customs?

"Write it on thine own life, and men reading it shall say, ' Lo, something greater than vengeance is here, a power mightier than coercion!' And then individual faith shall become a social faith; and to the mountains of crime around us, it will say, ' Be thou removed, and be thou cast into the depths of the sea!' And they will be removed, and the places that knew them shall know them no more.

. . . "A society has lately been organized here for the reform of prisons and their inmates. Their first object is to introduce into our prisons such a mode of discipline as is best calculated to reform criminals, by stimulating and encouraging what remains of good within them, while they are at the same time kept under strict regulations, and guided by a firm hand. Their next object is to render to discharged convicts such assistance as will be most likely to guide them into paths of sober and successful industry.

"John W. Edmonds, President of the Board of Inspectors at Sing-Sing Prison, pleaded for the benevolent objects of the institution with real earnestness of heart; and brought forward abundant statistics, carefully prepared, to show the need of such an association, and to prove that crime always diminishes in proportion to the amelioration of the laws. He urged the alarming fact, that from two hundred to two hundred and fifty convicts a year from Sing Sing were returned upon society, nearly without money, without

friends (except among the vicious), without character, and
nearly without employment. . . . Poor, unfriended, discouraged, and despised, in a state of hostility with the world,
which often has, in reality, done them more grievous wrong
than they have done the world, how terribly powerful must
be the temptation to new crimes ! . . . He said he had no
faith whatever in the system of violence which had so long
prevailed in the world, — the system of tormenting criminals
into what was called good order, and of never appealing to
any thing better than the sentiment of fear. . . . Of late
there has been a gradual amelioration of discipline at Sing
Sing.   Three thousand lashes, with a cat-of-nine tails, used
to be inflicted in the course of a month ; now there is not as
many hundred ; and the conviction is constantly growing
stronger, that it will be wisest, as a mere matter of policy, to
dispense with corporeal punishment altogether."

Let us pause !

That statement takes away one's breath. How can the
pen write it, or the soul think of it ? Yet we must. We
must think ; and not only think, but write and talk ; and
not only that, but we must act. We must " act in the living present, truth within, and God o'erhead."

Three thousand lashes with a cat-of-nine tails in a
month ! Three thousand !

This on the soil of the United States ! And the men
who inflicted the lashes were not called lunatics ! And the
government that countenanced such things is not called
insane, but is supposed to be a rational government ! Nay,
more, it is held up before the whole world as the star of the
earth ! And the nation is full of professing Christians !
All over it are people singing " that sweet story of old, when
Jesus was here among men."

Was this Jesus' method for healing sin ? Does he tell
us to cure sin-sick souls in this way ? Does he advise us to

turn upon these unhappy people, and thrash them, and scourge them, and lock them up under the caprices of hired keepers ? It is not done by his instructions.

How then ? Does common sense, or experience, teach us that harsh punishments, vindictive retributions, and unforgiveness, whether by individuals or government, are promoters of civilization, good-will, and peace ? It seems rather that love, just such broad, true, forgiving love as was in our Saviour, is a better civilizer than whips, gallows, penitentiaries, guillotines, and dungeons. Love, under the guidance of intelligence, is the great civilizer of mankind. It spreads over the lands, and touches hearts with new emotions. It reaches frontiers, and the barbarians subside before its power; it speaks to the masses, and wickedness flees from its presence; it whispers, and ignorance perishes. Intelligent love is the world's reformer. Prisons are the insignia of barbarism.

Since our public men are fond of going to Europe to study the best systems of asylum and prison management, let us introduce here an incident in one of their institutions. The revelations made by one of the women after her release from a Continental prison led to an official investigation. She showed the investigating officials the indelible marks of innumerable floggings which she had received from Louis Bassewitz, and his mistress, Louisa Rasch, the matron of the female department. Not only have men been flogged there, and subjected to all sorts of tortures, worthy of the fiendish ingenuity of an Apache chief, but delicate women have been whipped upon the most futile pretexts. Such was the terror which the threats of Bassewitz and Mme. Rasch struck into the hearts of the poor victims, that few or none of them ventured to prefer complaints against their inhuman tormentors. Painful as were the floggings by Bassewitz, the suffering caused thereby was slight in comparison

with the exquisite torture of the rod with which Mme.
Rasch frequently belabored the bare limbs of the prisoners
upon the most insignificant violations of the rigid prison
discipline. The rod itself was nearly four pounds in weight,
and consisted of innumerable small birch twigs, held together
by an iron band. Mme. Rasch, a powerful woman, had
often given her female victims fifty strokes with this terrible rod; and when the indescribable pain, as the rod descended on their bare hips, irresistibly wrested agonizing
screams from them, the severity of the punishment was
increased by the harridan, who seemed to be infuriated by
the cries of the helpless sufferers. One of the witnesses
before the officials testified as follows : "Had I not been
upheld by the sense of my innocence, and the stern desire
to avenge my wrongs by bringing to justice that man and
matron, I would have dashed my brains out after being four
or five hours within the walls of the prison. I was sent
there for one year on a charge of larceny, which has since
been proved to be entirely without foundation. After my
arrival, I was immediately turned over to Mme. Rasch, who
pushed me into a small, dark room, in the middle of which
stood a curiously-shaped wooden arm-chair. She rudely
pressed me into it, and, with leather straps, fastened my
arms and legs to it. I was so frightened that my heart
beat audibly. She then pulled my hair down, and did it so
carelessly that she hurt me. I uttered a faint cry, whereupon she struck me in the face. I may have struggled a
bit to free my hands : this seemed to enrage the matron
greatly. She almost hissed out, ' Wait, you hussy, you
shall catch it for this.' She then quietly cut off my hair
till my head was almost bald. I could not help crying.
She then ordered me to strip off my clothes ; and, when I
had done so, she suddenly pushed me towards a door covered
with a linen curtain. It was the bath-room ; and I fell hard

into the cold water, hurting myself severely against the wooden steps. The matron then pulled me out of the bath, and rubbed me off with a coarse hempen towel. Without saying a word, she pushed me to the wall, and fastened my hands and my feet in two iron rings in the wall and floor. I was petrified with terror, not knowing what was in store for me. I was shivering with cold, my skin having been but partially dried. Mme. Rasch went into an adjoining room, and returned with that rod. Before I recovered myself from the fear with which that terrible instrument filled me, the matron began beating me with it on the back and on the hips. Oh! I never experienced such dreadful pain in my life; and I broke into loud cries of despair, but she did not desist. My agony seemed to lend additional strength to her arms; and I fainted away, unable to bear the torture. How long she beat me after I fell into a swoon, I cannot tell. When I awoke, I was dripping wet. The matron had thrown a pail of cold water over me. I was almost delirious when she began to rub my smarting skin anew with the coarse towel, and I cried again; but the fierce threat of further birching silenced my voice. The matron said, that, having shown so obstreperous a spirit, she would lock me up for twenty-four hours in the dark cell. After I had put on the prison garb, she hustled me into an absolutely dark hole, where I sank down in utter exhaustion on wet and mouldy straw. Next morning Mme. Rasch brought me a tin-cup of water and a slice of stale brown-bread. I was so sick that I was unable to eat. I could hardly stir. In the evening I was taken to my regular cell, and fell into a fever. I tried to tell the doctor how I had been treated. He ordered me to shut my mouth, and said, that, in case I should manifest still further a refractory spirit, I would be disciplined again.

"Altogether I was seven months in the prison, and during that time received the rod eighteen times. I was a prey to such despair, that I often begged the matron on my bended knees not to torture me any more, as I was not strong enough to bear so much punishment; but she birched me only the more frequently. One day, in my misery, I began to cry and sob, when Bassewitz whipped me cruelly with a rattan. I told the doctor this, and he remonstrated with the warden; whereupon Bassewitz repeated the infliction. Many other women in the prison were treated with equal barbarity. Every morning, I heard, with a shudder, the screams of the girls as they were birched."

This was on a continent where bastiles and dungeons have long had sway ; but we are not far behind in prison discipline. Who supposes that "three thousand lashes with a cat-of-nine tails "'could be inflicted without swooning and agonizing misery on the part of the victims, such as is fearful even to the thoughts ? Whatever the crimes for which they were imprisoned, these crimes against them in their helplessness are greater. Their crimes were committed under temptations, and passion's besetting allurements; but these crimes against them are done in cool blood, in hidden situations, where they are powerless to shield themselves from the tempers of their assailants, who often become infuriated like Mme. Rasch, and, like people drunk with personal power, go on in these hidden cruelties.

That American people are not far behind the Europeans, we should soon learn if we lifted the curtain of silence from these up-ground, living tombs. Under date of June 24, 1873, a writer in one of our dailies says, "Editor of the ————. Will you allow me to say through the columns of your widely-circulated paper, that the most cruel murders ever committed in America have been committed in our jails and prisons; viz., Death in the shower-bath; death at the whipping-post; frosted feet while in the punishment cell, amputation, and a lingering death following. Some of the punishments inflicted on prisoners are of the most degrading character. I have had large experience as a prison officer. At no time, and under no circumstances, have I known the law of kindness to fail, when properly administered to prisoners. I never fail. God's loving kindness is ever faithful, ever sure. I have known prison officers to be killed by prisoners. In justice to the great and holy law of kindness, I can say that I have never known a prison officer to be killed by a sane prisoner where said officer had not inflicted on said prisoner wicked, cruel, and unnecessary punishment. I have had some fifteen years' experience as a prison officer, having at one time, six hundred and fifty convicted felons under my charge, and have never carried a pistol or weapon of any kind for one single hour when in charge of prisoners, and have never had cause to use one. No prisoner has ever resisted me, or attempted to, with force. No class of persons in our nation require the attention of the Christian community more than our prisoners do."

In this brief letter, there is much food for thought. He says, " the law of kindness, when properly administered." We who have lived in asylums can understand that phrase; for kindness in these places, from attendants and keepers, rests on a basis entirely unlike kindness in the outer world, and is usually so administered as to give the patient-prisoners a sense of degradation that never leaves him, and never will.

The above letter on prison discipline was not written in Europe, nor thirty years ago in Sing Sing; but is a thing of to-day, progressing at this moment on American soil. And the wail of the prisoners goes up as a discord in the ears of the Lord of Sabaoth, who has blessed our people beyond other nations.

Before any radical changes can be made in the inner lives of prisoners, either penal or medical, there must be radical changes in the ·dispositions of those who· supervise and rule these inner departments. The cupidity of the officers, and the tempers of the attendants and keepers, are the great obstacles to ameliorations. Of this reformers and philanthropists take little heed. They meet and "string out" the most beautiful resolutions; but who is to execute the resolutions? Angels should come down and do it; for men's tempers will not be suitable.

What shall we do, then ? Shall we let crime go unpunished, and lawlessness be free? We ·answer, that God in nature has established penalties for crime. It is our duty to instruct the people, and the children everywhere, in the natures of the penalties, and to train the intelligent world to *prevent* crime and lawlessness.

Prison discipline, model it as we may, can never be a missionary of the cross to thinking people. It holds a scourge in one hand, and the gospel in the other. It coerces and forces people to goodness ; but such goodness is never the real goodness, nor is this Christ's method for reformations. Something better, deeper, broader, more suited to the needs of souls diseased, must supersede this mode of punishment, or crime will ride more rampant, and evil prove more destructive. We should see that *crime* is *disease*, to be healed by *science* and *care*.

By present customs, insanity and crime are treated on similar principles. And, indeed, they are naturally related. Both are the result of perturbed mental faculties; and, though insanity is not necessarily criminal, all crime is, in some degree, insanity. The causes of these perturbations lie deep in the natures of people.

The crimes within prisons, there committed against prisoners, are not known to the world; for prison overseers do not report themselves, and the sufferers are withheld from reporting by various reasons. If now and then a case of tyranny finds its way out, people read of it, and pass it by as a thing of no moment; or a meeting for prison reform follows, speeches are made, and a few resolutions adopted. These are printed, and there is the end. The hateful tempers within the walls are not uprooted. The system is not cleansed. A few poisonous qualities may be disturbed, but only to settle back into new combinations; and still the prisons flourish, the *innocent* and *guilty* suffering together, and often suffering equally, by our practices.

There came one day, when the sun was shining gladly, and the earth was gloriously enrobed, a tall, strong officer of the law to the door of one of our Christian asylums. He bore in his arms a delicate, innocent girl. She was bound in iron shackles, and handcuffs were on her wrists. He sat her down in the public hall of the asylum. People gathered around her staring. The frightened girl looked at her wrists bound tightly together; and her fingers convulsed in agony, while tears rolled from her face in streams. "What is this?" she cried. "What is this you have done to me? Why have you disgraced me so? O God, my Father! what is this has come to me?" And the people stood by indifferently, caring nothing for her agony; for was not it an insane asylum, and was not she a patient? It was only a variation in the scale of commitments; one of those variations in which force was employed instead of deception. The greatest felon in the country would not have been carried to prison in a more ignominious manner than was this innocent Massachusetts girl.

There went up the asylum inner stairs one day a pale young man. His hands were tied, and a handkerchief was bound about his face. On his way up, hidden there from outward eyes, he was kicked, cursed, thumped, and pulled,

27*

till it would seem that the poor young man must be stunned and dazed beyond recovery, ere he could reach the hall where he was to be still further abused. A looker-on remarked, " He must be a fearful criminal." Lo ! a few days after there came a bowed old man, and asked to see his son. " He was a good lad," said the grief-stricken father ; " and I couldna' bear to have him brought away from me ; but the doctor said 'twas best. Ye'll be good to him, will na' ye ? "

So then it came out that he who was kicked up the stairs, and forced into prison by merciless hands, was no felon, but " a good lad," and sent from a kind home by medical advice, to be " treated " for mental disease ! A convict could not have fared worse ! We who have seen these things with our own eyes feel justified in saying, that, in our country, the innocent and guilty are treated alike in our prisons. Insanity and crime are placed on one stand. Prisons for both are uprising on every hand, reared for coming genera- tions. Between prisons for criminals, and asylums for the insane, few families are safe from supplying victims for imprisonment.

" But," says the world, " these imprisonments are neces- sary. The guilty must be shut up ; and the insane are not safe abroad."

On this reasoning people rest, while acts of fearful injus- tice are continually transpiring amongst us.

Not only are insane people treated like criminals during imprisonment, but also on the way thither, and in the methods of first taking them. The police and law officers handle them as roughly as if they were convicted felons. A man, a good husband and father, was taken from his bed by police force, and transported to an asylum, *for cure.* He was a man of spotless integrity, and irreproachable life, fallen ill because of his deep love for his family, and over- exertion in business for their sakes. Such a cause for illness should have entitled him to the utmost tenderness; and, whether his illness disturbed his bodily or mental faculties, his physicians should have considered the *cause*, and his worth as a man of truth and honor, and should have treated him with the utmost care medically, and with the highest respect as a man. Instead of that, they ordered him to an asylum. He went, as a criminal goes. The two policemen treated him as coarsely, and with as little civility, as they would have treated a thief or drunkard. When they wanted to pause for an hour, they locked him up. At night they threw him into a small out-house, where there was only a board; and on that board, bare of comforts or necessaries, they left him, under lock and key; and he had not even a pillow for his tired head. What right has a physician to consign an honorable man to such a fate? And who shall say that the insane and criminals are not treated alike?

It is said that the present condition of the insane is better than the former, when they were shut up in attics and cages, and kept in miserable conditions. It is also said that criminals are treated with more humanity than formerly. If we have made advances, let us thank God, and stride on in the work of reform. Let us take broader views of humanity, seeing that it is the highest work of God on earth, being part and parcel of his essence, made and fitted to move in him forever, in glory and freedom and seraphic universal love. Let us not suppose that intelligent beings, by being shut into solitude, can improve, either morally or physically; nor that society is thus rendered safe, seeing that the seeds of crime and other diseases are left outside to germinate and grow.

CHAPTER XXVI.

A NATURALIST placed upon his desk two germs, and over them he held a glass of immense magnifying power. He wanted to read those germs, and to discover what the Invisible was doing in them. He had already read many marvellous works of nature. He had read nature itself. He had learned that the whole universe, from the largest boundary to the smallest microscopic atom, is as an egg. From the globules of mist, up to the spheroidal earth, and to the distant and still larger spheroids, all is as an egg, — an egg within an egg; all full of life and law and glory and God. He had studied and thought of the earth in its vast circumference; with its heaving centre of fire; its melted, glowing rocks; its metals and varied secretions; its broad expanse of billowy foam; its motions, winds, and tides; its glory in light; its resistless, onward course; its moving among, and mingling with, other earths; and his soul filled with the wonders of that power, that, over all, in all, and through all, held the mighty reins, and guided the whole, clothing himself with his works as he would wrap about him the " drapery of dreams."

The soul of the naturalist grew larger ; and, as it expanded, he sought to know yet more of his mother earth. He extended and deepened his researches ; and behold ! he still found all things as eggs, and in all was life. Everywhere was life, expanding, growing, bursting, its forms decaying, but still renewing. And this life was God. It was the principle of creation, the light of the world.

The naturalist examined the productions of the earth. He studied the blades of grass, flowers with their dusty pollens, fruit, shrubs, weeds, animals of all kinds, and even the depths so wondrous, and behold! all were rich with life's rich eggs, joined in wonderful cohesion, with God-life moving in their midst.

The naturalist could not see God. He could not see the life; but he could see the works of life, which are the works of God. He could feel life within himself, and he knew it was God animating his existence. He knew the same God was in all living organizations; giving them life, animation, and reproducing seed.

Then he stood up reverently; and, glowing with wonder, he stretched out his arms, and said, "What! Am I, too, but an egg? Am I made up of eggs within eggs? Am I so full of life? Have I, within me, life that I cannot see, life intense, whose particles are beyond my microscopic power, beyond the power of any mortal vision, more subtle than any other power, yea, able to rule all other powers? Am I but clothing for this power? Then do I belong to it, to him! My hands, my limbs, my globular eyes with which I see, my soul, my body, the life within me, all are his! Nay, I am all his! Let me pause and worship! In all things I see his works, and everywhere they are life. Life, falling away and reproducing, forever in motion, moved by rule, and by laws fixed and firm, is God! And all these works are but as eggs! Let me go out and worship! I will cover my head here in his presence; and I will go out to adore!"

Then, reverently placing on his head his wonted hat, he went out — out — farther and farther through the fields, looking earnestly at all the wonders he had passed a life-

time without truly seeing. Now he saw them in a new
aspect; for a new light had broken into his mind, and the
mirror in which all these creations were reflected was a God-
given thought within himself. The friends and servants
accompanying him, seeing him so absorbed, dared not even
speak. So they went on till they reached the mountains.
There the naturalist paused; and looking about him, at
the slopes ascending, the fields waving with green, the
wooded heights, the valleys with their flowing streams, and
the white peaks beyond ascending to the clouds, he turned
his gaze abroad, and his soul swelled with wonder. Then
he stooped; and, picking up a piece of moss, he began looking at it, turning it from side to side, and peering at its
fantastic particles, as though some hidden treasure lay
within. His servant, alarmed, approached him, hat in
hand, and, bowing respectfully, said, " Master, what aileth
thee? Art thou mad? What seest thou in that twig? "

" God! " said the man, and placed it in his coat breast
button-hole.

Then, girding up his strength, he led the way up the
ascent. On and on he went, up and up, across ravines,
through woods, through ferns, through tangled bushes,
across high rocks, up where the free air played in whirl-
winds, where the eagle screamed, the high rocks piled, and
the cavernous roars on every side seemed full of spirits
playing with the old bards. Here the Unseen seemed visible in wildness, and nature lay as it had proceeded from the
word of God.

The naturalist paused. He listened to the deep sepul-
chral sounds, he heard the winds above him; and he said,
" Spirits and bards are these! There are spirits in every
thing; there are bards the wide world o'er. I hear them as
the voice of God."

Then, turning, he saw another mountain opposite. Its

wild, precipitous sides, its fissures where the tiny flowerets straggled through, its clumps of trees, its peaks beyond, hoary with venerable age, inspired the man as he stood looking from his height. The hat that he had worn as covering between himself and Maker, he now took off; and, holding it in his left hand, with his right he brushed his hair back from his brow, looked upward, downward, and around, and then again at the mountain opposite. The old, old mountain held its grand sway in dignity, unheeding its own beauty, its caverns, or its roaring winds. The naturalist stood and regarded it; then, drawing himself up to his full height, with reverence in his countenance, he stooped forward, and — bowed. Then he drew back, and waited; but the grand old hill returned not his salute. He paused a moment; then, planting one foot forward, as though to make a nearer approach, he drew himself up proudly, and bowed again, with a reverence deep and long.   .

Then his friends were alarmed for his sanity; and as his servant had approached him respectfully, so they drew near now. They gathered before him; and, with the rights of men who had been his equals, they looked him in the face.

. "Ay, surely, thou art mad! Dost thou worship a mountain?"

He turned his eyes to them, and said simply, "Nay. It is not the mountain I am worshipping, but the God I see within it; for it is the same God here as everywhere, the same that I saw at home. Creation is all the same. It is all life. Life is its spirit, life its essence; its manifestations are beings of life. It is all a living egg within an egg. These rocks, once molten particles, the drops of water everywhere, the trees, the air, the clouds, the vegetation, the skipping gazelle, the mountain acorn at my feet, this wrinkled moss, — all, when in life, are of tiny globlets filled with divine life. Dying, they throw themselves into fantastic forms;

but, living, their minutest atoms are full of the life we none of us may give, though we may take.   Let us ascend."

Then, covering his head, he turned and climbed.   His feet seemed tireless; and he went as if upborne by unseen wings.   His friends followed afar off, gazing at him as he uprose from cliff to cliff, never looking backward, but upward, onward, upward yet again.   Glacial snows beneath his feet, glacial ice and fissures, all were glided over as though they were but sunbeams in his path.   Friends and servants plied their staves, but all in vain.   They walked by sight, he went by tireless faith.   They climbed as men; he soared as a man who felt God within himself.   At length he reached the summit, the ice-clad brow; and, on its dazzling peak, he stood, alone.   Far down, his friends were panting, as they planted their staves.   Looking up, they saw him on the dazzling point; his hat, thrown off, was rolling far away; and his arms outstretched, as his head was lifted up, made him look as a human figure ascending to God.   And such he was!   He stood, absorbed, as one entranced; and his thoughts, emerging from the microscopic egg, went outward and upward in rapt expansion.

"And yet," he said to himself, "I do not see the limit. That great outer limit — where is it?   Where is the boundary of God?   Where the outer, farther, most distant rind of space, the great, outer shell, the grand circumference? Where?"

. When his friends reached him, he seemed ready to follow his hat down the backward slide, so eagerly his gaze was fastened upward.   They clasped him in their arms.   "Master, what aileth thee?   Thou art presumptuous."

He dropped his head, and fixed his deep, luminous eyes on theirs.

"Yes, I am presumptuous.   I thought to find God.   I see all earthly forms as eggs, full of life.   The earth itself is but an egg. The sun, the moon, the planets, are but eggs. The solar system is an egg, revolving ever. Other suns, and other systems, are eggs, and all go round together in one vast unity; but the limit — the· outer bound — in vain I try to find it — all in vain."

"Master," said they, "the limit thou mayst never know. There is no limit to God. Why seek him so far away? If thou shouldst find him there, he would be the same as here. He is unchangeable. Find him in thine own heart, master. He is there. Find him in thine own home. He is there, also; and thy Aurelia will marvel what has become of thee."

"Aurelia! Yes: I will go to her. I had forgotten her in thinking of God. Lead me down."

They took his hands, and carefully began the descent. His hair was flying in the wind, and his face was full of awe, unsatisfied.

"Master," said the servant, "wilt take my hat?"

"Nay. Let me descend from God's presence with only the covering that his Spirit gave me."

Then they went down, down, past all they saw in ascending; still down, till the green fields came in view, the old, familiar landscape spread before them, and every thing seemed to say, "Welcome back to us, O spirit searcher! The Spirit thou seekest is here."

He came to his own door at evening tide. His locks were wet with the dew, and his garments flapped limp in the darkening air. Aurelia met him at the door.

"My husband, I have been troubled for thee. Where hast thou been?"

He looked in her face a moment, saw their children gathered near, then, bending forward, he fell into her own outspreading arms.

"I have been" he said, "to find God; and, behold! he is here."

" Yes, my husband, God is here.　Wherefore didst thou seek him elsewhere ? "

" I thought to seek him in boundless space, as life in immensity, prolific in eternal thought."

" Thou art seeking higher than thou canst reach, my husband," said Aurelia, as she smoothed his damp hair, and drew off his limp coat.　" Thou canst not reach the Infinite with thy finite mind.　Thou must find him with such powers as he has given thee.　Find him in love, the love of *me* and *them.*"

Her finger pointed to the little ones, gathered near.　The father's heart was stirred.

" Thou art right, Aurelia.　Call them hither.　Let us kneel and pray."

Then, beneath that blest home roof, there went up such a prayer that the angels stopped to listen ; and God seemed very, very near, even as a part of the loved household. With infinite sweetness in his heart, the father arose ; and a flood of beauty filled his soul.　In solemn voice he repeated, " Thou art right, Aurelia : our God is here."

This was the naturalist who laid before him, on his desk, two germs, and held his powerful glass above them.　He had called his children around him.　He wanted to teach them the mysteries of life.　He drew them near.

" I have here," said he, " two little germs.　Very small they are, mere atoms ; but in them lies enfolded — what ? "

" Life," answered the eldest.　" I know you would say life."

" Right, my son.　Life lies dormant in these germs. Dead, apparently, they are ; but each of these little seeds is so wondrously made, that, in suitable circumstances, life would quicken in them, and they would expand and grow with all the organizations of their natures.　Worthless as they look, they have within them every element of growth ; and just one touch of electric warmth and natural force would start a power in them that could be checked only by death. They are organized. Look at them, and tell me what kind of life is in them. They are not alike."

One by one the children took the glass, and, peering through it, scanned the two magnified germs. At the one, and then the other, they looked, then handed back the glass.

"We cannot tell what kind of life. They are just alike."

"No, my children. The germs are not alike. Try once more."

Again they looked, holding the glass above the tiny specks, and unfolding the most marvellously wonderful constructions, as though a world was graven within, set with a signet of rare and wondrous value; but what kind of a world, or what the value, no mortal power could tell. The children handed back the glass.

"They are truly just the same, father."

The naturalist smiled. "Just so they seem to me, my children. I have scanned them long and earnestly; I discern no difference. But He who made them sees a difference, and they *are* different; for one would grow into a tree, the other into an animal."

The listeners looked incredulous, but the naturalist continued. "It is even so, my children. In these two germs I find no marks by which I can distinguish the tree or animal; but the Creator has planned them, and, by a magnetic touch, they quicken into life, and grow, by laws of nature working unseen by human eyes. Once, as you know, I went far up a mountain to find God. Now I cannot even find him here; but I know there is a power intelligent in these germs, just as there is in all germs, in all the earth, and in all the universe. This power is a unit in itself; but in its works it is multiplied, and various in forms and ways of in-

finite varieties.   Truly the mysterious workings of life are
wonderful ! ”

"Father," said the children, " do all things spring from
little germs ?   Do we ? ”

" All earthly forms, my dears, spring from germs.   We
were once but little germs, lying dormant in God's secret
storehouse.   He touched us by his own laws of love ; and in
an instant we sprang into life, endowed with every attribute
that would be ours through our existence.   Those attributes
we can never tear wholly from ourselves, though we may
curb, and guide, and govern ourselves by the laws of reason, thus directing our growth to forms of beauty and holy
symmetry.   The more I study the laws of nature, the more
deeply I am impressed, that, in the very incipience of the
germ, lies the stamp of its future.   In human germs, with
their wonderful, complex organisms, full of spirit and mind,
and passions that are to rule their quickenings and growth,
lie the elements of their after years ; and, in the impulses that
give them life, are the seeds of their after growth in good
or bad, to courses of life or soul death.   It seems to me that
a fact of such infinite importance should be known and understood by every being born for immortality.   Therefore
I have called you all together, to tell you the laws of life in
its beginning.   I tell you such things as I have learned.
God dwelleth in the secrets of life ; and those· people who
tamper with these secrets tamper with the holy laws of the
Invisible.

" You see these germs lying apparently inanimate.   With
one hand you might sweep them away as two worthless
bits ; but you sweep away a tree which might grow up to
beauty and usefulness ; and you sweep away an animal
which, also, would become useful in its place."

" No, father : we sweep away germs only.   This speck
is not a tree, nor that an animal."

"Not yet; but, under proper circumstances, they will be in the future, and the future is always before us. If *we* do not live to encounter its wants, myriads *will* live; and, in all the seed-sowing of the present, we should think of the future. Every germ of life that we destroy or deface or weaken now, destroys, defaces, and weakens the future."

"But, father, are we expected to preserve and care for every seed and bulb and root and graft of vegetation, or for every little egg and embryo of animals, of which you sometimes tell?"

"No," the father answered thoughtfully, "perhaps not in vegetation, or the lower classes of animal creations; but when we ascend to ourselves, with our natures planted deep in animal powers, yet ascending to God in intellects and affections, we are bound by life itself, and by God who is life, to watch, and guard from harm, each little germ! One hidden embryo, be it but a microscopic atom, has in it every element of the future man or woman. They who destroy or injure it, destroy or injure immortality. We all know that seeds, or germs, inherit qualities. The acorn becomes an oak, because the mother of the acorn was an oak, and the seed has inherited its mother's qualities. The germs of different animals grow to maturity in just such structures and natures as their parents had, because they, as germs, derived and inherited these natures. These are all quickened into growing life by instincts of nature, governed by natural laws; therefore, each is proper and perfect in its way. But when we ascend to men, we find new elements, and new powers governing each creation. Above instinct, we find reason and moral qualities. The quickening of germs can no longer follow blind instinct; for reason has usurped the place of instinct, and we must know the whys and wherefores and the hows of all our actions, creation among the rest. I tell these things, my children, because

28*

you *will be* men and women; and while in these tender years you are growing to assume life's duties, you should learn *what those duties are.*   I send you to others to learn your geographies and the higher branches of what men call learning; but the secrets of life I teach you myself, even as I teach you to pray and praise: for I believe the keeping of the laws of the secrets of life is more sacred than any outward form of religious worship; for these secrets are the foundation of human nature and existence.   They are secrets resulting from the laws of the unseen God whom men profess to honor, and have been established in nature as an integral and vital part.   When men die, all people are serious.   All feel that it is a solemn thing to enter upon that unseen existence from which there is no return.   But there is a moment of vastly more importance to every individual, a moment of more impressive grandeur and more ineffaceable stamp, when even the eternal destiny of each person is fixed."

The father paused; and the children, looking up inquiringly, asked, "Is it when people are born?"

"No: it is not when people are called *born.*   At birth the child is already a growing being.   It has obtained consistency and form sufficient to present it to the eyes of love. It has been already stamped with its mental as well as its physical characteristics.   Greater than death, greater than birth, greater than any event of life, is that moment, that second, when electric love flashing to electric love, wakens the eternal germ of one hidden, secret atom of eternal human life, and kindles it into an action that must resound through the never-ceasing passages of immortality.   That is a hallowed moment in the acts of Nature, when, in God's own way, a soul immortal springs to action, for weal or woe, for joy or sorrow, for usefulness or crime.   By its previous situation the human germ had inherited its physical character;

and, in this hallowed moment, its impulses and moral nature are stamped.

"After years may labor on children; the father may work for them, the mother may nurture them in love; society and religion may work together for them; but never, never, can the first instantaneous stamp be removed, and never can people be free from the passions and emotions then given them.

"The Bible recognizes God's secrets and their power. David says, 'Behold I was shapen in iniquity, and in sin did my mother conceive me; and the secret of Christ's pure and wonderful life lay in his pure and holy beginning. The Father did not leave him to the chance mouldings of after life, but made his character sure in the stamp of his creation. His strength to overcome all passion was derived from the quickening powers of his germ-life; and no temptations of manhood could warp or bend that holy nature."

"And why," asked the children, "does not God have us all made so beautifully?"

"Why," repeated the naturalist. "Why? If you ask me the *why*, I shall be lost, even as I was lost on the mountain when I sought God's limit. No man may know the limit, or the why; but this I know: We are right when we keep near God, and walk in his laws of nature. Human beings cannot sink to brutedom. They cannot fall from reason to instinct, but they can fall below it; and, to save humanity from such a fall, we need instruction. If we would be like Christ, we must be created by God's laws of purity and love."

"But, father, if Christ was created in a way by which he was more holy than we, then we can never be like him."

"We can seek to approach him in likeness, my children. And we can seek the laws of life in its secrets, that we may know how to create *our* children in more purity than *we* were created, and thus take the first step towards the great regeneration of the human race ; for this purpose, we need instruction in the laws of Nature. Every leaf that falls, every flower that blooms, does so by the laws of Nature. Every particle of dust, and every unseen element, is subject to these laws. Even so every germ that quickens into life is subject to these laws. Herein lie great truths, mighty truths, and truths that hold within them the eternal destinies of the human race, and the progress of nations. These truths I shall teach to you, my children, from time to time, even as I teach you all truths, as you become capable of understanding them. Let us now kneel down and pray."

If all fathers were like this naturalist, such truths would be disseminated among the children of our homes as would save them from temptations, crimes, lunacy, diseases, and a myriad of evils that now grow up in people, leading them to prisons, misery, and death. Thoughtful people view the increase of crime in our country with sorrow, and inquiries how to prevent it. Sabbath schools and pulpits have little power over large classes who never come under their influence; and some who do, seem to have no stamina within themselves by which to follow the good that is taught them. As a consequence, we have prisons, asylums, homes, penitentiaries, jails, houses of correction, houses of sin, reform schools, and every appliance for punishment; yet our people seem like the children of a father who is constantly flogging, while, the more he flogs, the more the children transgress. Something different is needed to save us from these evils; and instruction in themselves, such instruction as teaches them from youth the value of themselves as living creations of God, is needed.

In no way have nations more surely fallen into degeneracy than by the continued and successive creations of new generations, under emotions and influences and circumstances that carry death to the soul-powers of the human germs at the instant that they quicken them into life. As the children carry to manhood and old age the inherited traits of their ancestors, so they bear through time and through eternity the very impulses of the parental spirits that moved their earthly creators at their beginnings. Then, being thus begotten by ignorance, they are left to grope their way along, learning the alphabet of letters, but never the alphabet of life. It is derogatory to the intelligence of young people to suppose they can learn of every other subject in the universe, and have no curiosity with regard to the secrets of human reproduction. They do feel curiosity; and if they cannot be allowed to have pure, scientific instruction, they will seek the impure, and the consequence will appear in the increase of insanity, defilement, and crime.

Withholding scientific, proper instruction in life from the young does not promote their purity. It throws around these topics a veil of mystery that stimulates the desires of young persons for knowledge of what is carefully kept from them; and, in default of better instruction, they eagerly seek that which is written by base persons, which is as poison to them. A statement has just appeared in public prints, relative to licentious publications.

"A young man of New York commenced, single-handed, a crusade against the dealers in licentious literature. He had not much encouragement; the police winked at the traffic; many influential men were indifferent; and it was only by the most persevering efforts that he succeeded in getting any attention paid to his demands. At length he secured the indirect support of the Young Men's Christian Association, and of the leading men in the American Tract Society, and the hearty co-operation of the Assistant District Attorney. As a result of his efforts, six of the dealers were carried to the State prison, over half a million publications were seized and destroyed. In a single seizure, nine tons were captured. Enough has been brought to light to make it clear that these dealers have emissaries in every town, and canvassers in many of our schools, both male and female."

"This," says a New York paper, "is a matter which demands the attention of our public authorities everywhere. It ought not to be left to private individuals to ferret out this species of rascality. The American Tract Society are entitled to the support and commendation of the entire community, irrespective of sect or party, in the endeavor to arouse public sentiment on this subject, and in their effort, by establishing a cheap and illustrated literature, to supplant the obscene and vicious."

How can we read that, without seeing secret desires of young people for some light on these secret subjects. This traffic rests, like all trade, on the laws of demand and supply. There is a secret demand among our young people for these works, or there would be no supply. The stoppage of sales in one quarter will not stop the evil. Other printers will arise, other salesmen will be found; and, as long as the demand continues, the secret sales will go on. Universal, continued, and persistent instruction on these very subjects is the only remedy that will effectually cure the evil. Good, cheap, and illustrated literature serves its own good purposes; but it never touches these secret subjects, therefore the young are still in darkness. Our young people are too intelligent to be left thus ignorant.

In a nation where liberty is fostered till the people are imbued with its noble spirit, precautions and watchful care are needed lest poisons mingle with the good instruction, and freedom demand rights which are wrong. When freedom encroaches on the laws of *right*, she seeks *wrong*, and her beautiful name is tarnished.　When she prefixes *free* to *love*, and gives approval to the compounded word. she lays the foundation of practices that will destroy herself, filling her nursery with vices of every form.

Love, as it comes from God, is free, impartial, and universal; but we must receive it under laws that we cannot violate without penalties.　We have no right to inculcate ideas that lead us as unrestrained passions within may dictate; nor have we a right to permit ignorance by which our young people rush blindly into quagmires of destruction. Love has laws, and life has laws; and we must learn these laws, or we can never follow them.

Life and love are by nature blended in humanity, even as in God.　When we say, God is life, or God is love, we speak synonomous terms; for life and love have an eternal marriage in infinity.　They should be wedded in finite constructions.　Love gives birth to life; and life, when conceived, should be love.　But this love must be free from grossness, else the life will not be pure; and beings created with impure life will fall victims to insanity, disease, and crime, which is disease.

Of all diseases, crime is the most deadly, the most to be dreaded.　It cannot be driven out by harshness or prisons or chains or coercions.　It is a disease that works in the reason, the moral faculties, and the perceptions.　It can be cured only by intelligent love seeking its roots, and applying remedies there.　We shut criminals into prison; but crime still works outside, springing up in new victims; and all around us are people on whose vitals the secrets of crime are feeding.

Works of instruction on the physiology of ourselves should be, as we have said, universal in our public schools; and, in our homes, there should be text-books on the secrets of human life, seeing that every person is compelled by

nature to pass through these secrets.   If prudish people
cover their faces, and call it immodest to introduce works of
instruction on these subjects, let them watch the columns of
their newspapers, and then ask whether we have not already
cause to blush?   Throwing down the evening paper in disgust, a young girl said, " Father, why don't you take a better paper? "

He looked at her in surprise.   "That is a first-class
paper.   I can find no better."

" It isn't fit to read," she answered.   " It is full of murders and robberies and suicides, and all horrible doings."

" But, my dear, these sad things occur among the people ;
and it is the business of the papers to record them."

" Then I wish we had better people," the girl replied.

We should all say of our papers as she said, if we had
not become hardened by habit of reading them.   The dis-
gusting records of crimes, the lists of advertisements for
diseases that never should be, the statistics of our locked
institutions, and the records of our courts, show plainly
what terrible secrets are lurking beneath the current show
of morality.   Let legislators vote money to pay our
learned men for writing, and our publishers for issuing,
books of instruction to supply every family of every city,
town, ward, and district, with text-books on the workings
of life.   This would be far less cost than prisons, and all
the cumberings of courts in which to try unfortunate people diseased with sin.   Let government spend money to
teach and save the people, not to punish them with worse
than death.

The strength of a nation lies in the strength of its
homes ; but intelligent people can never have strong,
virtuous homes, till the beings born in those homes are
created, and reared also, by Nature's pure laws.

This science of life that should be taught in our homes

is deeply connected with every human being's welfare. It is ingrafted into our deepest impulsive motive power; and yet that science is utterly ignored in the education of the masses. Young people step within the bonds of wedlock, take upon themselves the holiest and most essential duties of earth, and become creators of immortal beings, without one sensible idea of what they are doing, or one iota of true knowledge of themselves, or of the helpless immortals they bring into life. Much weeping there is in consequence; "Rachel weeping for her children, because they are not," and sometimes weeping because they *are*. Cruel it is to mothers to compel them, or permit them, to bring into the world and rear offspring whose end must be in infamy, because of the moral infamy by which their conceptive births were stamped.

Much is charged at the door of Providence that should be charged to our own ignorance; and many parents ask resignation to the will of God, when they have unknowingly gone in the face of that will by their direct violations of the laws of Nature, that they might have learned, and would have learned, if society countenanced such knowledge. Little babes lie in the laps of mothers who have *not one true idea* of their inner systems, natures, or needs. The mothers know the piano, the fashions, and, mayhap, their housework; the fathers know how to make money. But of the little innocents that have come to them, they know nothing. By their stupidity they make the children ill; then they run for a doctor; the children live perhaps, — perhaps they die, and it is all laid to Providence; and, in all our enlightened land, none rise to teach the people that the fault is in their own ignorance.

Young people, and people in maturity, yield to vile debasements, and become as scum in our midst; and often this, too, is chargeable to ignorance.

On whatever subject we permit ignorance to rest its blight, we shall find the saddest of effects. And when that subject is our own selves, in any department of our natures, woe is ours. We cannot escape the penalties if we violate nature; and we have but one way to escape these violations, — that way is by instruction.

This instruction belongs to government, just as common schools belong to it. Government should cause the subjects of human life to be made the object of text-book instruction, till every family of every city and town throughout our broad land is made acquainted with the inexorable laws of Nature on these delicate, vital points. In no other way can the people of our country be saved from destruction.

To be forgiven for sin is the greatest · blessing a sinner can receive; but to be saved from becoming sinners is the highest gift intelligent people need.

Especially does this grand work of instruction belong to us as Americans. By every tie that binds us to humanity, by every ship that sails to the East or to the West, by our situation between the two borders of the immense Eastern hemisphere, by our enlightenment in science, our enterprise, our national vigor, our advance in freedom, and our free, untrammelled gospel, we are bound to start these mighty ideas, and to teach people the natural laws of their own lives.

There are no more new countries to settle. The earth is girdled with inhabitants. There is no large, empty space whither the good can flee as those Pilgrims came to Plymouth Rock. Henceforth we must all live in thickly-settled countries; and shall these countries be covered with people shut into cells and dungeons at a cost of law and expense to government that is fearful to contemplate? Or shall our governments expend to save the people? It would cost far less to instruct the nation than to support the heavy array of courts, and ponderous castles studding the land, as temples where the prince of darkness reigns. Let us open our eyes to these facts; and let us arise to demand instruction from our learned men, ere the seeds of corruption are so thickly sown as to destroy our people.

Thus, and thus only, we shall be spared the loathsome spectacles that meet us now in dismal corridors and miserable cells.

CHAPTER XXVII.

E have spoken of the nation as a mass of individuals, and of the cleansing of these individuals, as we
would purify the *drops* of water in order that the
ocean may be full of limpid purity.   There is
another view of a nation, in which all the people may
be ranked as one body, and the nation be as one individual.
This individual nation has its currents, its flows, its central
head of thought, its working departments, its consuming
departments, its intellectual and physical strength, its
healthy and unhealthy situations.

At this moment the question comes to us, Is this nation
healthy ?   And we answer, The blood is too much in the
head.   The extremities are cold.   In other words, the intellect and thought power is too centralized in the cities.
The rural domains are desolate and cold.

J. G. Holland says, "We find, that, in the world's
estimate, certain professions, callings, and trades are held
highest, held to be most respectable and honorable. So
the world rushes after them, rushes into them ; so half of
the world gets out of its place at once, and the world gets
made by its callings, and does not make itself at all.

"Now, the truth is, that every man is respectable, and
every power grows in man symmetrically, only when he is
in his place."

Mr. Holland illustrates this by the different classes of
horses.   He gives the qualities of family-horses, saddle-

horses, truck-horses, farm-horses, trotting-horses, and so on, and then proceeds to ask the propriety of fitting an elephantine truck-horse for the race-course, or of harnessing racers before a heavy load, or of training a farm-horse for a lady's saddle, or using the graceful ambler for a breaking-up plough. "All these horses," he says, "are beautiful in their places, but are spoiled out of place."

Then he adds, "What a lesson for us is there in this illustration! Bear me witness that the track of American public and professional life is crowded with human truck-horses, and saddle-horses, and farm-horses, and family-horses, all entered for the premium on speed, all making themselves ridiculous by the efforts they put forth to win it, and all spoiling themselves for the sphere to which their native individualities are adapted.

"Thousands of these unhappy men were started and stimulated in their courses by such general and indiscriminate counsels as I have alluded to. As boys, as young men, they were told to 'aim high,' and were particularly informed, that, if they pointed their arrows at the sun, the flight would be higher than it would be if they aimed lower, — another of those precious maxims, by-the-way, of which the world has too many; as if it were not better to knock from a Virginia rail-fence a respectable gray squirrel, than to spend one's shots on the blank, blue sky. No man who can hit any thing can afford to waste his arrows upon an object which he knows they can never reach. . . . His aim must be determined by the shape of his arrow, the size of his bow, and the strength of his arm.

"The professional and political lives are those which the great world of unformed mind is taught to regard, not only as desirable above all things, but as attainable by all men; and, being both desirable and attainable, to be striven for.

29*

The effect has been to crowd professional life with mounte-
banks and inferior men, and political life with demagogues.
It will not be disputed, I suppose, that there are more men
engaged in the professions of law and medicine than the
country has any need of; more than can obtain a respectable livelihood for themselves. The popular notion — the
popular fallacy — is, that, if a man is going to make any
thing of himself, he must be in public or professional life
of some sort.

"I hesitate to speak of the effect of these false ideas upon
the Christian ministry, because it is impossible to judge
how far they have been complicated with conscience, honest self-consecration, and motives of beneficence. . . . I
will not undertake to decide so delicate a question as this
matter involves; but I may be allowed to say, that it seems
to me a more Christian thing to be a first-rate Christian
lawyer, or a first-rate Christian farmer, or a first-rate Christian shoemaker, than a fifth-rate Christian minister. If a
young man becomes religious, and puts himself under the
law of love, it is not, therefore, necessary to his highest
efficiency in the Master's service, that he become a preacher.
Nay, the pulpit may be the place of all others in the world
where he would be the most likely to do damage to the
cause he loves. . . .

" I have sometimes fancied that the reason why so few are
adapted to the three varieties of professional life that we are
considering is, that there was no original provision made
for these classes of men. When Eve, our dear, over-
tempted grandmother, did that which 'brought death into
the world, and all our woe,' she did that which brought physicians into the world and all lawyers, and ministers. If
our race had not fallen, it would not have needed ministers
certainly; and a race that would do without ministers would
offer a very unpromising field for the professions of law

and medicine. I cannot help thinking, that, when the golden thousand years, which have been promised us so long, shall come, professional life will be much less desirable than it is now. Every man will be as good as a minister, and every lawyer will be—a man; and the favorite professional joke about the existence of an "alarming state of health" will become as serious as it is stale.

"But, at this day, it is in politics, quite as much as in the professions, that we see the effect of those unwise counsels given to the young, which have been noticed in this discussion. A poor boy rises to become a governor, as many a poor boy has worthily risen, — as many a poor boy, I trust, may worthily rise, — or he has become a member of Congress, or achieved some higher or humbler position in political life. To the young mind, these titles, and these positions, are so represented as to appear to be the prizes for which their possessors have striven; as a fitting and natural object and reward of their labors. The young have not been taught, by their self-appointed counsellors, that manhood is the highest human estate; that office can confer honor upon no man who is worthy of it, and that it will disgrace every man who is not. They have not been taught, that to desire office, and to labor for it for the sake of its honors and distinctions, is the meanest of all ambitions, and the most degrading of all pursuits. They have not been taught to distinguish between a self-made man and a self-made governor; and brought to understand that a self-made man is greater than a self-made governor; and that a self-made governor is less than a man. Vital distinctions like these have been ignored; and the consequence is, boys without beards may be counted by thousands, in this country, who have already begun their dreams of political distinction as a legitimate aim of life; and who are, of course, growing up into demagogues."

In addition to these overcrowded classes that Mr. Holland enumerates, there should be added another, more overdone, if possible, than the others. It is the class of writers. No persons have more powerful influence than writers for the public; but at the present moment the crowds seeking to behold their writings in print are innumerable, and myriads of them had better never touch a pen. That which is written for the public should proceed from the deepest and best thoughts of the deepest and best people. Public writers should be pure with God's own truths, warm with the very essence of simple, natural life, replete with solid qualities, and never the result of hot-bed cultivation. The present style of fiction is sentimental and highflown, to a degree that is actual poison to young minds, and, therefore, sin. The sentiments are highflown, the lovers are ecstatic, their loves are rhapsodies, the rooms of courtship are palace rooms, the dress of the lovers is faultless, their money flows in unearned, their language is mellifluous, their dispositions heavenly ; and, in every part of life, they are perfection. These are the pictures on which our young people feed, till their imaginations are colored by falsities never to be realized. They fancy their own loves tame, because the persons they love are only mortal flesh and blood ; and, according to these writers, poor people can never love, because they have not brown-stone fronts, and Brussels tapestry.

As to country people, if these writers picture them at all, they caricature them in uncouth style, make them appear verdant, and put in their mouths such language, that young people living in the country, and reading these stories, are almost afraid of themselves, and flee to the cities to avoid the stigma of "countrified."

Thus the writers, the editors, and publishers, feed the country on sentiments that help it towards ruin, by misplacing its young and vigorous people, starving the rural domains mentally, and over-stuffing the cities. Thus the beautiful, quiet country, the quaint old places, the valleys, the hill-sides, the mountain recesses, and the once beloved farms, where the dear old fathers and mothers dwelt, are deserted by the educated young people, and by the enterprising who are not educated. They go where they imagine higher spheres await them, and where they imagine life will run on golden wheels.

Thus the intellect is taken from the broad country where the air is pure with natural aromas, where the minds and and bodies, spirits and intellects, of men may bathe in Nature's fresh, pure atmosphere ; and people huddle into city passages, to live in miasmas, and partake of the diseases engendered there.

Why should the cities absorb the intellect, and the broad, beautiful country lie barren ? The circulation of thought thus becomes clogged and irregular, — too rapid and heated in the central marts, too stupid and slow in the extremities. Good men have less power, and bad men multiply, by this means.

Dante says, —

> " For where the argument of intellect
> Is added unto evil will and power,
> No rampart can the people make against it."

There is more danger from evil passions, where intellect is large, to lead them to their evil purposes. Let us remember this, and use our knowledge to plant, and train, and bring to fruitage, the trees of goodness. Then we can change the poet's theme, and say, —

> " For where the argument of intellect
> Is added unto goodness, love, and power,
> No rampart can ill people make against it."

CHAPTER XXVIII.

CONCLUSION.

WE have become a great and a powerful nation; but there is a power that can destroy us, and the name of that power is sin. Sin in the hearts, and in the systems, of individuals, works out its own corruptions. All the nations of the past have fallen under its influence. It is a disease that eats out the souls and bodies of humanity. Not only must we seek to stop it at its fountain, but we must open the avenues of purification wider all the way along where the rivers of society run. As a nation, we revel in money; but millions of it are used for purposes that destroy, instead of preserving, morals or physical health. Millions of dollars are expended for jails, penitentiaries, prisons, detectives, lawyers, sheriffs, asylums, houses of correction, and various devices for punishing; and into these the wayward are thrust, in the full belief, that, in these punishments, lies the healing of sin. Millions more are invested in churches, at which the masses may look, but into which they seldom enter. They feel that they have no rights there. The houses are the houses of a few, owned by private right, with pews set apart and owned by individuals for their own right. If strangers come in, they must wait at the portals for invitation to enter the house of — men, not God. God's portals are free as the sunshine of heaven.

We have a locking-out, as well as a locking-in. Society locks the masses out of churches; and, when they sin, it locks them in-to prisons.

When men build churches, why do they not make them a free gift unto the Lord? Why do they hold the seats as private property for those who can afford to hire or buy? Is it not enough that they have houses of their own, in which they and their families dwell as they list? In the houses of God we should all meet in common. Because a man has paid largely toward the building, or toward the pastor's maintenance, is no reason why he should have the undisputed right to a certain seat. The house is the Lord's, built especially for his worship, and not that a certain few may have private passage to paradise through its portals! If the men whose money has built and sustained the houses enter and find no place for themselves because the seats are already full of worshippers drawn hither on a lovely sabbath day, let these men stay without, and thank God, saying, "For this did we build the temple, that the people might have where to gather in worship."

This is the true spirit of Christ. If he should now appear in the flesh, and attend a sale or renting of pews, would he not drive out the money-changers, and say, "Ye shall not make my house a house of merchandise?"

But people say, "There are free churches, and free pews set apart in all our churches."

Perhaps there are, but only the very humble will attend worship under such circumstances. The class who most need religious influences will not take its outward observance in this way. Therefore they spend their sabbaths in ways of doubtful benefit, not choosing to advertise their poverty by attending free churches. Rev. Alexander McKenzie says, "That pew-rents are high is not the reason why common people do not all go to church. Those who are too poor to pay for a seat in church manage to pay for other things of less value."

This may be true. It may be that multitudes of people do not feel like depriving themselves of all other pleasures for the sake of a seat in church. We are apt to use our money for that which we like best; and it may be that myriads of the common people do not so love the pure worship of God as to be frugal in the comforts, luxuries, and necessaries of life through the week, for the sake of a place in the house of God on the sabbath. What, then, is the duty of Christians? Is it not to make religion free? If the people at large do not so love the worship of God, Christ's people should remove every stumbling-block out of the way, and love should flow out to those who need pure love. The houses of our Saviour's remembrance should be made free as the streets in which all people walk, that whenever the sabbath stroller sees a church-spire, he may know that there is a spot where people are free, where they have a right to turn in and listen, even as they have a right to walk the streets. Rich men pay by far the heavier amounts for building earthly highways, and the poor walk freely in them. Why should the highways to heaven be held under bondage of money? The rich and virtuous meet all kinds of people in the streets, and are not harmed thereby. Why should not they sit together in the streets that lead towards paradise, in the gates of the houses of God?

In all our churches, of all denominations, the rich and poor should meet side by side without thought of who owns or who does not own. The " publicans and harlots " should have equal rights with the righteous and pure ; for so, mayhap, the sinful and criminals will be healed of their soul diseases, and the love of God be increased. Christ would surely direct this method.

Our Saviour went out into the by-ways and hedges to find those whom the devout of his nation had left out. We should not only go out to them, but try to draw them in. The churches are under the control of those who profess to feel an interest in the welfare of the people. Let them prove this interest by opening the portals of the houses they control; for in this way they may help open the portals of heaven, and bring down upon us the peace thereof.

We talk of opening public libraries on the sabbath, that people may have places of quiet resort: it surely would be a better thing to open the doors of churches, and let the people walk in and hear the Word of God free, here, in this country, — this Cradle of Liberty! "Ho every one that thirsteth, come ye to the waters: buy wine and milk without money and without price."

We are told, that, in heaven, we shall all be as one. The criminals in their dark cells have this promise. But here on earth people will not accept the company of these men. The fine lady draws away her garments, the "priest and Levite walk by on the other side." Will they be willing to associate with the criminals on that other shore? There must be a great change in their hearts ere they accept a heaven in which felons and convicts and low people are found.

Enemies of our Saviour's gospel accuse our churches of being extravagant, corrupt, and worldly. Let Christians fling back their church doors, and say to all these, " Come in. Come and see what we are. Join your chants with ours, if we are good; if we are not, help to make us better."

Let those from prisons come; let the wretched come; let the strollers come; let the rich and poor come, and sit side by side. For these churches are way-houses, where all may be guided to heaven. If they are too costly to be made free, let them be made more simple. God does not

ask for rich houses. He asks for the heart. He asks for
love and kindness among the people, and he is glorified
thereby.

Thus is ended, "Bella; or, The Cradle of Liberty;" but
thus is *not* ended the labors of the people that this book
enjoins; for the people are to lift up these works, and
carry them on. We have written what we can in this
brief space; but that which should be written and done is
the work of time, and let people be careful, that, when they
take up these labors, they do as the God of nature directs.
For the year of jubilee is coming, the year when our freedom celebrates its first centennial year.   On that day,
when bells peal, and cannons echo, and children shout, let
there be no prisoners wailing in the midst.   Let there be
no houses locked to shut sufferers within, nor houses locked
to keep worshippers out, nor children created in thought-
less passion and with broken natures, nor people growing
up in ignorance, uncared for and untrained.   But from sea
to sea, over mountains and hills and plains, through cities
and through woods, where Eastern breezes blow through
homes, and Western winds clarify the air, let voices join in
one song of acclamation.   Mothers and fathers, wives and
husbands, children and parents, all shall join.   Then Bella,
with her curls once more growing, her eyes once more
shining, and her heart restored to happiness, shall sing
soprano over Mortimer's bass, while Harry, keeping sym-
phony in his grand old heart, shall shine in their midst
as the good and the true ever shine.   And this shall be
the song of the nation on that day, —

"Joy to the world !   The Lord is come !
Let earth receive her King !
Let every heart prepare him room,
And heaven and nature sing !

Joy to the earth ! The Saviour reigns !
  Let men their songs employ !
While fields and floods, rocks, hills, and plains,
  Repeat the sounding joy.

No more let sin and sorrow grow,
  Nor thorns infest the ground :
He comes to make his blessings flow
  As far as sin is found.

He rules the world with truth and grace,
  And makes the nations prove
The glories of his righteousness,
  And wonders of his love.

Joy to the world ! The Lord is come !
  Let earth receive her King ;
Let every heart prepare him room,
  And heaven and nature sing ! "